MAKING CHRISTMAS SPECIAL AGAIN

ANNIE O'NEIL

THEIR ONE-NIGHT CHRISTMAS GIFT

KARIN BAINE

MILLS & BOON

First Published in Great Britain 2019
by Mills & Boon, an imprint of HarperCollins*Publishers*
1 London Bridge Street, London, SE1 9GF

Making Christmas Special Again © 2019 by Annie O'Neil

Their One-Night Christmas Gift © 2019 by Karin Baine

ISBN: 978-0-263-26996-3

MIX
Paper from
responsible sources
FSC™ C007454

Printed and bound in Spain
by CPI, Barcelona

MAKING CHRISTMAS SPECIAL AGAIN

ANNIE O'NEIL

MILLS & BOON

This one goes out to my ladies who create!
Thank you so much Annie C, Karin and Susan
for, once again, being epically fabulous. xx

CHAPTER ONE

HELL'S TEETH, IT was cold.

For once the all-consuming distraction of lungs vs arctic winds hurtling in from the Highlands was welcome. Physical pain outweighed Max Kirkpatrick's rage just long enough to remember that for every problem there was a solution. This time, though…

Trust the festive season to send him another blunt reminder that, no matter how hard he tried, the universe simply wasn't going to let him put some good back into the world.

He'd genuinely thought he'd done it this time. He really had.

His eyes travelled the length of the scrubby inner-city hospital then scanned the former vacant plot. There'd been snow on and off for weeks and yet there were still patients wandering around with pets and still more in the greenhouse, fostering their plants as if they were their own flesh and blood.

He traced his finger along a frost-singed rose. The parents of a little boy who'd lost his struggle with cancer had planted it three years earlier when Max had only just started Plants to Paws. The lad had loved coming out here to play with the family mongrel. Golden moments, his parents had called them. Golden moments. They still came and tended it as if their son were still with them. In a way, he supposed, he was.

This week.

Max's disbelief that someone was going to destroy the garden shunted through him afresh. Gone were the piles of rubbish, the burnt-out car, the thick layers of tagging on the side of the Clydebank Hospital walls. In their place were raised vegetable patches, benches with the names of loved ones on shining brass plaques dappled about the small wildflower meadow and, of course, the greenhouse and extra-large garden shed he'd built with a handful of other doctors. They'd recently installed a wood stove for added comfort. That would go, too. Along with the bow-laden wreath someone had hung on the door, despite his protestations that it was too early.

He crouched down to pop a couple of stones back onto the rock garden one of the Clyde's long-term leukaemia patients had helped build. Her first ever garden, she'd crowed. She'd be gutted when she found out it was going to be demolished, all to help some fat-cat property developer.

As he nestled another rock back into place, a young Border collie ran up to him with the tell-tale wriggle of a happy dog. She rolled onto her back for a tummy rub. He took a quick glance around and couldn't place her with anyone within sight.

He gave her soft white belly a rub. 'Hey, there, little one. You're a pretty girl. Now, who do you belong to?'

'Some would say they don't *belong* to anyone.'

The female voice slipped down his spine like warm honey. Low and husky, it was the type of voice that could talk a man into anything if he didn't watch himself. Good job he'd put the emotional armour on years back.

Max was about to say he was very familiar with the way canine-human relationships worked, thank you very much, when a pair of very expensive boots appeared on the woodchip path. Expensive boots attached to a public school accent. Still Scottish, but he would put money on the fact their schools had had a mixer dance. The military school his stepfather had deposited him in strongly encouraged shoulder rubbing with the 'power makers', as the school head had liked to call them.

'Deal breakers' would've been a better moniker if today's news was anything to go by. He still couldn't wrap his head round the hospital reneging on their word. Sure, they needed the money, but obliterating Plants to Paws to let a developer build a car park?

Bam! There went three years of hard work. Not to mention the slice of peace that came from knowing he'd finally made good on a years' old vow to do what he hadn't done for his mother: offer a refuge from a life that wasn't as kind as it should have been. All for a bit of money they'd never see on the wards. Hello, cement trucks, sayonara Plants to Paws.

The puppy nuzzled against his hand.

'What's her name?' He had yet to look up.

'Skye,' the voice said.

She sounded like a Christmas ornament. Angel? Whatever. Too damned nice was what she sounded.

Her leather boots moved in a bit closer. Italian? They looked handmade.

'I think you'll find her "love me tender" routine is an act. Skye's always got an ulterior motive and, from the look of things, you're playing right into her paws.'

He didn't even want to know what that meant.

'Is she a working collie or one of those therapy dogs?' They'd been trying to introduce the therapy dogs into the hospital but, as ever, stretched resources meant the lovable fur balls weren't seen much on the wards.

'Working. Though she's still in training. Precocious. Just like her mother.'

Damn. This woman's voice was like butter. Better. Butter and honey mixed together. If he was to add a shot of whisky and heat it up it'd be the perfect drink on a day like this.

'What type of training?' he asked, to stop his brain from going places it shouldn't.

'Search and rescue.'

That got his attention. He had been expecting agility. Maybe sheep herding. A voice like that usually came attached to some land. Land managed by someone else. As he tilted his head up, the sun got in his eyes and all he could make out was a halo of blonde hair atop a stretch of legs and a cashmere winter coat that definitely wasn't from the kind of stores he shopped in.

Miss Boots squatted down to his level and the second their eyes met he stood straight back up.

Piercing blue eyes. A tousle of short curls the colour of summer wheat. A face so beautiful it looked as though it had been sculpted out of marble. For every bit of wrong she elicited in his gut, there was an equal measure of good.

'Are you a patient?' It was the only thing he could think to ask, though he knew the answer would be—

'No.' She put her leather-gloved hand out to shake his. 'Esme Ross-Wylde.'

He kept his facial features on their usual setting: neutral. Though society papers weren't his thing, even *he'd* heard of the Ross-Wyldes. Scottish landed gentry of the highest order. The Ross-Wylde estate came with about five thousand acres, if memory served. A couple of hours north of Glasgow. Before his mum had married The Dictator, as Max liked to think of his stepfather, she'd taken him there for one of their famous Christmas carnivals. Huge old house. A castle actually. Expansive grounds. Extensive stables. Skating rink. Toffee apples and gingerbread men. It'd been the last Christmas he hadn't been made to 'earn his keep'.

'So.' He clapped his hands together and looked around the sparsely populated garden. 'Have you brought Skye along to meet someone?'

She unleashed a smile that could've easily lit him up from the inside out. Good thing she'd met him on a bad day. On a good one? He might have had to break some rules.

'I was looking for you.' She held up a familiar-looking scarf.

'How'd you get that?' He knew he sounded terse,

but with his luck she was the developer. If she was trying to sprinkle some sugar in advance of telling him when the wrecking ball would swing, she may as well get on with it.

Esme was unfazed by his cranky response. She tipped her head towards the garden shed as she handed him his scarf. 'A member of your fan club gave me this to give Skye a go at "search".'

He glanced over at the shed and, sure enough, there were a couple of patients from the oncology ward waving at him. Cheeky so-and-sos. They'd been trying to blow some oxygen onto the all but dead embers of his social life ever since they'd found out the nurses not so discreetly called him The Monk. He rolled his eyes and returned his attention to Esme Ross-Wylde. 'I presume that means you're here for the "rescue" part?'

She shrugged nonchalantly. 'If you're interested.'

Skye's tail started waving double time.

If he wasn't mistaken, the corners of her rather inviting lips were twitching with the hint of a smile.

Something about this whole scenario felt like flirting. He didn't do flirting. He did A and E medicine in Glasgow's most financially deprived hospital. Then he slept, woke up and did it all over again. Sometimes he came out here and dug over a veg patch. There definitely wasn't time for flirting.

When he said nothing she asked, 'How do you fancy keeping Plants to Paws the way it is?'

His eyes snapped to hers, and something flashed hard and bright in his chest that had nothing to do with gratitude. It ricocheted straight past his belt buckle and all the way up again. By the look on her face, she was feeling exactly the same thing he was. An unwelcome animal attraction.

Oh, hell. If life had taught him anything, it was the old adage that if something seemed too good to be true, it usually was.

The Dictator had taught him that everything came with a price. Best to rip off the plaster and get it over with. 'What's the catch?'

'Charming.' Esme quirked a brow. 'Is this how you win all the girls over?'

'It works for some.' Dr Kirkpatrick's shrug was flippantly sexy.

'Not this girl.' Her hip jutted out as if to emphasise the point she really shouldn't be making. That she fancied him something rotten and her body was most definitely flirting without her permission.

'Suit yourself.' His full lips twitched into a frown. Something told her it was for the same reason her mouth followed suit. They'd both been burnt somewhere along the line and if she was right, those burns had been slow to heal. If at all.

She sniffed to communicate she would suit herself, thank you very much, but the butterflies in her belly and the glint in his eye told her Max Kirkpatrick knew the ball was very much in his court.

He wasn't at all what she'd expected when she'd heard about an A and E doctor who'd set up a multi-purpose garden where patients could grow carrots and play with their pets. For some reason she thought he'd be older. Like…granddad old. And not half as sexy as the man arcing rather dubious eyebrows at her.

She called Skye to her and gave her head a little scrub. Here was someone she could rely on. Even as puppies, dogs were completely honest. Constant. Loyal.

Men? Not so much. Something she'd learned the hard way after her entire life had been splashed across the tabloids as a naive twenty-year-old who'd been taken for a fool. These days the Esme Ross-Wylde people met was friendly, businesslike and, despite the inevitable tabloid update on her charitable activities, able to keep her private life exactly that. Private. Which was a good thing because the rate of knots at which she was mentally undressing him would've won a gold medal.

'Are you going to tell me what the catch is or are you going to make me beg for it?' His frown deepened. As if he was fighting exactly the same onslaught of images she was. Sexy ones that most definitely shouldn't be drowning out any form of common sense.

Normally sponsoring a struggling charity was incredibly straightforward.

Normally she didn't feel as though her entire body was being lit up like a Christmas tree. Flickering and shimmering in a way she hadn't thought possible after years of protecting her broken heart. All of which was tying her insides in knots because feeling like a lusty teenager was not a safe way to feel. And yet…she couldn't tear her eyes away.

C'mon, Esme. You know the drill. Find a charity. Offer a lifeline in the form of a Christmas ball. Donate a couple of service dogs after two weeks of training up at Heatherglen. Job done.

She forced herself to answer. 'From what I hear, you might need my help.'

The doctor crossed his arms and squared his six-foot-something form so that she could see nothing else but him. Classic macho male pose. Designed to intimidate.

Although…she wasn't really getting that vibe from Dr Kirkpatrick. It was more protective than aggressive. There was something about the ramrod-straight set of his spine that suggested he'd done some time in the forces. Her brother had had the same solid presence. Unlike everyone else, who was bundled up to the eyeballs, Max Kirkpatrick wore a light fleece top bearing the hospital logo over a set of navy scrubs and nothing else. A normal human would've been freezing.

A normal human wouldn't be messing with her no-men-for-Esme rule. This guy? Mmm… Dark chestnut-brown hair. A bit curly and wild. The type that was begging her fingers to scruff it up a bit more. Espresso brown eyes. The fathomless variety that gleamed with hints of gold when the sun caught them. Everything about him screamed tall, dark and mysterious. And she liked a mystery.

No!

She did not like mysteries. She liked steady and reliable. Although…steady and reliable hadn't really floated her boat the last few times her brother had presented her with 'suitable dating material'.

Dr Kirkpatrick broke the silence first. 'Any chance

you're going to explain this rather timely offer to rescue me?'

Ah. She'd forgotten that part. An oversight she was going to blame on Skye for unearthing the softer side of this impenetrable mountain of man gloom towering over her. Sometimes being short was a real pain.

'I run the Heatherglen Foundation. I founded it after my brother—an army man—and his service dog were killed in a conflict zone.'

A muscle twitched in his jaw. She'd definitely been right about the military.

She continued with more confidence, 'I am particularly interested in helping charities that use animals as therapy and who, more to the point, are in danger of closing. It's relatively straightforward. I select the charity, and in a few weeks the foundation will be hosting a Christmas ball, where the bulk of the funds raised will be donated to said charity, and ongoing support from the Heatherglen Foundation will also be provided.'

'Sounds great. Have a good time!' Max said in a 'count me out' tone.

'But—it'll save Plants to Paws.' Didn't he want his charity to survive? 'The ball's just before Christmas. It truly is a magical event.'

He rolled his eyes. 'So…what? Is this your stab at being Scotland's very own Mrs Claus?'

'There's no need to be narky about it. I'm trying to help.' She didn't like Christmastime either. Her brother had been killed on Christmas Eve and ever since then her favourite time of year had been shrouded in painful memories, but it didn't mean she took it out on others.

Quite the opposite, in fact. The Christmas ball was her attempt to recapture the love she had for the festive season. Ten years and counting and it still had yet to take.

He opened his hands out wide. 'How would you feel if the one thing you'd poured three years of hard graft into was going to be paved over for a pay by the minute car park? At *Christmas*.'

'I'd do everything in my power to save it.'

'Trust a stranger I've never met to save a charity she'll most likely never make use of? I don't think so.'

She was hardly going to tell him to search the internet because, depending on which site he hit, he could definitely get the wrong impression. She took a deep breath and started over. 'The donors are personally selected by me. People who believe in giving back to communities that have treated them well.' The look he threw her spoke volumes. He wasn't biting. She spluttered, 'Think of it as your first Christmas present.'

'I don't trust things that come in pretty wrapping.'

The way he looked at her made it crystal clear he wasn't talking about ribbons and sparkly paper. He was talking about her.

Now, *that* was irritating.

She wasn't some little airhead who bolstered her ego by doing seasonal acts of charity.

He shoved up his sleeve to check his watch. 'I've got patients to see and bad news to dispense, so if you don't mind...?'

'I *do*, actually. I mind very much.'

He rolled his finger with a 'get on with it' spin.

What was with the attitude? Founders who believed

in their charities tended to drop it. Not this guy. Either he'd been royally screwed around at some point or was just plain old chippy. Even worse, somehow, in a handful of seconds, Max Kirkpatrick had slipped directly under her thick winter coat, beneath her cashmere sweater and burrowed right under her skin, making this interaction feel shockingly personal.

The Heatherglen Foundation wasn't a platform for her to prance about Scotland, giving away her family's money. It was the one good thing that had come out of the most painful chapters in her life. As quickly as she'd been unnerved by his attitude, she'd had enough. She wasn't going to beg this man to take her money. He didn't want it? He couldn't have it.

She wiped her hands together as if ridding them of something distasteful. 'I came here with a genuine offer of help and a list of donors as long as my arm. If you're not interested in stopping Gavin Henshall from paving Plants to Paws over, I'll be on my way.'

He blinked. Twice.

Ooh. Had she found a chink in the strong, silent man's armour?

'I suspect it'll take more than a few thousand to keep Henshall at bay.'

He was right. She told him how much the last charity she'd sponsored had received.

He blinked again. 'Can we skip straight to the what do I need to do to get the money part?'

Blunt. But it was a damn sight better than being dismissed as a bit of society fluff.

Her frown must've deepened because he suddenly

folded into a courtly bow before unleashing an unexpectedly lavish charm offensive. 'I do humbly ask your forgiveness. Etiquette school clearly failed me. I didn't mean to be rude, Miss Ross-Wylde. Or is it Mrs?'

'Ms,' Esme snipped.

His eyes narrowed. Probably the same way hers had when he'd stiffened at the mention of Gavin Henshall.

He'd found her chink. She'd found his. Normally this would be her cue to run for the hills. But something about him made her want to know what made him tick. *Sugar.* Why couldn't Max Kirkpatrick have looked like a troll or been long since married to his childhood sweetheart? She checked his ring finger.

Empty.

Her heart soared so fast she barely knew what to do with herself.

Explain the details. Accept his refusal—because he will refuse—then leave. Problem solved.

She crossed her arms, aiming for nonchalant, not entirely sure if she'd hit her mark. 'I've just been up to speak to the hospital administrator, who has agreed to stall the sale until the new year. If the Christmas ball goes to plan, the hospital is happy to leave Plants to Paws as is.'

'In perpetuity?' Max obviously had his own set of conditions.

'Precisely. The only thing—'

He huffed out a laugh. 'I knew there was a catch.'

She let her eyebrows take the same haughty position his had earlier. 'The only thing, Dr Kirkpatrick, is that

I require the head of each charity to select two patients whom you think might benefit from a service dog.'

'Oh. You require it, do you?'

She ignored him and soldiered on. 'We can offer the patient two weeks of one-to-one training at the canine therapy centre, all expenses included, and a follow-up care package if they have financial difficulties.'

His expression didn't change, but she could see he was actively considering her offer.

'What sorts of things do your dogs do, apart from search and rescue?' Max asked.

She smiled. She might have trouble bragging about herself, but she could big up her dogs until the cows came home. 'We have service dogs specially trained to work with epileptics, diabetics, people with cancer, people with mobility problems. I imagine you see the full gamut of patients in A and E. I'll forward you a full list of the services we can provide. We also have emotional support dogs, who work with people suffering from PTSD or anxiety.'

He nodded. 'Would I have to play any part in this?'

Normally he would, but no way was she inviting Max Kirkpatrick to Heatherglen. He was setting off way too many alarm bells. Before guilt could set in, she reminded herself that she made the rules. She could also bend them.

'Apart from attend the ball to receive a big fat cheque?' She shook her head. 'Not necessary. We're an all bells and whistles facility, so...' The lie came a bit too easily. She always invited the charity founder to join the patients and their families up at Heatherglen, but two weeks in close proximity with Max Kirkpatrick at this time of year, when the castle was romantically bedecked for the festive season? Not. Going. To. Happen.

Her mouth continued talking while her brain scrambled to catch up. 'We run the training sessions at our canine therapy training centre. There's also a medical rehabilitation clinic my brother runs in the main building. I have a week-long slot from December fifteenth up until the twenty-third of December, when we hold the ball. I understand the timing could be awkward with Christmas and family obligations, but as the developer is so keen to get construction under way, I thought we'd best get cracking. The patients could take the dogs home over the holidays then return for a second week of training sometime in January. If that suits.'

She watched his face go through a rapid-fire range of emotions. All of which he erased before she could nail any of them down.

'I'm fine with that,' he said evenly. 'As long as we make a few of my guidelines clear.'

Esme couldn't help it. She laughed. 'Excuse me, Dr Kirkpatrick. If I'm not mistaken, I'm the one helping you here and as such—'

'As such,' he cut in, 'I don't want you steamrolling my charity into something it isn't.'

'And what makes you think I plan on doing that?'

'Bitter experience.'

The second the words were out of his mouth Max regretted them. Hearing Gavin Henshall's name had a way of catapulting him straight back into the scrawny fourteen-year-old kid who'd mown lawns, taken out rubbish and thrown himself at all the rest of the chores his stepfather had set him as if his life had depended on it, only to discover he'd changed the goalposts. Again.

Military academy, apprenticeships over the summer holidays, boot camp. No matter what he'd done or how hard he'd worked, he had never been permitted into the house to shield his mum from the emotionally abusive relationship she'd unwittingly married into.

Not that he blamed her. They'd both fallen for Gavin's smooth lines. He'd promised her love, respect, a house with a big garden on the right side of town. A proper education for her 'shockingly bright boy', the son he'd always hoped to have.

How the hell Gavin had convincingly passed off the lies still astounded him. The only plus side of the cancer that had taken his mother's life was that it had freed her, at long last, from Gavin. It was more than he'd been able to do.

He shook his head and forced himself to focus on the here and now.

Esme Ross-Wylde didn't strike him as a steamroller socialite. The type of do-gooder who blithely floated round the city flinging gold coins for the 'have nots' to do her bidding. Sour memories teased at his throat. Money brought power and no one had made that clearer to him than Gavin. *'You earn your keep? You're in. You don't? You'll have to learn how to make a real man of yourself.'*

'What's your role in all of this?' Max had already been hit by one bombshell today. This one—the Henshall H-bomb—was making it harder to harness any charm. If he was going to tell everyone who cared about Plants to Paws it was going to survive, he needed to trust it was a genuine offer. Trusting a woman who could clearly cut and run from any scenario that didn't suit her was a tall order.

'Apart from being Mrs Claus, you mean?' She pursed her lips in a way that suggested he'd definitely hit a sore spot then said, 'As well as running the foundation, I'm a vet and an animal behaviour specialist. I also pick up poo, in case that's what you're really asking.'

It was all he could do not to laugh. Brilliant. Esme Double-Barrelled-Fancy-Boots picked up poo. It was a skilful way to tell him there was a vital, active brain behind the porcelain doll good looks. A woman who wanted to be mistress of her own destiny as much as he'd worked to be master of his.

'That it?' He knew he was winding her up, but…his flirting skills were rusty. Rusted and covered in a thick layer of dust if he was being honest.

Her smile came naturally, clearly more relaxed when talking about her work. 'The vet clinic is the only one in our area and the therapy centre's busy pretty much round the clock. The service dogs are trained to aid patients with specific tasks they are unable to do themselves. Like press an alert button for someone having an epileptic seizure, for example. Much like a dog who works on a bomb squad or for drug detection, they are not for the general public to cuddle and coo over.'

'That's the therapy dog's job?' Max liked hearing the pride in her voice as she explained.

'A therapy dog's main role is to relieve stress and, hopefully, bring joy—but often on a bigger scale. Retirement homes, hospital wards, disaster areas. An emotional support dog tends to provide companionship and stress relief for an individual. People with autism, anyone suffering from PTSD. Social anxiety. That sort of thing.'

Max nodded. The smiles on the faces of patients when they were reunited with their pets out here in the garden spoke volumes. Pets brought joy. Too bad people couldn't be counted on to do the same.

She continued, 'We're obviously highly selective, but find that dogs who come from animal rescue centres are particularly good for emotional support, learning and PTSD. The bigger dogs are wonderful with ex-soldiers who might need a service and emotional support dog all in one big furry package.'

He gave a brisk nod at that one. A few guys from his platoon could probably do with a four-legged friend. He still didn't know how he'd managed four tours in the Middle East without as much as a scratch. Physically, anyway. Emotionally? That was a whole mess he'd probably never untangle. 'And your brother? The one with the medical clinic?' Max crossed his arms again. 'How much of a say does he have in who I choose?'

A flicker of amusement lit up her blue eyes. One that said, *You think I let my big brother push me around?*

'My brother's a neurologist, but his clinic is predominantly for rehabilitation. The foundation has pretty much always been my baby, so...' There was a flicker of something he couldn't identify as she paused for breath. Something she was leaving out. When she noticed him watching her she quickly continued, 'You'll see for yourself when you come up to Heatherglen—' She stopped herself short.

'I was under the impression I wasn't invited.' He wasn't hurt by it. Had been relieved, in fact, but…he had to admit he was curious. And he wasn't thinking about the castle.

Her cheeks were shot through with streaks of red. 'Normally the head of the charity comes up, but I just assumed with the dates I have available being so close to Christmas… I just— I didn't think it would be feasible for you to come along and observe, so…' The rest of the sentence, if there had been any, died on her lips.

Max pulled up the zip on his fleece and glanced across at the hospital where an ambulance was pulling in. His break was coming to an end and this was already getting more complicated than it should be. No point in watching the poor woman squirm. She obviously had a big heart and he shouldn't play hard to get. The future of Plants to Paws was on the line. 'Don't worry about it. My dance card's been full for a while.'

'I see.' She tucked a stray curl behind her ear.

Max's thumb involuntarily skidded across his fingertips wondering if her hair felt as soft as it looked. He forced his voice into fact-finding mode. 'So where would the patients stay? If we go ahead with this.'

'At Heatherglen.' Esme reluctantly met his eye. 'The castle has been partly remodelled as a residential clinic and we've refurbished the old stables as a training centre and kennels.'

'No more hunts, then?'

Her brows dived together as her eyes finally met his frankly. 'You've been to Heatherglen?'

'Not for a long time.' He felt her eyes stay on him as he knelt down to give Skye another cuddle. The last thing he was going to tell her was that that long-ago day at Heatherglen was one of his handful of good memories from his childhood. Guilting her into an invitation she didn't want to give wasn't his style. Especially if it meant the ultimate outcome was helping patients with the added bonus of sticking one to Gavin Henshall. The money he'd give to see the look on Gavin's face when he found out he wouldn't get his precious car park.

'So...' Esme's voice trickled down his spine again. 'Does this mean you're considering my offer?

He stood up and looked her square in the eye. 'If it means saving this place, let's do it. How do I get in touch with you?'

Esme shook her head. She might need her ears checked. Did Max Kirkpatrick just say he wanted to touch her?

An image pinged into her mind. Ice skating by moonlight. Her mittened hand in his bigger, stronger hand. The two of them skating away beneath the starlit sky until he pulled her to him and... She screwed her eyes shut and forced the image back where it had come from.

'Email? Phone?' he prompted.

Oh. Right. That kind of contact. She handed him a card. 'From here it's pretty easy. We'll do two video calls with you and the patients once you've picked them.'

'For what purpose?'

'It's how we introduce the dogs to the patients before training at Heatherglen gets under way. It gives me a good feel for who they are before they arrive. If you could take part in the calls, that would be greatly appreciated.'

'Why do you need me?'

Esme bridled. If he was going to persist in questioning every single thing she said and did, she was right to keep him away from Heatherglen. 'If a couple of video conferences and formal wear is too much of a sacrifice to secure two free, incredibly talented service dogs for patients who would normally have to wait years to receive one... I completely understand.' She gave him her most nonchalant smile, hoping it disguised just how intense she was finding all of this. The penetrating looks. The pointed questions. The downright yumminess of him. The last time someone had had this visceral effect on her... *Oof...* She shuddered as she felt Max's dark eyes continue to bore into her.

'Why do I need formal wear for a conference call?'

'It's for the Christmas ball. You're req—' She stopped herself from saying *required*. She didn't like being bossed around and had the very clear impression he didn't either. 'It's really useful if the founder of the charity comes along and speaks with the donors.'

'Schmooze, you mean.' A flash of a smile appeared. 'You might want to reconsider that. It's not really my forte.'

'So I noticed,' she said dryly.

He laughed and once again that strangely comfortable feeling she got from banter with him made the day seem a bit less cold.

'I can pick any patients I want?' He asked.

'Doctor's choice.' She nodded. 'The harder the better.'

Her eyes dropped to just below his waist.

Oh, good grief.

Work. She should think of work. Work was not sexy. Complicated patients to match to hard-working service dogs. Also not sexy. Big brothers. They definitely weren't sexy. Work, complicated patients and big brothers. Okay. Her heart rate began to decelerate. She liked bringing in clients Charles knew nothing about. He was far too serious for his own good and this was her annual chance to pop a little spontaneity into his life. And her own.

She followed his gaze as it drifted across to the hospital, his mind obviously spinning with options.

She got the feeling he was going to test her. Good. Maybe *this* would be the year that signing over the proceeds from the charity ball gave her back that magical feeling she'd lost all those years ago when her brother had been killed in action, she'd married a hustler and just about everything else in her life had imploded.

'You're not going to bend on the Christmas ball thing, are you?' A smile teased at the corners of his mouth.

'Nope!' She grinned. 'And let me know if you don't have a tuxedo. You'll need one for the ball.' She gave him what she hoped was a neutral top-to-toe scan. 'You'd probably fit into one of my brother's if you don't have one. I'm sure we could stuff socks in the shoulders if you don't fill it out.'

What was she on? He'd make a fig leaf look good. Which was an image she really shouldn't let float around her head quite as gaily as it was.

'If I go formal, I wear a kilt, thank you very much.'

A kilt! Yum. She had a weakness for a Scotsman in formal kilted attire. Her brain instantly started undressing and redressing him. What she saw she liked very much. Too much. Was it too late to uninvite him to the ball as well?

Yes. Yes, it was. Besides, as much as seeing Max Kirkpatrick in a kilt could very well tip her into the danger zone of dating outside her brother's 'pre-approved' choices…she needed him. The donors loved hearing about the charities from the founder.

'A kilt will do very nicely,' she said primly.

He gave her a sharp sidelong glance as if he'd been following her complicated train of thought, then took a step back and said, rather formally for someone who'd just been flinging about witty banter, 'In which case, Ms Ross-Wylde, I'd be delighted to accept your offer to participate in two phone calls and the ball.'

It was a pointed comment. One that made it clear he'd understood loud and clear she hadn't asked him up to Heatherglen. A wash of disappointment swept through Esme so hard and fast she barely managed to keep her smile pinned in place as she rejigged her vision of what the next few weeks held in store. Training patients. Absolutely normal. The hectic build-up to Christmas. Ditto. The Christmas carnival being set up out at the front of the castle that would, once again, be a good opportunity to practise with the dogs and their handlers.

It was ridiculous of her to have imagined for as much as a second that she might finally make good on that fantasy to skate by moonlight, hand in hand, with someone who genuinely liked her for herself. Let alone share a starlit kiss.

'Delightful.' Brisk efficiency was the only way she'd get out of this garden with a modicum of her dignity intact. She called Skye to her side. 'We'll expect them on the fifteenth and you on the twenty-third in Glasgow.'

She turned and gave a wave over her shoulder so he wouldn't see the smile drop from her lips.

Stupid, stupid girl. The last time she'd let her heart rule her actions she'd ended up humiliated and alone. She'd been a fool for letting herself think that Max Kirkpatrick could be the one who would bring that sparkle of joy back into Christmas.

CHAPTER TWO

MAX WASN'T SURE who was more nervous. Him or the twelve-year-old kid squirming like a wriggly octopus on the wheelchair beside him. His eyes flicked to the chair behind them. Euan's mum was there. Carly. Timid as ever. Gnawing on a non-existent fingernail, her eyes darting around the office he'd managed to commandeer for the video call.

The poor woman. She didn't look as though she'd had a good night's sleep in years. The same as his mum back in the pre-dictator days. Getting Carly here today had been a feat and a half. How on earth she was going to get two weeks off work was beyond him.

'You ready for this?' Max asked. He wasn't. He was no stranger to sleepless nights, but he definitely wasn't used to erotic dreams. Or a guilty conscience. There was a hell of a lot more information he should've told Esme that would've explained his spiky behaviour when she'd appeared at Plants to Paws last week, but having jammed himself into an emotion-proof vest quite a few years back, sharing didn't come easily. Sharing meant being closer to someone. Opening up his heart. There was no point in doing that because he'd learnt more than most that opening up your heart and trusting a person meant someone else got to kick the door shut.

It had happened with Gavin. And with his fiancée. Now very much an ex-fiancée. And out on the battle-fields of Afghanistan where lives had been lost because he'd trusted his commanding officer and not his gut.

He gave Euan and Carly as reassuring a smile as he could. They were living breathing reminders that if everything Max had been through hadn't come to pass, Plants to Paws wouldn't exist and Euan wouldn't be getting this once-in-a-lifetime chance to get his life back on track. Not the world's best silver lining, but... *'Start small, aim high.'* One of his mum's better sayings. *'Forgive him, Max...'* being one of the worst. There was no chance Gavin Henshall deserved his forgiveness. Not after everything he'd done.

Euan's mum fretted at the hem of her supermarket uniform. 'Could you run us through what the call's going to involve again, please?'

'Absolutely. It'll be similar to the one Fenella's going to have tomorrow.'

'She's the poor woman with epilepsy?'

Max nodded. Fenella had first came into A and E on a stretcher after a horrific car accident. Since then the forty-one-year-old had come in with cuts and bumps after experiencing severe epileptic seizures resulting from the head trauma she'd suffered. The poor woman was nearly housebound with fear. A service dog could change her life.

'She'll be getting a dog specifically trained for her requirements.'

'And Euan's dog will be trained to help with his… situation?' Carly asked.

Bless her. She never could bring herself to say PTSD.

'My crazy brain, Mum. My *crazy* brain!' Euan pulled a wild face and waggled his hands.

The poor woman looked away. She blamed herself for what her son was going through, as parents so often did, when, in reality, the attack on Euan had simply been very, very bad luck. The kind of bad luck that could change his life for ever.

Max looked Euan square in the eye. 'Esme knows what happened and will find a dog that can be there for you. It'll make being at home on your own more relaxing.' He glanced at Esme's email again, trying not to picture her lips pushing out into a perfect moue as she concentrated. He cleared his throat and continued. 'She mentions having a chat with the headmaster at your school. Some therapy dogs are permitted, so…if you need it, he might be coming along to school with you.'

Euan's antsy behaviour suddenly stilled. The poor kid. The past couple of times he'd shown up in A and E had been for black eyes and cuts from fights at school. Despite the best efforts of the headmaster, it definitely wasn't Euan's safe place.

His story set the bar for cruel cases of mistaken identity. He'd been walking home from school about eighteen months ago when a local gang had mistaken him for someone else and had near enough pulverised the life out of the poor blighter.

Even in the war zones he'd been in, Max struggled to remember a kid who'd met the wrong end of a fist to such ill effect. He was a poster boy for PTSD. He bunked off school regularly. He had frequent panic attacks. His nightmares woke everyone in the flats around them, the screams were so piercing.

Carly was a single mum and worked shift hours so couldn't be there for him when he needed it most. He was a scared kid with no one to back him up and the only way he knew how to deal with all that fear was rage. With waiting lists longer than Max's arm, Euan needed someone beyond the psychiatric profession on his side. Someone to give him a bit of confidence. A reason to see the bright side of life. Someone with the unerring loyalty of a dog.

Max glanced up at the clock. 'Right. It'll be a short call. Enough time to meet the dog, find out his or her name.'

'I hope it's a boy. A huge bulldog!' Euan's eyes gleamed with possibility.

'There's only one way to find out.' Max pressed the button and waited for Esme to answer.

Seeing Max Kirkpatrick's face appear on her screen brought back a whole raft of emotions Esme thought she had dismissed a week ago. So she'd thought he was hot. So what? Lots of people were hot. Like…um… movie stars. And models. And ex-soldiers with dangerously sexy hair working in inner-city A and Es who were doing their damnedest to keep their hearts off their sleeves.

But now that she was seeing him again?

Heart hammering. An entire swarm of butterflies careering round her tummy. A flock of birds might as well have been circling her head. She tore her eyes away and did her best to focus on the young lad sitting next to Mr Extra-Gorgeous with a cherry on top.

The boy he'd selected, Euan Thurrock, really pulled at her heartstrings. Skinny. Buzz cut. Looked ready for a fight, but it was so easy to tell there was a scared little boy hiding beneath all of that bravura. She couldn't imagine having to live in the same neighbourhood where he'd nearly lost his life. When the proverbial rubbish had hit the fan when she'd lived in Glasgow, she'd had a five-thousand-acre estate to hide in. Euan had to confront his biggest fears on a daily basis. She wasn't entirely sure she ever had.

She glanced at Max then looked back at Euan. 'So, are you ready to meet Ajax?'

Euan punched the air. 'Ajax sounds awesome. Like an attack dog. Is he a Rottweiler? A Doberman Pincer?'

Esme smiled. 'None of the above, I'm afraid.' She whistled the dog over and watched Euan's face melt with affection when the golden Lab popped his furry face up to the screen. 'Euan, meet Ajax.'

Despite having done 'the big reveal' hundreds of times, Esme felt the familiar sheen of tears glaze her eyes. It wasn't just the dog's adorable face as it tried to make sense of what it was seeing on the screen, and this dog was particularly adorable. Dark brown eyes, black nose, fluffy golden fur and ears that quirked inquisitively at any unfamiliar sounds. It was Euan's face that caught her heart and squeezed a few extra beats out of it.

Seeing this tough kid's eyes light up to see something that represented hope would've turned anyone into a puddle. It was an expression that said he believed someone was finally, unequivocally on his side.

She gave Ajax a treat then asked him to sit beside her. 'So, Euan, d'you mind introducing me to your mum? She's the adult coming to stay with you, right?'

Euan's mum gave a nervous wave as Max and Euan pulled their chairs apart to make room for her to scoot forward. 'This is Carly,' Max said, his voice a bit thick with emotion if she wasn't mistaken. 'She's all booked up to join Euan next week.'

'Actually...' Carly put her hand to her mouth then dropped it '...I've got a wee problem on that front.'

Max's eyes went wide with concern. 'Is everything all right?'

She shook her head. 'My bosses have pretty much said if I leave at this time of year, I can expect not to have a job when I get back.'

Esme was shocked. She always covered costs and rarely had problems with employers. 'Would you like me to make a call?'

Carly shook her head again. She looked as timorous as she was sure Euan felt. 'I don't want to make a fuss. I'm afraid the job's a bit more important than the dog.'

Esme bit down on the inside of her cheek. If only she'd had the training centre in Glasgow, as she'd planned all those years ago.

If only the world was populated by nice, honest men

who didn't spend their new bride's trust fund on night-clubs instead of training centres.

Before she had a chance to say anything, Max jumped in. 'I'll go.'

The look of sheer gratitude Euan threw him near enough tore Esme's heart out of her chest. When Euan got himself together enough to give Max a fist bump, neither of them managed to meet the other's eye.

Esme's chin began to wobble. She cupped her hands over her mouth.

Max straightened up, looked back at the video screen and what felt like straight into Esme's soul. 'If that's all right? Wouldn't want to mess around your well-laid plans.'

There was an edge to his voice, but it was a protective one. An edge that spoke of a fierce protectiveness that wasn't going to let Euan experience one more disappointment.

If Esme hadn't fancied Max before, she...well, she was really going to have to command her heartstrings into place. No fawning, or drooling, or looking with dopey-eyed fondness at a man who so clearly wanted to be warm, kind and open but, for whatever reason, couldn't.

One week ago, her instinct had been to keep him as far away as possible.

In the last five seconds her entire nervous system had done a one eighty. Take away the rugged good looks, the hands she would've paid money to see hold a puppy and that chestnut hair just begging her fingers to play with it—and underneath it all was a solid, reliable and trustworthy man.

Which was perfect. So long as he stayed at the end of a video call. Which was no longer happening.

Right! So. She started a mental to-do list with just one very important item: do not fall head over heels in love with Max Kirkpatrick.

This was her most vulnerable time of year and, as such, she had to be on her guard.

'So!' She scribbled some nonsense onto a pad no one could see then gave Max a bright smile. 'Just a few little rules and regs to cover.'

'I would expect nothing less,' he said with a…oh, my…rather sexy smile. The type that said he could see right through her and back again.

Rule number one was going to be tough.

Esme gave what she hoped was a briskly efficient nod and ran through a few things, including what clothes to bring, what sort of weather to expect and asking about any dietary requirements.

Max looked at Euan. 'I think just about anything beyond a sausage roll will be a new one on this lad.'

Euan jabbed him in the ribs. 'I'm not that bad. I've heard of…um…sushi.' He abruptly leant in and whispered something to Max.

Max answered quietly then gave the lad's head a slightly awkward scrub. 'Maybe we can scratch the sushi.' The two of them threw each other a shy grin.

If there was any time to wish for some Christmas magic, now was it. Esme had a feeling it wasn't just Euan who needed a bit of TLC from a service dog. Max looked as though he had a wound or two himself that could do with being salved.

Esme glanced down at the stray pup one of their physios had found who was curled up at her feet. Dougal. Maybe she could convince Max to give him a forever home? Dougal was cuddly and responsive enough that he'd easily be a therapy dog, but...

When she looked back up at the screen Max was all business. Times. Schedules. Anything else they needed to bring. She answered his questions as efficiently as possible, all the while telling her hammering heart that she could do this. She could survive a week with Max Kirkpatrick. Besides, the second her brother Charles laid eyes on him she knew he wouldn't pass the big brother approval check list. Not that Charles was officially in charge of who she dated but having a second opinion after her disastrous elopement had seemed pretty wise, all things considered.

She followed Max's hand as it stuffed a few of his wayward curls back into submission.

What Charles didn't know...

As they signed off, Esme looked out the window towards the castle, merrily twinkling away in the early evening gloaming. It looked like something out of a fairy-tale. It was far too easy to imagine that long dreamed-of kiss under the starlight with all of the glittery warmth still swirling round her chest. Glittery warmth brought to life by one dark-haired, reluctant hero.

Good grief.

What had she just agreed to?

* * *

'How long's it going to take, Doc?'

Max gave his back-seat passenger a quick glance. 'As long as it takes, Euan.'

About eight days with any luck. Then he wouldn't have to go through the hoop-jumping Esme had no doubt set up for him. Attending Euan's training classes. Ensuring Fenella, his other 'volunteer', was all right as her elderly mother couldn't come along either, owing to previous commitments. Day in. Day out. Dining together. Training together. 'Fun time.' Whatever the hell that was. Together.

Bonding.

He didn't bond. He assessed, treated, then moved on. Precisely why he'd opted to work in A and E after hanging up his camos. Move 'em in, move 'em out. Zero time to bond.

Bonding made you start Plants to Paws, mate. You're going to have to own it one day.

Unbidden, an image of Esme introducing the dogs via the video call to Euan and Fenella popped into his head. He was pretty sure he was the only one who'd caught the little surreptitious swipes she'd made at her cheeks when the patients' eyes had first lit on the pooches. He was positive he was the only one in the room who'd itched to reach out and wipe them away.

'D'you think Ajax is going to be allowed in the castle?'

'How would I know? Do I look like I was raised in a castle?'

Euan snorted then asked, 'Hey, Doc, I was supposed

to do a maths quiz today. Epic thanks for getting me out of school, mate!'

Max glanced into the rear-view mirror of his clunky old four-by-four and meet the lad's eyes. 'I'm not your mate and this isn't a jolly, pal. There will be homework tonight. Of that you can be sure.'

'Why're you so tetchy?' Euan countered in a tone that suggested he was well used to cranky adults.

'I'm not tetchy.' Max's knuckles whitened against the steering wheel.

'Actually,' Fenella gently cut in, 'you are a bit tetchy.'

Max harrumphed. Whatever. So he was a bit out of sorts. Spending a week with a fairy dogmother who, via numerous phone and video calls, had managed to do all sorts of things to the steel walls he'd built round his psyche wasn't exactly something he'd been looking forward to.

Not to mention the annoyingly inviting visions that kept popping into his head of Esme in a ski suit. Esme in a onesie sprawled in front of a roaring fire. Esme in nothing at all.

He pulled off the multi-lane motorway that led north from Glasgow. The fastest option. 'We'll go the scenic route,' he growled.

Esme checked her watch. Again.

'The more you look, the longer he'll be,' her colleague Margaret teased, then gave Esme's shoulder a little pat. 'Don't worry. Lover boy will be here soon.'

Esme gave a dismissive click of her tongue. Good thing they were friends as well as co-workers.

'He's *not* lover boy! And I'm definitely *not* worried.' Esme flounced away from the window. Worry wasn't her problem. Lust was. And the last person she was going to tell was Margaret—a woman on a single-track mission to get Esme to date someone 'interesting'. Just because Margaret was now madly in love, it didn't mean Esme had to be as well.

'What's he like? Your sexy doc? And don't trot out the line about how you can't say until Charles meets him because we both know what the men he approves of are like.' She feigned an enormous yawn to show just how interesting she thought his choices were.

Esme laughed. Her brother did have a tendency towards introducing her to men who…well…lacked lustre, but she'd told him she wanted a man who didn't have a single surprising thing about him. He'd taken her at her word. Not that he played cupid all that often, but when he did? Suffice it to say there had yet to be a love match.

'Ez? C'mon. Details, please.'

'I told you. He's a Glaswegian A and E doctor.' With gorgeously curly brown hair and the darkest, most fathomless brown eyes she'd ever seen. He'd been a bit stubbly when they'd had their last video call. She could just imagine his cheek rasping against hers when he— No! No, she could not.

Margaret grabbed a gingerbread man from the tray Mrs Renwick, Heatherglen's long-term cook, had given the therapy centre staff and held it in front of her face. 'Won't you tell your dear friend Mags something more interesting about the big handsome doctor?'

'Who said anything about him being handsome?'

Margaret just about killed herself laughing. 'You didn't have to. The way your cheeks go bright pink each time you come off a video call with him tells me everything I need to know.' She began to chant in a sing-song voice, 'Esme needs some mistletoe!'

Esme picked up another gingerbread man and stuffed it into her friend's open mouth.

'Do not.'

Margaret tugged on her staff hoodie. When her head reappeared she grinned. 'Suit yourself.' She pulled on a gilet over her hoodie. 'I'll see for myself in a few seconds.' She flicked her thumb towards the window. 'Lover boy's here!' Before Esme could protest—again—Margaret was on her way out the door, saying she'd get the dogs ready.

Esme tried to ignore the tiny tremor in her hand as she took a distracted bite of the gingerbread man, her eyes glued to the battered four by four that would give their new vet Aksel's bashed-up staff vehicle a run for its money. His arrival had been a godsend at the busy veterinary clinic. Running it and the canine therapy centre was a Herculean task and Aksel tackled everything Esme put his way with a fabulous mix of pragmatism and care. Mind you, Aksel was so loved up these days they could've issued him a wheelbarrow and a workload for ten men and he would've accepted with a smile.

Her thoughts landed in a no-go zone. It was a bit too easy to picture Max gazing at her in the same adoring way Aksel lit up whenever Flora, the rehab centre's physio, appeared.

The last time Esme had looked at someone like that she'd lost her heart and hundreds of thousands of pounds of her family's money. Not to mention her dignity, sense of self-worth and, yes, she might as well admit it, since the divorce papers had been finalised, nearly nine years ago now, she'd found it hard to believe she was worthy of love. All the compliments Harding, her ex-husband, had lavished on her had turned out to be lies. Lies she'd vowed never to fall for again.

Her tummy flipped when she caught a glimpse of Max behind the wheel.

She bit the head off the gingerbread man.

The next week was going to be a test of sheer will-power.

Via the Clyde's administrator, she'd learnt that Max had done several tours in the Middle East. Two more than her big brother, Nick had done. As a surgeon in conflict zones he would've seen enough horror to make that difficult-to-read face of his even more practised—giving away no more than he was comfortable with, which, in her case, was just about nothing.

She'd get there in the end. She always did. She loved teasing apart the complicated webs of her clients' personalities. Not that she ever bothered turning the mirror on herself. She knew what her problems were. Trust. Trust. And trust.

The car slowed as it climbed up the hill towards the castle. She craned her neck to watch as the passengers rolled down their windows and took a look. Max was the only one not to stick his head out of the window. As ridiculous as it was, she was a bit put out. Heatherglen

Castle was more than a pile of rocks thrown together to impressive effect. It was her home.

The huge stone structure was framed by a crisp blue sky, the dozen or so chimneys puffing away with fires as the weather had turned so cold. Though some of the rooms were enormous, she and her brother had done their absolute best to make the castle feel as cosy and inviting as possible for the residents. Residents like Max who—because they were running at capacity—would be sleeping in her and Charles's private wing. Just. Down. The. Corridor. When they'd put Euan's mum there it hadn't been a problem. When the thirty-something mum had turned into Mr Tall Dark and Utterly Off Limits, Esme's stomach had swirled with far too much delight.

Silly stomach. Just because a good-looking man is on the grounds, it's no reason to behave like a goofy lust-struck teen.

The car pulled up outside the clinic.

Right! Time to get to work.

Hamish, Mrs Renwick's grandson, tucked a stack of files under his arm as she walked into the reception area then pointed at her jumper. 'You going to leave any of those for us?'

She flashed him a guilty smile when she saw the crumbs. 'Of course, silly billy. I was just doing a quality control test.'

'Of Nan's biscuits?' He didn't bother to disguise his disbelief that she could say such an outrageous thing.

Her guilty smile turned sheepish. They all knew Mrs Renwick's biscuits were insanely delicious.

'Can you take this plate back to the pooches, please,

Hamish?' She handed him a platter of dog-bone-shaped biscuits made to a special dog-friendly recipe. 'Make sure Dougal gets one. He adores them!'

'Aye aye, boss.' Hamish gave her a jaunty salute and headed back to the kennels. He was openly enjoying his work experience at the clinic. She hoped he followed up his dream of becoming a vet one day.

She hurriedly wiped the gingerbread crumbs off her jumper and tuned into the loud laugh of a boy as the door opened and banged shut. Euan. A woman's delighted giggle followed up the boy's. *That would be Fenella.* Good to hear everyone was in such a good mood.

Before she could come out from behind the reception desk the door to the clinic flew open, slammed against the doorstop and whacked back again, only to meet a human doorstop. She shivered against the blast of cold air and looked across in time to catch the divot between Max Kirkpatrick's eyebrows furrow in apology. 'The door caught a draught.' He scanned the large reception area in slow motion. There were the usual accoutrements of a veterinary clinic. Dog food displays. A wall full of indestructible toys. Educational posters.

As Max's eyes narrowed and the divot between his eyebrows deepened, she suddenly saw what he saw. An insane riot of Christmas decorations covering absolutely everything. Hamish may have gone a bit OTT with the tinsel and glittery snowflakes. 'You certainly like your Christmas decor,' he said dryly.

'Not your cup of tea?'

'Not so much.'

She gave a nonchalant shrug. Drowning in tinsel wasn't everyone's idea of Yuletide joy. She was more of a warm twinkly lights and a few well-placed baubles girl herself but ever since Nick had been killed on Christmas Eve and the news of his death had reached them on Christmas Day thirteen long years ago, she'd struggled to recapture the love she'd always had for the festive season.

She glanced behind him. 'Where're your patients?'

'Outside.' He flicked his thumb over his shoulders, those dark eyes of his not leaving hers for as much as a millisecond. 'They're having a snowball fight.'

'Brilliant!' She clapped her hands. 'Some say it's good for the soul.'

'Some say it's good for getting pneumonia.' His eyes left hers and landed on her jumper. It featured three polar bears ice skating along a river up to the North Pole. 'Nice jumper.' His eyes were not on her belly button.

'Thanks.' She tilted her head, forcing his eyes back up to meet hers. 'I bought it in town if you want one.'

'It isn't my usual colour palette.'

She snorted. The man was dressed in top to toe navy blue.

'At least you're honest.'

'Some say to a fault.' He dropped her a wink that, judging from his follow-up expression, he hadn't planned to drop.

Esme looked straight into his eyes and just as they had that first time they'd met, they released a hot, sweet glittery heat that swept through her bloodstream with a not-too-subtle message. Max Kirkpatrick floated her boat. She gave herself a little shake. This wasn't a dating session, it was the beginning of a series of rigorous training sessions for the dogs and the new residents. And yet...

She forced her cheeky grin into a look of pure innocence. 'Any chance you're open to being converted? To the Christmas thing?'

A shadow tamped out the glints of fun in his dark eyes. 'I'd say about as likely as one of Santa's reindeer swooping down and taking me for a ride.'

No wiggle room in that response.

She rolled her shoulders beneath the thick wool of her jumper. Rough against smooth. Would she feel the same sensation if Max were to slip his hands...? *Stop that!*

She wove her fingers together and adopted a pious expression as she began the lie she told herself every year. 'I happen to love Christmas and all of the ancillary—' her voice dropped an octave *'—accoutrements.'*

They both looked surprised at her foray into 'bedroom voice'. No one more so than Esme. The last thing Christmas was was sexy. Hot chocolate, cosy fires and Christmas trees, definitely. Sultry voices and shoulder wriggles in silly Christmas jumpers? Not even close.

The fact she even looked forward to the holiday was little short of a miracle.

Ever since Nick's commanding officer had shown up at their front door on Christmas Day all those years ago, Esme had been trying to convince herself it was still the best day of the year. Impossible when they'd been told the rebel forces had taken advantage of the holiday to set intricately built tripwire bombs across the village where Nick had been stationed. Even tougher when they'd found out the only reason Nick had been out and about had been to deliver presents to a bunch of young soldiers who'd been finding it tough to be so far away from home.

Ever since that day Christmas had been like participating in a dreary panto. Each of them going through the motions, pretending they were happy, when all they wanted to do was weep for the golden boy they'd lost. Not that 'they' were much of a they any more. Esme's doomed romance had taken up the first year after Nick's death.

Her mother had reshaped her grief into a near pathological need to enjoy life. Parties, swanning around the globe, scandalous affairs that had quickly led to the end of her parents' long and happy marriage. Her father had passed away three years after Nick had and their mother was now married to a Greek shipping magnate, so it was just Esme and Charles now, neither one of them doing all that well at re-injecting joy into Christmas.

No doubt as a former soldier, Max had his own particular days he didn't like. Unlike her, he didn't seem all that interested in trying to tap into any tendrils of Christmas cheer lurking somewhere in his heart. For the past thirteen years it had been like a mission for her. Which maybe defeated the purpose—pounding a square peg into a round hole—but there was something about Christmas that sang to her and she wanted to find that music again.

From a very early age she had believed that Christmas was magical. The decorations, the frenzied build-up, the secrets. More than any of those, though, she'd always loved the *giving*. Much more than the receiving. Seeing the joy on someone's face when they opened an unexpected present, or a child who had their first proper spin round the ice rink at the Christmas carnival, or someone's eyes widening as the first snowflake of the season landed on their mittened palm...she loved it. She just wished that the joy of the season touched her heart the way it used to.

All of which reminded her... She lifted up the tray of biscuits resting on the counter. 'Are you so anti-Christmas that you'd refuse a homemade gingerbread man?'

Max rolled his eyes at her as if she were the lost cause.

Well, to each his own. At least he knew his mind. Honesty was clearly his policy and he stuck to it even if it did make him look like a Scrooge. She could respect that. A slow grin crept back onto her lips. Even Scrooge saw the light in the end.

CHAPTER THREE

TWO SECONDS.

Two measly seconds was all it took for Max to start working on an exit plan. Impossible, given his idiotic instinct to volunteer as Euan's guardian, but how the hell was he meant to survive? Esme was a walking, talking Christmas minx. One who, without as much as a how do you do, had him dropping winks and staring at her boobs. Classy. He really suited the whole 'landed gentry' surroundings. Not.

If he didn't watch himself he'd have her over his shoulder, out the door and high-tailing it around Heatherglen on a quest for mistletoe. He'd bet her lips tasted like peppermint. Or whatever it was Christmas was meant to taste of.

Sugar and spice and all sorts of things that were wickedly nice.

He stuffed his hands in his pockets. He shouldn't be thinking about what anybody's lips tasted of. He should be thinking about Euan and Fenella and their dogs and the time he'd no longer have to spend with them in A and E because of this excellent opportunity to turn their lives around. A much more practical line of thought.

A woman wearing a gilet with her name and the therapy centre's logo stitched onto it pushed through the swinging doors that led to the kennels. Margaret. She was thirty-something. Dark-haired. Rosy-cheeked, from the cold most likely. Her eyes pinged from Esme to Max then back again. Margaret smirked. Esme glared.

If he was any good at reading women's signals and, like his flirting skills, they were rusty, Max would've bet cold hard cash Esme had told her that he was a crusty old man. Esme had obviously lied. Not that he slathered himself in youth potion or hunky man juice or anything, but he was relatively confident he was a step up from the abominable snowman's granddad.

Perhaps the exchange of meaningful looks between the women meant Esme was staking a claim on him.

He quickly pulled the plug on that idea. Esme was a beautiful woman and an heiress. She doubtless had queues of men ready to slip a ring on her finger.

Something instinctive told him the socialite scene wasn't her gig. Anyone who announced she picked up poo wasn't someone who fancied being a pretty bauble for some man to parade around on his arm. Maybe that was why her clinic was hidden away up here in the Highlands. Down in Glasgow or Edinburgh she could be at the doorstep of so many more people who would benefit from her therapy dogs. He had something teasing at his memory he couldn't quite bring to mind. Something he'd skidded over on the internet when he had been researching her work here at Heatherglen. A romance gone bad, perhaps? Whatever. Not his business.

As if she'd been reading his mind and wanted the thoughts to stop, Esme cleared her throat.

'Margaret,' Esme said pointedly, 'may I introduce you to the man behind Plants to Paws, Max Kirkpatrick?'

'Hello, Max,' Margaret said, a merry twinkle in her bright blue eyes. 'It's *very* nice to meet you. Esme simply hasn't been able to stop talking—'

Before Margaret could elaborate, Esme cut in with a very polite, stagey voice, making great use of her enunciation skills. 'Margaret, don't you think it would be lovely if we got the dogs ready to meet the new residents? Max here was just on his way to get them.'

Margaret's eyes pinged between the pair of them before she answered in the same stagey, highly enunciated voice, 'Why, yes, Esme, I think it *would* be lovely.'

'Great!' Esme gave a decisive nod. Margaret didn't move. Esme tilted her head towards the kennels.

Margaret threw an apologetic look in Max's direction. 'We normally wait for the residents to be in the room before we bring the dogs in.'

He took that as his cue to leave. Which was just as well, because it was all he could do to keep a straight face. Not that he was certain the women were having a non-verbal *he's mine* fight over him, but...it certainly felt that way. It'd been a hell of a long time since anyone had played tug of war for his attentions. No offence to Margaret, but if he were remotely interested in having his heart shredded to smithereens again, he knew which way the pendulum would swing. Not that falling for Esme was an option.

He'd adored his ex. Had loved her to within an inch of his life. She'd been all for his plan to save up money to buy his mum a house. Had supported his extra tours of duty. The overtime. The delayed returns. He'd thought she was amazing. Right up until he'd discovered her largesse was easier to bear because she'd been having a full-on affair with her boss. Not that she'd offered him the ring back or anything, but the fewer reminders of what it was like to have his emotions in someone else's power the better.

After he'd managed to brush most of the snow out of Fenella's hair and Euan's hood, they went back to the reception area, where Esme was wearing a very professional, very controlled smile.

They made a quick exchange of names, handshakes and the obligatory offering of gingerbread men. Both Euan and Fenella were so excited they could barely stand still.

'Have you had a chance to settle into your rooms yet?'

Fenella and Euan exchanged quick looks before Fenella answered for the pair of them. 'We've not seen the barracks yet, no.'

Esme's eyes shot to Max's.

Oops. He should've warned her he might've been teasing them on the ride up. There may also have been a mention of dungeons and castle keeps.

She twisted her lips into a little moue before that cheeky grin surfaced again. She'd rumbled him. 'I think Dr Kirkpatrick may have been preparing you for a Christmas surprise.' She nodded towards the castle. 'Your rooms are in there.'

Euan threw Max an incredulous look. 'You mean we're staying in the castle?'

'Looks like it.' Max gave the back of his neck a swift rub. It was nice to be giving good news for once.

Euan put his hand up for a fist bump. 'Result, Doc!'

Max met his fist bump and then, to make sure the kid still knew his place, pulled him into a loose headlock and gave his head a light knuckle-dusting. Euan seemed to like it. Poor guy. He didn't have a dad to rough and tumble with. Someone to have his back when he needed it. Snap. At least Max had had the military. Brothers in arms and all that.

When he looked up, he caught Esme looking at him and Euan with that soft smile of hers. One that rammed an arrow straight into his heart. It wasn't often a woman saw his soft side. Then again, it wasn't often she stuck around long enough to find out he had one. After things had gone so apocalyptically wrong with his fiancée, he had decided he wasn't built for relationships, so didn't see the point in letting a woman know he had a heart thumping in his chest. Anyway, moving on...

Esme suggested Fenella and Euan pick a toy and a couple of bags of treats each from the display rack before they met their dogs.

Euan looked at her with disbelief. 'You mean...we just take them?' He threw an anxious look at Max.

'I told him everything was gold plated here.' Max said, as neutrally as he could. There was no chance in the universe these two could afford some of the high-end collars and doggie coats on display so he'd wanted them to know things were for looking at but not for coveting. A valuable lesson his stepdad had made a point of impressing on him right from the start. He wanted cool trainers? He'd have to earn them. No time for a job and military academy? Well, then, looked as though he'd have to do without.

Euan's eyes were practically glittering with possibilities. Max's hand went back to his wallet. He'd pay if necessary. Just the once. It was, after all, Christmas.

'They may not look like it, but these are tools that will help you work with your dog. So, while you're here, these are free,' Esme explained, without the slightest air of a have giving to the have-nots.

Max's respect for her went up another notch.

'Don't worry about stocking up on treats for ever. We'll be sending along food and treat parcels once a month to keep you going for at least the first year as we're well aware you weren't prepared for this sort of expense. If it's too much at the end of that, we'll set up a support programme. For now, though, help yourselves. Think of this as an all-inclusive Christmas pressie.'

Fenella laughed. 'Don't say that to Doc Kirkpatrick. He hates Christmas.' She put on a voice to mimic Max's. 'Nothing comes for free in this world.'

Euan guffawed and gave Max a light arm punch. 'Yeah. I tried to get him to wear some reindeer antlers on the way up and he near enough decked me.'

'Is that so?' Esme's eyebrows shot up.

'Well…not literally but, yeah.' Euan gave a very serious nod. 'Doc Kirkpatrick and Christmas are not BFFs.'

'Any particular reason?' Esme kept her tone light, but she clearly wanted to know. He couldn't blame her.

'Nope.' No one needed to know just how miserable a time of year Christmas was for him.

'He's always working double shifts at the Clyde.' Euan explained.

There was a reason for that. Double shifts didn't let the demons in. Euan was trying to give him an out. There was hope for the kid.

'All work and no play,' Fenella teased, 'makes Doc Kirkpatrick a…' She ran out of steam. 'Well, you're not exactly dull, are you?'

Max could practically see the wheels turning behind Esme's sparkling blue eyes. As if she was already gearing up to change his Scrooge-like ways. Was there a challenge the woman didn't like?

'As none of this is relevant to service dogs, shall we get cracking?'

Esme narrowed her eyes as if she was staring straight at the chip on his shoulder. Oh, hell. She wasn't actually going to try to wheedle some Christmas cheer out of him, was she? To his surprise, she gave him a nod that indicated she knew exactly what he was talking about. That she understood pain and loss and everything that came along with it but she, unlike him, was trying to muddle through to the light at the end of the tunnel.

It was the type of look that made him wonder if his approach—no light, no tunnel—was a bit too blunt. He was the first to look away.

'Right, then.' Esme clapped her hands together and pointed to the displays. 'Why don't you two get a lead each and some treats? The dogs already have specialist collars that we'd like you to use. They've tried and approved of pretty much all of the treats on the wall, so take your pick.'

Max noticed Esme sending him a curious look after another round of victory air punches from Euan. He moved in closer, lowered his voice, his eyes flicking to Euan as he spoke. 'The kid's had a rough ride. That's why I didn't tell him about staying at the castle. I like to keep expectations low. Makes anything good that happens a welcome change.'

'Ha!' Esme laughed. 'That's my policy when it comes to men!'

'Good policy,' Max said darkly. He didn't like the thought of her with other men. He also didn't like that he didn't like it. He shouldn't care and he did. Which was precisely why keeping Esme at arm's length—further if possible—was the only way he'd get through this. Basic training had been easier.

Esme shot him a look so full of hurt he knew she'd taken it the wrong way. Before he could fix it, Margaret bounced through the double doors and cheerfully interjected, 'You ready, boss?'

Esme gave herself a little shake as if it would flick the pain away. 'Absolutely. It's time for Fenella and Euan to meet their dogs in real life.'

As she turned to go there was only one thought in his mind: This was a woman he would never allow to walk away. Which was why letting her think he was a bastard was for the best.

Now that Esme had properly humiliated herself in front of Max, she was as grateful to be around the dogs as she was hoping Euan and Fenella would be. Normally this was her favourite part—introducing the dogs to their new companions. This time, though, she was still stinging from Max's glowering response to her dating comment.

What had he been trying to say? That she'd always disappoint? That she'd never be enough? Hurt became anger. How dared he? He didn't know her. Another Harding MacMillan. She scowled. At least he didn't seem to want anything from her.

Against her better judgement, she glanced at him. He looked away.

Oh, yes. She'd read the comment right. He had no time for her except when it suited him. At least his affection for Fenella and Euan seemed genuine.

She snorted. Honest like a dog. She loved dogs, and dogs were trainable so—

No. Don't even go there.

'Any chance we're going to get this show on the road?'

Humph! Impatient like a dog.

'If you'll follow me,' Esme snipped. Margaret went to fetch the dogs as Esme showed Euan and Fenella into a large room that was a bit like a sports hall. Big, airy, more than enough room for a large group of dogs to be trained and, of course, for their new owners to learn how to handle them.

'Now, a word of warning—mostly to Max rather than the two of you,' Esme began. 'No offence.'

He put his hands up. None taken. Of course. He was ex-military. He could take it. Then again, the look on his face when Euan had fist bumped him. It was as if he'd won the lottery. There was definitely a big old softie lurking under that tough-guy exterior of his. Probably just as well it didn't extend to her.

She forced herself into work mode.

'Right! In a wee while we'll give Max a dog too, so he can experience the same training as you are. First things first, though…your dogs are precisely that. *Your* dogs. They need to bond with you and only you.'

She scanned the small group again, her confidence growing as her professionalism came back into play.

'The most important thing to remember when you meet your dog is that you are their new best friend and you are going to establish a bond that, up until this point, they've only had with their trainer. Margaret and I are the main handlers, but we tend to raise a lot of the puppies down in the village so that they grow up in a home environment. They've been well socialised. What that means is you are going to have to make extra-sure that the praise they seek is yours. That the only treats they receive are from you. That the cuddles they want are from you. So this means, no matter how much you want to spread the love with Max…'

Her eyes flicked to his and she instantly wished they

hadn't. *Spread the love?* Was she mad? No. She needed to make her own point now that he'd made his.

'You can't. No treats. No cuddles. Nothing.'

There. Line drawn.

If Esme was trying to make a point, Max heard it. Loud and clear. Any chemistry he might've felt humming between the two of them had run its course. Fair enough. He'd been a jerk. She wasn't one to beg. Good for her. Too bad he hadn't had that same ability back when he'd kept hoping his stepdad would finally realise he was a good kid, or that he had been hallucinating when his fiancée had told him there was someone else. Someone worth loving. He felt a scowl form. Being here was reopening a whole ream of memories he'd hoped to never revisit.

He made himself tune back into what Esme was saying.

'Are you ready for me to bring the dogs in?'

Euan and Fenella were so excited he thought their heads would pop off if they nodded any more vigorously. Even he had to admit it was pretty damn sweet. When Margaret brought the dogs in, it was all he could do to keep the tears at bay. And that was saying something.

Margaret dropped the lead to the biggest of the two dogs and said, 'Go, Nora. Go to Fenella!'

Fenella dropped to her knees and immediately embraced the large, creamy-haired goldendoodle. 'You're absolutely gorgeous, aren't you lovely? Look, Max! Isn't she gorgeous? No, I mean don't look. She's all mine!' Then she burst into giggles and dug into her pocket to give Nora a treat. Nora took it then licked Fenella's face.

There it was. A forever bond made in a second.

Euan was equally over the moon. Max had thought the lad would've tried to put on more of a cavalier attitude. Pretend he kind of liked the dog. But when the big old bandy-legged golden Lab bounded over to him and offered a paw? Instant love.

Max gave his jaw a rub then shoved his hand through his hair, willing the scrubbing on his scalp to keep the bottleneck of feelings exactly where it should be. Suppressed. Churning away in his gut. Wherever. Anywhere but on display.

'It's pretty amazing, isn't it?' Esme had appeared by his side without him noticing. Little magical Christmas nymph that she was. She probably had elf dust or something like that in the small treat pouches she had hanging off her belt. 'I always cry.'

He looked down at her and, sure enough, she was wiping away a couple of tears. One glistening liquid diamond from each eye.

'How do you do it?'

Her eyebrows furrowed together. 'Match them up, you mean?'

He nodded.

'That's relatively easy. Well, you obviously have to have the dog trained up for the right job. Then I read the profiles that you send and...' She gave an unreadable shrug. 'I just get a feeling.'

Against his better judgement, he laughed. 'Female intuition?'

Her eyes dropped to half-mast and moved from him to the dogs. 'No. Past experience, a wealth of knowledge and a finely tuned instinct for my dogs and the types of people they'd suit.'

Well, that told him.

They silently watched Fenella and Euan play with their new dogs as Margaret showed them, in turn, how to get the dogs to sit, shake paws, high five. No doubt they'd get to the 'serious stuff' in a bit. For now, it was bonding time.

Damn. He hated to admit it but these two were experiencing exactly what he had hoped would happen when his mum had told him there was a new man in both of their lives. She'd organised a picnic in Glasgow's Botanic Gardens. Proof, if he'd needed any, that this was no casual boyfriend and that he definitely wasn't from their neighbourhood.

Max had brought along a football and a chest bursting with hope that this time he and his mum might've found 'their guy', as she'd liked to put it. She'd never brought men home. Said it wasn't right as she wasn't just seeing someone for herself. It was for both of them. She'd get Max the dad he deserved after she'd made such a poor choice the first time round.

A fresh wash of guilt poured through him. He should've told Esme he knew the developer. He'd tried to convince himself it didn't matter because he would've fought whoever was trying to crush Plants to Paws. But there was a part of him that wanted to crush Gavin Henshall, too. No. Even that was wrong. Not crush, just…

'Forgive him, Max.'

He looked across at Euan, whose dog was lolling on

his lap, his tongue hanging out of his mouth, his eyes glued to Euan's. He wanted that.

Bonding. He'd been desperate for it with Gavin.

And he was never going to get it.

Without his having noticed, Esme appeared beside him, her eyes solidly on Euan and Fenella.

'I know,' she said softly. 'That's why I do this. Pure love with absolutely nothing expected in return.'

He chanced a glance in her direction and when their eyes met? He saw it. The clear-eyed gaze of some-one who understood exactly what it felt like not to be enough. And at that instant he fell a little bit in love with Esme Ross-Wylde, though every part of him knew there was no chance of a happy ending. Not for guys like him. Not with girls like her.

Esme shot him that impish grin of hers. 'Right, then, pal. It's your turn.'

'My turn?'

'Yup. We've got a dog for you to do some training with, so you don't feel left out. He can stay in your room with you, just like the others' will, or he can stay here in the kennels. On his own. Crying himself to sleep at night.'

'Yeah, I don't think so.'

Esme said nothing.

'I live in a flat. I work all the time. I don't have a life that's got room for a dog.'

He decided not to remind himself that he'd made the life that didn't have room for dogs, or other humans for that matter.

'No one's asking you to fall in love with him,' Esme

said neutrally. Her eyes told a different story. She was daring him not to.

'Do what you must,' Max said.

'Nice attitude, mate.'

His stepfather's voice rang loud and clear in his head. One of the many things he hadn't been able to shake from his past. The low rumbling voice. The biting quips that never failed to make him feel lower than the mud on Gavin's shoe. *Time to earn your keep, mate. Pull up your socks, mate. Off to military school, mate. Maybe they'll know what to do with you.* As if he were a lost cause before Gavin had even tried to like him, let alone love him.

Euan's laugh pulled him back into the room. He followed his eyeline, then heard Fenella get the giggles as they all watched Margaret jog in with the scruffiest puppy he'd ever seen. The little puppy was wearing miniature red velvet reindeer antlers and a jumper covered in snowflakes. He could've scooped the little mess of fur and quirky ears up in one hand and barely felt the difference. If he was into scooping up puppies and going all doe-eyed, that was.

Esme's grin split into that superstar smile of hers. 'Max? I'd like you to meet Dougal. Your very own fur buddy for the next fortnight.'

'Ha-ha, very funny. Pair the big lunk with the tiny mongrel.'

Esme feigned dismay. She picked the puppy up and nuzzled him, holding his face to hers, both of their eyes all wide and innocent. 'How on earth could you say no to this poor orphaned pup? All alone at Christmas with no one to love him?'

Hell. He knew what that felt like too. Esme was really punching each and every one of his buttons today and he wasn't even on the patient roster. He felt Euan's eyes on him and made the mistake of letting some of the hope in the lad's eyes transfer to his own heart.

'Hand him over.' He held the puppy up so they were eye to eye. 'It's you and me, pal. What do you think of that?' Dougal licked him on the nose and barked.

CHAPTER FOUR

'ALL RIGHT IF I hang out with Euan and Fenella until we set off?'

'Go for it,' Esme chirped a bit too enthusiastically, trying to resist the urge to touch Max's arm, his hand, his anything really because each time they so much as brushed a pinkie finger…fireworks. For her anyway. Twenty-four hours in and, despite her best efforts, that same heated attraction that had lit her up from the inside out the first time she'd laid eyes on him refused to be tamped down. If anything…it was worse.

She watched from a distance as Fenella and Euan showed Max the tricks they'd just learned in the clinic. They 'shot' their dogs to get them to play dead. He laughed appreciatively. Then they 'shot' him, after which he picked Euan up and tried to carry him away, only to have Euan's dog cut in and 'save' him as they'd done in one of the practice sessions. If she hadn't known better, she would've thought he was a father trying to do his very best by his son. Did he want children of his own? Marriage? Though he came across as gruff and spiky with her, Fenella and Euan clearly adored him.

They must think he was heaven sent. They probably thought a lot of things. None of which probably included being scooped up in his arms, flung onto a four-poster bed and having their wicked way with him.

Nope. She hadn't thought of that once.

He glanced over and caught her eye. The gold sparks that lit up his brown eyes whenever he let himself relax became shadowed.

Well, then. At least she knew who, of the two of them, wasn't fizzing with frissons.

'Shall we get going?' She rubbed her hands together then pointed towards the path they would be taking.

Max passed on the instructions to Euan and Fenella then walked over to her as if she were an obligation to fulfil.

Esme's heart sank a little. She didn't want to be an obligation. She wanted to be... Her breath formed into a little cloud as she huffed out a frustrated lungful of air. She wanted to be loved, that's what she wanted. What she didn't want was to have it be unreciprocated, so she needed to nip this whole *light my fire* vibe in the bud.

'The place hasn't changed much since I was here last,' Max observed.

'Oh, yes!' She clipped Dougal's lead onto his collar and tried to match Max's long-legged stride. 'I thought you'd mentioned you'd been to Heatherglen.'

He nodded soberly. 'Twenty-three years ago.'

'And how many days?' She joked.

'Seven.' There wasn't a trace of humour in his voice.

'Sounds like quite a memory.'

'It was. Is. My mum brought me here.'

About a thousand questions poured into her heart as he scanned the brightly decorated stalls surrounding the ice rink at the centre of the Christmas carnival. His eyes took on that faraway look she often saw in her brother when he was thinking of Nick or their father. It was almost as if she could see the memories shifting past his eyes. First the good ones...then the harsh reminder that there would never be more.

She'd been so gutted when Nick had been killed she'd entirely lost sight of who she was. Her father had become a workaholic. Charles had poured himself into med school as if his life had depended on it. Her mum had filled the empty hours with parties and, eventually, other men. She'd never felt more lonely.

She had became two people. A diligent student determined to become the very best vet she could be and a dedicated party girl who'd thought getting lost in the mayhem of yet another mad night out on the town was the only way to stem the grief she felt. Harding Mac-Millan, the leader of Glasgow's most elite pack of party people, had sensed her weakness, her desperation to feel loved. She'd stepped straight into his web of lies and deceit, willing it to fill the dark void of loss in her heart.

'Are the stables the only thing that you've revamped?'

Neutral territory. Phew.

'Apart from some of the medical elements we've added to the castle, you're exactly right.' Esme pulled a knitted hat out of her pocket and put it on. 'My parents were big fans of tradition so Charles and I tried to keep everything as it was. As you can see, the skating rink's a bit bigger, but...' she held her hands out as they approached the entryway to the carnival '…it's still toffee apples, chainsaw sculptures and mulled wine for all!'

Euan ran over, with Ajax in tow. 'Are we going in?'

Esme smiled at his undisguised enthusiasm. If Max had been anything like this as a kid, no wonder the memories had stuck. 'We're going to save the Christmas carnival for another time, if that's all right. We'll definitely have a go as we need to help you operate in crowds and tricky situations together. We'll also head into town one day. Maybe take you to the Christmas market. And there's always the Living Nativity to think about. Who thinks Max would make an excellent Joseph?' Esme shot him a playful smirk. Her first in the past twenty-four hours.

He shot a 'yeah, right' look back at her and there it was…that buzz of connection that crackled between them like electricity. If a right place and a right time for a kiss presented itself…

This way danger lay.

Esme nodded at the dogs. 'Are you two all right with them? Happy with the training so far?'

A chorus of 'Yes' and enthusiastic 'More than' filled the wintry air. Esme and Margaret had already done a lot of one-to-one work with them. Esme focused on the drills Fenella's seizure dog knew whilst Margaret had been tasked with showing Euan all the tricks of the trade his dog could help him with when he was feeling panicky or depressed.

The grin on Euan's face near enough hit ear to ear. 'I love him!' He dropped down low so he was eye to eye with the golden Labrador he had been assigned. 'Ajax and I are going to rule the world!'

Esme laughed good-naturedly. 'How about we see how the two of you do on a woodland walk first? Plenty of distractions out there. Squirrels, hares, deer. Maybe reindeer.'

Ajax gave Euan's face a lick and when he raised a paw to shake hands with the boy, he laughed without an ounce of the self-consciousness he'd arrived with. Now, *that* was satisfying.

'Do I have to keep my dog on a lead?' Fenella asked.

Esme nodded. 'Everything we're going to be doing for the next week ensures you are developing a relationship with your dog.'

'Do you think Ajax would like cake?' Euan's gaze travelled over to a parade of food stalls at the Christmas carnival. 'I love cake.'

Esme laughed. 'Cake is definitely not on their menu. Think of Ajax as an athlete. You want him to be in top health, right?' Euan nodded solemnly and blocked Ajax's view of the cake stall. It was easy to see he would let no harm come to his new furry friend.

Esme pointed to a path leading off into the woods. 'I thought we could go down to the pond for now. Another big lure for Labs and goldendoodles. Even in the winter. But remember! You're in charge. Let's see how well you two can do at making sure they resist all of the temptations along the way.'

She held out a lead to Max. At the end of the lead was Dougal wearing yet another Christmas jumper. 'Happy to tag along with me and Wylie as back-up?'

Wylie was a huge old St Bernard who leant in protectively towards Esme's leg. When Max didn't immediately take the lead, a thought struck her. 'Are you all right with dogs? I can't believe I didn't ask. With Plants to Paws I just assumed.'

'No, it's not that.'

'What is it?'

Max tilted his head towards Wylie. 'Loyalty. Hard to find it these days.'

The click and cinch of eye contact that followed hit Esme hard and fast.

From the shift in his stature she knew in her very core that Max felt it, too.

When she finally spoke, she barely recognised her own voice. 'Should we get a move on? I think Fenella's got an appointment with one of the physios in an hour or so.'

Esme set off at a crisp pace, reminding herself with each step that Max wasn't here to find a new girlfriend. He was here to make sure his charity didn't get paved over. Eyes on the prize. Just like her ex had had his eyes on her family money. Suddenly, the air felt a little bit chillier.

'What sort of behaviour do they have to exhibit to be a service dog?' Max's attempt to start up some casual chitchat wasn't exactly stellar but it would definitely beat the ice-queen vibes coming from Esme.

Esme briefly considered the two dogs walking beside them. 'Probably the same traits it takes to be a good soldier. Commitment. Hard work. Intelligence.' She glanced at him. 'You were in the services, weren't you?'

He nodded. She'd obviously done her research. 'Army. Twelve years.'

'As a medic or a soldier?'

'Started as a soldier but worked my way into the Royal Army Medical Corps.' He hadn't been able to stand waiting for someone else to help when one of his fellow soldiers had been injured. Mashing your hand on top of a wound rarely helped. Telling them you were there for them counted for something. Listening to their final goodbyes. As a nineteen-year-old soldier with his own emotional scars, Max had wanted something practical he could do. Medicine had rescued him from the deep morass of helplessness he'd felt ever since the Dictator had entered his and his mum's lives.

'You must've seen a lot of awful things,' Esme said.

He nodded and scrubbed at the back of his neck. They all had. At least he'd been able to walk off the plane when they'd landed back in Scotland.

'Have you chatted with Andy at all?'

Max had heard Euan introducing his dog to him the first night. 'The chap in the wheelchair?'

Esme nodded.

'Euan and he seemed to have struck up a friendship and I didn't want to interfere. He has that ex-military look about him.'

'Army. He was one of my brother's best friends.'

'Charles?'

'No. Nick.' An air of sadness cloaked her words. She

shot him a sad smile. 'You aren't really friends with the internet, are you?'

He shook his head. 'Not really. For twelve years I lived and breathed the military and since then I've been deeply involved in the A and E unit. The internet fuels gossip. I don't like gossip.'

She huffed out a disbelieving laugh. 'That would make you a rare breed.'

Shards of pain lanced through those pure blue eyes of hers and if he were the sort of man who knew how to make them go away, he would've. It was a cruel reminder that the only thing he'd learnt over the years was how to push people away.

'Nick was my older brother. Much older. He was in a canine dog squad in the army and one day... Christmas Eve, actually...things didn't go so well.'

All the little pieces he'd been trying to put together fell into place. The castle as a rehab centre. The rescued mutts. The repurposed search and rescue dogs. Those intense looks she sometimes had when she held a dog close. All of this was for their brother.

'He must've been an amazing man.'

'He was my hero.'

The depth of emotion in her voice punched him right in the solar plexus, loosening up the muscles that held his own story deeply embedded in his heart. He wanted her to know she wasn't alone. That he understood pain and loss. His mum had been his best friend up until when his stepdad had entered their lives. A man whose method of putting a relatively wayward kid back on track was to ship him out to a military academy instead of letting him live in their new home, as promised. How the same man had verbally subdued his jolly, full-of-life mother into being little more than a timorous mouse, frightened to say or do anything that might embarrass her social-climber husband. As the dark thoughts accumulated, Dougal nosed his thigh. He gave the dog's head a scrub. The pooch definitely had a sensitive side. That was for sure.

As if the move had also jostled Esme, she gave herself a little shake, popped on a smile and asked, 'What made you choose the Clydebank Hospital? Pretty rough area of town.'

'It's where I grew up.'

'Oh. Um…are your parents still there?'

'Nah.' He cleared his throat because it still choked him up to say the words. 'My mum passed. Three years ago now.'

There was no point in mentioning his father. Step or otherwise. Neither had treated his mum the way she'd deserved.

Cancer had stolen his chance to give her the house he had bought for her. It'd taken him twelve years of service to buy it outright. He'd meant it to be a refuge from the Dictator and his constant micromanagement. As far as Max knew, he'd never laid a hand on her, but guys like that knew how to bruise and hurt in other ways. Gavin had been chipping away at his mother's self-worth for years. He hadn't wanted a wife. He'd wanted someone to feel small so he could feel big. It was a miracle she'd had any confidence left at all in the end. Or the generosity in her heart to forgive a man he didn't think he ever could forgive.

At least her battle with cancer had been swift. A cruel mercy. The day she'd died, Max had put the house on the market. He'd thought of making it a shelter, but he simply hadn't had the funding to keep one up and running. He'd used the money to establish Plants to Paws instead. His mum had loved gardening. It had been the one place she'd known her husband couldn't fault her.

He needed to bring up his relationship to Gavin before a single penny came his way from Esme, but for now he was enjoying the thoughtful silence she'd chosen in lieu of asking, *And your dad?* Like her therapy dogs, she seemed to know when to push and when to back off. If he wasn't careful he'd be pouring out all his secrets but he knew more than most that putting his heart in someone else's hands was always a bad idea. So he followed Esme's earlier lead and sidestepped the real stuff.

'Where'd you find this cheeky chappie?' He pointed at Dougal.

'A couple of our staffers found him. Cass and Lyle. Someone had abandoned the poor wee thing.' She gave the dog a goofy grin and he barked his approbation. 'Up until a few days ago he was staying with our physio, Flora, but she's moving in with Aksel—the new vet— and they already have an assistance dog for his daughter, so…' Esme looked up to the wintry sky as if for inspiration.

'Because he's so young and such a little scruffball we weren't sure he'd be up for much training, but he seems pretty adaptable. Aksel caught him trying to purr next to a cat the other day.' She laughed, her features softening as she unclipped his lead and gave him a bit of a cuddle. 'Poor Dougal. He deserves someone who will love him exactly the way he is. A little broken. A lot in need of love.'

Something told Max she was describing herself. She sure as hell was describing him. Though he could hardly believe the words as they came out of his mouth, he said them anyway. 'Want to talk about it?'

'About Dougal?' Esme knew he'd been asking about her, but she was hardly going to pour her heart out to a man who had more control over her emotions than she cared to admit. 'Nothing to say really. His past is a mystery.' Her eyes flicked towards Max. *A bit like you.* Adopting what she hoped was a fun, interested look, she asked, 'So what's your kilt like? I'm not familiar with the Kirkpatrick tartan.'

'Probably because it's Lowland. I'm guessing the Ross-Wylde tartan is—forgive the pun—cut from a different cloth.'

It was as it happened. Highlander through and through. But that didn't mean he could tar her with a brush of superiority. 'I don't use my name to get things I haven't earned.'

His eyes widened. There had definitely been bite to her bark and Max wasn't a man to stand around getting attacked. 'You certainly seem happy to use it when it comes to flinging your money about.'

Everything in her stilled.

'Don't say that.'

Max's spine realigned into ramrod position. 'Sore point?'

'Something like that.'

She saw him reeling through the possibilities of what could make the poor little rich girl so touchy about money. When she failed to explain he asked, 'Is this why you fund the charities through the ball instead of donating it all yourself? Gives you a bit of emotional clearance so you don't have to feel responsible for anyone and they don't have to come crawling to you for more?'

He was hitting close to the bone. Too close. And he wasn't bothering to sugar-coat it.

She flicked her hair out of her eyes and tucked it back underneath her hat.

'How I run the foundation is nothing for you to worry about, Max. It's a charity event, not a Princess Charming Ball.' Instead of stropping off, which she should have done, she lashed out, 'And don't think for a minute I need to find a male version of Cinderella to make me happy.'

'No?' countered Max, the space between them diminishing as the heated intensity between them increased. 'What do you need to make you happy?'

Her heart was pounding so hard she could barely hear her own thoughts let alone the sounds around them.

Someone like you?

'Max!' Euan was running towards them. 'Come fast! It's Fenella!'

Max took off with the practised speed of an athlete. Esme scooped up Dougal's lead and, as best she could, ran behind, silently adding, *Make self immune to grumpy but sexy Scottish doctors* to her list of things to do.

When Max reached the clearing, he could hardly believe what he was seeing.

Fenella's dog, Nora, was nudging herself under Fenella's head as she came to the end of a seizure.

'She was fitting, Doc.' Euan said, breathless and a bit pale from fright. 'I stuck my glove in her mouth so she wouldn't bite her tongue or anything, but she spat it out. Too mucky, I guess.'

'It's all right, pal.' Max dropped to his knees and did a quick check of Fenella's vitals. 'You've done the right thing in finding me. From the look of things, Nora here knows what she's doing.'

'Absolutely.' Euan looked awestruck. 'I know we saw her in the practice hall, but this was the real thing. It was like she knew it was going to happen.' He looked up as Esme jogged into the clearing. 'Did you know Nora makes herself into a cushion?'

Esme gave Nora a quick pet and a treat as Fenella slowly came to. 'Absolutely. That's what she's trained to do.'

Max helped Fenella sit up. 'You all right there, hun?'

The post-ictal phase was always a bit tricky. The person who'd had the seizure could feel perfectly fine or often exhibit signs similar to those of a stroke. Headaches, slurred speech, nausea and fatigue. In rare cases, some epileptics could suffer from post-ictal psychosis and suffer from paranoia or extreme fear. Usually the anomaly occurred in people who weren't taking their medication.

'Yes, I...' Fenella looked a bit confused and then, when her eyes lit on Nora, it was as if everything pinged into place. 'I felt a bit woozy and the next thing I knew, this one was being my pillow.' She ran her hand through the dog's fur and automatically reached to her pocket to get her a treat. 'Good girl. You're a clever girlie, aren't you?'

'She was!' Euan jumped in. 'Out of, like, absolutely nowhere you fainted. But you weren't fainting. You were having a seizure, I guess, and it was like Nora knew exactly what to do. She broke your fall. Then she stuck herself under your head while you were fitting. No offence, but it was really cool.'

Max glanced across at Esme. She looked concerned for Fenella but pleased her new service dog had fallen straight into her new role. She was actively avoiding eye contact with him. Served him right. He'd been an ass. Sticking his nose where it didn't belong. He should tell her about Gavin. It would break just about every rule in his play-your-cards-close-to-your-chest handbook, but he felt he owed it to her to even the emotional playing field. He got it. Sometimes things were personal. Luckily for his emotional armour, taking caring of Fenella took precedence.

'Did you take your AEDs?' Max asked. Antiepileptic drugs helped but weren't a failsafe, especially if they weren't taken regularly or weren't the right dosage. Having seen her in his A and E several times for sprains and cuts sustained while she'd been fitting, he knew she had struggled for years to find the right balance of medication.

'Yes.' She looked away, rubbing her elbow.

It didn't sound like a one hundred percent yes, but he wasn't going to embarrass her in front of everyone if there was a story behind her not taking it. Or, as was often the case, she might need to change meds. They weren't a one-pill-fits-all type of medicine.

'Did you hurt yourself?'

'No more than usual.' She held up a lightly scraped hand then qualified her answer. 'I probably would've cracked my head on a stone or something if it hadn't been for Nora.' She wrapped her arm round the dog and nuzzled her face into the fluffy goldendoodle's coat. After a few moments, Max quietly asked, 'What do you think set this one off?'

Fenella shot him a sheepish look. 'Lack of sleep most likely. I've been so excited the past few days, I've hardly slept a wink.'

He nodded. 'Perhaps it'd be best if we all head back to…um…'

'The castle?' filled in Esme, with the ease of someone who'd grown up in one.

Had it been more burden than blessing?

Esme glanced at her watch. 'Max mentioned you have an appointment with Flora, our physio. Shall we head back, get you a cup of tea and some quiet time before then?'

Fenella nodded, grunting a little as she sat up properly. Max reached out to steady her. Poor woman. Had to be tough being taken by surprise by seizures just when you thought you were having the time of your life.

'Are you two still all right having your dogs with you in your rooms? We can take them back to the kennels for the afternoon if you need a break.'

They both asked if they could have their dogs stay with them. Esme grinned a naughty little sister grin.

Which did beg the question, 'Is that not *de rigueur*?' Max asked, sotto voce. 'Having the dogs in the clinic?'

'Oh, it is,' she answered breezily. 'It just annoys my brother. Speaking of him, if he has time later on, Fenella, it might be a good idea for you to meet Charles and talk through your medications.'

'It's just the one right now. I'm sure it's fine.' Fenella looked uncomfortable about the suggestion, which instantly put Max's protective streak into high gear.

'Does he know much about epilepsy?' Max asked. A bit too defensively from the look of Esme's own bristly demeanour.

'He's a neurologist, so he's pretty good at understanding why brains work the way they do. I'm not criticising any of the medical treatment you've received at the Clydebank, Fenella. They obviously have specialists there who are helping you and Max, here, of course. I'm just covering our bases as you are our guest. We want to make sure you receive all the treatment you need. If there's anything we can do—'

'Don't worry.' Max helped Fenella get back to her feet. 'Easy does it, lassie. Why don't we take this step by step and get this woman some rest first?'

He tried to block out the sharp looks Esme kept sending him, but the odd one or two pierced straight through to his conscience. Now he definitely owed her an apology. What had got into him? Accusing her of flinging gold coins at people for her own amusement. Dismissing her sensible offer of a fresh set of eyes on Fenella's case.

If she knew even half of the reasons why he swung from one end of the emotional spectrum to the other she'd…hell, he didn't know. Send him packing most likely. It seemed to be the remit.

His stepfather had lured him in with all the bells and whistles that had appealed to a twelve-year-old kid from the wrong side of the tracks. Tickets to premier league football matches, nights out at the scary films his mother couldn't bear, slap-up meals at the finest burger joints in town. It had been kid heaven. Until it hadn't been. And had set him up for a lifetime of keeping people at arm's length until they proved they were the real deal.

Ironically, it had been Gavin's constant demands that he 'earn his keep' that had pushed him so hard in the military. Had made him the top-rate soldier and surgeon he knew he'd been. Gavin hadn't thought he had what it took? He'd vowed to show him.

He would have as well if he hadn't had a conscience. Or carried around those little-kid hopes and dreams that one day he'd be good enough. Worth loving. He supposed it had been that same little boy's belief in love that had made him blind to his fiancée's affair. Being so oblivious had made him feel every bit as weak as he'd felt when Gavin had shipped him off to military academy, instead of taking him to their new home, as he'd promised.

A few more proofs that truth and justice rarely reigned—dodgy commanding officers, innocents rigged up with IEDs, the cruelty of poverty had closed the book on the matter. Being wary of whatever met his eye was his modus operandi. Being suspicious of whatever touched his heart was critical. It hadn't exactly made him A-list boyfriend material. A handful of one-night stands he wished he hadn't had had been the clincher. So life as the Monk had begun. Which, of course, immediately made him think of all the people who were relying on him back at the Clyde to save Plants to Paws.

His conscience gave him a sharp kick in the posterior. His emotional baggage shouldn't be a factor. Normally it wasn't. Not with the chaos he encountered in A and E every day. And yet...here it was, front and centre. His hypersensitivity did beg the question, did he want Esme to think well of him?

He stuffed his hand through his hair. No need to ponder that one. It was an unequivocal *yes*. Which meant the next week was going to hoist this festive season up amongst the worst ever.

You could try being nice.

'Go on, then,' he said when Esme shot him another *look*. 'Give your brother a call.'

And there it was. The first chink in his 'don't ask for help' armour. If you don't ask, you don't need. And if you don't need, you're never disappointed. It was a little pact he'd made with himself when the Dictator had asked him to put a value on himself the very first Christmas they'd spent together. Turned out the pair of them had disagreed.

It hadn't been a very nice Christmas.

When Esme's smile of thanks hit him on full beam, he began to wonder if his pact had flaws.

CHAPTER FIVE

ESME CAREFULLY PLACED the enormous tabby back into Mrs Elsinore's arms. 'It might be an idea to cut back on Theo's treats. The extra weight could be contributing to his arthritis.'

Mrs Elsinore looked horrified. 'But, dear, we have a routine.' She talked Esme through morning treat, morning breakfast, elevenses treat, lunchtime and so on.

'No need to veer from the routine, it's more a question of reducing—' Something, or rather *someone* caught her eye just beyond the exam-room window. A six-foot someone tugging a hat over that touch-me-now hair of his. Was it time for the afternoon walk already? Not that she hadn't been counting down the seconds or anything, but the last few patients in the vet clinic had mercifully managed to steer her thoughts away from Max. Not any more!

'What was it you were saying about routine, dear?'

'Yes. Right. Routine.' Her gaze involuntarily drifted back out the window. Max was laughing at something Margaret had said. Margaret looked so relaxed and at ease with him. The total opposite of how *she'd* been. By turns uptight, weirdly flirty, downright snippy.

He glanced over towards the window and caught her eye. He raised his hand in a half-wave but turned the instant Margaret said something. Something *hilarious* from the look of things.

Ruddy Margaret.

Wait. *What?* She loved Margaret. Margaret was her friend. Her friend who had a boyfriend and was no threat at all. Not that she was feeling competitive. It wasn't as if she wanted to date him. Or press her hand to his chest to feel his heart beat. Or find out if his lips were as kissably delicious as they looked.

'Esme, dear…shall I carry on as normal, then?'

'No. I mean…cutting back a wee bit on Theo's treats would be advisable.' Esme gave her face a quick scrub with her hands. 'Apologies. I'm a bit distracted today. New residents…'

Mrs Elsinore looked out the window and smiled. 'With residents like that I think I'd be distracted, too.'

Esme blushed instantly. 'What? Him? Oh, no…he's not…'

'Don't deny it, dearie,' Mrs Elsinore tutted. 'He is. Now, if you tell me what else you want me to do with Theo that'll free you up to go on out there and be distracted a bit more up close and personal.'

Esme pretended she hadn't heard that part.

A few dietary tips and one prescription for glucosamine tablets later and Esme was pulling on her staff puffer jacket and heading out to where residents and their dogs met for the afternoon walk.

Margaret waved her over when she saw her. 'Big favour.'

'Sure.' Especially if it involved being nowhere near Max. He was currently at the far end of the barns with Hamish and Dougal. Max didn't look as pleased as Hamish was about Dougal's new Christmas jumper.

'Woohoo! Esme.' Margaret waved her hand. 'Eyes over here, please.'

'I wasn't—'

'Yes, you were. Which brings me to my favour. Do you mind taking Max for the next couple of hours?'

'What?'

'He's brilliant, but Euan keeps deferring to him for everything and we need to take a walk where Euan's sole focus is Ajax, not Captain Gorgeous.'

'He's not—'

'Esme.' Margaret stopped her cold. 'He totally is and there's absolutely nothing wrong with fancying him.'

There was. There were a thousand reasons and probably another thousand right behind those.

'Hey.' Margaret forced her friend to look at her. 'Not everyone's Harding MacMillan. Go on a walk with the man. What's the worst that could happen?'

She was about to launch into an extensive list of all of the bad things that could happen, even though Margaret knew the whole sordid story. Before she had a chance, Margaret had called Max over, explained the situation then told them where the group would be going so Max and Esme could go elsewhere.

When Margaret walked off and left the two of them standing there Max huffed out a laugh. 'Feels a bit like a set-up, doesn't it?'

'If you're not interested in taking a walk with me, I'm more than happy to take the dogs on my own.'

'Hey, easy there. I wasn't suggesting anything of the sort, I was just saying—' What was he saying? That being alone with her made his brain go all sorts of crazy? That sleeping down the corridor from her meant not sleeping at all? That he wanted her?

It was that simple.

All he had to do now was find a way to get his body to fall in line with his brain, which was telling him to step away from the beautiful woman and everything would be fine.

Esme tightened her lips then pointed towards a path. 'If we go that way towards the old castle ruins we should stay clear of them. I'm perfectly happy to go on my own, though.'

'No. I wasn't saying anything like that.'

'Well, what were you saying?'

'I was just saying your colleague has a way of making everything sound like a date whenever she matches the two of us up.'

Esme rolled her eyes then grudgingly laughed. 'Margaret has a way of doing that. She sees herself as my personal matchmaker.'

He didn't push for details, opting to let silence do the work. If she wanted to talk about her love life, she would. If she didn't, she wouldn't. As plain as that.

After about ten minutes of briskly paced walking, Esme threw up her hands. 'It isn't that I don't find you attractive, all right?'

Despite himself, Max laughed. She'd obviously been having a conversation all by herself. Again, he decided not to push for details. Lord knew, the more he was pushed, the less he wanted to say.

'I don't date clients.'

'Who said anything about dating?'

Esme glared at him. 'You did. The thing about Margaret making everything sound like a date?'

Max rubbed the back of his neck. This was one of those complicated conversations he had no way of winning. Did he want to take her out? Not particularly. He didn't do dating. Was he attracted to her? Absolutely. More than he had been to anyone, to be honest. There was something about Esme's combination of vulnerability and fiery strength that spoke to him. A kindred spirit who may have started off in life on a different path but, like it or not, they were on the same one now.

'You're right. This is a professional relationship. Nothing more.'

'Good,' Esme said, sounding absolutely miserable. 'I'm glad we've cleared that up.'

All of a sudden, they heard someone calling out, a loud piercing scream. It sounded like a name.

Esme scooped up Dougal and took off at a run. Max did the same, with Wylie loping along in his wake. The screams stopped abruptly. Esme pointed towards a gated field. 'A lot of villagers use this field as a shortcut to get up to the ruins. Maybe someone's dog was hit. Let's tie up the dogs here. I'll ring Aksel to come and collect them and bring the four-by-four in case we need to take anyone back to the vet or the clinic.'

All the tension tightening her features over the 'dating incident' had re-formed into exacting focus. This was not a woman fazed by crisis. Once the dogs were secured and Esme had made the call, they ran across the field, Esme leading the way. When they got to the far end, Max's doctor brain kicked into high gear. A woman was curled around a grey lurcher absolutely covered in blood. She was moaning and crying her dog's name over and over. When she looked up at them, they could see she was also covered in blood. She sobbed, 'Help! Teasel's been cut!'

'Janet, it's all right. We're here now.' Esme dropped to her knees beside them. 'Are you hurt?'

'I'm not sure. I had to jump over the fence after him and I think I twisted my ankle.'

Esme shot a glance up at Max. 'If I take the dog, can you look after Janet? She works down at the pub and has had this wee thing for…what is it, Janet four and a bit years now?'

'Five!' wailed Janet. 'We were out for his birthday walkies.'

'Well, then, we'll have to make sure we look after him with extra-special care, won't we? Why don't you sit up and we can take a look?'

Max could see what Esme was doing. Putting both of the patients at ease. Her voice was calm and steady. Her energy completely soothing. Animals read humans much better than people did and Esme had an impressive ability to match her energy accordingly.

'Sure thing.' He took his fleece off. 'Here, use this for Teasel.'

Janet clung even more tightly to her dog as Esme

reached out to take him. 'I'm afraid to let go. He was chasing a deer. I tried to get him to stop.'

That explained the screaming.

'When he leapt over the fence, the barbed wire snagged him.' She sobbed again. 'It's ripped a huge wound from his chest to his belly.' She tried to pull herself up to standing, still reluctant to let go of the dog. Max reached out and caught her as she stumbled. Esme deftly grabbed hold of the dog and cradled him in Max's jacket.

'All right, darlin'.' Max eased her back to the snow-covered ground. Not ideal, but until he knew what was wrong it'd have to do. They also weren't so far away from the castle that he couldn't carry her if necessary. She was a wee snip of a thing compared to some of the muscled soldiers he'd hoisted fireman style for over a kilometre.

Esme pulled off her puffer jacket. 'Here. Use this for Janet. She's had a shock.' The dog whimpered and Janet jumped up towards him.

'Hey,' Esme soothed. 'Teasel's whimpering is a good thing. It means his windpipe is intact.'

Janet fell back to the ground using both her hands to clutch her ankle. 'I think I sprained it or something.'

Max saw blood around her ankle, swiftly rucked up her waterproofs and carried out a quick examination. She didn't have a compound fracture or any obvious cuts so that was something, but she'd need X-rays to rule out any fractures. He felt further up along Janet's leg and was satisfied that her ankle had received the brunt of the fall and nowhere else. 'You don't happen to have X-ray facilities in the clinic, do you?'

'Yes.'

'Brilliant.' He checked Janet's pulse and suggested they keep her off her leg until he could do a proper examination. 'Looks like you got your own set of cuts as well. We'll check on the status of your tetanus jabs and get these cuts cleaned up. I don't think you'll need stitches, but—'

Janet pulled her wrist out of his hand. 'I'm not leaving Teasel! What if he's nicked an artery—what if—?' Janet became consumed with tears as she considered the very worst outcome.

'Hey.' He pulled her to his side as Esme carried out her own examination. The last thing one doctor needed was another doctor's patient jumping in at what could be a delicate moment. From the look on Esme's face, it was grim.

Max cocked his ear at the sound of a vehicle.

'That'll be Aksel.' Esme didn't look up as she wrapped the dog tightly in his coat. 'He's going to be up with the dogs—can you guide him in, please? The less movement for this little guy, the better.'

'Absolutely.'

Esme could hardly believe it had barely been a couple of hours since the mere idea of going on a walk with Max had filled her with horror. Now? She would happily have him along—day or night. Not that she was always encountering incidents like this harrowing one, but if she ever had to face the eye of a storm with someone, it was Max Kirkpatrick.

His military cool and first-class medical knowledge were exactly what you would want in a crisis. He'd even showed his soft side when Janet had dissolved into tears. Dug a clean handkerchief out of his pocket and everything. The man might see himself as solid mass of impenetrable man mountain, but her gut instinct had been right. He had a heart the size of Scotland.

'How's he coming along, Esme?' Janet asked through a speaker in the viewing room.

Esme tied off the delicate stitch then looked up. 'Only a few more stitches to go and then he can have a proper rest.' It was a highly edited way of describing what had been a difficult surgery. Teasel had had to be anaesthetised while she'd assessed the extent of the tissue damage. She'd had to debride some of the most heavily damaged areas right next to the wound and multiple layers of tissue had needed suturing but, luckily, they'd avoided having to put any drains in.

Despite Esme's insistence that Teasel would be receiving the very best of care, Janet had point blank refused to leave her dog. The best she'd agreed to was sitting in the large windowed room just outside the surgical area in the veterinary clinic, with Max in attendance. It wasn't standard practice, but…as the accident had happened on Heatherglen land, Esme felt an added responsibility to both patients.

With Janet and Max looking on, Esme had poured her concentration into the surgery as she'd painstakingly stitched Teasel's shockingly long wound back together. The barbed wire had done a real number on him, from his throat to his belly. He had miraculously managed to escape nicking his jugular vein. If he had, the nurses wouldn't be prepping a recovery kennel for him.

The nurse who was working with Esme turned off the microphone and asked, 'Shall I ask Max to try and get her to go up to Heatherglen now?'

Esme shook her head. She wasn't going to admit it, but having Max there was strangely soothing. She didn't want to have to worry about Janet while she was working on Teasel and with Max there, she didn't even feel an ounce of concern. 'It's not like it happens every day and she's been through such a shock. Teasel's her baby. I can understand her not wanting to leave him.' Dogs were family in her book. You didn't abandon family when they needed you most. Having a mother who'd abandoned ship at her lowest ebb had taught her that the hard way. Having a brother who'd been there to pick up the pieces had confirmed it.

She glanced up and caught Max's gaze. A warm heat swirled round her belly with such intensity it was as if he'd slipped his hands under her scrubs. This was not the time to be distracted. Even so, she hadn't been able to help taking the odd glimpse at him. He had either been readjusting Janet's position so that her foot was elevated, giving her a proper blood-pressure test with a pump Lyla had run down with from the clinic along with some ice packs, or running her through a ream of questions all designed to keep Janet's eyes off the rather gruesome injury.

Max was a picture of calm, quick thinking, levelheadedness in what could have been a difficult situation. Mercifully Janet's injuries hadn't been serious. She had a few cuts of her own, which Max had cleaned and put antibacterial cream on before lightly dressing them. He'd also called her GP and checked on her anti-tetanus status. She'd need a booster.

Half an hour later, when Teasel was resting in his kennel and Janet had been assured for the hundredth time that he'd be asleep for the next few hours and that they'd call straight away if there was any news, she finally agreed to let Max take her in for X-rays.

Esme had only just finished up at the surgery when she saw his vehicle leaving the castle grounds heading into town—to the GP's surgery and on to Janet's, no doubt.

She looked down and realised both of her hands were pressed tightly against her pounding heart. If she didn't watch herself...

Margaret came out of the front door of the clinic and locked the door behind her. 'Fancy a drink down in the village?'

'No,' Esme said a bit more dreamily than she'd intended. 'I'm all right here.'

Margaret followed her gaze as Max's four-by-four wended its way down the long drive. 'Oh, you are in trouble!'

Yes, Esme agreed silently. Yes, she was.

Charles stopped Esme as she was about to enter the kitchen.

His big-brother expression turned serious. 'The snow's just started, it's pitch black and it's icy.'

'Thanks for the weather report, Charles.'

He gave her a don't-be-daft look. 'I'm trying to tell you it's not safe to go out driving.'

Easily falling into her role as kid sister, she shot back, 'I happen to be an excellent driver, thank you very much.'

'Where are you going all dressed up like that?'

His eyes dropped to her flirty, swishy, feminine skirt. She never wore skirts. It was usually scrubs, workout clothes or pyjama bottoms at this time of the evening, unless she was meeting Margaret in the village for a glass of wine or, on very rare occasions, heading to Fort William or Glasgow for a dinner date. Yawn-fest more like. She silently vowed never to take her brother up on another suitable suitor again.

Though her features remained stoically neutral as he waited for an answer, she could feel tiny tendrils of heat creep into her cheeks. 'I'm just on my way to see Mrs Renwick. Everything else is in the wash.'

'Yeah, right.'

'Why are you so grumpy?'

'I'm not grumpy.'

He was. He was very grumpy. Which was annoying as he'd been in an absolutely brilliant mood when he'd come back from his medical conference a couple of months ago. It'd made a nice change from Dr Too Serious for His Own Good. Maybe he should go to another one. It would keep his prying eyes away from the fact she just might have accidentally on purpose put on something slightly more feminine in case she accidentally on purpose ran into a certain Max Kirkpatrick.

Since he'd come back a couple of hours earlier it was as if they were slowly circling one another, neither one willing to make the first move. Not that she even knew what kind of move was going to be made. If they were simply going to be friends, fine. She just wanted an end to this silly friction that existed between them. Working together today had helped, but when he hadn't bothered to find her after he'd come back from town, she'd gone into another one of her insane spirals of insecurity.

Was she good enough? Wasn't she? Was it time to simply grow up and not treat every single man who showed a flicker of interest in her as a potential pariah? Maybe in this case work was work and pleasure was a figment of her imagination.

Either way, she wanted the tension to end. She respected him and there was absolutely no reason why they couldn't be friends. She gave her brother a supercilious sniff then swished through the swinging kitchen doors before Charles could say anything else.

Esme was immediately drawn to the platters of Christmas biscuits covering the long kitchen counters, then sent her most winning look at Mrs Renwick. 'Yum. How many may I take?'

Mrs Renwick gave Esme her loving equivalent of a glare and placed yet another tray of perfect Christmas biscuits on the marble countertop. 'One. The rest are for the baskets I'm making up for the Christmas market.'

'Which ones are these again?' Esme reached out to take one of the little pink cloud-like treats, only to have her hand lightly slapped away.

'You know perfectly well they're peppermint divinity, Esme. Heaven knows, you've eaten enough of them each and every Christmas.' Esme dodged another tray of hot biscuits. 'Off you go. I'm busy here. Scoot.'

'Why can't I stay here with you?'

'Because you must have far better things to do than watch me mass-produce my Christmas biscuits.'

True, but…also…false. Nothing was holding her interest. Ever since Max had returned and *not* hunted her down, she'd felt listless. She took a biscuit and watched Mrs Renwick at work.

After a few minutes of being stared at, her honorary aunt gave an exasperated sigh. 'Esme Ross-Wylde, you are underfoot. Why don't you go to the lounge and talk to some of the residents?'

'Ha! No thank you.'

Mrs Renwick gave her a sidelong glance. 'You like seeing the residents.'

'That's true.' She took another biscuit. She did like spending time with them. Honestly, she did, it was just that *he* was out there and as he'd avoided her when he'd come back he obviously didn't want to talk to her. Then again, what if he thought *she* was avoiding *him*?

This was ridiculous. What was she? Twelve? There was no way she was going to get through the rest of the week unless they resolved the whole tension thing. But how?

It wasn't as if she was going to saunter up to him and say, *Hey, Max! Just so you know—I've got loads of trust and confidence issues thanks to my ex-husband. We got married when I was nineteen. I know…young, right? Anyway, I was grieving after my brother's death at the time, and the rest of the family were dealing with Nick's death in their own ways...you know how it is.*

One thing led to another—we eloped, he stole half of my trust fund and set up a nightclub, but made it seem like I was reneging on my promise to set up a canine therapy centre I'd told the universe I was going to establish in honour of Nick's death. Yeah. I know! Not very nice. It makes a girl paranoid. So, anyway...the thing is... I'm really attracted to you and it freaks me out. So sorry if I'm being weird. Friends?

Yeah, that definitely wasn't going to happen.

Maybe she should bring a thank-you present for everything he'd done today. She scanned the kitchen. 'Is there anything I could take out to the residents as a night-time nibble?'

Mrs Renwick picked up a gloriously over-the-top chocolate cake. 'Here. Take this and leave me in peace.'

'Perfect.' She leant in and gave Mrs Renwick a kiss. 'Thank you, Christmas Fairy!'

When she left the kitchen the first person she laid eyes on was Max. He was at the doorway to the media room, staring intently at something. She poked her head in to see what was so interesting.

'Wow.'

Euan and Andy were playing some sort of scuba-diving treasure-hunt game, their two dogs curled up beside their armchairs. It looked as though the forty-something soldier and the twelve-year-old had been friends for life. Playing. Cheering one another on. It was all quiet and modulated, but...there was a kinship there. Two broken souls finding a safe place to be happy.

Sensing her rather than looking at her, Max said, 'This definitely falls into the category of things I thought I'd never see.'

'You're not wrong,' Esme agreed. 'I never thought I'd see Andy this interactive again.'

Max shot the pair a nervous look. 'Should I get Euan out of there?'

'No. Not at all, it's just...' She rested her head against the doorframe and watched the ex-soldier offer gentle instructions to Euan as he navigated the game. A splashing sound came out of the speaker and they both flinched. Then fist bumped each other. 'They've both found someone who understands what they're going through.'

Max nodded, his eyes still on the pair. 'They've each got PTSD for fairly different reasons, though.'

Esme's heart softened. This definitely wasn't virgin territory for him. 'I guess you know a fair few soldiers who came back from their tours seeing the world through a different lens.'

He scrubbed his hand along his jaw before answering. 'Everyone comes back from a conflict zone seeing the world differently.'

Not an insight exactly, but...she supposed she'd seen Glasgow as her 'conflict zone' after everything had gone wrong with Harding. It made hiding out up here too easy. Maybe it was time to see about that satellite clinic she kept promising herself she'd open one day.

They watched for a few moments as the game progressed. There was a third unused console sitting on a footstool. Esme pointed at it.

'You not playing?'

'Nah.' He shook his head, loosening those loose curls on top of his forehead again. 'I'm no good at fantasy.'

Oh, she would've bet actual money that he was very good at fulfilling fantasies.

Esme! Stop it. Your mind is very, very naughty. Especially when she was within a ten-foot radius of Mr Tall, Dark and Scrumptious here.

She shifted her weight to her other hip and balanced the cake on her left hand.

'After seeing you in action today, I would've thought you'd be good at anything you set your mind to.'

Uh-oh. That had come out more flirtatiously than she'd anticipated. Mostly because her eyes were on the same level as that yummy-looking mouth of his.

Her tooth caught her lower lip as she felt Max's dark eyes glint then take a leisurely inspection of her. Nice and slow from her hair, to her eyes, to her lips, to her…

'You always walk around your castle with a chocolate cake?'

'Yes.' She gave him a goody-goody smile. 'It's my evening ritual. It's required actually.'

'Oh?' That increasingly familiar little hitch of his eyebrow let her know he was back in flirt mode.

'Yes, that's right. Cake-bearing duties are obligatory for poor, beleaguered Highland spinsters who rely on their big brother's largesse for a roof over their heads.'

He snorted. Rightly so.

She had inherited plenty of money when her father had died. The trust fund thing had been awful, but her father had been clever enough not to give his children access to vast lump sums. Charles had inherited the castle in line with tradition, but it wasn't exactly as if he was pushing her out the front door. Quite the opposite, in fact. Both of them loved it here, but they would've traded it all if they could have had their brother back. It was one of the reasons Charles had suggested they turn it into a clinic. A way for them to work together, honour their brother, and make their home a place to heal.

Max's eyes dropped to the cake again. 'Are you planning on sharing any of that, or are you just going to walk round and show people what they aren't getting?'

The atmosphere between them went taut. Max wasn't talking about cake. Margaret's words coquettishly danced to the fore: *'What's the worst that could happen?'*

She was safe here. This was her home. She wasn't going to elope and give him all the PIN numbers to her bank accounts. Apart from that, Max Kirkpatrick simply didn't seem the type of man who would have any dealings with lies and deceit.

A mad urge to go with her gut instinct seized her. She swooped her finger into the thick icing then stuck the whorl of buttercream into her mouth, making a show of enjoying the rich icing as it melted on her tongue. 'Mmm...'

'Looks good.' Max's voice was as rough as his stubble. Not that she'd touched it. Yet. When she finished the icing she reached out to touch his cheek. He grabbed her wrist and swept her finger through the chocolate buttercream for a second time. 'Uh-uh.' He said. 'My turn.'

Esme's insides turned as hot as lava as he pulled her finger towards his mouth. *Oh, mercy.* He was going to— *Oh...* he did... He drew her finger into his mouth. It was hot and wet, and his tongue was making short work of that icing, but his eyes had not as much as blinked. This had to be one of the sexiest things that had ever happened to her and they were both completely clothed. She dreaded to think what would happen if they were naked.

No, she didn't. And that was a problem. She didn't dread it at all.

Just then Wylie bumbled over and gave her a nudge.

Max let go of her wrist.

'Your bodyguard?'

'Something like that.' Gulp. 'Want a proper slice?' She raised the cake.

'No.' He shook his head, his voice still thick with whatever it was that had just happened between them. 'Not hungry.'

'Neither am I.'

'Give it to the lads.'

'Okay.'

And just like that Esme walked into the media room, handed the video-game players the cake and two forks then walked straight back out again.

'Want to see my Christmas tree?' she asked Max.

'Is that a euphemism?'

'No. But it can be if you'd like it to be.'

Much to her astonishment, Max followed her as she silently led him towards the small sitting room in her and Charles's private wing. This, she was beginning to realise, was going to be a very different Christmas indeed.

CHAPTER SIX

'THIS DOOR HAVE a lock?'

Max knew they were in the private wing, but private also included Esme's older brother and the last thing he wanted was to get a black eye as a result of what he was about to do.

'No.' Esme swallowed. 'But my bedroom does.'

'So does mine.'

'Mine has mistletoe.'

'I don't need a reason to kiss you.' He smiled at her shocked expression. Finally! He'd called a spade a spade and put that humming buzzy friction crackling between them out in the open. He wanted her. She wanted him. The only question was where. 'Is Dougal in your room or mine?'

'He's in mine with Wylie. I think they're brand-new BFFs.' She held out her hand. 'Let's go to yours.'

He took her hand but didn't move anywhere. Instead he pulled her to him and did what he'd wanted to do since that first moment he'd laid eyes on her. Cupped that perfect chin of hers between his thumb and forefinger, tipped it up and kissed her. She was every bit as sweet, hot and delicious as he'd imagined.

When she parted her lips and their kisses deepened, he felt things happening inside him he definitely didn't want her big brother to see.

'My room,' he rumbled. 'Now.'

She didn't need telling twice.

Moments later they were in the room, locking the door and tearing each other's clothes off. Kissing as if their lives depended on it. His top first. Her jumper next…a bit of a stall as he relished the sensation of touching that creamy, freckly, décolletage of hers. His hands skimmed over the very nice lace of her bra and he was rewarded with a moan as her nipples turned into tight nibs under his touch.

Her skin was every bit as soft as he'd imagined. Staying steady and in control was almost impossible. In true 'everything's magic at Heatherglen' style, someone had already been in and lit the fire in his room so enjoying the bit-by-bit exposure of Esme by firelight was little short of heaven.

'Let's slow it down,' he said when Esme started fiddling with his belt buckle.

She instantly froze beneath his hands. 'What? Why?'

He smiled at her aggrieved expression. 'I was just saying we have plenty of time—twelve days before Christmas.'

'It's seven, actually.' He could see her begin to withdraw emotionally. 'So…you don't want to do this?'

'Quite the opposite, darlin'. I've wanted you from the

moment I laid eyes on you.' He dropped kisses on her forehead, her nose, her lips then said, 'The way I see it, once we start, there's no turning back. So we either agree that this is something that won't affect our "day jobs" while we're here or we walk away now.'

Esme actually whimpered. Which was just about the sweetest thing he'd ever heard. 'I don't want to walk away…'

'There's a lot you don't know about me.' A lot he didn't want her to know. He'd been trying to leave the angry guy from the past behind for a long time now and he thought he'd finally done it, but…this whole business with Plants to Paws had dug up a bunch of unresolved feelings. Something about Esme made him want to wrap them up once and for all.

'Well…' Esme traced the pad of her fingertip along the stubble above his upper lip '…there's definitely a lot you don't know about me.' Her eyes provocatively flicked to his. 'But it doesn't seem to have stopped us from liking each other.'

As her finger traced round his lips then dipped into his mouth, he couldn't resist drawing it in deeper and giving it another swirl as if it were still slathered in chocolate icing. When he let go of it, he said, 'That's very true. Maybe we could call this getting-to-know-you time?'

'We could do that…'

He ran his thumb along the bare swoop of her waist to her hip and watched a smattering of goose pimples shift along her belly just as he'd thought they might. 'Am I sensing there is another part to that sentence?'

* * *

Esme had a choice here. She could tell Max the truth. Tell him she was scared. Scared of being betrayed. Of being taken advantage of. Of not being enough.

She could also tell him she was so ready to rip the rest of his clothes off she could hardly see straight. An urge she hadn't felt in years.

And yet here she was, standing in his arms with nothing on but her bra and her skirt while he was still mostly clothed. Which was strangely sexy. No. Not strangely at all. Everything about Max Kirkpatrick was sexy. The touch of his hands. The warmth of his skin. The way his eyes looked at her like she was the most beautiful thing he'd ever seen.

Max deserved an honest answer. One that she could live with, too.

She flattened her hand against his chest, just itching to tease her fingers through the sparse whorls of dark hair around his nipples, but stopped herself. Teasing him when she hadn't yet said yes was little short of cruel. To both of them.

She waited until she could feel the beat of his heart beneath her palm. It was fast. He was as nervous as she was. And as excited. She could tell that easily enough by leaning into him. Cotton trousers didn't hide much in the way of male arousal. Before she shifted her hand down and felt it, she had to make a decision.

He wasn't Harding MacMillan. Or any of the exceedingly bland men she'd dated to avoid heartbreak since. Max Kirkpatrick was one of a kind. Something deep within her told her he wanted nothing from her

apart from honesty and respect. All of which spoke
to the very essence of who she was. The fundamental
spirit of how she wanted to live her life. Courageously.
Openly. Honestly. Would this be her chance to restore
that bright flame of confidence, which she'd once felt,
flickering in her heart again?

She tilted her head up for another kiss. He saw the
questions in her eyes and knew it would be the decid-
ing factor. The kiss he gave in response told her all she
wanted to know. It was everything she'd ever wanted in
a kiss and more. Soft then responsive. Inquisitive. Passionate. Hungry. Wanting absolutely nothing of her but
that she enjoy his touch. Could she handle seven perfect
days of Max and then watch him walk away?

When he shifted both his hands to her waist her
goose pimples turned her insides to liquid gold. She
pressed up against him so that her hips were just below
his. 'Yes,' she said. 'If we keep it low key with the staff,
I'd be grateful, but other than that? Let's dispense with
the seven swans aswimming.'

Max didn't need any more encouragement. He swept
his hands along her bottom, down to her thighs, and
pulled her up so that her legs circled his hips so quickly
she hardly had a chance to catch her breath. Didn't care
if she did. She was already light-headed with her decision to give herself to this man. He was half untamed
wild man, half cultured Casanova.

The light stubble on his cheeks brushed against her
cheek as he carried her to his huge four-poster bed then
laid her down on the thick linen bedding. She almost

purred in response. Rough with the smooth. That was life, wasn't it? That was Max.

'It's a very nice room.' Max said, thinking she was cooing about the bedding.

'It's much nicer with you in it.'

A rakish smile crept onto his lips. 'Did you put me here by accident or design?'

'Neither,' she said with an innocent smile. 'Dr Sinclair does the room assignments. He thought you were going to be a thirty-something single mum. When he heard you were ex-military he said I'd be as safe as houses.'

'Is that what he told you?' His eyes lit up with a dangerously scrumptious glint.

'That's what he assumed.'

'Shall I show you what you can do with his assumptions?' Max began undoing his belt buckle.

'Yes, please.'

What followed was by turns heartfelt, carnal and utterly luxurious.

Max had never experienced lovemaking like this before. It felt by turns entirely new and utterly familiar. As if he'd been waiting his whole life to find this. To find her. To hold Esme in his arms. Not that she lay still long enough for him to give her a cuddle. No, she was busy exploring his body as if she'd found Atlantis itself. He didn't mind being a stand-in for the mythical place. Not by a long shot.

She was busy tracing his abdomen at the moment. With her tongue. By the time she hit that divot between his ribcage and his hips, her blonde hair tickling the wake of where her hot, wet mouth had just been, he wanted nothing more than to turn the tables. It was his turn to pleasure her. Tease every tiny moan and groan of which she was capable out of her. Bring her to the climax he could already sense building inside her.

Before she could dip any lower, he pulled her into his arms and flipped her onto her back, her hair splayed out around her like a halo, her blue eyes glistening in the firelight. 'Now it's your turn.'

As she had earlier, she pressed her palm to his chest as if to bond their hearts. When she was satisfied that the beat of his own heart matched hers, he kissed her so hard and with such depth of emotion he could have disappeared into the kiss and never come back again. From the intensity of her response, she was feeling the same way.

After an utterly decadent spell of exploring her body he was barely containing his own heated tension. When she arched into the taut length of him it was all he could do not to thrust himself deep inside her and find his climax. It would come easily and quickly, as he suspected hers would as well. But he didn't want that for Esme. He wanted slow, and intense and meaningful. Then maybe another round that was hot and fast. Yet another that was dirty and dangerous. And then they could spend the rest of the time they had left figuring out all the other ways the two of them made sense.

As if reading his mind, she smiled at him with such desire in her eyes he felt his heart seem to nearly double in size. Quadruple. Whatever. All he knew was that he cared about her. Knowing she felt the same way was worth its weight in gold. There was something vulnerable about her he wanted to protect. Something fiery in her, brave even, that he wanted to nurture. Though they had come from different worlds, he felt he knew her and that with each passing day there would be discoveries that would only make knowing her even more enriching than it already had been. So long as he didn't do anything stupid like fall in love—

'Stop thinking.' Esme held his face between her hands. 'I want you inside me.'

This was the one time in his life he felt utterly obliged to do as the lady wished.

After a scramble for protection and an intensely pleasurable few moments ignoring Esme's cries for him to stop what he was doing with his fingers because she couldn't hold back much longer, Max was certain she wanted him as much as he wanted her. He positioned himself so that the thick tautness of his desire finally dipped between her legs. Her hips were urging him to enter her. He somehow managed to exhibit a bit more restraint than Esme, who was virtually glittering with frustrated desire under him. When at long last he finished teasing her, he pushed inside her. Both of them groaned with pleasure. If there'd been any doubt before, it was a certainty now. They were made for each other. Their bodies moved in a synchronicity he had never experienced before. An undulating cadence that built and strengthened and empowered.

He wanted to let loose. He wanted her to feel him

completely inside her. He wanted to bring her to a climax she would never forget.

'Do it,' she whispered. 'Take me.'

There was absolutely no hesitancy or fear in her voice. Only pure, undiluted desire.

He did as she bid.

When the moment of fulfilment came Esme cried out his name and Max actually saw stars. He almost laughed. If he told Esme she'd insist it was a Christmas star. He'd tell her sometime why it was such a complicated day for him. But for now he just wanted to hold his slightly breathless, incredibly beautiful, Christmas angel in his arms. That was more than enough Christmas magic for him.

Esme would've happily stayed snuggled all warm and cosy in Max's arms for the rest of the day. Longer if her tummy wasn't rumbling. Thank goodness he was still asleep and couldn't hear all of her mere mortal noises because last night…last night had been straight out of the heavenly bodies notebook. He was right. Once they'd had a taste of what intimacy was like between the pair of them? Catnip. Once hadn't been enough. Or twice. It was like discovering herself all over again. Discovering just how magical a connection between two people could be had been little short of revelatory. If not a tiny bit scary. He was perfect. And she was scared of perfect because she'd thought she'd had perfect once before and how wrong she'd been.

Even so, something told her she had to find a way to start trusting her instincts again. It had been over ten years since Harding had well and truly pulled the wool over her eyes. Surely she'd learnt her lesson by now. If what her gut was telling her was true, Max was the real deal. Complex. Loving. Generous, sharing, caring, sensual. She gave his hand, which she'd been using as a mini-pillow, a kiss. Yes, he was all that and more. The big, strong soldier was vividly on show every time he scooped her up and flipped her this way or that on the bed. But there was also a tender, unbelievably sensitive man whose hands could… Ooh…goosebumps.

When her phone alarm went off before the sun had even thought about coming up, she was tempted to throw it out the window, but duty called. Max's hand reached out to bat at the snooze button, but she swatted it away and turned the alarm off. 'Uh-uh. Sorry, pal. I've got a long day of surgery ahead.'

'Surgery?'

'Yup.' She rolled over so she could face him, pulling a sheet up to her mouth in case she had morning breath.

'What are you doing?'

'Hiding my morning breath from you. Hey. Stop that! Don't. OMG, what if I kill you with morning breath?'

Max made a big stagey inhalation then grinned. 'Delicious. Just like a candy cane. Now, out with it. What's with the surgery?'

She grinned, pleased that he was interested, and sat up, pulling a swirl of sheet around her as she did so. 'Well! I have a knee surgery for a Great Dane.'

'Sounds interesting.'

'It will be. It's an ACL surgery. Almost identical to the ones they do for top athletes.'

He arced an eyebrow. 'Cruciate ligament on a giant breed. Definitely interesting. Can I tag along?'

Her eyebrows scrunched together. 'Don't you want to be with Euan for his training?'

He gave his jaw a scrub. 'They're going on some sort of outing today with Margaret. To a shopping centre, I think. I've noticed Euan tends to defer to me when he's nervous about something and seeing that he and I aren't going to be attached at the hip when we get back to Glasgow, I was wondering what you thought about the idea of letting him get on with things?'

Esme leant in and gave him a soft kiss. Margaret hadn't needed to farm him out for babysitting. He'd been well aware of what had been going on all along. 'You're much sweeter in real life than you let on.'

He growled and pounced on her until they were a kissing, cuddling, giggling tangle of legs, arms and duvet. When they flopped back onto the pillows with a contented sigh, Esme reluctantly climbed out of bed.

'Right! I'd better get across the hall before my brother sees me do the walk of shame.'

Max jiggled his eyebrows. 'Is this a frequent occurrence?

'Pah! Hardly.' Like never. 'Not even close. But he'd probably have a heart attack if he saw me tiptoeing out of a man's room. After last time—'

She clapped her hands to her mouth.

He traced a line from her throat to the little divot between her shoulder blades. 'Want to talk about it?'

She didn't. But as she'd actively avoided talking about her past to every single man she'd ever dated before, perhaps it was time to see what happened if she was as open and honest as she wanted the men in her life to be.

'Later?'

'How about after work? I'll pick you up at yours.' He winked. She blushed. It was settled.

She was going to have a date to discuss her evil ex-husband with her lover and it felt like the right thing to do.

She gave his hand another kiss. 'Sounds good.' She quickly pulled on her clothes for the run down the corridor.

'You're sure you're cool with me watching you in surgery today?'

'Why wouldn't I be? You watched yesterday.'

'Yesterday I hadn't seen you naked.'

'Good point.' It wasn't very fun thinking of what lay ahead when all she wanted to concentrate on was the here and now, but... 'Not to throw ice on this or anything, but I do live and work here. As you'll be leaving in a week, maybe we'd be best keeping it quiet?'

'Sounds sensible. Your wish is my command.'

Oh! That was easy. There were a thousand ways he could've responded to her request to keep things quiet, but the way Max had taken on board what she'd said made her feel as though she'd really been listened to. Maybe this was what adult relationships were like. Honest. Straightforward. And super sexy.

Max pulled her in close so that she was standing between his legs as he sat on the edge of the bed. Mmm...

He smelt of warm bedding and cloves and some sort of special man scent. *Yum.*

He pulled her in for a kiss then held her a few inches back and spoke in an exaggerated brogue. 'All right, then, ma wee lassie. Just be warned, if anyone tries to swoop in and claim you, I'll tilt my lance for ye.'

Swoon!

If she didn't watch herself, it would be very, very easy to fall for this man.

'Excellent. I shall get Wylie to do the same on my behalf.' She was quite sure the St Bernard would know how to keep other women at bay. Slobber them to death most likely. 'Speaking of that, I'd better let poor Dougal out. He and Wylie need a quick spin round the block before I head off to the clinic. Interested?'

He shook his head. 'I've got a few phone calls to make to the Clyde and I'll have breakfast with Euan as I'll be abandoning him all day.'

He pulled her in for a final kiss and when they finally came up for air she knew she'd have a big challenge ahead of her in regard to keeping this romance under the radar. Hiding the way she felt about him would be little short of impossible.

CHAPTER SEVEN

EVEN WITH HER entire body buzzing from the last twenty-four hours, Esme was not going to be kept from her morning cup of coffee. She was in the middle of frothing up some milk when Margaret walked into the staffroom with the daily schedule.

One look at Esme was all it took. 'Ooh! I see why you blew me off last night.'

Esme's plan to not tell anyone lasted about two seconds before she cracked. 'It wasn't strictly planned but…' Her smile stretched from ear to ear.

'Finally.' Margaret accepted the proffered latte and took a big slurp before giving Esme's arm a congratulatory pat. 'I was going to have to reclassify you as a virgin if you hadn't got some action soon.'

'Crickey.' Esme play-sulked because she was too happy to actually sulk. 'I didn't think I was that dire a case.'

Margaret rolled her eyes. 'Oh, believe me, Ez. You were definitely on the brink of being sent to a nunnery.' She shot a surreptitious look out the door towards the main reception area. 'So what is he? Short term or long term?'

Her gut said long term. Her head told her otherwise. 'Short terms. Obviously.'

'Why obviously? He's hot. And you look all loved up, so…if it works, why cut it short?'

'Cut what short?' Max appeared in the doorway. 'Sorry, ladies. Was I interrupting something?'

'No!' they both shouted, then burst into giggles, which, of course, answered his question.

Esme choked out something about coffee, which Max accepted with a bemused grin. She busied herself making the coffee, praying he wasn't noticing Margaret's eyes ping-ponging between the pair of them as if she was expecting cartoon love hearts to blossom out of thin air and float round the staffroom. She wasn't *that* loved up.

Max took the cup of coffee from her and when their fingers brushed, she blushed.

Okay. Maybe she had a *crush* on him. Big time. But that was normal when a girl had had such a lengthy hiatus from romance. A Christmas dalliance, she reminded herself when her eyes travelled across the room to the mistletoe hanging in the doorway.

Margaret took another big slurp of her coffee then asked, 'Shall I run you through what I'm doing with Euan and Fenella today before I leave you two love-birds to it?'

Max choked on his coffee. Esme's cheeks flamed.

'That would be lovely, Margaret.' Esme had her public-school voice back on. 'Please. Do tell us.'

With an unapologetic grin, Margaret launched into a detailed explanation of the trip they'd be taking to the shopping mall, where Euan in particular would have a chance to deal with the loud noises. They'd work with how the dog could help in stressful situations. 'It's getting so close to Christmas it's going to be very busy.'

'Six days,' Esme said, a bit too aware of the countdown to Christmas.

Max gave a little involuntary shudder. 'You sure you're all right with the pair of them on their own? It might be a lot for Euan to take on board.'

'He needs to get used to dealing with these things and if we ease him in with these baby steps, it'll be much more useful once you get back to Glasgow.' She pulled her mobile out of her pocket. 'I've got one of these and know the staff at the shopping centre well, so if there are any problems I'll give you a tinkle. You two enjoy yourselves in surgery.'

'Oh, we plan to,' Max said, rubbing his hands together.

'I'll bet you do,' Margaret said, then swished out of the room.

Esme shook her head. For heaven's sake! So, she'd had sex. No need to make a song and dance out of the whole thing. She glanced at the clock on the wall to gauge just how much time they had before her first dog came in for surgery.

Max looked at Esme as her smile widened. 'What?'

A few hours in, Max had to admit that watching Esme at work was on a par with observing the finest surgeons at work in war zones. He'd never thought veterinarians were less skilled than human doctors, quite the opposite in fact, but he'd never really taken on board how much more complex it was because her patients couldn't explain where it hurt.

Didn't seem to matter to Esme. She appeared to have a sixth sense about them. And their owners. She was focused, exacting and utterly intent on bringing about the best results for her patient. After Max had popped on a set of the clinic's scrubs and a fleece, he parked himself in the corner as Esme kicked off the day with the promised cruciate ligament surgery for Arthur, a Great Dane who was virtually eye to eye with Esme when standing. Which wasn't long, because she liked to keep their distress to a minimum.

After Arthur's rather astonishing surgery, she neutered a cat and a dog, removed a large growth from a chocolate Labrador's spleen, sewing him up with the same exacting stitches she'd exhibited on Teasel, and plucked a rather painful-looking thorn from a bloodhound's paw without eliciting as much as a whimper of discomfort from the dog.

This, on top of an emergency extraction of a chicken bone stuck in a Chihuahua's throat, operating on a bulldog's cherry eye whilst singing 'Rudolph the Red Nosed Reindeer', much to the delight of the vet nurses, and taking off the bandages and pronouncing good health to a ferret who had suffered a serious cut after getting stuck in a bit of guttering.

Unlike most of the human surgeons he'd met, she was also completely soppy. And not just with puppies. Any animal that entered her exam room or surgery brought that soft, dewy-eyed expression to her face as if she'd never before seen anything so utterly adorable. No wonder their patient roster was filled to bursting. All the pet owners absolutely adored her!

The bell tinkled above the main door to Reception just as Esme was dropping off a prescription for an arthritic lurcher. A woman wearing riding clothes, including her helmet, rushed in, carrying a heavy cardboard box. 'Help! Please! Can you help!'

'Mrs McCann? What's happened?'

'It's Honeybear!' wailed the ashen faced woman.

Esme rushed over to her side to help her, her entire body stilling as she saw what was inside. 'Max?' She threw him a quick look. 'Could you do us a favour?'

He came over and looked inside. It was a smallish dog—a beagle—who looked as though it had been hit by a car. He was alive, but bleeding from a bad cut on his right hip, and was panting in clear distress.

'Would you mind bringing Honeybear back to the surgical room? I'll be right behind you.' He heard her ask the nursing staff to get the woman a cup of sweet tea and to see if they could call Aksel to come in a bit earlier than the afternoon shift they had him scheduled for. She also asked them to ring Arthur the Great Dane's owners and tell them he was doing just fine in Recovery and could be collected at the end of the day.

The second she was in surgery she was a picture of undeterred focus. Surgical cap, gown and mask on. Her instructions were crisp, thoughtful and modulated. Every single member of her team was made to feel like that…a member of a team. Which was every bit as sexy as Esme naked in his bed. He liked a confident woman. He liked Esme. More and more as the day progressed. All of which meant saying goodbye come Christmas Eve was going to be a wrench, but… He stuffed the thoughts away. No need to think about it now.

'You don't have to stand back if you don't want to.' Esme smiled across at him. 'Since you brought her in, you're part of the team. If you scrub in, you can come on over to the table and see how the real doctors do it!' She dropped him a wink. 'All right, Honeybear, let's get you on the table, shall we?' Deftly she inserted an IV drip into the front paw one of her nurses had just shaved. They also fitted an oxygen mask to her small muzzle. 'Lainey? Can we please get some samples?'

'What are those for?' Max asked from the scrub sink in the adjacent room. Nothing was going to stop him from being a part of this.

Esme worked as she spoke. 'We need to see what the packed cell volume is, total solids, glucose and BUN.'

'Same as for humans? The BUN levels?' Max asked.

'Exactly. Dogs need kidneys every bit as much as humans. If this little chap's kidneys can't remove urea from the blood, the same things happen to him as happen to a human.'

She didn't need to spell it out. It was bad. The critical diagnostic test would indicate whether or not they needed to worry about liver damage, urinary tract obstruction or even gastrointestinal bleeding.

'The IV includes painkiller as well as fluids,' Esme

explained. 'Apparently he was running alongside Mrs McCann when she was out for her daily ride on Hercules.'

'And he is…?'

'Her shire horse. She likes to go for a bit of a hack through the woods up here on the estate but something spooked him and he kicked out. Unfortunately, Honeybear was caught, the poor wee thing. It's all right,' she cooed at the dog, who was beginning to feel the effects of the sedative she'd just given him. 'All right, darling.' She grabbed a pair of scissors and a stack of swabs. 'Let's see what's going on in here, shall we?'

Half an hour and a set of X-rays later, the prognosis was better than expected.

'What would your assessment be, Dr Kirkpatrick?'

Max had been so absorbed in the examination he answered instantly. 'Initial observations are to keep an eye on the laceration on his right hip, presumably from the horseshoe. Perhaps the horse's hoof should be checked. There might be a loose nail in there judging by the jagged edge of the cut. I would give Honeybear a tetanus shot if they aren't up to date. His pelvic fracture will need external stabilisation. It doesn't appear to be displaced, but…' He glanced at the X-rays hanging on the wall again.

'If he were a patient in my ER, I would advise one or two days in hospital to stabilise. He'll need monitoring because of the damage and swelling. There's always the possibility that there's some internal bleeding we haven't caught yet.' He wove his fingers together on top of his head as he leant in for a closer look. 'The blunt trauma of the injury will cause significant bruising and swelling so any chance of haematomas or clotting will need to be reduced.'

Esme nodded, only her bright blue eyes visible above her mask.

'So…you wouldn't put him down despite the catastrophic injuries?'

Max stood bolt upright. 'No. You wouldn't do that to a human! Put them down just because of a bit of recovery time.'

Soft little fans of crinkles appeared at the sides of Esme's eyes. 'Very good, Doctor. A few more years of university and you'd make an excellent veterinarian here at the CTC if you ever decided to change over.' The soft, approving look he knew was just for him sparkled with delight, then abruptly shifted back into professional mode as there were about four other staff members waiting for Honeybear's actual assessment.

'He'll definitely need a bit of time to recover from the shock before we do anything other than make sure this cut doesn't bleed any more. The only other thing is that once the swelling goes down, the pelvic fracture could require stabilising surgery rather than observed cage rest. Although… I agree. If we can avoid surgery, it'd be better for this little one. Possibly seven to ten days' cage rest would do the trick, which would mean…' Her eyes flicked across at a large digital clock and calendar. 'It would mean, if all goes well, you just might be home in time for Christmas with your mum! It's what everyone wants, isn't it? To be home for Christmas with their loved ones?' Her eyes flicked to Max's just in time to catch his inevitable wince.

He felt awful. She wasn't to know his stepdad used to make Christmas the unhappiest time of year. From day one Max had never able to put a foot right in his stepdad's immaculate home. Or say the right thing. Or give the right presents. So much so the frequently made suggestions that he stay behind at the military academy to make sure he was on top of his studies had soon become the easiest option to keep his mum out of an ever-increasing line of verbal fire.

When she shot him an *Are you okay?* look, he excused himself. There was a side door out to a small covered porch just outside the surgical ward. He tugged on a gilet and went out into the wintry air and sucked in a deep breath. He cursed himself under his breath. He couldn't help feeling like that twelve-year-old boy who'd wanted nothing more than his stepfather's love. The eighteen-year-old boy intent on hating everything about him. The man who *bah-humbugged* his way through Christmas just to keep the dark memories at bay.

Time to grow up. Flinching and wincing and bracing himself against any and all things Christmas didn't change a damn thing. He looked in the window to the room leading to the operating theatre and saw Esme carefully carrying Honeybear in her arms, deftly shifting him into one of the fleece-lined kennels. His heart squeezed so tightly he could barely breathe, and he knew it wasn't the north wind that was making it so.

Perhaps he'd reached a crossroads. A point where he had to stop withdrawing from life, from relationships, friendships even for fear of messing them up. Sure, he'd taken a step into more intimate territory with Esme, but there was an automatic expiry date built into that. December the twenty-third—the night of the ball.

He barked out a laugh. Trust him to make sure he didn't have anything good to look forward to on Christmas Day.

He didn't have an immediate solution for the Christmas problem, but he knew it was time to change how he thought about relationships. Which meant moving on from that boy desperate for love. The young soldier intent on proving he was worth the wait, only to find out his efforts had been for naught. He wanted to open his heart to Esme. It wasn't right to keep her at arm's length, as he had everyone else in his adult life. What was the worst that could happen? His heart might break a little? Maybe this time the pain would be worth it.

He looked back at exactly the same moment as Esme crossed to the window, presumably to look for him. When she saw him her face lit up, her forehead lightly furrowed with concern. She put her hand up to the window. He reached out and pressed his to meet hers. When their eyes met? Magic.

Yes. She was worth the risk all right. Worth that and then some. Bring it on, Christmas. This A and E doc was ready to get his jingle on.

The last patient of the day was a very poorly Pomeranian called Snowy, who had stolen a mince pie off her owner's kitchen table. A quick injection to clear her stomach did the trick. Not very nice for poor old Snowy, but Max, much to Esme's amusement, had the giggles.

'This the sort of thing that tickles your funny bone?' she asked.

'No, sorry.' He tried to wipe that adorable smirk from his face and couldn't. Which, of course, made her laugh.

Esme gave Snowy an apologetic cuddle. The poor wee thing could've died from eating the mince pie, which was toxic to dogs. It was no laughing matter. She gave Max his next 'quiz' as he'd requested throughout the day. 'Any idea what comes next for this little one?'

'An IV for fluids and mild food like rice or scrambled eggs for the next couple of days?'

Esme beamed. 'Got it in one.' She held the little fluffy dog up in front of her and asked it, 'What on earth could be so funny about watching you get sick that made big old Dr Max have the giggles?'

All of which set Max off again. 'It reminds me of weekends at the Clyde. I know I shouldn't laugh. It's not funny. But at this time of year there is always someone at an office party who manages to overdo it and in they come and out *it* comes and...well...' He crossed over to Esme's side and gave the fluffy pooch a tender little scrub on the head. 'I'm glad there's a happy ending.'

A warm swirl of happiness shifted round Esme's heart as she watched Max's features soften. It was similar to the look he got whenever Euan texted him to say he and Ajax had aced something. He'd sent Max a selfie about an hour earlier from the shopping centre, surrounded by crowds. Euan's smile was bigger than he'd ever seen it. Max had been so proud he'd looked fit to burst. She wondered if he'd look even more proud if he had children of his own one day. A wife.

She swallowed down the thoughts because even considering putting a ring back on her finger was absolutely
ludicrous. Particularly given the fact she was going to
bare her soul to him tonight and whatever this was between them might very quickly become past tense.
She'd thought of countless reasons to change her mind
and every bit as many to stay on course. The smile on
Max's face was one of them.

'All right, then! I'll get one of the nurses to set Snowy
up with a drip.'

Half an hour later, after Esme had done a final round
of checks on everyone, she and Max were the only ones
left in the clinic. She pulled off her surgical cap, ran her
hands through her hair and gave it a good old shake.
'Phew! What a day!'

Max was looking at her with an odd expression on
his face.

'What? Do I have something on my face?'

'Nope.' He pulled her to him, hip to hip, her breasts
brushing against that big man chest of his. 'Nothing but
pure perfection.' He dipped his head down and gave
her the slowest, softest, most sensual kiss she could
bear without her body turning to complete jelly. When
he finally pulled back, which was too soon, he dipped
his forehead to hers. 'Mmm… I've been wanting to do
that all day.'

Esme's butterflies swiftly adorned themselves with
feather boas and started dancing to sexy music. 'Is there
anything else you've been wanting to do all day?'

'There most definitely is, ma wee lassie.' Max's voice
swept through her like wildfire. If there had been blinds

to draw on the big glass entryway to the veterinary clinic she would have drawn them immediately and torn off his scrubs in record time. 'I think we should have pizza.'

Er... It wasn't entirely what she was expecting to hear but, okay. 'You're hungry?'

He circled his arms round her waist and leant back with a big grin on his face. 'Yup. And you must be too after a big day like that. Impressive stuff, Dr Ross-Wylde.'

Despite herself, she blushed. 'We tend not to go by "Doctor" in the veterinary world.'

'Well, you should. It's extraordinarily difficult to diagnose a patient who can't speak to you. I thought we played a bit of a guessing game in human diagnostics, but you take it to another level. Impressive.'

She play-punched him in the arm. Getting compliments for doing what she loved most was great. Getting them from Max was some seriously divine icing on top. Speaking of which... 'Fancy any more of that chocolate cake of Mrs Renwick's, if there's any left?'

She pressed close to him and felt his response to the naughty glint in her eye and the low purr of seduction in her voice. Who knew she could be a sex kitten? Who knew this would be the man to bring it out of her?

'Pizza first,' he said, though she could feel his arousal though his scrubs.

She kissed one of his nipples through his top. Then the other. 'Don't you want to take a hot shower first? Wash off the day and get ready for the rest of it?' She tried to slip her hands under his top to get better access to that scrummy chest of his. Windows be damned!

He held her out at arm's length. 'Compromise?'

'Depends on the compromise.' She wriggled in closer, unable to shut down the primitive need to feel the warmth of his body.

'You said you had something you wanted to share with me so I thought perhaps I should as well.'

The part of her that had zero confidence in herself instantly wanted to shrink away but she forced herself to hold eye contact.

'Sounds a bit scary.'

He gave a light shrug and a soft smile. 'Not if you're eating pizza.'

She almost laughed. When he put it that way...

He held open the door for her and tilted his head towards the castle. 'I saw a wood-fired pizza van out by the Christmas carnival. Thought maybe we could get ourselves some and then tuck ourselves away somewhere warm to eat it.'

An idea struck.

'I know *exactly* where we should go.'

Max smiled and held out his hand towards the door. 'Right, then, m'lady. Lead the way.'

CHAPTER EIGHT

'It was sweet of Euan to offer to look after Dougal while we came up here,' Esme said as she climbed the stairs without as much as breaking a sweat.

'He's a good kid.' Max took a peek out of a window he was passing. Three stories and counting. 'This is an awful lot of stairs to climb for a pizza date.' Max wasn't complaining. But he was bewildered. 'Are you sure you've not put the dungeon at the top of the castle?'

'Ha! No. There *is* a dungeon in the old castle. A poor little girl was stuck in it the other week, but Cass and Lyle saved her.'

'Who's going to save us if we get stuck up here?' Max joked.

'My big brother,' she said brightly over her shoulder.

'Does he step in to save you from all your bad dates?'

The smile dropped from her face and she picked up her pace. 'Just a couple more flights to go.'

Well, that put him on ice. Or perhaps he'd just jumped the gun on the 'something she wanted to talk about'.

A couple of minutes later he and Esme were standing looking out over the whole of the Christmas carnival and beyond. It was a sparkling mass of light and laughter and...even he had to admit it...it was magical. They must've been a good four or five storeys up. Five, most likely as he could see the roofing of the rest of the castle alongside them. The room was small, octagonal and incredibly cosy. A deep cushioned bench seat had been built under the windows that ran around the room.

They were just about level with the star on the enormous Christmas tree at the centre of the carnival. To their right was the skating rink. Beyond that were the twinkling lights twisting through the maze with a miniature castle in the centre rising up as a goal for the happy carnival-goers. Snow was falling lightly. It was truly a winter wonderland.

'It's amazing, isn't it?' Esme whispered as she tucked herself onto the window seat. 'I used to sneak up here as a kid with Nick and Charles and we'd watch everyone on the skating rink.'

'Then you probably saw me one of those nights.'

She shook her head, still trying to reconcile the big, strong man beside her and the young boy who had come here with his mum. 'I wouldn't have thought something this Christmassy would have been your thing.' She was teasing, not accusing, so he decided to just go for it.

He sat down beside her and took one of her hands in his, both their eyes still trained on the scene. 'It was when I was twelve.'

Esme gave his hand a squeeze. 'Want to tell me about it?'

'Yes,' he said, surprised at the raw emotion in his voice. 'Yes, I do.'

* * *

Esme listened, wide-eyed, as Max told his story. She knew he must've had a rough childhood, but the more she heard the more her heart ached for him.

'And you didn't mind being a latchkey kid?'

Max shook his head. 'It was the only life I knew. Besides, we were happy, Mum and me.'

'Even though she worked all those crazy shifts at the factory?'

'Yup. She was pretty strict about what I was and wasn't allowed to do and, lucky her, I was one of those dorky kids who always wanted to make her happy.'

Esme swatted at the air between them. 'I can in no way imagine that you were ever a dorky kid.'

'Well…' he acquiesced. 'Maybe in the privacy of my own home. I had my tough-kid image to look after on the mean streets of Glasgow after all.'

'You weren't in a gang or anything like that?'

'No. But there were gangs and the last thing you could show was weakness. I was hardly going to brag to all the other kids that I knew how to roast a chicken and make Yorkshire puddings.'

'Wow!' Esme's eye pinged open. 'You can cook?'

'Had to if I wanted to eat. My mum used to leave me recipes. You must have a huge kitchen here. What can you make?'

She shot him a bashful look. 'True confession? Mrs Renwick always did it so well and Mum wasn't all that interested, so I never really learnt.' Before he could reply she said, 'I suppose I could learn. I wonder how long it would take?'

Max laughed. 'If you're planning on replacing your job with a pinafore, please don't. I like you just the way you are.'

'Really?'

Max shot her an inquisitive look. 'Of course. You're an amazing woman. Anyone who thinks otherwise can jog on to the land of no return as far as I'm concerned.'

'Thank you. That means a lot.'

She hadn't meant to sound as bone-achingly grateful as she did, but… Harding MacMillan hadn't liked her just the way she had been. He'd liked the bells and whistles and had merely tolerated her as a means to an end.

Max picked up another piece of pizza, his gaze drifting back out to the wintry scene.

'What was so magical about the time you were here with your mum?'

'It was our last proper Christmas together.'

The sentence came out harsh and blunt.

'Did she—did something happen to her?'

'She got married.'

'Isn't that normally a good thing?'

'It is if the man in question is after a twelve-year-old son.'

'Oh, Max.' Her heart squeezed so tight for him she could barely breathe. As a young boy who'd never known a father's love, it must've been complete torture. 'Did he not even try?'

Max tossed the remains of his slice of pizza into the box and closed the lid. Thinking about his stepdad clearly wasn't good for his appetite.

'I used to call him the Dictator.'

That didn't sound good. 'And now?'

She saw something flicker in his eyes. A moment's hesitation as if he were debating whether or not to tell her something. 'I call him Gavin Henshall.'

Everything in her stilled.

So this was what he'd wanted to tell her. He was using her to get back at someone.

'Is that why you agreed to accept my help?' There was no chance he didn't hear the wobble in her voice.

He scrubbed a hand through his hair, looked out the window then back to her. 'I should've told you that first day. It's been eating at me ever since.'

'Why didn't you?' She forced the roar of blood in her ears into submission. She'd shared a bed with this man. If she was going to find out she'd been a pawn in something, she at least wanted to hear why.

'Because it was so personal. As you've probably noticed, sharing what's in here...' he thumped a fist against his chest '...doesn't come easily. Gavin changed my life and not in a good way. My mum's, too. But I didn't want you to think I was after revenge when what I really wanted was to save Plants to Paws.'

Her hammering heart slowed its cadence. He was being honest. Looking her straight in the eye. If it was revenge he was after...well, he'd hardly be telling her now, would he? Before he'd seen as much as a penny. And then the proverbial penny dropped. He was telling her now because he didn't want her to find out later and with that revelation her heart opened far wider than she'd let it open in years. She knew how hard it was to separate rage and pain. She'd had her own fair share of teasing the two apart over the years and a castle to 'hide' in to do it. Max had literally been on the front line and despite the incalculable amount of good he'd done, she could now see it was his past that was tearing at his heart.

'Well.' Esme sniffed imperiously. 'If he isn't a very nice man, I'm doubly glad we're keeping Plants to Paws as it is.'

The relief in Max's eyes brought tears to her own.

'At the beginning, when he was courting my mum, he was all right. She'd made it very clear that we came as a package.' He huffed out a laugh as his eyes travelled back out to the skating rink. 'She used to date a man for at least six months before they were even allowed to meet me. Said she had to vet them to make sure they were top-grade father material. It made me think I was this special kid. Worth waiting for.' His unhappy tone made it clear that special was the last thing he'd been made to feel.

Esme bristled on his behalf. 'Every child should believe they're safe. Protected. Your mum sounds amazing. Not all single parents are so discerning.'

'Not all single parents met slimeballs like him.' There was no mistaking the bitterness in his voice now.

'Did he hurt you?'

He scrubbed his hands along his trousers as if trying to get rid of a bad feeling. 'No. But he used to... I think the term they use now is psychological abuse.'

'To you?'

'Mostly to my mum. Which killed me. Because I was powerless to do anything.'

'Why powerless?'

'He always had an answer or a comeback that I couldn't respond to. He was a master of manipulation. And he shipped me off to military academy as soon as he could.'

'How awful.'

He tilted his head to one side, as if weighing up whether her response was valid. When he lifted his eyes to meet hers his eyes burned with fury. 'It was. But not for the reasons you'd think.'

Esme pushed both pizza boxes away and wrapped her arms around her knees. She was desperate to throw them round Max but the last thing she thought he'd want was pity. He must have felt so helpless watching the person he loved most in the world fall prey to the man who had promised to look after her. Both of them. A Jekyll and Hyde from the sound of it. 'What sort of things did he do?'

'Before they were married, he promised her a house on the nice side of town and a chance to be a stay-at-home mum. Host dinner parties, tend the garden, which she loved, that sort of thing.'

'That doesn't sound too awful.'

'It is when everything comes with conditions.' His smile was grim. 'She didn't get a choice of which house or where. Who she hosted at her parties. Which types of foods she could make. The clothes she could wear. The topics she could discuss when she was allowed to talk.'

Ouch. Her own marriage had been a bit like that. Indulgent at first. Indulgent until there had been a ring on her finger. The fact Harding had managed to fool her seemed insane now but, in hindsight, they'd all been reeling from Nick's death and Harding had brought some focus to their lives. Something to look forward to. A wedding. Grandchildren. If only she'd known how devious his 'courtship' had actually been.

Harding, who laid claim to some mysterious title, had insisted they go to the *right* balls and the *proper* restaurants and be seen with the *best* people. The types of people who tended to travel with paparazzi in tow. He might've even tipped them off, for all she knew. She'd been so naive, sad and lonely down there in Glasgow, away from her family and so desperate to feel loved she'd gone along with it all.

If Max's mum had felt that way... She wrapped her arms even tighter round herself. The poor woman. The only blessing was she hadn't had the tabloids smearing her misery all over the front pages.

'Are you cold?' Max started to take off his fleece.

'No, just...' *Just reliving some of the worst memories of her life, that was all.* 'Please. Go on.'

'Well, as I said, one of the first things he did to rip away any link to her old life was to pronounce me a bad seed in need of some proper schooling, so he sent me to a military academy.'

'Bad seed? The chicken roasting, Yorkshire pudding making latchkey kid was a bad seed?'

He shrugged. 'I could've hung out with a better crowd, but where we lived there weren't exactly choice pickings. It was all a bit rough and ready on our estate. In all honesty, military academy suited me. I got on pretty well there and I kept thinking that the better I did, the sooner I could come home and make sure Mum was all right. It was pre-mobile phone years for kids so I couldn't call home, wasn't sure if she got my letters. I was completely powerless.'

'You said he didn't hit her, right?'

'No, but he may as well have for all the damage he did. *Not...*' he held up his hands '...that I would ever, ever condone hitting someone. Or putting them down. Just as vicious. Just as cruel. He was always picking on her. What she wore. How she set the table. Belittling her in front of guests when the whole time he was the one who was small and insignificant.'

'Social climber?' she guessed.

His grim expression told her all she needed to know.

'I'm so sorry you both had to go through that. Did you get her out in the end?'

Much to her astonishment, Max's eyes glassed over. She let him wrestle with his emotions rather than pressing him to speak. She knew the courage it took to admit something hadn't gone the way you'd wanted it to. The core-deep fear she'd felt when she'd finally told her father what her ex-husband had done had been the scariest, most isolating sensation she'd ever experienced.

The love and unconditional response she'd received in return had set the bar high. Too high, some might say, but...waiting for someone who would love her that unconditionally was critical. She reached out and took one of Max's hands in both of hers. She pressed her cheek to the back of it then gave it a soft kiss. Was he that special someone?

'It's my worst regret.' He sighed and balled his hands

into fists. 'I enlisted because I knew there wasn't a chance in hell he'd let me back into that house so I thought if I made enough money to buy her a house she could get out. Be free. Tend the garden any damn way she wanted to.'

Ah…the garden. That's where Plants to Paws came from. Her own eyes filled with tears as she thought of just how much it must've destroyed him to learn that the charity garden was going to be paved over to make way for a car park. And by whom. She made a silent vow to double the guest list. Come what may, they were going to save Plants to Paws and ensure it was there for the patients at the Clyde for ever.

'So did you get the house?' Esme asked quietly.

He shook his head. 'Cancer hit first and though I'd bought the house she was in a hospice and she passed away before I could even show it to her. At least I got to be with her then. My stepdad didn't handle the messy business of dying all that well so he wasn't around much.' A sad smile teased at his features. 'It was back to just the two of us in the end. She was so weak I bought her one of those miniature Japanese gardens. You know the little zen ones with stones and a bonsai tree and whatnot? She tended that thing as if her life depended on it.'

'Oh, Max.' There was nothing she could say to make any of it better. Her own experience with pain had taught her sometimes it was best not to say anything at all. Being there and listening was the best thing to do.

'After she died, I began to notice more and more patients wishing, above anything, that they could grow something. Keep something alive since they were powerless to do the same for themselves. So I sold the house to build Plants to Paws.'

No longer able to hold back, she wrapped her arms around him. 'I'm so sorry you've been through that. Let me assure you we will do everything in our power to make this the best Christmas ball ever. Gavin Henshall be damned!' She threw a fist in the air, hoping to tease out a bit of relief from the sadness he'd been carrying all of these years. There was a change. The tiniest flicker of something she couldn't put her finger on shifted through his eyes as he pulled her to him for a kiss.

Max had never once considered the possibility that feeling vulnerable could also make him feel strong. Opening up to Esme in the way he had had paid emotional dividends he'd never considered. There'd been a moment—right when he admitted he'd known who Gavin Henshall was all along—when he'd thought he'd lost her, but she'd silenced whatever was going on in that head of hers and heard him out. For that alone, Esme would always have a special place in his heart.

'C'mere.' Esme beckoned him over to the long wooden counter. 'What shoe size are you?'

'Eleven.' He couldn't help smiling at Esme's puckish face. After his big emotional purge she'd said she was more than happy to carry on talking but he'd had enough and suggested they do something she wanted to do. So here they were, preparing for an after-hours ice skate. He was bound to spend more time on his rear than his feet, but...what the hell. Her eyes had glittered with excitement at the idea so there was zero chance he was going to say no.

She handed him the skates then pulled a pair off of the shelf for herself. 'I can't believe we're doing this!' She clapped her hands and let out a quiet little 'Woohoo!' She'd promised the security guards they'd be as quiet as dormice. The fact she was Esme Ross-Wylde and had arrived carrying a big plate of Mrs Renwick's Christmas biscuits had had a lot more to do with receiving their go-ahead than keeping the volume down.

The pair of them went out to the moonlit skating rink…completely free and clear of any marks from the evening's crowds. Perfect for a bit of midnight mischief.

'I haven't done this for years!'

'Why has it been so long?'

Max recognised the shadows of sadness instantly.

'I used to come out here with my brothers.' She sighed and put a tidy bow on her second lace and clapped her hands to her knees. 'I haven't really told you about Nick, have I?'

'No. But if it's too difficult to talk about…'

'It is, but… I think the two of you would've got along. He was army. Like you. Worked in the canine bomb disposal unit.'

Max nodded. It was pretty easy to see where this was going.

'He was killed on Christmas Eve when I was eighteen and Charles was in the throes of med school.'

'That's rough.' And explained why she was so desperate for Christmas to be magical. She was trying to recapture a time that used to be. A memory of when life had been perfect. A bit like him, he supposed. Pretending Christmas wasn't happening never made the pain go away, so perhaps she had the right idea. Try and try again. One day it just might work.

'He was my hero. He was so much older than me, everything he did seemed amazing. When he died we all fell apart. Dad worked himself into an early grave. Charles buried himself in his medicine and I…'

Her voice caught as he saw tears form in her eyes. He put his arm around her and swept his hand along her cheek. 'It's completely understandable if you were sad, darlin'. Losing someone you love is pure heartache.'

Esme looked him straight in the eye. 'I was more than sad. I lost the plot.'

'I doubt that. Grief is a powerful emotion. Sometimes it is difficult to know how you're coming across to the world when everything seems so grey.' The only thing that had saved him after his mum had passed was Plants to Paws. Knowing he was putting some good back into the world after channelling so much hate in Gavin's direction.

Esme took one of his hands in hers and said, 'There's something I have to tell you.'

He nodded for her to go ahead. She'd been amazing when he'd bared some of his darkest memories to her and she deserved his full attention.

'I met a man shortly after Nick was killed. He said all the right things, did all of the right things. He made me feel safe. Cared for in a world I wasn't so sure about any more. If Nick, my amazing strong, incredible brother, could be killed, what else could happen?'

A surge of protectiveness shot through him. 'This man didn't hurt you, did he?'

She shook her head and covered her face with her hands. 'It's more embarrassing now than anything.'

'Hey.' He crooked a finger under her chin and ran his thumb along her cheek. 'Like I said, I like you just the way you are.'

She gave his arm a squeeze. 'I know. And that means a lot. In fact, it was your honesty with me that made me want to tell you my story. I owe it to you.'

Esme was trembling as Max took her hands in his and said, 'You don't owe me anything, love. Not one thing.'

'That's exactly why I *want* to tell you. Because you don't want anything from me. This man did.' Before she chickened out, she took in a deep breath and told him everything. 'I married him at the ripe age of nineteen. We eloped to Gretna Green, if you can believe it. Such a cliché!'

He gave a small shrug. 'You were young, and clichés are clichés for a reason. It was meant to be romantic, right? An act of love.'

Bless him. He was trying to find a silver lining. Little did he know this particular cloud was completely shrouded in darkness.

'It was romantic,' she admitted miserably. 'And then pretty quickly it wasn't. Mostly because there wasn't love. Not that I knew that yet. At his suggestion, I quit veterinary school and we—meaning I—rented a ridiculous penthouse in Glasgow. When we went home and told everyone, my family were actually pretty amazing.

We'd all been so sad after Nick's death it was great to have a reason to celebrate. And Harding took his time before his true colours were revealed.'

'Harding MacMillan? Isn't he the guy who's always on the covers of those socialite magazines?'

Esme looked at him in surprise. 'You read those?'

'You'd be surprised what pops up as reading material in the staffroom on a night shift.' He gave a self-deprecating laugh then admitted, 'It's not my usual fare, but I recognise the name.'

'If you'd been reading those same magazines eleven or twelve years ago you would've also recognised my name.'

He shook his head. 'They don't make much of a show in the Middle East conflict areas. Anyway, most of the stuff that's in those magazines is salacious gossip. Even if I had read it, I would've taken everything with a grain of salt.'

She fretted at the knitted cap resting in her lap. Being betrayed in the way she had had opened up all the wounds she'd thought were healing after Nick's death. Turned out…they hadn't even begun to heal. The entire experience with Harding had only served to magnify the pain she'd felt at the loss. 'Harding made me feel completely useless. And when, after it was all over, he sold his story to the tabloids with his own special spin, it made my life a living hell.'

Max stiffened. 'Why? What happened?'

'Not that he'd put it this way, but it turned out all of the wooing—fancy dinners, nights out on the town, weekends away—were all paid for with credit cards on the brink of being maxed out. He would fill one up then apply for another. Long story short, he married me because he wanted money. My family's money.'

A bitter laugh caught in her throat as she remembered the day she'd found out how his family came to be 'titled'. His father had bought the title years ago, along with one acre of woodland back when his business had been flourishing. He had since sold the same acre and title when the business had been failing. Not that Harding had bothered to tell anyone about the change of circumstances. If he hadn't been so deceitful about his family's lack of finances, she might've felt sorry for him, but Harding MacMillan had been one hundred per cent snake. A snake whose venom had no antidote.

She met Max's solid, kind gaze and shivered. Could this be the man she could finally put her trust in?

Max tucked a lock of her hair behind her ear then snuggled her hat back on her head. 'Wouldn't want you catching cold,' he explained, then continued after a moment's thought. 'You know it's not your fault, right? He was preying on a vulnerable young woman. I'm surprised he's not in jail.'

Her lips thinned. She would've pressed charges but… she'd given him her card. A joint account. It hadn't really been theft when it was a joint account. It would've boiled down to a case of him against her and Harding was very persuasive. It was how he'd convinced all the paparazzi to appear every time they'd gone to dinner or a club. She'd thought it was coincidence.

A sour taste filled her mouth as the worst of the memories returned.

'Because I wasn't at uni any more, I wanted to do something amazing for Nick. His service dog had meant the world to him and I'd heard about soldiers suffering from PTSD who needed their own service dogs so I decided to open a clinic to help them do that.'

'Which you did.'

She shook her head. 'No. Remember, this was years ago, in Glasgow. I became obsessed with the idea. I was working crazy hours with a local organisation to learn how to train the dogs so Harding "volunteered" to take over setting up the clinic. Leasing the facility, kitting it out. That sort of thing. I was so wrapped up in the dogs and trying to drum up publicity for the service sog centre that I didn't bother checking up on him.' She felt absolutely sick remembering it all. How the man could've done what he had, knowing it was in aid of her brother's memory.

'Did he get you a site?'

'Oh, he did that all right.'

'You don't sound like you were very happy with it.'

'I was at the time. It was all so romantic, and he had made such a show of wanting to take anything stressful out of my hands so that I could focus on the dogs and helping soldiers.'

Max nodded. He'd fallen for a lot of stuff, too. It had made him wary, but it had also taught him that anyone could fall for a conman.

'He said he didn't want me to see it until the grand opening. That he wanted to see the surprise in my eyes. Oh, he saw surprise all right. So did all the society magazines.'

'I thought you said you'd invited the media.'

'I had. He'd found my list, cancelled them all and replaced them with his people. So, there I was, ready to cut the ribbon, glass of champagne in my hand, the whole nine yards... Harding had hung this huge, ridiculous red velvet curtain in front of the building and when he pulled it open...' her voice caught at the memory but she continued as if she had just swallowed sour milk '...instead of my humble canine therapy centre there was a gaudy, glitzy nightclub called Wylde.'

Max swore under his breath. That was a whole new breed of low.

'So, of course, once the legitimate papers got hold of the fact I'd opened a nightclub instead of the service dog centre, they dismissed me as just another airhead heiress who had more money than sense. It still makes me furious for not having seen through him before I put that stupid ring on my finger. Sure,' she acquiesced, 'it was a whirlwind romance. Maybe...three or four weeks? Insanity really, but I thought he loved me when all along it turned out it was my money he loved.'

Much to her embarrassment, tears began to trickle down her cheeks. And then flow. She hadn't cried about this in years but telling Max was strangely cathartic. Cleansing even. She'd felt so small back then. Humiliated and worthless. But she'd changed. She'd finally made something of her life. Which was a lot more than she could say for Harding. If her mother's short emails were any sort of guide, Harding was still living with little beyond his charm to keep him afloat. A hollow life if there was one.

Max pulled out a clean cloth handkerchief and handed it to her. Her heart squeezed tight. He was such a gentleman. Why couldn't she have fallen for someone like him back then? She thought back to the story he'd just told her and realised he probably wouldn't have been in a chivalrous place back then. Perhaps, despite the pain, they'd each needed to go through these tribulations to become the people they were now. A bit wiser. A bit more wary.

'I presume your family took him to task,' Max said after wiping away a couple of her stray tears.

She shook her head. 'I didn't want them to. It would've compounded the whole poor little rich girl thing having my family swoop in to rescue me. Particularly given the fact that, at the time, Mum was showing up at one too many nightclubs herself.'

'Did Harding actually think you would go for it? The nightclub, I mean?'

She shrugged. 'My best guess is that he thought I was so under his spell I would go for it to make him happy. He thought the service dogs thing was a fad.'

'Sounds like he didn't know you at all.'

She gave him a sad smile. 'We can definitely agree on that. The whole thing was so humiliating. Afterwards, once we'd split up and I'd come back here, it still took ages to shake everything off. The tabloids were paying people to get staff jobs here at Heatherglen. Undercover maids hoping to find me curled up in a weeping, sobbing ball in the corner of my gold-plated bedroom. That sort of thing. The last thing I wanted the world to see was me being pathetic, so I got myself back into veterinary school and set up the clinic properly. With no publicity.'

Max laughed and gave his head a rueful shake. 'That's my girl.'

Despite the seriousness of the talk, Esme blushed. His girl? She liked the sound of that. Even if it was just a saying, there was something safe and comforting about talking with Max that she'd never felt with another man. It felt *real. Genuine.* As if there was nothing she could tell him that would make him think any less of her.

'I'm hoping he didn't get to any of your money in the end.'

'Oh, he did. Not all of it obviously,' she snorted and looked at the castle, glittering like a jewel in the crown. 'The joint account we shared was actually my trust fund. I never really spent much from it. Unlike Harding, I wasn't really one to splash the cash about.' She qualified the statement, so Max didn't get the wrong idea. 'I'm not unaware that I have grown up with a privileged lifestyle. I mean, how many people get an ice rink and an entire Christmas carnival outside their castle at Christmas?'

Max laughed appreciatively. There was warmth in it. As if he didn't care if she was worth a billion or tuppence. It was her he liked, not the trimmings she came with.

She shook her head. 'I still can't believe I fell for such a superficial poser.'

'Everyone has someone who pulls the wool over their eyes.' Max gave her back a soft rub and dropped a tender kiss on her forehead. 'He really put you through the mill, didn't he?'

'Yup!' She stood up, using one of Max's strong shoulders as support to keep her balance on her blades, and gave him a proper smile. 'But that was then and right now we've got a skating rink calling our names.'

They spent the next hour having an absolute ball, whirling and racing and falling down and kissing. It was every bit as fun as it had been when she'd sneaked out with her brothers to do exactly the same thing, minus the kissing part obviously.

That night when they made love it felt even more intimate than it had the night before. There was true sentiment behind the soft touches, the caresses, the deep, emotionally charged kisses they shared.

She was falling for him. Head over heels. The practical part of her knew she needed to put on the brakes and acknowledge that this was nothing more than a no-strings-attached fling. There was no way it could work in real life. His life was in Glasgow, hers was very much here at Heatherglen and, well, there was all the magic of Christmas that would melt away in the spring.

And yet...there was a tiny sliver of hope she hadn't felt in years. Hope that she might finally leave her scars from the past where they belonged. In the past. Hope that true love *was* real. That she deserved it. She stared at the lights twinkling on the tiny Christmas tree by the fireplace. Honestly? She wanted to believe in Christmas miracles. And Max was the man she wanted by her side when all of it came to pass.

CHAPTER NINE

'SOMEONE LOOKS HAPPY,' Charles growled as he dug his spoon into a rather enormous, well-sugared bowl of Mrs Renwick's delicious porridge.

'Someone else looks like they woke up on the wrong side of the bed.' Esme smiled benignly in return. She was in a gorgeous floaty love bubble. Four days in and her days with Max had morphed into a lovely little routine. Sometimes he spent time with her in the vet surgery and at others they worked on training with Euan and Fenella. Max usually had his meals with them, but he always, every single night, crawled under the covers with her. Not even a grumpy older brother whose mood had plummeted daily since he'd returned from his medical conference could burst the particularly lovely mood. 'Would you pass the blueberries, please?'

'They're out of season,' Charles snapped.

'So's your mood,' Esme chirped, tacking on a 'tra-la-la-la-la' to prove her point.

Charles grimaced, ate a spoonful of porridge, then pushed it away.

'What's up with you?'

'Nothing. Busy day, that's all.'

She was about to retort that all their days were busy but it didn't mean they had to be miserable but she opted for the kinder, gentler version of her kid sister self. She, after all, had three more glorious days of naughty nights and flirty days ahead. Charles, on the flip side, showed no signs of even as much as casting the slightest glance at a woman, let alone falling in love again. 'Anything I can do to help?'

'No. Thank you, though.' He pushed up and away from the kitchen table then turned back. 'I had a meeting with Fenella, by the way. I've put a call through to the Clydesbank to send up her records. She's agreed to let me take a second look at her meds.'

'Oh! Great.' Her gut instinct was to run out the door, find Max and tell him immediately, but the fact she and Max had agreed to keep their romance low key kept her in her chair, smiling dreamily up at her brother. 'You're the best.'

He narrowed his eyes. 'Are you sure you're all right?'

'Never better.' She took a huge spoonful of porridge so she couldn't answer any more questions. The truth of the matter was, no matter how much she told herself she shouldn't, she was falling in love.

Max was spending the day with Euan and Fenella as their training with the dogs intensified. He was being absolutely brilliant, ensuring they felt they were receiving proper support, asking questions for them when they were too shy to do so themselves. They were lucky to have a man like him in their corner. She was lucky to have a man like him in her bed! And utterly insane to let a man whose life was so solidly based elsewhere into her heart.

The morning at the veterinary clinic whooshed by and, as Aksel was now on hand to help, she was treating herself to an afternoon at the Christmas carnival where they were going to put Euan and Fenella's dogs through their paces.

She had just changed out of her scrubs into a cosy pair of leggings and a thigh-length jumper with a Christmas tree knitted into the pattern when she heard a knock on her office door.

'Come in.'

Her heart skipped a beat when she saw it was Max. 'Hello there, you. How's tricks?'

'You're looking festive as ever.'

She skipped over to him and gave him a quick peck on the lips. 'Mmm…chocolaty.'

'Margaret just made us all hot chocolate before "The Big Adventure".'

Esme pulled a sad face. 'I wanted to be the first one to make you hot chocolate! It's the one feather in my cooking cap.'

'Not to worry. I'm sure I'll be up for another before I head back south.'

Her sad face gained traction. 'I can't believe it's all coming to an end so soon.'

'I know.' Max pulled her into a cosy hug. 'It's not going to be nice, saying goodbye.'

She pulled back so she could look him in the eye and asked the one question she'd vowed to herself she wouldn't. 'Do we have to? Say goodbye?'

'I don't really see another way around it. Your life is here. My life's in Glasgow.'

'You don't fancy practising somewhere up here?'

The second the question was out she regretted it. It wasn't fair to ask him to change his life because of what they'd both known would, at best, be a festive fling.

He swept her hair off her forehead as his own brow crinkled. 'I think you know the answer to that, but let's talk about it tonight.' He tilted his head towards the door. 'We've got a very eager Fenella and Euan waiting out in Reception with their hounds, ready for the carnival.'

Though he sounded the same and looked the same, Esme's stomach twisted with anxiety. She'd overstepped the mark. Pushed when she should've accepted the situation for what it was. Doing her best to mask her misplaced disappointment that he hadn't immediately suggested that they scrap all their sensible, practical plans so they could get on with the business of falling in love, she said, 'Absolutely. Let's get on out there and enjoy some Christmas cheer, Heatherglen style!'

Max would've had to have been blind not to see the splinters of dismay pass through Esme's eyes when he put off answering her question. A dodge was a dodge and with her history, looking shifty was never a good thing. Of course he wanted to drop everything and stay in the magical world of Heatherglen—a place whose sole remit appeared to be making dreams come true. Whether it was to recover from PTSD, heal from a traumatic injury or meet that one faithful companion who would never lie, never cheat, never say one thing and mean another…

Damn. He was either going to have to grow a backbone and test the remaining elasticity in his heart or stick to his guns and go with their original plan: enjoy the here and now—then get back to real life.

Esme was bright enough as the group walked towards the Christmas carnival, each with a dog on a lead. Dougal, as ever, was lavishing love on whoever looked at him.

Esme threw Max the odd smile, but he couldn't see the light hitting her eyes like it normally did and it was killing him.

Of course he wanted whatever was blossoming between them to continue. More than anything he wanted to throw caution to the wind, pull her into his arms and tell her he loved her. Because he did. He knew it right down to the very last fibre in his body. He loved Esme Ross-Wylde heart and soul. So…what was the problem, then?

She'd been amazing when she'd heard his story. Didn't seem to give a monkey's that he'd come from a poor background. Or that he'd had a complicated, messy upbringing. Just as he loved her exactly the way she was, she seemed to care for him solely because of the man he was now.

So why was he holding back his feelings and, more importantly, his concerns when he knew honesty was the best policy with her? The only policy. The one way to know if Esme believed in him. Loved him even.

And then it hit him. Somewhere, deep inside him,

he still hated Gavin Henshall for all he'd done to his mother. Worse than that, he was still beating himself up for not finding a way to forgive the man as his mother had asked him to. Forgive him and move on. It had been her last request and he'd failed her. Failed himself. And if it weren't for Esme's timely intervention, he'd very likely be failing everyone at Plants to Paws as well.

Esme had had an awful time with her brother's death and her subsequent marriage. She'd harnessed her anguish and turned it into something good. He'd thought he'd done the same with Plants to Paws, but without Esme? He'd be back at the Clyde clearing out the greenhouse and telling everyone the bad news. Again and again in his life, money and power had trumped good intentions. Could it be that love and its ally, forgiveness, were more important than both?

The thought hit him with the force of a lightning bolt. Was he strong enough to accept that having to start over didn't necessarily equate to failure? That the journey was every bit as important, if not more so, than the outcome? That he might be hurt by love again but that it was completely worth the risk?

Unless the answer was a solid yes, he wouldn't be able to love Esme the way she deserved to be loved. With all of his heart. Because there'd always be a part of him wondering if he'd done enough to deserve her. Acknowledging that simple fact just about killed him. He watched as Esme led their motley crew towards a small log cabin where people could make gingerbread houses. After everyone entered, she looked back. 'Aren't you coming?'

He shook his head. 'I've got something to do. Can I meet you later?'

She gave a little nod, her features closing in on each other. Proof, if he'd needed it, that she knew something wasn't quite right.

'Are we okay?' she asked.

The anxiety in her voice near enough slashed his heart in two.

'We're okay,' he said, because he couldn't say what he wanted to. That he loved her. That he was going to have to find a way to reach down into his past and pull out some of his darkest memories, confront them, and pray that he came out stronger.

Esme poured a pile of cereal into her bowl then sloshed some milk in. It looked revolting. And it was her favourite cereal.

Something weird was up with Max. They'd spent the night together, but he'd not brought up whether or not he wanted to see her any more after Christmas. Something about the intensity in the way he'd looked at her, touched her, had made her feel as though he was memorising her in preparation to say goodbye.

All of which had her in a particularly foul mood.

She stared at the cereal then at Wylie. 'Want my cereal?'

He wagged his tail. She gave it to him.

She looked around the kitchen for something else to eat. Her eyes eventually landed on her gingerbread castle. Why make a house when you can build a castle? she'd thought. Fenella and Euan had thought it was hilarious. Max had given it a glance, her a smile and then told her he wouldn't be joining her in the veterinary clinic today as he'd volunteered to cover Lyle Sinclair's medic shift at the ice skating rink. Lyle wanted to tag along with Cass, who was due to rehearse for the Living Nativity down at the village. Fussing more like. Doting. Caring, adoring, lovesick man that he was.

She'd thought it was adorable about twenty-four hours earlier. Today? Not so much. She wrenched off the gingerbread turret and took a bite.

There was a light knock on the kitchen door. Max stuck his head into the room. 'I was just going to make a call to the Clyde then head out to the skating rink. Everything all right?'

'Not particularly,' she said, tacking on a petulant smile. He blinked his surprise.

Okay, fine. It wasn't a particularly mature way to respond, but she wanted Max to feel as bad as she did. She pulled a section of the wall off her gingerbread castle and chomped down on it.

Charles appeared behind Max, who let him through to the kitchen. 'Good to see healthy eating is still the order of the day,' he said in a remarkably similar strain of crankiness. 'May I?' He nodded at the castle.

She shrugged. 'Help yourself.'

He did, and the castle collapsed.

Her expression must've been one of pure fury because both Charles and Max made their apologies and left. It wasn't the castle she was cross about. It was not having the guts to have it out with Max and find out what was going on with him. She'd thought they were good at being open with one another. Telling each other the truth. And here she was exactly where she didn't want to be. Feeling scared. Panicked she wasn't enough. Would never be enough for someone when all she wanted was to be enough for one man. For Max.

A horrible thought landed in her head. What if the only reason he was doing this was to make sure he got the money for Plants to Paws? Surely he knew her well enough to know she didn't offer lifelines like the Christmas ball with strings attached. The fact they seemed to adore each other's company was just an added bonus.

All of which meant she was being ridiculous. A bit of insecurity went a long way in her case, and it was time to keep it in check.

Doom and gloom would get her nowhere. It was probably nothing. Max was a busy man, who was doing his best to be as present as he could be here as well as keep tabs on his very busy life back in Glasgow. A life he'd dropped to give two of his patients this amazing opportunity.

See? Proof, if she'd needed any, that she was being ridiculous. He'd made just about the sweetest love to her a girl could imagine only a handful of hours ago. No one could be that intimate, that loving and also be looking for an escape plan.

Right! She took one last bite of her gingerbread castle, wiped her hands then announced to Wylie that it was time to go out and make the world a better place. No point in spreading her ridiculous mood any further than this kitchen. She knelt down so she was eye to eye with her big, furry bear of a dog. 'I'm being silly, aren't

I, Wylie?' He rubbed his nose against hers. 'He's *not* Harding. All this silly insecurity is nothing, right?' He licked her chin. 'Well, that settles it. Just a blip on the old emotional barometer.' She called him to heel and together they walked to the veterinary clinic. When she passed Max, who was on his way to the ice-skating rink with the reflective safety vest on, she waved and smiled. She'd apologise for being such a grump later. In bed. He threw her a confused wave in return but seemed happy that her mood had improved.

'See, Wylie? Nothing to worry about. Absolutely nothing at all.'

With half an eye on the skating rink and half an eye on the veterinary clinic, Max's gut was churning with indecision. Should he tell her why he hadn't brought up their relationship last night or would it scare her off? Carrying around rage and fury over something he would never be able to change was not going to help anyone. Least of all him and Esme. He wanted to give this a shot. Be the man she deserved. Woo her properly. Take her out. Show her his favourite places in Glasgow. Discover her favourite walks up here. Hold hands at the movies. It'd be tough with his schedule at the Clyde but putting a few thousand commuter miles on his old four-by-four was worth it. Especially if he were to accept in advance that there was always the possibility it might not work out. Once the charity ball was over and he was back to work, they might discover their lives were simply too different for them to be a perfect match. It didn't mean their time together had been for nothing, but it did mean talking about the future at this juncture was a bit of a moot point. Live in a fairy-tale for ever? Sure. Why not? Commute two hours there and back every day to hold hands with his girl? Maybe yes. Maybe no.

He looked up as a few squeals erupted from the ice rink. A gaggle of girls had collapsed into a giggling heap of jewel-coloured winter jackets and scarves. They looked as though they didn't have a care in the world.

He wondered if Esme had ever had a chance to be that silly. The other night she'd told him that, as children, the local paper had always taken a picture of them going to church on a Sunday and had made note of the times they didn't. Never mind the fact they'd often been down in Glasgow, working for a soup kitchen. No wonder she cherished those stolen moments of fun on the ice rink with her brothers. No one to perform for.

For every ounce of him that had bones to pick with his own childhood, he wouldn't have traded it for hers. At least his most tumultuous years had only been under two people's radars. His mum's and his stepdad's. The press? It must've been awful. And incredibly impressive that she'd managed to turn it back round in her favour in the form of her annual Christmas ball.

It was tomorrow night. Maybe that's why she'd been so crisp this morning. It was a lot to organise. And the pressure had to be immense. They'd have to raise a lot of money if they wanted to put Gavin and his car park plans out of the picture.

He sensed someone approaching from behind him. 'Well, here she is.' He put his arm out and while Esme didn't snuggle close in to him her smile was sincere enough. She was all kitted out in her canine therapy centre winter gear and he was on duty so fair enough. She gave him a little hip bump. 'Sorry about earlier.'

He looked at her blankly. 'What do you mean?'

'Oh, don't be silly. You know I snapped at you.'

'I suspect your plate is rather full with the ball to-morrow.'

'It is,' she agreed, 'but that wasn't what I was grumpy about.'

'Want to talk about it?'

She scrunched up her nose. 'Not really. I was being silly. Imagining things.'

'About?'

'Absolutely nothing.' She gave his hand a squeeze. 'Just…sorry. I don't want there to be anything funny between us, seeing we haven't got much time left.' It was all he could do not to pull her into his arms and tell her he was confronting his very worst demon so that maybe they wouldn't have to call it a day. That Christmas, for once, would be the herald of good things to come for both of them.

He followed her eyes as they travelled out to the skating rink. She was watching a middle-aged couple skating along hand in hand. 'That's a first date.'

'How do you know?'

'He's showing off for her.' Her voice took on a dreamy quality. 'And the way she's looking at him… it's like she's won the lottery.'

Esme was right. The woman was beaming. More so when her beau pulled a bit ahead of her to do a bit of a jazzy move. Judging by his windmilling arms, it wasn't going to plan. The woman pulled ahead to do her own move. She put her arms out ballerina style, gave a couple of strong strokes of her skate blades and lifted her back leg into a lift when all of the sudden the giggling teens and happy couple collided and became a sprawled mass of bodies in the centre of the rink.

Max was on the ice with his medical bag in seconds. His rubber-soled boots didn't have brilliant traction, but they got him where he needed to be.

Max could hear Esme instructing the rink monitors to clear the other skaters from the ice.

The teens were examining themselves for injuries.

The gentleman was sandwiched between them all as he had tried to fling himself protectively over his girlfriend. When he rolled off, he howled in agony. 'My shoulder!'

Max shot a quick glance at his partner, who looked a bit dazed but was pushing herself up to a seated position. 'Can you let me have a look?'

The man stared at him blankly. 'Only if you can make it stop.'

Max made a quick examination. 'You've popped your shoulder out, mate. I don't think your wrist is looking all that brilliant either.'

'It's my shoulder that hurts most. Make it stop. Make. It. Stop.' The man's breathing was coming in short, sharp huffs as he tried to grapple with the pain. He launched himself forward so that his forehead and shoulder rested on the ice bearing some of his body weight.

'It's not the easiest way to treat you, pal. What do

you say we try to—? Oops. Okay. Stay as you are if that helps you to breathe.'

Esme appeared beside him. 'I've called an ambulance from the hospital up the road. They'll try to get here in twenty minutes or so.'

'Brilliant. I should be able to get everyone triaged before they come. Relocate this chap's shoulder, at the very least.'

'Anything I can do?'

Max did a quick scan of the group who were still sprawled on the ice. One teen was clutching her elbow. Another had her hand pressed to her forehead with a bit of blood appearing between her fingers. The woman who'd been trying to do a trick move was squeezing her knee into her chest. He tilted his head towards his medical bag. 'Do you mind popping on some gloves and pressing some gauze to that poor girl's forehead? I'll examine her in a second.'

'On it.'

Esme was swift and efficient. It was a shame vets weren't allowed to treat humans. Esme was every bit as confident with people as she was with animals. So much so he was happy to turn his full attention to the poor bloke and his shoulder, knowing she'd call him if something urgent was required.

'What's your name?'

'John.'

'All right, John. It looks like you've dislocated your shoulder and possibly fractured your wrist in your valiant attempt to be a bodyguard for your friend here.' Max shot a reassuring look in John's girlfriend's direction.

'That's my wife of over thirty years, I'll have you know!'

'Thirty years?' Max did a quick check on whether or not there was blood flow to John's arm. 'What's your secret?'

'Exactly that,' John huffed through his pain. 'Not having any secrets. Never once told her a lie. Jeanie's my absolute best friend. What she sees is what she gets. Isn't that right, darlin'? Oh— Ow!'

'That's right, lovebird. Nothing but honesty.' Jeanie gingerly pressed herself up to her hands and knees and began to crawl over.

'Hold steady there, John. Just checking for any other breaks or fractures. It looks like it's mostly your shoulder, although that wrist is beginning to swell.'

It was important he reduce the shoulder displacement quickly as that would no doubt swell as well. If that swelling were to cut off blood flow to the hand, it wouldn't be a very merry Christmas.

Jeanie crawled across to her husband. 'Are you all right, love?'

He tried to sit up and howled in pain.

'I'll take that as a no.' She shot Max an anxious look. 'It's our wedding anniversary. I was trying to show him how spry and delightful I was still was, even though I'm all wrinkly and grey-haired now.'

Max started talking John through the steps they'd need to take to alleviate the pain.

'You're as beautiful as you were the day I met you, darlin'.'

'If you can just hold still now, John, I'm going to check your vitals before I administer any pain medication.'

'Will it take long? We've got lunch reservations at the pub.'

Max smiled. 'I'm afraid you'd be best cancelling. I'll pop your shoulder back into place in the next couple of minutes, but you'll need X-rays to make sure there aren't any tears to the musculature and a stabilising sling at the very least.'

Esme was back at his side. 'What can I do?'

Max glanced at the ice rink as he slipped on the blood-pressure cuff. No one else was there but John and Jeanie.

Esme explained, 'My elves helped me escort everyone off the ice. We've got them wrapped in blankets and waiting by the hot chocolate hut. I hope that's all right. I've also put a call in to Lyle. He's had similar medical training to you so can lend a hand if the ambulance gets caught up in traffic or anything.'

She was an amazing woman in a crisis. No surprise, given how incredibly calm and methodical she was in her own surgery.

'Doc! You're killing me.'

Max glanced down at the blood-pressure cuff that he'd been pumping up. 'Sorry, mate. Good news. Your readings are strong. We can administer some morphine sulphate to see if that helps ease the pain. We've also got some nitrous oxide in this kit here if I'm not mistaken. Just need a couple of more checks before we administer anything.'

'Please! Anything! No, Jeanie! Don't make me move.'

Jeanie had been trying to get him to sit up but the

only way he could bear the pain was to put pressure on his shoulder. It looked like he was kowtowing to them all. John's peculiar position meant getting pain medication straight into the shoulder would be impossible. 'I'm going to have to inject into your gluteal muscles. Is that all right?'

'I don't care, just do it!'

'Oh, my poor big macho man. Leaping to my rescue like that.' Jeannie looked at Esme with tears in her eyes. 'Look what a hash I've made of showing off for him. Now his poor lily-white bum— Ooh, Doctor! Be quick about it or he'll get sunburn.'

'I'll be fast.' Exposing a man's derriere for any length of time on a sunny but very cold winter's day wasn't in anyone's best interest.

Esme was grinning. 'Is this your first date?'

'Oh, no,' said Jeannie as she stroked her husband's hair. 'He's been my man for over thirty years now. We had our very first date here, in fact. On this very day thirty-five years ago. That's why we picked this date for our wedding day.'

'I thought it was because you wanted a winter wedding,' John said, the painkiller clearly beginning to take effect.

Jeannie batted away the comment with a smile. 'It's because of our happy memories here. Of course, it's a bit different now. Why, back in the day...'

Esme kept them talking while Max got himself into position to do the shoulder reduction. 'It all sounds very romantic.'

Max laid out a thick wool blanket on the ice. 'Right, John, I'm just going to roll you over onto your back here.'

After another round of agonised *No* and *Please Stop* and a couple of things not suitable for children, they got him there. Max slipped the face mask onto John that would allow him to breathe in some nitrous oxide. 'When you want to take a breath with the nitrous oxide, you press this button here. A few deep breaths and it should help your nervous system relax a bit.'

'What if it doesn't?'

Max shot a quick glance at Esme, who was waiting to hand him equipment from his medical kit. 'There's stronger stuff, but if we can avoid it, it'd be best.'

'You can do it, John,' his wife encouraged him. 'You'll not want to be on the strong stuff as we've got dinner with the Carmichaels on Christmas Eve, then there's the Boxing Day lunch with the bridge club. Don't forget we're hosting the Hogmanay drinks do—'

John turned to Max, 'We might need that extra bit of painkiller if she carries on reminding me of all our social engagements!'

'John, you rascal. You know you love them. Just as much as you love me.' She planted a kiss on his cheek as if it settled the matter. Which, apparently, it did as John was visibly more relaxed. 'Right, then.' Max rubbed his hands together. 'Let's get this shoulder back where it belongs.'

After manipulating the arm to a ninety-degree angle then gently levering his forearm to the side, he felt the shoulder shift back into place.

'There you are.'

'That was it?' John looked at his arm, clearly expecting more.

''Fraid so, pal. There are more dramatic ways, but this one hurts the least.'

'Sounds like the voice of experience.'

'Army rugby.'

John nodded as if that explained everything. 'Our lads play rugby. They've dislocated just about everything that moves!'

'Well, don't try too hard to catch up with them. From the sound of things, you've got a busy Christmas schedule. Want to stay fighting fit for the wife, don't you?'

The silver-haired gent laughed. 'That I do, son. Thank you. You've rescued me from a world of pain.' After putting his arm in a sling and some ice on his wrist, John allowed himself to be gently helped up and escorted off the ice.

After the ambulance had come, and they'd gone through everything with Lyle Sinclair for the record, the rink opened again. Esme crooked her hand into Max's elbow and grinned up at him. 'Fancy a spin?'

'Maybe not today.'

'Good answer,' she said. 'I was thinking we could head into town and see the Living Nativity. Cass is in it and a couple of the lads from the vet clinic.'

'I'm not really sure the nativity is my thing.' He backpedalled when her smile dropped. *This may not last for ever, but you have it in your power to be kind.* 'But if you think it'll be fun, count me in.'

* * *

Esme could hardly believe how transformed Cluchlochry looked. It was straight out of a fairy-tale. Glittering lights everywhere. Tasteful decor binding the different shopfronts and buildings together in a harmonious seasonal aesthetic. She didn't think she'd ever seen so many holly and evergreen swags looping from window ledge to window ledge. It was gorgeous.

'So where's this nativity?'

'Just across there on the market square. Oh!' Esme clapped her hands. 'Look! Cass is Mary! She told me she was going to be the donkey.'

'I would've thought you'd have volunteered Wylie to be the donkey.' Max gave Esme's faithful canine companion a scrub on the head.

Esme smiled as Max moved Dougal's lead from one hand to the other so he could hold Esme's hand. He led them all across the square and found a place near the front where they could see the full tableau.

The Living Nativity was just that…a life-sized version of a nativity scene, with local villagers and their livestock standing in for the miniature versions of Jesus, Mary, Joseph, the three kings and, from the look of things, a candlestick maker—a woman Esme recognised from one of the shops who sold all sorts of products to do with bees.

Cass was glowing as Mary. As promised, Lyle had fashioned an old ladder, which wouldn't have looked out of place in a stable, into a perch for Cass so her leg wouldn't hurt. The tableau was only for an hour but even so…as she was still recovering from her injuries sustained during a search and rescue mission at the site of a massive explosion, there was no point in taking risks. Cass was so fiercely independent it was wonderful to see her allowing someone to help. Across the crowd from them Esme could see Flora and Aksel gently steering his daughter and her service dog to the front of the display so Mette could enjoy the new 'cast'.

The whole scenario made Esme feel peaceful. Content in a way she'd never felt before.

Just a girl out with her man, looking at the Christmas delights.

See? She *had* been ridiculous this morning, thinking Max was hiding something from her. Here they were, out in public, and he was more than happy to hold her hand as if they'd been a couple for ever. A warm, swirly, happy heat whirled though her when he popped a scratchy kiss onto her head. It was time to trust again. *Time to love.* She could hardly believe she was thinking it, let alone believing it.

She was in love with Max. Whether or not they could make anything of their relationship remained to be seen, but if this season was about anything it was about having faith. Faith and hope. Believing in the impossible.

'It's amazing, isn't it?' Esme looked up at Max.

'Absolutely. I've never seen anything like it. Do you see, they've even got a few wee early lambs over there?' Max pointed out the furry little beasts whose tails wriggled with delight when their mother was led into the small pen. 'They've done a brilliant job.'

'Apparently they need someone to stand in for one of

the three kings on Christmas Eve. I'm already signed up to be Mary.' Esme looked up at Max. 'Do you fancy coming back up here after the ball?'

It was a loaded question and, from the look on his face, one Max clearly hadn't expected. She'd actually wanted to ask him up for the whole of Christmas but was so used to being cautious the Christmas Eve invitation was about as brave as she could get.

'I'll have to check in with the hospital. See what sort of rosters they've put me on.'

'Of course,' Esme said brightly, quickly turning back towards the nativity. She didn't want Max to see the disappointment in her eyes.

'I did tell Andy I'd like to have a chat with him before I headed back to Glasgow.'

'You mean Euan's new bestie? Those two seem inseparable.'

'I know, a pair of odd bods, aren't they?'

She almost said you could say the same about the pair of them, but Max started rattling off a list of things he needed to do tonight before he packed up and headed back to Glasgow to dust off his kilt. Not quite the romantic gesture she'd been hoping for, but she'd been the one who'd insisted they bring Wylie and Dougal along to the Live Nativity, even though he'd suggested they leave them behind, so perhaps this was what real relationships were all about. Give and take. Compromise. Balance.

She twisted round so she was facing Max and gave

his scarf a little tug. 'Sounds good. Shall we head back
see if we can rustle up some you and me time tonight?'

He gave her a decidedly wolfish wink. 'Absolutely,
my dear. Time's awasting.'

CHAPTER TEN

MARGARET PULLED THE strings tight and tied off the corset. She looked over Esme's shoulder into the full-length mirror and beamed. 'Oh, Esme. You look absolutely *amazing.* You're so lucky your family tartan brings out your blue eyes. Mine makes me look all pale and revolting.'

Esme laughed. 'It does not. You look beautiful. Green tartan and dark hair? A perfect combination. Besides—' she pointed out the obvious '—you're only wearing the sash and your parents won't be there. You could take it off if you want to. I won't tell if you won't.'

Margaret grinned. 'I just might do that.' Margaret picked up a bit of gingerbread from the remains of Esme's gingerbread castle then sighed as she looked back at Esme. 'You look like a blinking princess. Perfect, seeing as you're about to be in the arms of your Prince Alarmingly Charming.'

'Don't be ridiculous.' Esme swatted at the air between them then gave another little twist in front of the mirror. As silly as it was, for the first time in years she actually cared whether she looked beautiful or not.

The setting for the ball had been specifically chosen to match the charity—the Kibble Palace at the Glasgow Botanical Gardens. She knew Max's mum had loved it there and had thought it would be the perfect place to tell Max she loved him. A spray of nervous energy gripped her chest as she silently walked herself through the plan. Host the ball. Give Max his cheque. Then, once all of the madness of the ball was over and done with, she'd say those three perfect words: *I love you.*

Plants to Paws would be saved, so he wouldn't 'need' her any more. His reaction would tell her in an instant whether or not he felt the same way about her as she did about him.

Tendrils of insecurity began to seep into place despite her very best tentions. Despite spending the night together, Max still hadn't brought up whether or not he thought the idea of seeing each other after he headed back to Glasgow was a good idea. He didn't strike her as the type of man who would ghost a girl, but... No.

She stared at her reflection and gave herself a stern frown. Max Kirkpatrick was a gentleman. It could be that he didn't want to see her any more, but there was no chance he'd just up and leave her. A man who kissed a woman the way he'd kissed her when he'd left Heatherglen that morning was a man who would be coming back for more.

Margaret barked a loud and very unladylike laugh. 'What are you grinning at?'

'What? I'm not grinning.' She was. She was definitely grinning.

'You look like the cat who got the cream. Mind you,

I'm perfectly happy, but with a man like Max about to appear in a kilt? I'd be grinning like the Cheshire cat as well.'

Esme tried to wipe the smile from her face but couldn't. 'He is rather scrummy, isn't he?'

There was a familiar knock on her bedroom door and, as usual, Charles didn't bother waiting for a reply before sticking his head in.

'We could've been naked!' Esme chided.

'Hmm. Well, you aren't.' Charles was clearly distracted. So much so she wondered if he would have even noticed if they'd been naked. 'You lot ready to head down to Glasgow?'

'Come on. Let's see you in all your finery.' Margaret beckoned Charles in. He gave a half-hearted turn in his dress kilt then jangled the keys. 'All right, ladies? Your carriage awaits.'

'Is it a pumpkin now or is that at the other end of the evening?' Margaret loved winding Charles up. It used to be because of a lifetime crush on him. Now it was just for fun. Being loved up with the local GP did that to a girl. Made her permanently happy. Esme was pretty sure being in love with a Glaswegian A and E doc did exactly the same thing to her.

They both grinned at him.

Charles rolled his eyes.

Poor Charles. Esme hoped he found someone to love, too. Even though hers was still in the baby-steps stage, meeting and falling in love with Max had already filled her with brand-new confidence. It wasn't a pushy, braggart's confidence. It was more…peaceful. Settled. As if love had finally made her whole.

'Where's Max?' Charles scanned the room. 'I thought he'd be coming with us.'

Esme put on her best casual voice. 'He left late this morning. He said he had a couple of meetings in Glasgow so he drove Euan and Fenella back down. I'm sure he'll be there early. He said there was something he wanted to talk to me about, so…'

Charles shot her one of his intense, protective, big brother looks. 'What kind of talk?'

Again…that clammy feeling she couldn't quite shake pushed to the fore. 'It's probably nothing.'

'Like a sparkly diamond engagement ring kind of nothing?' Margaret cackled, and wriggled her fingers dramatically.

'Don't be daft!' Esme shot Margaret a thanks-for-nothing glare. 'He was here for Plants to Paws.'

'Yeah, right. You keep telling yourself that,' Margaret said dryly as she pulled her pashmina from the sofa and wrapped it round her shoulders. 'What do you think of Max, Charles?'

'Why?' Charles's big brother mode flicked onto high alert. 'What's he done?'

Esme glared at Margaret. She hadn't yet spelled things out to Charles. He was so protective. He still saw her as that messed-up nineteen-year-old, so she had wanted to be crystal clear what was happening with Max before she'd said anything.

She gave Charles an innocent smile. 'Nothing beyond looking forward to presenting him with a big fat cheque for his charity tonight.'

'I'll bet you're hoping to present a lot more than that,' whispered Margaret.

Despite herself, Esme giggled. Charles barely noticed, thank goodness. Margaret started humming 'The twelve days of Christmas', which made her giggle even more. That's more like it, Esme thought. Giggly, girly fun in advance of a beautiful Christmas ball. A big brother who was focusing on the right things. Fingers crossed, tonight would be the perfect evening before what could be the perfect Christmas.

'Forgive him.'

Max heard his mother's voice as clearly as if she were sitting right there on the bench beside him. In his mind's eye he looked up towards the hospice room where she had spent her last days then readjusted the lavish Christmas wreath with a rueful smile. What a difference a week made. Never mind the castle, the top-rate medical and canine facilities and the Christmas carnival. The only thing—the only *one*—he was impressed with had blue eyes, blonde hair and had pushed at the elasticity of his heart and mind so hard and fast he had no choice but to decide if he was up to changing.

'I know you find it hard to believe, but he loved me in his own way.'

Max's heart rate accelerated as an image of his stepfather closing the door on him when he'd returned from his first tour of duty popped into his mind.

'Always remember that the love we share is so much

bigger than anything else. It has the power to heal. To lift. To inspire.'

His mother's words had been the inspiration behind Plants to Paws. If all went well tonight, the place could virtually run itself from now on so he'd need something new to work on. And for the first time in a long time he looked deep inside himself to get answers.

He needed to forgive Gavin. *Wanted* to forgive him. Unless he let go of all that rage, he was not fit to love. Not properly. He closed his eyes tight and pictured the complexity of feelings he had about Gavin as a grenade. The hurt, the anger, the fear. For well over half his life he'd let Gavin define whether he was a success or a failure. And in Gavin's world success meant money. Power. Failure meant living in a run-down inner-city estate where, no matter how hard you worked or how kind you'd been, you were at the mercy of developers who thought nothing of paving over another man's hopes and dreams.

His mental grenade went incandescent with pent-up fury.

Then he mentally pulled the pin.

Two seconds later?

The sun came out from behind a cloud.

Yes, he was still Max Kirkpatrick. Still an A and E doctor in an inner-city hospital. A soldier who'd served his country. A doctor who'd saved many lives. He was also a man who was in love with a woman who deserved his whole heart. Would letting go of his past be as easy as willing it to be over? He sure as hell hoped so. It was time to get on with his life. Live the future he'd always dreamed of. A future he hoped with every fibre in his being included Esme.

An entire glitter bomb exploded in Esme's bloodstream when she finally saw Max enter the ballroom.

The man most definitely knew how to wear a kilt. Yum.

As she worked her way through the crowd, thick with Scotland's most generous donors, she was vividly aware that the only person who really mattered to her tonight was Max.

'Hey, you.' She touched his arm.

When he turned and saw her, that heated buzz of electricity she now knew she didn't want to live without swept through her. It was time to change her life. Stop hiding out at Heatherglen and finally open the clinic in Glasgow she'd always dreamed of. Margaret and Aksel could run the Heatherglen site. She and Max could forge a life here. It'd be perfect.

Max leant in and kissed her cheek, the moment briefly closing out the rest of the world as she inhaled the scent that was so specific to him. The outdoors. A hit of citrus. Male inner strength.

With his cheek brushing against hers, he whispered, 'You look beautiful.'

She stepped back and gave a shy little twist in her dress. A nod to her family's tartan, the double skirts were in two shades of blue, the darker of the two rucked up so that the thick satin cornflower blue underskirt was visible as well. The under-bust corset was surprisingly comfortable now that she was used to it. It had been woven by a local woollen mill and showed off the family tartan to full effect. The appreciative look in Max's eyes meant wrestling into the ensemble had been worth the effort.

'Gorgeous, darlin'.' He dropped her a wink. 'Any chance you'll save a place for me on your dance card?'

They were hardly the words of a man who was about to tell her to take a hike so she crossed her fingers that he had decided they should see each other once the ball was over. Besides, it was Christmas. He couldn't possibly break her heart at Christmas, could he? She gave him a coquettish smile. 'If you're lucky, I might even save you two.'

Charles came up to them and said something about wanting to introduce Max to someone. She watched as they worked their way through the crowd, wondering...hoping... Charles would see everything in Max she saw. A passionate man committed to making the world a better place despite the way life had kept knocking him down. No matter how many times it had happened, he'd still got back up again.

There was a part of her that was still shy of marriage, but her heart was speaking loud and clear. A life with Max Kirkpatrick would make her a better person. A happier person. Living with fear, not trusting anyone to come too close, never feeling worthy enough to deserve being loved for herself and herself alone...it had depleted her.

With Max she felt like a newborn colt. Better even. Giddy, full of verve and willing to take on a thousand new challenges she would have never considered before she'd met him. A life that, perhaps, stretched beyond the gates of Heatherglen. Perhaps they should start tonight. Maybe, after they'd talked, she'd suggest they spend the night in Glasgow...give her a taste of all that lay ahead of them.

Max nodded and listened as Charles spoke.

'Do you understand what I'm trying to say?'

'Loud and clear.' There had been no malice in Charles's words. One could argue it wasn't even personal. He'd explained how far Esme had come. How this was a vulnerable time of year for her. That she was more trusting than she should be. Though Charles hadn't spelled it out, Max understood what Esme's very protective older brother was saying with laser-sharp clarity.

Hurt my sister and you'll have me to answer to. Your best bet is to back off. Now.

Hurting Esme was the last thing on his mind. Being pulled to one side as he had been—being pointedly reminded he was here to receive charitable aid for Plants to Paws and nothing more—was like a sharp knife finding that sweet spot between his ribs. Or, more pointedly, a wrecking ball to his plan to finally open his heart to Esme and say yes, to everything. Yes to dating. Yes to love. Yes to trying to build a future together. He knew it wouldn't be perfect. Not right away anyway. He lived here, she lived at Heatherglen. Neither of them could just drop their lives. But he had shored up enough strength over the past week to admit to her he was flawed, and she hadn't slammed the door in his face. Quite the opposite, in fact.

He looked across to where Esme was talking with Charles and a group of donors. She really was a remarkable woman. She had made all this happen. And she did it every year. Every day if you counted the animal's lives she saved, the humans she empowered with service dogs. How a woman like her could've thought for a second she wasn't worthy of love...

Now was the time to make the call. Was he in or was he out?

He soaked in the beautiful surroundings, the waiters floating about the place with trays of luxurious canapés and delicate crystal flutes of champagne. Charles hadn't said as much—and certainly didn't strike him as the type to judge—but this wasn't Max's world. These were Scotland's movers and shakers. The power people. He was a grassroots man. A guy who rolled up his shirtsleeves, grabbed a shovel and got stuck in. He gave a mirthless laugh. He was the guy who picked up the poop. Esme deserved someone who wanted more. Pushed harder. Thought bigger.

He was happy where he was. Serving Glasgow's not so finest. It was where he belonged. All of that boiled down to one thing. He would never be the man Esme deserved.

For the next hour or so, no matter how hard Esme tried to make good on that promise to dance with Max, she simply couldn't get anywhere near him. Again and again their eyes caught, but donors were virtually queuing up to talk to him about Plants to Paws. Those who couldn't get to him made a beeline for her. Told her what an inspired idea it was. Wondered if there were ways they could make similar gardens and pet visiting areas outside other hospitals. It made her feel so proud. All the charities she had championed were incredible, but this one had a special place in her heart. Before she'd as much as taken a sip of her champagne they'd surpassed their target. If things continued along these lines, Max would be able to set up ten Plants to Paws. It was truly inspiring.

Once again she sought him out in the crowd. She hoped this would be the proof he needed to finally realise just how valuable, strong and incredible a man he was. She hadn't been blind to his insecurities. To the little boy in him still trying to prove he was worth 'investing in'. He didn't only deserve all the money that was pouring in, he deserved every ounce of love she had for him. He probably didn't even know how much he'd helped her. Being here, feeling so confident in front of the media and the donors, she realised Max had helped her reach a place where she was finally able to see Harding MacMillan for what he truly was: a small, conniving, opportunistic man. If he hadn't pulled the wool over her eyes he would've pulled them over someone else's. His actions were a reflection of who he was…not her. And that simple revelation made all the difference.

All too soon it was time for speeches. Esme managed to pull Max away from a group of well-wishers and asked if he was ready to head up to the podium.

'Absolutely, I just…'

There was something off. Something he wasn't telling her.

'Max? Is everything all right?'

'I need to tell you something.'

'Miss Ross-Wylde?' The maître d' touched Esme's elbow and pointed towards the stage. 'Everyone's glasses are being charged for the toasts.'

'Of course.' She turned back to Max, whose expression had shifted from agitated to resolute. As if he'd made a decision and wasn't going to change his mind. 'Do you mind if we talk after the speeches?'

Before he could answer she was being ushered up onto the podium.

Esme's speech of thanks to the donors was short but entirely heartfelt. '...in closing, without you this inner-city haven would have been paved over. A car park or a garden? You have spoken loud and clear. Thanks to your generosity, every single one of the Clyde's patients will now have a permanent lifeline to a beautiful garden where they can grow vegetables or flowers, play with their pets, or simply sit and watch the world go by as they go through their journey in hospital.' As the audience applauded, she beckoned Max to step up to the podium. Plants to Paws existed because of him. He should be the one in the spotlight.

After making a few heartfelt comments of thanks, Max turned to Esme and raised his glass of champagne. 'My biggest thanks, of course, go to this beautiful woman right here. Without her...' His Adam's apple dipped and lifted as he swallowed and started again. 'Without her, a young lad's dream to put some good into the world would not have come true. In our time together she has shown me just how strong she is. Which is why I know she will continue to be a beacon of inspiration for all the people she will meet now that our time together has come to an end.'

Esme felt as though she'd been hit by a truck. What was he talking about?

He continued, 'I would like to propose a toast to a woman who I hope continues her incredible work. I know she will continue to bring change to people's lives. And I would like her to know that I will always remember her and the kindness she has shown Plants to Paws. The patients—'

A loud buzzing started in Esme's ears. *Always remember her?* Was this it? The last night she'd ever see him? She forced herself to tune back in again.

'…with her busy schedule I suspect our paths won't cross again, but she can rest assured that she will always be remembered.'

Esme grabbed hold of the podium, the floor no longer feeling stable beneath her feet.

Max was breaking up with her. And though no one here knew it, except perhaps Margaret whose eyes were all but popping out of her head, he was humiliating her in public. Just as Harding had done.

'Ladies and gentlemen, if could you all please charge your glasses and join me in a toast to Esme Ross-Wylde…'

He lifted his glass, took a sip without losing eye contact, then leant in to whisper, 'I'm so sorry.' Without waiting for a reply, he gave the crowd a quick wave then left the room.

It didn't make sense. None of it did.

Esme felt as though ice had filled her body. Once more she'd been played. Once more she'd misread a man from the moment she'd met him. Once again her heart was breaking. Only this time she knew she wouldn't be able to put it back together again.

Suddenly, urgently, all she wanted was to be back in her safe haven. Back at Heatherglen with her dogs and her big brother, where she was safe. If she never saw Max Kirkpatrick again it would be too soon.

CHAPTER ELEVEN

EVEN UNDER HEAVY attack from enemy fire, Max's heart had never beat faster. He was leaving the woman who was more than likely the love of his life.

Though his flat was miles away, he walked through the Botanical Gardens and back to his neighbourhood to see if it would give him any perspective. A few freezing hours later he was none the wiser.

Defeat weighted his every footstep and when he finally got home, he fell into a restless sleep.

He woke up feeling exhausted and empty. He forced himself out of bed, into the shower then out the door to Plants to Paws. It was where this whole debacle had begun. It was where he'd lay it to rest with a few hours' hard labour.

When he eventually returned home, covered in earth from a few hours of digging and planting some fruit trees one of the patients had brought in, he glanced at the racks of newspapers outside a shop near his flat. There she was, right on the front page. The photographer had captured her perfectly. Beautiful. Capable. Strong.

And he'd just hurt her in the worst way imaginable. In a situation where she couldn't do anything other than paste on a smile and bury her pain.

The self-loathing he felt at that moment was powerful enough to consume him but something rose in him that said, no. Enough. Esme deserved more and he was the man to give her what she wanted. Love. Pure, unconditional, everlasting love.

He raced back through the conversation he'd had with Charles. Had Esme's brother ever told him to back off? No. Had he said he thought Max wasn't a worthy suitor? Quite the opposite. He'd said he respected him. Admired what he did.

Then how the hell had he heard what he had? That he wasn't worthy?

Because it was his biggest fear.

Well, he didn't want to let fear run his life any more. It had for far too long and today it was going to end.

If Esme decided she didn't want him in her life any more after what he'd done he'd have to take it. But he wasn't going to just let her walk away without letting her know how he really felt.

He dug into his pocket for his car keys and a short while later hit the motorway for Heatherglen.

He loved Esme. More powerfully than he had loved any woman. If his life had taught him anything it was that standing by and doing nothing was the worst course of action. With grim determination he punched an address into his sat-nav and set off on the make-orbreak journey.

* * *

Esme drew up a dose of anaesthetic and was just about to put it into the IV bag already hooked up to Boopsy the Labrador when Aksel put his hand on her arm to stop her.

Esme stared at the syringe then looked at Aksel. She could only see his eyes thanks to his surgical mask and cap, but he looked alarmed.

'What?' They urgently needed to put the young Lab under after an X-ray had revealed his lethargy and lack of appetite were due to a tennis ball being lodged at the top of his intestines. Proof, if she'd needed any, that having fun came with consequences.

'You've prepared the wrong dosage.'

'No, I haven't.'

The vet nurse who was with them winced, then showed Esme the dog's chart. 'He's only twenty kilos, not forty.'

Esme dropped the syringe as if it were on fire.

She'd let herself get so distracted by her emotions she had compromised the poor dog's life.

The roiling ball of fury she'd been wrestling with ever since the ball last night had nearly overshadowed her number one vow: to care for and protect the animals she treated with every ounce of her being.

The nurse picked up the syringe, disposed of the contaminated needle and waited for instructions.

The last thing she wanted to do was harm someone's beloved pet. It was the final surgery of the day. She'd managed to hold things together so far, but endangering a poor, innocent creature because she couldn't focus?

Unacceptable. She looked Aksel square in the eye and did something she'd never done before. 'Can you do the surgery? I think I need to sit this one out.'

He agreed and mercifully didn't go through any ridiculous show of hugging her or asking if she was okay or if she wanted to talk about it. She never, ever wanted to talk about this again.

She tugged on her thickest parka as the snow was falling *yet again*. Normally she'd be thrilled. Snow on Christmas Eve! Today it was just *irritating*. She glanced across at the Christmas carnival. It was all laughter and lights and couples holding hands and looking adoringly into one another's eyes.

She needed a walk with a dog. It was the only medicine that would get her to see straight. Especially as she had the Living Nativity to do tonight. Charles had said he'd ring to cancel for her, but she didn't want her big brother stepping in to fix things for her. She was a grown woman. A grown woman who should be able to deal with the fact she'd let a lying bastard into her heart yet again. From here on out? Total. Nun.

A few metres out from the clinic, Margaret ran out to meet her. 'You taking Wylie for a walk?'

That had been the plan but if she admitted that, Margaret would want to come along and that would involve talking.

Wylie took hold of the lead dangling from Esme's hand and tugged it. Margaret knew that meant it was walkies time.

'I'm coming whether or not you want me to,' Margaret said.

Esme huffed out a sigh.

Margaret gave her scarf another whirl round her neck and met Esme's speedy pace. 'Just so you know, I'm as cross as you are.'

Esme wheeled on her. 'Cross? You think I'm *cross* with him?' Her fist slammed against her chest. 'I trusted him. I opened up my heart to him. I *loved* him.'

'Charles? Of course you love Charles.'

Esme stopped cold. 'What are you talking about?'

Margaret returned her perplexed expression with an equally confused look. 'What are *you* talking about?'

'I'm talking about Max leaving the ball without as much as a thank you very much.'

Margaret shot a nervous look at the castle. 'Did Charles happen to tell you about the little talk he had with Max before the speeches?'

'No.'

Margaret's features morphed into a full-on wince. 'I thought you knew. That's why I didn't say anything.'

'About what?'

Margaret scrunched her forehead, clearly debating whose loyalty to play to.

'Margaret! What did Charles do?

An hour later Charles zipped Esme's fleece up to her throat as if she were a five-year-old. She batted his hands away. If she didn't love him so much she would give him a punch in the nose. If she were that sort of woman. Which she most definitely was not.

He pulled the zip up anyway. 'You're sure you want to do this?'

'Of course.' She tugged herself free and pulled on the burlap dress the Marys had been wearing. 'I promised the nativity committee I would do it. Unlike *some of us*, I do not let people down by telling them one thing then doing another!'

'I didn't realise you liked him in that way!'

'Even a blind person could see I loved him! Surely you were aware of it enough to give him that big brother talk of yours.'

'Wait. You love him?' Charles looked dumbfounded.

'Yes,' She'd never felt more certain of anything in her life. 'I love him, and I want to date him and go on holidays with him and wear silly Christmas jumpers with him. For many years to come, if possible.'

A clock chimed on the mantelpiece.

'Are you sure you want to be in the nativity? You're a bit high-strung. Do you think you'll be able to sit still?'

Esme glared at her brother. *Honestly.* 'If Mary could ride a donkey to Bethlehem when she was nine months pregnant, I can do an hour in the market square. And then I'm going to get in the car and drive to Glasgow and tell Max I love him.'

'You should ring him. It's snowing. The four-by-four hasn't been serviced in—'

'Uh-uh!' She cut him off. 'This is something that has to be done face to face. A phone call isn't good enough. Besides, you're the reason I'm in this stupid mess.'

'I didn't say anything!' Charles threw up his hands.

'According to Margaret, you told Max I was a fragile little piece of china that deserved the very best life had to offer!'

'Isn't that what a big brother is supposed to say to potential suitors?' Charles looked so bewildered it almost endearing. Almost.

'Don't you get it?'

'Obviously not.' He threw up his hands and plopped down on the couch.

'You scared him off! If you tell someone like Max—a man who's been trying to do right by the people he loves—that he isn't good enough—'

'I never told him he wasn't good enough, I just said…' The penny dropped. He scrubbed his face with his hands. 'I think I owe Max an apology.'

'Good! Then you can come along to Glasgow and dig me out of any ditches if we hit any black ice.' Before Charles could protest, she pinned on a bright smile. 'Right! Let's get this show on the road.'

The crowd round the nativity was especially big. The magic of Christmas Eve had wrapped everyone in its embrace. As it was snowing, it had been decided that rather than take up one of the villagers' very generous offers to let her toddler be the baby Jesus, Dougal was standing in instead as he had a built-in fur coat.

Wylie had on a pair of antlers and was lying with his head in Esme's lap as she knelt by the manger. Charles was one of the three kings. She eventually had to stop looking at him as his eyes were laced with such concern it was about to do her head in. Breaking down in front of the whole of Cluchlochry wasn't part of the plan.

About twenty minutes in, the crowd started murmuring and parting as if they were letting someone through. Her eyes widened as Mrs McCann's shire horse appeared. It was dressed up like a camel one of the three kings might've arrived on. Only...all the kings were there. Charles, Hamish from the clinic and Lyle. Wylie lifted his head and gave a friendly woof. Dougal jumped up in the manger and began wriggling in that happy way he had when he saw someone he knew.

When she looked up and saw who this unexpected arrival was, her heart leapt straight into her throat.

Max.

Her gorgeous, manly, wonderful Max. He was wearing his kilt, which had to be ruddy cold as it was beginning to snow. Big fat flakes fell on her face as she fruitlessly tried to blink away her tears.

He got off the horse and handed the reins to Mrs McCann, who gave him an utterly adoring smile.

What on earth was happening? The last place she'd thought he would've wanted to be was with her.

Wylie, sensing she'd been thrown completely off-kilter, pressed his big furry nose against her thigh.

'I think I owe you an apology,' Max said when their eyes met.

Emotion stung at the back of her throat. 'I think you might've got that the wrong way round.'

His forehead furrowed. 'No. I'm pretty sure it's me who needs to apologise for leaving you at the ball.'

She shook her head. 'And I'm relatively certain I know the reason why that happened.'

She heard an uncomfortable cough come from the three kings' corner of the stable. *Charles.*

He stepped forward. 'Perhaps you two would like some privacy?'

None of the villagers moved. Esme couldn't help it. She laughed. A real-life Christmas drama! She looked at Max whose face read pretty easily. Yes. Some privacy might be nice. Esme searched out one of the publicans from amongst the crowd. 'All right if we nip inside by the fire for a wee bit?'

He nodded and a path was cleared.

Once inside the pub Esme pulled one of Max's big strong hands into hers. 'I thought you had just left. I was terrified I'd never see you again.'

Max's features softened. 'That was definitely one of the plans.'

'One of...?'

He tilred his head from side to side. 'I had a few.'

Esme's chest tightened. *Please, please, please, let one of his plans be with her.*

'The one I like best involves a lot of travel.'

Her hands flew to her mouth to stem a host of follow-up questions.

'I went to the Clyde this afternoon and asked them if I could split my shifts between there and the hospital up the road from Heatherglen. I thought... I *hoped* you might be interested in seeing what we had between us might bring if we saw each other a bit more regularly.'

Her heart skipped a beat. 'What are you saying?'

'I'm saying I love you, Esme. I don't want to stop seeing you. One night away from you with all that in-security and fear tearing at my heart and...' He folded his hands over his heart. 'I don't want to live like that. I'm prepared to fight your brother for your honour if need be.'

'Luckily that won't be necessary,' Esme assured him, the smile on her face nearly stretching from ear to ear.

'You're the one I'm meant to be with. I will do everything in my power to convince you that I'm the man for you if you'll have me.' He went down on one knee, holding both of her hands in his. 'You are my heart, my soul and everything I could have imagined that would make me a better man. Please say you'll give me a second chance.'

A different kind of tears welled in her eyes. Christmas was meant to be a time of giving. Of opening up one's heart to those you loved, and she loved Max. She'd let fear and her complicated past override what she knew to be true. That she and Max loved each other. She'd fled that ball like a frightened girl. She was a woman now. It was time to start acting like one. She leant forward and kissed Max with every ounce of passion she could muster.

When they started hearing applause coming from the pub windows they both laughed. 'Looks like privacy is hard to come by here in Cluchlochry!' Max waved at the crowd, who cheered.

'Would you like to come back to Heatherglen for some hot chocolate? I think we probably need to talk a bit more.'

Relief flooded Max's features. 'I'd like nothing more.'

When he rose and pulled her into his arms for another soft kiss, a chorus of 'Ahh...' and a second round of applause cocooned them in the village's heartfelt delight. This, Esme thought as she pressed her hand to

Max's chest to feel the cadence of his heartbeat, was where she belonged. With this man who would love her and stand by her side through thick and thin. 'What a way to turn round one of the worst Christmas Eves ever,' she whispered.

'Just wait until you see what I have in store for Christmas morning,' he whispered back in a voice that left little to the imagination.

She slipped her mittened hand into his, rested her head against his shoulder and smiled. Christmas was back exactly to where she'd been hoping to find it. In her heart. She looked up at the sky and sent a special prayer to her family who were no longer with them, knowing that they would be over the moon for her. Letting go of the grief she'd carried all these years would take time but filling that void with love was the very best Christmas gift of all.

After three mugs of hot chocolate and hours of heart-felt conversation, Esme and Max were agreed. Honesty was not only the best policy; it was the *only* policy. Charles had generously volunteered to look after Dougal and Wylie for the night, but when Max and Esme awoke on Christmas morning, Esme sneaked into her brother's room to take them into the sitting room for a yuletide cuddle.

'I think Dougal looks good as a reindeer,' Esme insisted as she adjusted the antlers headband she'd perched on top of his little puppy head.

'I think Dougal will do anything to bring a smile to your face.' Max pulled her close to him and gave her a kiss. 'Which makes two of us.'

'Good!' Esme clapped her hands and pulled out a present from behind her back. 'Now it's your turn.'

Max opened the present and let out a huge laugh. 'Seriously? This is what you want me to wear?' He held up the jumper. It was probably the most awful Christmas jumper he'd ever seen in his life. Pom-poms. Blinking reindeer nose. Sequins. Everything that would normally send him running for the hills.

'I had it made specially.' Esme fluttered her eyelashes. 'You wouldn't want to make me sad by not wearing it, would you?'

Max laughed. 'Of course not, darlin'.' He pulled it on and held out his arms. 'Look good?'

Esme nodded. 'Perfect.' She pulled another package from under the tree.

'What's that?'

She giggled. 'One for me! I knew Charles would never buy one so I got one for all of us.'

'You goof.'

'I know, I just... I love Christmas so much and after years of trying to pretend I was having a brilliant time, it finally it feels right.'

'I hope that's because you are precisely where you belong.' Max pulled her to him and gave her a deep kiss. 'With me.'

'Exactly.' Esme grinned. 'Now...' She unfurled her own jumper. 'What do you think of this?'

'You've never looked more beautiful.' Max said dryly.

'And you've never looked more handsome,' she quipped. 'Shall we take a look in the mirror?'

When they went over to the large gilt mirror hanging above the fireplace they both started giggling. 'We look ridiculous,' Esme said, barely able to control herself. 'Ridiculous and perfect.'

Max frowned at their reflection. 'There's something missing.'

'What?' Esme shot him a panicked look. 'You don't have any more secrets up your sleeve, do you?'

Max ruffled her hair and gave her a soft kiss. 'No. I am so sorry about everything that happened at the ball. The best-laid plans and all that. It was stupid of me to want to wait until Christmas Eve to tell you. I made a real hash of things, didn't I?'

'Nothing you didn't fix.' Esme gave his hands a reassuring squeeze. 'Nothing you can't spend the rest of your days making up for,' she said in a much saucier voice.

'In which case...perhaps you'd like to hear my proposal?'

Her cheeks instantly went pink. 'Oh, Max, I love you so much, but you know how I feel about that.'

'I do,' he said, popping a kiss on his finger then transferring it to her nose. 'And I respect it. Which is why I was thinking we might do something a little different.'

'What kind of different?' She might not want to dive into a white frock anytime soon, but that certainly didn't mean she wanted to try anything too off piste. She was, after all, a traditional romantic at heart.

'This kind of different.' He held up his pinkie finger and crooked it. 'I want to be your pinkie promise forever man.'

She giggled. 'Is that even a thing?'

'It is if we make it a thing.'

She stilled when she realised he was absolutely serious. 'What do we have to say?'

He shrugged. 'Nothing formal like wedding vows… Shall I go first?'

She nodded, too choked up with emotion to say anything back.

He crooked his pinkie with hers, looked straight into her eyes and said, 'Esme Ross-Wylde, I love you. You make the world a better place to live in. And one day I'd like to live in it with you by my side.'

'One day?'

He laughed softly. 'All the days if I'm being completely honest, but… I want to make sure what we have makes you the happiest woman on earth.'

'It does.' It was out before she could stop it.

'Good.' Max dipped his head to kiss her, his lips brushing against hers as he finished. 'Then let's take our time. Because all of mine is all of yours. Happy Christmas, love.'

'Best. Christmas. Ever.'

They sealed the promise with a kiss, knowing in each of their hearts that Christmas would for evermore be the happiest, most blessed day of the year.

CHAPTER TWELVE

Two years later

'I CAN'T BELIEVE it's snowing!'

'I can!' Margaret laughed. 'Everything you've wished for since you and Max got engaged has come true. It's like that engagement ring of yours came with magical powers.'

'Only the magical power of love,' Esme teased. She held up the beautiful seasonal bouquet the florist had crafted for her. It was a bountiful mix of heather, holly berries and scarlet roses, dappled with fronds of spruce with miniature pinecones as seasonal flourishes. 'Are you going to be the one to catch this?'

Margaret laughed. 'You can count on it.'

There was a knock on the door. Charles came in when Esme had made sure it wasn't Max trying to get a sneak peek at the bride.

'How's my wee sister doing on her wedding day?'

'Amazing.' She smiled up at him then across to the pictures of her father and Nick. 'I wish they could be here.'

'They are.' Charles gave her a warm smile then pointed to his heart then her own. 'They're here with us.'

'I still can't believe Mum came home.'

'I know! Yet another Christmas miracle!' He laughed and crooked his arm. 'Ready to go and meet your groom?'

'More than ever.'

When Esme came through the small chapel doors and into the cosy church festooned with garlands, Max could hardly breathe. Two years together and she still took his breath away.

Behind her, bearing the rings, were Dougal and Wylie. Behind them were Margaret and a string of bridesmaids dressed in deep evergreen-coloured dresses. But he only had eyes for Esme. Her eyes glittered with anticipation as she walked past the packed congregation towards the altar. There'd be even more people at the reception. Testament to the respect Esme had garnered in her community and beyond. He could not have been more proud of her than he was at this moment.

When Charles handed Esme's hand to him with a stern but loving reminder to take care of his sister, Max answered solemnly. 'I will take care of her until the end of time.'

Esme gave his hand a squeeze and smiled up at him. 'Are you ready for this?'

'More than ever.'

'Do you think they'll let us skip ahead to the kissing the bride bit?' he whispered.

'Don't you worry.' Esme's smile grew. 'We've got a lifetime of kissing ahead of us.'

'In that case…' Max and Esme turned to the minister and nodded. They were ready, hand in hand, to embark on the rest of their lives together, taking a special handful of Christmas magic along with them as they went.

* * * * *

THEIR ONE-NIGHT
CHRISTMAS GIFT

KARIN BAINE

MILLS & BOON

For Richard Rankin xx

CHAPTER ONE

CHARLES ROSS-WYLDE WAS a selfish, cold-hearted liar and Harriet Bell was better off without him. At least, that was what she'd spent the last twelve years telling herself.

The reality of seeing him again was very different from the scenario she'd imagined. She'd been shocked to see him here, but so far she'd resisted slapping him, throwing a drink in his face, or announcing to the rest of the conference attendees that *he* was the reason she couldn't risk loving anyone again. Perhaps she'd matured or, more likely, hadn't expected to feel anything other than pure hatred towards him.

She watched him now from the other side of the room as the assembled medical community enjoyed the tea break between lectures. It gave her time to study him unnoticed and decide what she wanted to do—if anything. If she chose to she could walk out of here and he'd be none the wiser, with nothing changing their current status quo.

Impossible when there was so much she wanted to say, so much she wanted him to explain.

Physically, he hadn't changed much from the man who'd once promised her their lives would be spent together except he looked older...more manly.

He was still trying to sweep that floppy dark hair back into a neat style befitting a professional man, though she remembered all too well how it had looked first thing in the morning tousled by sleep. And, as always, he was dressed impeccably, the navy suit tailored to his exact measurements. The beard was new, the dark shadow along his jawline making him look even more masculine, if that was possible. It suited him—as did the glasses he was sporting.

Damn it, he was still gorgeous, and apparently still able to make her heart flutter maniacally as though she'd just run a marathon.

'They really should have an open bar,' she muttered to the bewildered woman serving refreshments to the masses, turning away from the view of her ex-fiancé and wishing for a tot of whisky in her coffee.

Not that she drank often, but she'd make an exception to help her escape memories of her and Charles—good and bad. She'd have to make do with an extra spoonful of sugar in her tea to help with the shock.

'I didn't expect to see you here.' That soft, Scottish burr capable of rendering her into a gibbering wreck tickled the back of her neck. He'd found her.

Harriet fumbled with her cup and saucer, spilling the contents over herself right before she turned around to face him. 'Charles. What a surprise.'

'Sorry, I didn't mean to startle you.' He grabbed a

napkin from the buffet table and started dabbing at the stain darkening the front of her dress.

'I can do that, thanks.' She didn't mean to snap but she couldn't bear to have him touch her after all this time when she didn't know what emotions it would unleash.

'Sorry.' He handed over possession of the napkin so she could tend to the ruined dress herself. 'It was just nice to see a familiar face. How have you been, Harriet?'

There was no sign of remorse for the relationship and future he'd thrown away. He was talking to her as though they were old school friends, who had no real emotional connection and had simply happened to run into each other.

She set the wet napkin and coffee back on the table and took a moment to consider her response. If she kicked off and made a scene it would be clear she'd never got over him and that would most likely send Charles running. She didn't know what she wanted from him, but it wasn't that.

'Oh, you know, keeping busy. You?' She plastered on a smile, willing to play along with this game until one of them broke. Her, probably.

'The same. I took up a placement in Glasgow to complete my medical training and set up a clinic at Heatherglen. It was initially to help army veterans, but we've extended to provide state-of-the-art medical facilities for physical and emotional rehabilitation to a wider range of patients.'

'Sounds impressive.' Inheriting his father's fortune

and the family estate had signalled the end of their engagement so it was difficult for Harriet to be as enthusiastic about his accomplishments as she should have been.

'I wanted to do something worthwhile to honour my brother and father, but it takes a lot of upkeep. I don't get to make as many trips to London as I'd like.' His older brother, Nick, had served with the military in Afghanistan. Unfortunately, he'd been killed by a roadside bomb before Harriet had had the chance to meet him. That family tragedy, followed by the death of his father about a year later, had proved too much for Charles and their wedding plans.

'I'm the same, too many responsibilities here to even take a holiday these days.' Needless to say, she hadn't been back to Scotland since his father's funeral, when Charles had gone back on his promise of making a life with her. At the time she'd believed grief had driven his decision, but when he'd failed to follow her back to London she'd soon realised he was serious about no longer wanting to marry her. It was difficult to reconcile that man who'd broken her heart with the one stood before her now, making small talk.

'So, you did stay here after all? I'd hoped you would.' He was smiling so Harriet didn't think he was trying to rub salt into the wound he'd inflicted on her that day. She'd never received a proper explanation as to why he'd called things off. Goodness knew, she'd been desperate for one, but she'd eventually had to accept the simple truth that he didn't want her any more. She'd seen that happen between her own parents when she'd been young and had watched her mother torture herself trying to figure out what she'd done wrong when her father had walked out on them. There was no way she was spending the rest of her life beating herself up about it, the way her mother had until her death.

'Yes. I'm an orthopaedic surgeon.'

Top of my field, she wanted to add, piqued by the fact he'd never bothered to check up and see what she'd been doing. Then again, she hadn't done that either, afraid she'd start obsessing over him or what could have been between them. In his case it seemed it was merely down to a lack of interest.

'Neurologist,' he countered. 'I thought it made sense to take that path, so I'd be able to better treat veterans.'

What a team they would have made working together but perhaps she wouldn't have pursued her career so doggedly if they had married. When she and Charles had been together she'd imagined she could have it all—a career and a family. She'd thought they were a team, on an equal footing and willing to share the responsibilities of raising children. Except the moment Charles's circumstances had changed he'd backed out and left her to pick up the pieces of her broken heart. She'd paid the price for his actions.

Perhaps she'd had a lucky escape. If he'd proved so unreliable further down the line, he could have left her raising their children alone once he'd decided he didn't want her after all. As it was, she'd poured her heart and soul into her career because that was the one thing she could count on always being there. Things happened for a reason and she had no regrets when it had moved her focus back onto her work. It didn't look as though he had any either.

They fell into an awkward gap in conversation, neither apparently knowing what to say to the other but not wanting to make the first move in walking away.

'Could all attendees please make their way back to their seats for the next talk, please?'

The announcement over the loudspeaker filled the silence on their behalf and left them with the decision of whether to say goodbye temporarily, or for ever.

'Listen, why don't we go for a proper drink? The hotel bar should be quiet enough with all the reprobates locked in here for another few hours of telling us things we already know.' Charles rested his hand lightly at her waist, leaning in so his comment reached only her ears. She could barely feel the pressure of his fingertips on her skin, but it was sufficient to awaken every erogenous zone in her body until she was sure she'd follow him to the ends of the earth.

'Sure,' she squeaked.

Damn, she was in trouble.

Charles didn't know what he hoped to gain by getting Harriet on her own, except having her to himself for the first time in over a decade. When he'd spotted her across the room there had been no great plan, just a need to be near her. Much like the first time they'd met in medical school and had instantly become inseparable. Being each other's first loves, they'd become seriously quickly. In hindsight, that youth and inexperience would never have worked in a world where tradition and duty to the family name was everything. He'd just wanted to be with Harriet and had given no thought to Heatherglen back then.

Now he considered himself lucky she'd agreed to go for a drink with him instead of throwing a cup of hot coffee in his face.

'There's a seat in the corner. I'll get the drinks. White wine?' He led her into the bar, where one or two other hotel guests had sought refuge.

'Yes, please.' Even that knowledge of her preferred drink brought back memories of times together it was difficult to ignore. Those early student days of being silly and partying too hard. Later, when it had been a bottle of wine to accompany a romantic meal they often hadn't bothered to finish...

'Charles, what are you doing?' he muttered under his breath, and stole a glance back at Harriet as she settled into the corner.

Those days of acting only in his own interests were supposed to be far behind him. He didn't make any decisions now without thinking through how it might affect those around him. It had been a tough lesson to learn when the consequences of his past actions had come at the price of his brother and father's lives. He'd sacrificed his relationship with Harriet for her benefit—his first act of selflessness when he'd inherited Heatherglen. Not that she'd known, and he couldn't have told her it was because he'd wanted her to stay on in London and pursue her career instead of getting dragged into his mess. She would've insisted on going to Scotland with him.

Although, seeing her now and realising everything

he'd lost, regret weighed heavily on his shoulders along with his threefold burden of guilt.

Approaching her this evening and getting her to agree to join him for a drink had been entirely for his own benefit without considering her feelings. Yet, so far, she'd shown him nothing but friendliness in return. It was entirely possible he'd over-inflated the idea of what they'd had together in his head and she'd forgotten him the second she'd got on that train without him.

'You look good, by the way. Have I said that already?' He'd certainly thought it as he'd headed back to her.

Harriet had always been pretty with her slim figure and long, dark blonde hair but now she was a stunningly beautiful woman. The emerald-green dress she was wearing wasn't particularly noteworthy except for the womanly figure it clung to, accentuating her every curve. It was understated and sophisticated, but on Harriet it was as sexy as hell.

'You haven't but thank you.' She sipped her wine, leaving a trace of ruby lip gloss on the rim of her glass, and...he really needed to keep his libido in check. She was his ex-fiancée, not an anonymous one-night stand.

'So, are you married? Any kids?' He took a gulp of lager, making the question as nonchalant as he could. Why should it matter to him what her marital status was, other than cooling his jets if he found out there was someone waiting for her at home?

'No. I decided my career was the only long-term relationship I needed in my life. I'm too busy to fall for all that again.'

Ouch.

Harriet's brown eyes glittered with a dark challenge for him to bite back. Charles didn't want to go down that route, going over old ground and spoiling the moment they were having now, but she deserved some sort of explanation.

'What about you? Did you settle down?'

'I'm too busy with the clinic and, to be honest, Mum isn't the best advert for marriage. I'm not sure what number husband she's on now since Dad. Three, I think. She spends her days sailing around in his superyacht. We don't see very much of her. I think Heatherglen holds too many sad memories for her.'

'I know the feeling.' Harriet took another sip of her wine, apparently needing to dull the mention of his family home with alcohol.

'Harriet, about all that…' There had to be some way of saying 'It wasn't you, it was me', without sounding completely insincere.

She saved him the trouble, reaching out her hand to still his, which was currently ripping up the cardboard beer mat. 'This is much too serious a topic for this evening, Charles.'

Suddenly his mind was spinning, trying to come to terms with the way his body was responding to her touch after all this time apart and to what she was saying to him.

'I don't do serious any more.' She held him with her ever-darkening gaze, making no attempt to break contact.

'No? What *do* you do?' He leaned in closer, hoping

that if she was actually coming on to him, it wasn't simply a ploy to get revenge.

'I have fun, Charles. You do remember how to do that, don't you? If so, I'm in Room 429.' With that, she got up and walked away. Leaving Charles with his mouth open, his heart hammering, and battling with his conscience, which was telling him that following her was a really bad idea.

Harriet's legs shook on her way towards the elevator. She'd never been so brazen in her life and couldn't even blame it on the alcohol when she'd only had a sip. From the moment she'd seen Charles, she'd wanted what they'd had in the past. Wanted him. What she didn't want was to rake over the ashes of the past and be reminded of how he'd rejected her. It was important to know he was still attracted to her. As though that would somehow erase the previous damage he'd caused her self-esteem.

One night with her ex, on her terms, might give her closure on the relationship that had spoiled her for any other.

Except he hadn't immediately jumped up and begged to take her there and then. She'd merely succeeded in humiliating herself and now had an extra chapter to add to their tragic story.

She jabbed and jabbed at the button for the lift, wishing it would somehow make it come faster. Then it would swallow her up and transport her away from view as soon as possible.

'Harriet, wait!' Charles shouted after her as she

stepped inside the lift. It was tempting to let the doors shut in his face and be done with him once and for all, but he jammed his foot inside and stole that option from her.

The only scenario worse than being stood up when you'd offered yourself on a plate to a man was having him tell you why he didn't want to sleep with you. She fought off the tears already blurring her vision because she was determined not to re-create their last mortifying goodbye.

'Are you sure you want to do this?' His brow was furrowed, and she could see he was actually contemplating her proposal, not attempting to let her down easily at all.

That reassurance buoyed her spirits once more, along with her intention to seduce him. 'It's not a big deal, Charles. We're both single, hard-working professionals who want to let off a little steam in a hotel room.'

Now that she knew she had his interest, she stepped so close to him they were toe to toe.

'We both know it would be more than that.' There was a thread of resistance left in his words, yet his eyes and body were saying something different.

They'd spent enough time together for her to know when he was aroused, and vice versa.

'It doesn't have to be.' She didn't have to fake anything to convince him she wanted this no-strings fling when her breathy voice was a natural reaction to having him so close again.

'I know I hurt you, Harriet. Sleeping together now isn't going to change that. It isn't going to change anything. I'm still going to go back to Heatherglen and your life is here.' He was pointing out the obvious to her, they weren't getting back together no matter what happened tonight. It wasn't an outright rejection, though, because he was reaching out to her, caressing her cheek with his thumb, letting her know this was her decision. She was all right with that, safe in the knowledge she was in control of what happened next.

'I'm not looking to rekindle a romance. The past is done with but it's clear that the chemistry is still there between us.' She stroked a finger down the front of his shirt, revelling in the desire darkening his eyes until they were almost black. This was what she wanted— confirmation that she still affected him as much as he did her. More importantly, she needed this to give her some closure.

She'd used Charles as an excuse not to let anyone else get close to her but recently she'd begun to wonder if she was missing something in her life. If she was ever to entertain the notion of a serious relationship, or even a family, she had to put Charles's memory to rest first. One more time together and a chance to say a proper goodbye should finally close that chapter of her life.

'As I remember, that was never a problem for us, but we do have a long, complicated history. Is it really a good idea to go back there?'

'Now isn't the time to start getting chivalrous, Charles.' Harriet let her finger trail down until she reached his belt buckle, then started to undo it.

Charles let out a groan. 'I just don't want us to do anything that will end up with you getting hurt again.

I can't give you any more now than I could all those years ago.'

'All I'm asking for is tonight. I'm not going to beg.' She popped open the button on his trousers then stopped. If he wanted more he was going to have to say so.

'One night?'

'We never got to say goodbye. Let's think of it as us both getting closure.'

'Going out with a bang?' he asked with a smirk, but he was close enough she could hear the hitch in his breathing. Clearly, he wasn't as composed as he was making out.

'Something like that. A one-time offer never to be repeated or spoken of again.'

'Deal.' His voice was a growl as he wound his arm around her waist, pulled her tight to his body and covered her lips with his.

Just like that the touch paper was lit, their passion reignited in an instant. The kiss so urgent and demanding it took her breath away. She didn't remember Charles being quite so...masterful. Perhaps it was that knowledge they were being reckless that added an extra frisson to their passion. This was definitely the last time they'd be together and would be a sweeter memory, she hoped, to hold onto than the last one.

He backed her against the wall of the lift, his mouth, his tongue never leaving hers. Arousal swept through her, showing no mercy or regard for their location or history. Harriet felt along the wall for the control panel and hit the button for the fourth floor. Charles paused their amorous reunion to hit the one for the second floor instead.

'My room's closer,' he whispered against her neck, and she felt the effect of his warm breath on her skin all the way down to her toes.

The thing about being her past lover was that he remembered exactly where to strike to make her weak at the knees. He knew all her sensitive spots and she shivered with anticipation at the thought of him using that advantage. Two could play that game and it wasn't long before they were both gasping with pleasure as they began to reacquaint themselves with each other. If either of them had booked the penthouse suite she doubted whether they would've made it out of here without consummating their renewed acquaintance.

The doors opened, and they were soon fumbling their way down the corridor, steadfastly locked in their passionate embrace. Charles smiled against her lips as he tried to unlock the room door behind her. They were giggling young lovers again, driven by their hormones and lust, and Harriet was ignoring her adult brain telling her otherwise.

'Have you got any protection?' As they fell through the door her mind was racing ahead. She didn't want to interrupt a crucial moment to track down some condoms in case it gave either of them time to think about what they were doing and change their mind.

'Somewhere.'

He backed her over to the large bed, raining kisses along her neck and collarbone until she fell onto the mattress in a puddle of ecstasy. With one hand he fished in his pocket for his wallet and produced a foil packet. Harriet was glad he didn't have a drawer full of condoms by the bed stocked up for a weekend of bedroom antics with faceless women. A hook-up had come as much of a surprise to him as it had to her but now it was happening she was glad one of them had come prepared.

She helped him shed his jacket and set to work unbuttoning his shirt, longing for the feel of his skin beneath her fingertips. Finding that patch of hair on his chest reminded her how familiar his body was to her but, oh, how she wanted to get to know it intimately again. Her hands at his fly, she began to undo his trousers.

'Harriet? I want to make this last,' he gasped as she pulled him free from the constraints of his clothes.

'I want you. Now,' she demanded. This had to be on her terms, so she remained in control. The only way she could justify bedding her ex was to treat him as casually as he had her. She had needs and though she'd taken lovers since Charles, only he could give her what she truly wanted.

Charles didn't protest. Instead, he slid his hand beneath her dress and tugged her underwear away. With their clothes half on, half off, and Harriet's dress hitched up around her waist, she waited with bated breath for him to sheath himself. There was something daring and incredibly sexy about the spontaneity of it all. She was risking everything she had by bedding him one more time when he'd had the power in the past to topple her world around her.

'I guess we do have all night to get to know each other again.' Charles smiled at her in the darkness and

Harriet arched to meet him at their most sensitive parts. She wanted their bodies to do all the talking tonight. That way there could be no confusion about what she expected from him. This was only about sex. An area she knew he excelled in.

They clung to one another, perspiration settling on their skins as they raced towards that moment of utter bliss they knew they could find with each other. Harriet was already on her way to hitting that peak as though she'd been waiting for twelve long years to do this with him again. Those years apart certainly hadn't diminished their appetites for one another, not on her part at least. No other man had come close to satisfying her the way Charles had. Perhaps because she'd never allowed herself to get as emotionally involved with a man as she couldn't bear the pain that came with it, or perhaps because he'd been the best lover she'd ever had.

He knew exactly where to touch her to drive her crazy and exactly where she needed him to be. Charles too seemed to be making up for lost time, lust setting the heady rhythm of his every stroke inside her. It was as out of control as she'd ever seen him, or indeed had ever felt herself.

When her orgasm came it hit fast and hard, and as Charles's cries echoed hers she knew she never wanted this night to end. There was no more living in the past when the present was so much more enjoyable.

CHAPTER TWO

Two months later

EVERYTHING AND EVERYONE on this road trip had been telling Harriet to have a merry Christmas. From the radio presenters accompanying her on this journey, to the few strangers she'd encountered along the way, to the very weather, they'd been insisting she should be enjoying Christmas Day.

There was a fat chance of that happening, thanks to Charles, and now she was about to ruin his day too. She was happy to do this alone and more than capable. The only reason she was coming all this way was to give him the chance to step up to his obligations this time instead of walking away. He could tell her face to face if he didn't want any part of this, then they wouldn't have to see each other ever again.

The drive to Scotland had been long but uneventful thanks to the lull in traffic. Most people had chosen to stay at home celebrating with family and loved ones. How ironic when she had neither, but next year things would be different. Her whole life was about to change if she didn't take steps to secure the one she already had.

The closer she got to the Ross-Wylde family estate, the harder and faster her heart pounded and her stomach churned. Both from the conversation she had to have with Charles, and the last one they'd had at Heatherglen. She'd never imagined returning to the very place where she'd left her heart.

Road signs directed her towards the clinic that had essentially stolen Charles from her. Where he'd committed to setting up a life as the director there and Laird of the estate, instead of as her husband.

The drive up through the hills to her destination was as familiar to her as the last time she'd seen it, albeit through tear-filled eyes back then. It was dark now, the winter night so all-consuming it had swallowed up the colourful patchwork of countryside she knew surrounded her. All that remained were the inky shadows of the trees towering on either side of the winding road leading to Charles's ancestral home.

Buildings new and old appeared in view but her focus was entirely on the castle itself. With lights blazing in every window and the porch decorated with Christmas wreaths and garlands, it was a welcoming sight. An invitation to visitors that at least one of the residents might come to regret. She hadn't called or texted ahead so she had the element of surprise and could gauge Charles's true reaction to her news.

Harriet parked her car behind the others, which all had a dusting of snow like icing sugar on a sponge cake, and it was obvious no one had left the premises today.

They'd been too busy having a good time, to judge by the sounds of music and laughter filtering through the crisp night air as she made her way to the entrance. There was a twinge of jealousy thinking of him celebrating the festive season here with family when she had no one. She rested her hand on her belly—flat for now. In another few months it would be a different story.

This wasn't about forcing him back into her life. She'd managed quite well without him these past years and she wasn't expecting anything from him now. Harriet wasn't that naïve. A baby hadn't been part of the deal, but she wanted to do the right thing by informing him of the pregnancy at least. With his track record she didn't believe he'd want to be involved and so she would let him know she didn't need anything from him. Her plan was simply to tell him and walk away, leaving them both with a clear conscience over the matter.

Before she could make her way up the stone steps, a door further along the castle burst open and all the warmth and excitement from inside spilled out.

'Oh, sorry. I didn't realise there was anyone out here. Are you here for the clinic?' The petite, smiling blonde looked familiar.

'Esme? Is that you?' She'd only been a teenager when Harriet had last seen her, but there was no doubt that was who she was looking at. It was those dazzling blue eyes, so much like her brother's, that gave away her identity.

'Yes? Can I help you?' There was no sign of recognition from the woman who'd almost been her sister-in-law but for all Harriet knew Charles could've had a procession of fiancées over the years. She couldn't be certain Esme would even remember her if she introduced herself.

'Esme, will you close the door, please? You're letting the cold in.' Charles's irritated voice sounded from inside right before he marched out to see what the commotion was on the doorstep.

It was then Harriet wondered what on earth she'd been thinking by turning up here tonight instead of waiting to speak to him on his own. In truth she hadn't been thinking clearly at all the second she'd seen the positive pregnancy test in her hand. She'd simply packed a bag and headed off to Scotland rather than spend the day considering what the consequences of their night of passion meant for her.

'Harriet?' He peered out into the darkness, glass of whisky in hand.

'Sorry. I didn't realise you'd have company.' She was prepared to walk away from the heated conversation she'd imagined having inside rather than discuss it in front of an audience.

'Harriet? Harriet Bell?' Esme let out a squeal and launched herself at Harriet, hugging her so tight she could no longer feel the cold, or much else.

'Esme, put her down.' Despite their more mature years, big brother Charles still spoke to her the way all boys did to their irritating little sisters. And, as all little sisters tended to do, Esme ignored him completely.

'What on earth are you doing here? It's been, what, ten years?' She had her arm around Harriet's shoulders now, steering her past the main entrance to the house to a side door.

'Twelve, but who's counting?' She managed to dodge answering the question when it was apparent Charles hadn't shared any details of even having met her at the convention. There should have been no reason for him to do so when they'd agreed to forget it had ever happened. Something they could no longer afford to do.

'It's good to see you.' Charles kissed her chastely on the cheek as she entered his ancestral home, probably for his sister's benefit. If he'd answered the door he might not have let her over the doorstep. This definitely hadn't been part of the arrangement.

'You too.' The brief contact was enough to fluster her and she hoped she could explain away her reddening skin with the cold.

'We use the main house for the clinic now. Esme and I have private rooms in another wing. We converted the old servants' quarters downstairs into a small kitchen and informal lounge. It affords us a little privacy from the comings and goings at the clinic. Now, can I get you a drink? A mulled wine or hot toddy to warm you up?' He swilled the contents of his whisky glass, filling the air with scent of cinnamon and warm spices.

'No, thanks. I'm driving. I'd take a cup of tea, though.' She didn't want anything, but she was hoping a trip to the kitchen would get her some privacy to speak to Charles alone.

'Ooh, what about a hot chocolate? I can make you a double chocolate with cream and marshmallows.' Esme's special sounded delicious after the poor service-station efforts they'd dared to charge Harriet for during the stops she'd made on the way here.

'That would be lovely, thank you.' This was all so civilised and bizarre. The Ross-Wyldes were acting as though she was a neighbour who'd just happened to drop by, not an ex-fiancée who'd turned up out of the blue after an extended absence. Either they were incredibly well mannered, which she knew, or they were too worried to ask why she'd come.

Lovely Esme slipped off towards the kitchen and Charles offered to take Harriet's coat for her. She supposed she was staying longer than she'd imagined.

'So, you were just passing by, huh?' He was smiling as he helped her out of her jacket.

She'd panicked when it was clear she couldn't blurt out the real reason she was here on his doorstep. He knew there was no 'just passing by' when London was an eight-hour drive away, yet he didn't seem put out by her unexpected arrival.

'I know this wasn't part of our deal and I'm sorry to intrude on you on Christmas night. I didn't realise you'd have a house full of people.' Even alluding to the 'arrangement' seemed salacious outside the anonymity of the hotel now, when they were in his home.

Charles, however, didn't appear perturbed if his smile was anything to go by. 'Oh, don't worry. You've saved me from another game of charades. Esme insists on covering all the clichés of the season.'

'That explains the outfit.' Now they were in better lighting she could see what he was wearing. The gold paper crown suited him, but the ugly sweater was a far cry from his usual dapper suits. Although he did look pretty cute in it.

'A present from little sis. She made it herself.' He rolled his eyes and Harriet knew he'd suffer the indignity of being seen in it rather than hurt Esme's feelings. If only he'd taken such consideration over *her* feelings when he'd broken up with her, she mightn't have been so intent on getting closure with that one last night together.

'That's lovely. It's so thoughtful for someone to put all that time and effort into making a gift.' To her, Christmas had become just another day. There weren't many presents beyond the odd box of chocolates or a bottle of wine from a grateful patient and she didn't bother making an elaborate Christmas dinner just for one. She preferred to work whenever she could, this year's exception giving her the chance to make the journey here.

'I guess. I'm sure she'd have made you one too if we'd known you were coming.'

Harriet could tell he was curious about what had brought her here when they'd severed all contact after that unforgettable night in his hotel room.

She cleared her throat. 'I came because there's something we need to discuss.'

'In that case, we should go somewhere quiet. We're winding down from our Christmas party and there are still a few people here.'

'That would be better.' She didn't want an audience for what was a very private matter.

'What are you two still doing, standing in the hall?

Charles, bring Harriet in so she can have her hot chocolate by the fire.' Esme tutted as she chivvied them towards the lounge, but Charles resisted leaving the hallway.

'I think Harriet would prefer somewhere more peaceful after her long journey.'

She saw the disappointment on Esme's face and didn't want to hurt her feelings when she'd been so welcoming. 'I can always make time for a hot chocolate first.'

Charles seemed to understand what had brought on her change of heart and stood back to let them enter the living room in front of him.

There were a few couples engaged in conversation by the table of food along the back wall and a ruggedly handsome man, who got to his feet when he saw them, sitting by the fire.

'Harriet, this is Dr Max Kirkpatrick. Max, this is Harriet Bell, an orthopaedic surgeon visiting from London.'

Charles made the introductions, giving little detail away, but Harriet realised it would be impolite for him to say she was the fiancée he'd dumped on inheriting the family silver. Introducing her as 'an ex I hooked up with recently at a medical conference' wouldn't have been the ideal ice-breaker either. The extra bodies in the room, however, did mean she was forced to delay her news a bit longer.

'Nice to meet you.' She shook hands with the man, who couldn't keep his eyes off Esme, and Harriet detected a reciprocal attraction between them. He wasn't the last man she remembered Esme being head over heels about, but she knew better than most that love didn't last for ever. These two still had that glow of new romance about them, which suggested they were in that phase when they found it hard to keep their hands off each other.

'You too. Esme, didn't you say you needed a hand with something in the kitchen?' Max wasn't very subtle about wanting some alone time with Esme, but Harriet didn't begrudge them their privacy. You had to take the good times when you could find them.

'Yes, I think I did.' Esme set the hot chocolate on the table and hurried out with him, giggling down the hall.

Harriet couldn't help but glance in Charles's direction, when they'd been as keen to spend time together not long ago. To find he was looking at her with that same longing was unravelling all the tension that had set in on the drive until her limbs felt more like spaghetti. One word and she just knew they'd both agree to another no-strings tryst. Except that word wouldn't be 'baby'. It was going to change the way he looked and felt about her, and probably not for the better.

'I should probably let you meet some of our staff here.' Charles led her over to the source of the chatter she'd heard from outside.

'Harriet Bell.' She shook hands with the group and introduced herself.

'Cassandra Bellow.' The pretty American set down the plate of canapés in her hand to greet her.

'Cassandra is one of our past patients and this is Lyle Sinclair, our medical director.' Charles didn't have to tell her these two were a couple either when they were glued to each other's sides.

'I'm Aksel Olson. I work with Esme.' The large hand pumping hers up and down next belonged to a bear of a man who couldn't fail to make an impression. The muscular build and Scandinavian accent coupled with the long air gave him a definite Viking vibe.

'Nice to meet you,' she said, before Charles moved her swiftly on to the woman standing next to him.

'Flora. I'm a physio at the clinic.'

'Hi.' She was definitely the gooseberry here but, then, so was Charles, who didn't seem to have a significant other in the mix. Something that hadn't gone unnoticed and brought her a sense of relief she hadn't known she needed. It hadn't entered her head that he might have met someone in the weeks since they'd last seen each other. Certainly, it hadn't been part of the deal that they couldn't date anyone else. They weren't supposed to see each other again. Thankfully, things wouldn't get any more complicated than they already were.

'And you've already met Esme and Max.' Charles didn't attempt to hide his disapproval as they reappeared with huge smiles on their faces.

'Are you staying in Cluchlochry?' Charles asked, as she attempted to drink her hot chocolate through the cream and marshmallow topping. It tasted as over-indulgent as it looked, and she just knew she was wearing a cream moustache as a result. As confirmed by Charles's smirk when she lifted her head to reply.

She did her best to wipe away all traces with the

back of her hand. 'Probably. I didn't really think that far ahead.'

It would be suicidal to attempt a return trip tonight when she was ready for bed. There was bound to be a B&B in the village where she could put her head down for the night.

Charles frowned. 'Not everywhere would be willing to take guests in on Christmas night and those that do will be booked out. We get a lot of people who come for the Christmas market and stay on for Christmas itself.'

'You must stay with us, Harri. There's plenty of room.' It was Esme who offered her refuge, not her brother. Although Harriet wanted to protest, she couldn't face getting back into her car again so soon.

'Esme, I really wish you wouldn't invite every waif and stray into Heatherglen as though it's your personal rescue centre. We converted the stables for your pet projects.'

'No offence taken,' Harriet muttered.

'Sorry. That was directed at someone else.' He nodded towards the furry bundle currently rolling around at his feet.

'Oh, he's gorgeous. What's his name?' She knelt down to stroke the curious-looking puppy with tiger-striped brown fur, which was wearing its own ugly little sweater.

'Dougal. He was half-starved when we found him, but Aksel nursed him back to health. Esme's trying to find him a home now.'

It was Flora who filled her in on his sad background, which just made him even more adorable.

'My sister has issues about turning anyone away.' Charles muttered.

'Harriet is neither a waif nor a stray. She's a friend who's very welcome to stay.' Esme overruled her older brother, using Harriet as a pawn in their sibling rivalry.

'I didn't say she wasn't. I was simply making a point, Esme.'

Harriet set down her cup. 'It would probably be easier if I look for somewhere in town to stay.'

This wasn't what she had planned at all. By this stage she'd expected to be on her way home, with Charles thanking his lucky stars for escaping the parent trap.

'No!' Both Ross-Wyldes expressed their indignation at the suggestion.

'I thought you said you wanted to talk to me about something?'

'We have so much catching up to do, Harri.'

The group watched the pair vying for her attention with as much fascination as she was, and Charles discreetly manoeuvred the argument away from the spectators over to the far side of the room.

'Charles is just trying to make a point—badly—about him being the king of the castle here. He runs the clinic and I run the veterinary practice and canine therapy centre across the way.' Esme punched him not so playfully on the arm.

'Oh, I think you mean Laird, Esme—but, yes, this isn't about you. Forgive me, Harriet. I'll take you up and show you to one of the spare rooms. Dear sister, perhaps you'd be so kind as to get Harriet something to eat too?'

He batted his eyelashes at Esme and Harriet knew

it would be enough to persuade her to do anything. Especially when he was wearing those glasses and that jumper, which made him look more like the Charles she'd known instead of the suave version she'd met at the conference. She hoped that would keep some of the most recent, more erotic memories at bay so she could stay focused on the reason she'd come all this way.

'I would love to—but I'm doing it for our guest, not you, Chas.' Esme fluttered those same long dark eyelashes in response. They were so alike it was probably why they'd fought for as long as Harriet had known them. Deep down it was obvious how much they loved each other, and she wished she'd had a brother or a sister to fight with, love unconditionally, and have to hold after she'd lost everyone else.

'We keep a few rooms made up just in case of emergencies.' Charles led her up the stairs to one of the bedrooms. She couldn't help but wonder which door led to his.

'Do you get many late-night, uninvited women calling in on you?' she teased, when he was such a stark contrast to the man who'd literally sent her packing in a previous lifetime.

'No, I don't, but sometimes we get patients arriving too late to be admitted to the clinic, so we put them up here for the night.' Her teasing fell flat with him, but she supposed his defence from her insinuations was understandable when she was accusing him of having loose morals. She knew nothing about him any more.

'I'm sure it's most appreciated. As it is by me.' She had to remember he was doing her a favour by letting her stay when she had no right to be here. Their risky behaviour in London had been her idea and as such she was fully prepared to take on the consequences single-handedly.

'Bed, bathroom, wardrobe. All the essentials.' He did a quick tour of the room before turning back to her. 'Do you need help bringing in your luggage?'

'I just have an overnight bag in the car, but I can manage that myself. As I said, this was a spur-of-the-moment visit.'

'Ah, yes. The talk. Is this about what happened in London? I must admit it's been harder to put out of my mind than I'd imagined too.' He was moving towards her and Harriet's heart leapt into her throat at the thought of him kissing her again. She wanted it so much but that's not what had brought her here.

'I'm pregnant, Charles.'

His outstretched arms immediately fell limply to his sides. 'Pardon me?'

She sat down on the edge of the bed, wishing it would swallow her up. 'That night in London… I'm pregnant.'

Charles collapsed onto the mattress beside her. 'But—but we took precautions.'

'The first time,' she reminded him with as much of a smile as she could muster when she was wound up tighter than a drum, waiting for his reaction.

The second time had happened later, when they had both been naked under the covers and he'd reached for her, keen to do things at a slower pace and drive her wild with want before he had his way with her again. The third time, in the early hours of the morning, when she'd reached for him, knowing they would have to part again.

Conception could have happened at any point during those few passionate hours together. They'd simply been too wrapped up in each other, literally, to care. Well, they would now.

He dropped his head into his hands and she waited for him to process the information.

'Are you sure? Have you done a test?'

'Yes, Charles. I wouldn't have driven all this way otherwise.' She understood this was a shock to him, her too, but questioning her common sense wasn't going to make the situation go away.

'I gave up on plans for a family after we broke up. With very good reason. I don't have time to spare for babies and all the baggage that comes with them.' He was on his feet now, pacing the room like a caged animal. Trapped and unsure how to get out.

'Believe me, becoming a mother wasn't in my immediate plans either but here we are. I only came here to tell you about the baby because I thought it was the right thing to do. I didn't say I wanted anything from you. You had no room in your life for me, I wouldn't expect it to be different for your child.' If he thought she'd waited until she was at the peak of her career to seduce him, get pregnant and force him back into her life, he'd really forgotten who she was.

'That night was supposed to be a bit of fun. One last hurrah before we went our separate ways again. A baby means the complete opposite. We'll be tied together for ever now. If I'd wanted that I would've saved us the heartbreak of splitting up twelve years ago.'

'Okay. You've made your point. I don't think there's anything left for us to say.' She should never have come here. Despite whatever flicker of hope she may have harboured for a different response, Charles had proved he hadn't changed. He still had the capacity to let her down. She'd managed this far on her own and she was sure she could raise this baby alone too. It was preferable to Charles feigning interest, only to have him bail out later and make their child suffer too.

Harriet was pregnant. It was his fault for not protecting her, for getting carried away, and not thinking about the consequences of his actions. Again.

When she'd turned up on the doorstep tonight he'd hoped it was because she'd wanted a replay of that night in London. Perhaps an extended version that would have taken them into the New Year instead of one night. Mostly because he hadn't been able to get that time together out of his head, but this was a whole different scenario.

He was waiting, hating this ridiculous sweater more than ever, for Harriet to give him some sort of clue what he was supposed to do next. Instead, she slowly rose from the bed, crossed the floor and walked out the door. It wasn't the response he'd expected but some space would be good. Esme could keep her entertained and when he'd digested the news they could sit down and plan the next move.

Any second now Esme would come bowling up the

stairs and deliver a knock-out punch once she heard what had happened. He was surprised Harriet hadn't done just that after the way he'd spoken to her. It had been a knee-jerk reaction to finding out he was going to be a father and one he'd apologise for once this sank in. He was angry at himself, not her, when his selfish needs had resulted in this life-changing news. The last thing he'd ever wanted to do was complicate her life.

Harriet's response to his outburst was reminiscent of that awful day of his father's funeral. She hadn't slapped him then either, the way most women would have. Silently crying, she'd simply packed her things and walked out. He hadn't seen or heard from her again until that conference.

At the sound of a car engine running outside, Charles rushed to the window in time to see Harriet driving away. It was déjà vu, except he couldn't claim his actions, or lack of them now, had been in any way for her benefit.

'Charles, what the hell have you done?' Esme arrived, as he'd known she would, temper flaring, fists balling, ready for a fight.

'Not now.'

'You must have said something to make her leave like that. Are you really just going to stand here and watch her go? Again?' That was the ultimate question. What they were going to do about the baby, how he felt about Harriet and what they did next were incidental if he let her go without a fight again. She was a successful surgeon in her own right with no need for him or his money. He was the one standing to lose out here.

'Tell everyone to go home. The party's over.' He left Esme to break up the gathering before dashing downstairs to retrieve his own car keys. His child wasn't going to grow up thinking its father was a disappointment, like the rest of his family had.

This was one time he could do the right thing without waiting until it was too late. He couldn't live with any more guilt and regret. Losing his father and brother had taught him not to be selfish, and unless he wanted to lose his child too he had to think about the needs of its mother. That didn't include being upset by her baby's father. Not when she'd driven the whole way to Scotland to tell him personally on Christmas Day. Something a person would only do if they had no one else to turn to.

CHAPTER THREE

'DID YOU HONESTLY expect him to react any differently? What were you hoping for? A happy-ever-after? Stupid woman!' Harriet chastised herself in the mirror as she drove away.

She'd given him the chance to be involved in the baby's life and he wasn't interested. End of story. It was his loss. She knew where she stood and that wasn't with Charles by her side. She could raise this child alone. It would be better for her and the child. At least it was apparent she'd be parenting on her own from the beginning, unlike her poor mother.

Coming here had been a reminder that night in London had been nothing more than a fantasy. The real Charles was entrenched in family tradition and duty with no room for anyone else in his life. Harriet was an independent city girl. She didn't belong here. She hated the fact it still hurt that he didn't want her, whatever the circumstances.

Perhaps she'd convinced herself something had changed between them after their escapade in that hotel room, and not merely on a physical level. Deep down she'd hoped he'd be pleased to see her again because, even before realising she was pregnant, she'd wondered about rekindling their relationship. Sentimentality and lust over common sense, but she hadn't been thinking with her head lately. That's how she'd ended up in this mess.

Charles Ross-Wylde had altered the course of her life again, sending her down a road she'd never planned to take. Now she simply had to make the best of it, the way she had the last time. Only instead of becoming a successful surgeon, her next goal was to become a good mother too.

Bright lights began strobing around her, disturbing the pitch-black night. A glance in her rear-view mirror revealed a car, flashing its headlights at her and now blaring its horn. Someone from the house had followed her and was trying to get her attention. Esme, no doubt, had figured out something was amiss and was coming to persuade her to go back. There was no way Charles would've told his sister about the baby when he didn't want it messing up his life. It was likely to be her good heart making her chase after someone who was virtually a stranger now.

Although Harriet had no intention of going back with her, she would put Esme's mind at ease because she held no bad feelings towards her. She indicated and pulled into the side of the road. The sooner they said their goodbyes, the sooner she could leave Heatherglen behind her for ever.

She stepped out onto the grass verge, but the headlights continued to blind her as she waited for the driver to get out. It wasn't until the very tall, very male silhouette drew closer that she realised it wasn't Esme who'd flagged her down.

'I have nothing to say to you. At least, nothing very ladylike,' she threw at Charles, hurrying back towards her car. He probably wanted her to sign some sort of gagging order to prevent her from claiming her unborn child had any right to the estate.

Her attempt to open her car door was thwarted as Charles grabbed her arm and spun her around. 'I'm sorry, Harriet. I reacted badly.'

'You think?' She tried to wrench her arm out of his grasp. It was going to be harder to continue hating him if he insisted on touching her, reminding her of an intimacy they could never have again.

'Come back to the house so we can talk.' He didn't let go of her, but he did loosen his grip.

'Why? You've made it clear you don't want to be part of this.'

'I'm sorry. It was a shock to the system, that's all. We both know I was a very willing participant that night, and the following morning.' His cheeky grin did things to her insides, which apparently shouldn't be acted on.

Goodness, she needed him to stop teasing her with enough delicious memories to block out the more hideous ones. Twice now he'd let her down in the most callous way. The last time she'd forgotten not to trust him and had let her hormones do the talking she'd ended up pregnant.

'I should've called instead of coming here.' That was

one thing she was sure about and something he'd agree with when she'd spoiled his Christmas.

'No. I'm glad you came. Look, it's late and freezing cold out here. Why don't you just come back to the house? The talking can wait.'

It was tempting when her stomach was rumbling and the tip of her nose was so cold she was convinced it had turned blue. She thought of the lovely roaring fire in the lounge and the banquet of food spread out and going to waste. Pregnancy apparently had lowered the price of her pride. If she went back with him it would be for the baby's sake. They had things to sort out. It was the whole reason she was here. It definitely wasn't anything to do with the man still holding her, dressed in that ridiculous sweater his little sister had knitted for him.

'I don't have anywhere else to go, I suppose.' She didn't fancy traipsing around town, knocking on doors and hoping to find room at an inn.

'That's settled, then. You're coming home with me.' If only he meant that as something other than a polite host she'd be reassured he'd had a change of heart where the baby was concerned. This was more about him saving face in front of his family and friends. She shouldn't get too carried away with the idea that he'd finally stepped up to be the man she'd always believed he was deep down. For now, she'd take advantage of the food and lodgings being offered because it suited her and meant she'd no longer be putting her unborn child at risk out here in the Scottish wilderness.

'Fine.' She got back into her car, but nothing had

changed. Except perhaps his conscience getting the better of him at letting the mother of his child disappear into the night.

Harriet followed Charles back to the house, resolving to take herself straight to bed and avoid any further confrontation. When he slammed on his brakes as they approached the house, she almost ran into the back of his car. As it was, she nearly gave herself whiplash having to make her own emergency stop.

'What the hell are you playing at, Charles?' she shouted as she wrestled her seat belt off, about to jump out and give him hell. That's when she saw him bolting across the driveway, not even taking time to close the car door behind him.

She got out and followed him over to the side of the road where the house lights didn't quite manage to reach. It wasn't until she was standing over him that she realised what it was his headlights had picked up along the drive. Charles was hunched over the body of a woman who was clearly having some sort of fit. Stranger still, there was a dog lying next to her, providing some sort of cushion for her head.

'Fenella? Can you hear me? It's Charles, Esme's brother.' Charles checked the woman's pulse while he tried to get some sort of response from her.

Harriet knelt beside them and brushed away the debris of Christmas presents scattered around her, and anything else she could hurt herself on while her body was jerking uncontrollably on the cold ground. 'Is she one of your patients?'

'One of Esme's clients. She's epileptic so we'll just have to wait this out with her.'

When someone was having a seizure it was important not to restrain or try to move them in case of injury. All they could do was make sure she didn't hurt herself and time the fitting in case it developed into something more serious. A fit lasting more than five minutes could lead to brain damage.

'I don't think she hurt herself in the fall. I can't see any obvious injuries.' Harriet checked as best she could and loosened the scarf around Fenella's neck.

'That'll be down to Nora, the dog Esme trained with her. She would've alerted Fenella that the seizure was coming and positioned herself underneath to prevent her hitting her head.'

'That's amazing.' She'd known what Esme did for a living but actually seeing it in practice made Harriet see what a valuable service she was providing to the people who came to her. As was Charles. Despite her personal issues with him, there was no denying the good he was doing at Heatherglen between the clinic and the canine therapy centre he'd set up with his sister.

'The convulsions are slowing now. She should be back with us soon.'

'I'll go and alert the others so we can get her inside out of this cold.' Harriet hurried inside to inform Esme and Max so they could organise a transfer for her into the clinic. When she came round, Fenella would be tired and probably confused about what had happened. She'd be spending the night under medical observation and so would Nora.

* * *

By the time Fenella had been admitted to a bed in the clinic for the night and Esme had taken Nora to the kennels, Harriet was emotionally and physically exhausted. Charles had gone out to park the cars and lock them so she thought she could sneak off to bed unnoticed.

With a foot on the first tread of the staircase she thought she'd got away with it until Charles called her back.

'Harriet, you don't have to hide away from me up there. Come and get something to eat. You deserve it after the night you've had.'

Her stomach rumbled and made the decision to stay for her. 'I did miss dinner.'

'It's important for the baby's sake that you don't skip meals.' At least he was acknowledging her condition, even if it was only to scold her.

The house was unfeasibly quiet compared to the raucous atmosphere she'd arrived to earlier. 'Is Fenella okay?'

Charles led her to the kitchen where the worktops were laden with covered leftovers. 'She'll be fine. Apparently, she was coming to deliver a few Christmas presents to the staff but she really shouldn't have been out walking alone in that cold weather. I'm going to look into the medication she's on and see if I can reduce the frequency of the seizures. I'll get onto Clydesbank Hospital again and get a rush on her records. In the meantime, Esme is spoiling the dog something rotten for doing such a good job tonight.' The smile on his face showed the pride he had in his sister's achievements.

'Does Esme know about you-know-what?' She pointed to her belly, afraid to mention the baby again and end this fragile truce, but she didn't want to put her foot in it if she ran into Esme at some point.

'No. One thing at a time. Now, turkey sandwich?' He uncovered the carcass of their earlier dinner and Harriet was so hungry she could've attacked it with her bare hands.

'Yes, please.'

'Help yourself to a drink.' He waved the huge carving knife in the direction of the fridge, where she found a bottle of non-alcoholic grape fizz. She poured two glasses in the hope he wasn't just going to sit there and watch her eat. Thankfully, he placed two plates of sandwiches on the table and they both sat down.

'This is really good. Thanks, Charles.'

'I'm sorry about what I said earlier, Harriet.'

After a couple of bites, they talked over each other, Charles surprising her with his topic of choice.

'You were being honest. A baby isn't in your plans.'

He set down his half-eaten sandwich. Harriet's appetite too had waned at the reminder of their earlier conversation. 'It's been a long day and I wasn't prepared for that kind of bombshell. I shouldn't have been so short with you.'

'Believe me, it came as a shock to me too. Why do you think I jumped into my car and started driving here, Charles? I didn't know how to react any more than you do, but the important thing is where we go from here.'

An apology for his behaviour on this occasion was

progress and more than he'd offered the last time he'd spoken to her so harshly.

'Okay, so you're a couple of months gone?'

She nodded, though she'd been so busy she hadn't noticed the first missed period. 'I honestly only came to tell you about the baby so no one could ever say I kept it from you. I mean, joint parenting between London and Scotland simply isn't feasible. Plus, I intend to continue with my medical career.' Motherhood and her job could co-exist if organised properly well in advance.

Charles took a drink as he contemplated his response. 'I want to *be* a father. I just didn't think it would happen. Although seeing everyone around me settling down and starting their own families has made me realise I did want that once. I know this wasn't planned, but it's really a blessing. I mean, this child will be the heir to Heatherglen. This is a legacy that should be passed on to the next generation. I can't let you walk away with my baby when I'd want to be more than just a weekend dad. Family is everything to me and I want my child close.'

It was such a turnaround Harriet's head was spinning. She should've considered the Ross-Wylde obsession with family tradition before coming here. Of course the Laird of Heatherglen would want an heir and she'd made it all so easy for him. There was nothing to say he had to want her along with the baby. As was clear when his first thoughts were about passing on his legacy. She'd left herself open to becoming collateral damage for a second time.

Did Charles think he could somehow get custody of

their child and keep her out of the picture altogether? She hadn't anticipated having a custody fight on her hands but if he insisted, she'd do everything in her power to make sure this child had a stable influence in life. Experience had taught her that Charles wasn't reliable enough for that role.

'How do you suppose we do that? It's not practical for either of us to travel up and down the country on a whim and my schedule is not nine to five, Monday to Friday. What are you going to do, kidnap me? Lock me up in the attic until I give birth and dispose of me when I've outlived my usefulness?' She snorted. It might sound absurd but right now he was making her feel little more than a baby-making machine. This wasn't supposed to be about him. She had to fit in a life of her own somewhere, not spend every spare minute making sure Charles was happy.

'I don't think we need to resort to that, but you could move in here. The house is big enough that we could live our separate lives and share child care.' He'd managed to come up with a practical solution to co-parenting that suited him. Her initial suspicion was that he'd only suggested the move because he knew she'd never agree to it. Heatherglen held so many sad associations for her that she couldn't imagine waking up every morning in the very place where their fairy-tale romance had turned into a nightmare.

Then he would be free to make a legal bid for custody and who wouldn't think a child would be better off with his prestigious side of the family and their millions in the bank? A cold sweat broke out over Harriet's skin at the fight she could have on her hands for a baby she hadn't realised she wanted so much until now.

'You know that's not an option, Charles. My life and my career are in London.' Unlike him, she'd never left.

'Hear me out. The country would be so much better to raise a child than the city. You have no family there and look at the land we have around us. At least here you'd be surrounded by family and friends.'

'Your family, your friends, your home and your rules, I expect.' She wasn't going to let him control her. There was no way she was giving up her independence to be locked away in a tower, so the Laird and master of all he surveyed had unlimited access to his heir. What was in that for her?

'Esme would be the baby's family too. Everyone else who lives and works at Heatherglen would soon become a friend to you. Not to mention those mutts my sister keeps around the place. I'm sure a child would appreciate growing up around her four-legged friends much more than I do.' There was a hint of tension surrounding the matter and she could imagine how irked he'd be finding puppies peeing on his antique rugs. She'd be tempted to agree just to see his face when that happened.

'I told you, I'm not flushing away my career because I'm pregnant. Being the mother of your children is no longer enough for me in life, as hard as that might be for you to believe.' His ego had grown to match the size of his bank balance if he thought he was enough for her to turn her back on the success she'd worked so hard to achieve.

'I'm not asking you to give anything up for me. It would be for the baby.'

'Emotional blackmail won't get you anywhere, Charles. I'll raise this child to understand women can have it all these days. You did me a favour, you know, dumping me like that. If you hadn't, I would've left London there and then and moved here with you. I would never have had the career I have now.'

'Why do you think I did it?' he mumbled as he cleared the dishes away. That was the first time he'd offered any explanation for his actions, but he wasn't making any sense.

'You told me you no longer wanted to marry me, that you had Heatherglen and didn't need me once you inherited your father's land and title.' Not his exact words but it was the gist of his rejection after his father's funeral and sufficient to send her back to London alone with a broken heart.

'Did you honestly believe I was able to switch off my feelings for you so easily? I knew you'd insist on moving back here with me and I didn't want you to give up on your medical dreams. This place cost my father his life. I knew the mess and the hard work I had waiting for me here. I didn't want to inflict that suffering on you too.'

Harriet could see he was being sincere and felt as though her heart was breaking all over again. For that young woman who'd believed she wasn't good enough for the love of her life, and for the grieving son who'd had the weight of the world on his shoulders.

'I had no idea.' Her voice was but a whisper as she came to terms with the knowledge it had all been a lie, albeit with the best of intentions. All these years she'd hated him when he'd acted out of love for her. Yet there was a slow burning fire starting deep inside her that he'd taken the choice away from her about her future.

'Yes, well, we can't go back even if we wanted to. This is about moving forward.'

'Wait. You made that decision for me to return to London and now you're dictating I move here because it's more convenient for you? Control freak much? Are you so bored and lonely out here you've decided it might be nice to have an ex with benefits on site?' She couldn't sit here any more when she wanted to smash things, including Charles's face, for he was being so damned noble and breaking her heart without giving her a valid reason. There was no doubt she would've moved to Heatherglen with him because she'd loved him and nothing else had mattered. It was a shame he hadn't felt the same way about her.

'I know you're angry, but it worked out for the best, didn't it? Until now.' He gave a sad smile, which she wasn't sure was for her or himself.

It was a revelation to find out his behaviour, in his eyes, had been in her best interests. From the outside it would seem his plan had worked. She was financially stable, living in London with a career she'd dreamed of, but she'd never been able to trust again. Despite his scheming, fate had brought them together in the end, expecting the baby she'd always imagined having with Charles. Except now the circumstances didn't include parents who were in love or anything like it.

'My career isn't up for negotiation.' She wasn't budging on that point and he couldn't make her. If he had sent her away to build on her career, that time apart would've been wasted if she was expected to give it all up now.

'We have the clinic here. It would be a real coup to have someone of your calibre with us. Heatherglen could offer you a flexible position to fit around your needs and a home for you and the baby. Come and work here. It sounds like the perfect solution to me.'

'Of course it does. You win this way. It's your home and it doesn't inconvenience you. You get to play daddy on a full-time basis on your doorstep and get an orthopaedic surgeon thrown in too. However, it's asking a lot from me to give up everything at home to move here.' Regardless of Charles's wealth and the unspoilt land around Heatherglen, Harriet didn't know if this was the best environment in which to raise a child, or even to live in herself. She knew nothing of life in the country or how isolated she might feel here. However, she did know that Heatherglen hadn't brought her happiness in the past and the family ties that kept Charles here weren't what she wanted for her baby.

What scared her most, though, was having all those feelings resurfacing for Charles and being trapped here with them. One night had been difficult enough to forget, even before she'd realised she had a souvenir of the event.

'It's not a competition, Harriet. Don't you want us to do this together? It would be a partnership without the inconvenient distance between us.' He made it sound so straightforward, but it was that distance that would keep her sane now they were back in each other's lives.

'Do you really have need for an orthopaedic surgeon here? I mean, I'm not trading in a full schedule for the odd consultation here and there. I'm not taking a demotion.' The whole point of this exercise was to ensure parenting wouldn't affect her working life. She couldn't help thinking this was going to end up with her in that stay-at-home mum role she was trying to avoid.

'As a matter of fact, I have a patient at the moment I could use your help with. If you find clinic life and motherhood aren't enough for you, I'm sure every hospital within a hundred-mile radius will be queuing up to have you on their books. You could consult, run your own clinics. Whatever you need.' He was being so damned reasonable it was difficult to argue with the options he was laying out before her. It was being around other people she found most appealing. Life in London was busy, hectic, and she did everything at breakneck speed, but that was because she didn't have anyone at home to make it worth her while to slow down to enjoy time out from it all. That was going to change in a few months, whether she was ready for it or not.

'Why should I believe you're not going to change your mind again?' There was no way of predicting the outcome if she took this gamble but there was every chance she'd be the one to come off worse out of this arrangement.

'I've lost a brother, a father and a fiancée because of this place. I don't want it to cost me the chance of being a father too. You know I can't leave here, there's just too much responsibility involved, but I want my child to know I'll be there for her or him. Your moving here would give me the chance to do that.'

'It's a lot to put on my shoulders, Charles, and after everything we've been through...'

'Marry me, then. I can provide you both with everything you could ever need. I know you need something in return to offset everything you'd be trading in to come here.'

'Don't be ridiculous.' It was like a slap across the face for him to toss a proposal of marriage in there so casually, as if it meant nothing, when the last time he'd asked her that question it had meant the world to her.

Her mother had passed away not long after they'd started dating and Charles had represented everything she'd thought she'd have in her new life. Marriage and stability were all she'd wanted then but he had obviously never held it in the same regard when he'd used it as a device to keep her dangling on a string.

'It's not unheard of for a couple to get married for the sake of a baby. I would give you equal rights to the estate, the clinic and anything else you wanted.' He was offering everything except love and devotion, the only things that could ever convince Harriet marriage would be a good idea.

'No.'

His shoulders slumped when she torpedoed his marriage of convenience idea, but he'd a lot to learn about the woman he was dealing with now. This one wouldn't be so easily swayed into the life-changing decisions he made on a whim.

'When are you due back at work?'

'Not until January. Why?'

'You could spend the rest of your break here. A trial run if you like. You could get to know the staff and patients at the clinic and see where you could be working if you gave it a chance.'

'See if you and I can live together in the same place without coming to blows?' She didn't know how to get out of this situation she'd created by coming here in the first place. If she left now, Charles would be sure to look into the legalities surrounding the baby's parentage and she didn't want him or her to get caught in a tug of war between them. It might be best to do as he'd suggested and stay. That way she could do her best to make him see how impossible it would be for her to fit in here. She would be reasonable and, when it didn't work out, she could say she'd tried to do things his way. Once she was back in London and the baby was born it would be too unsettling for them to uproot again.

If she stayed, it wouldn't be the clashes between them she was sure would keep her awake at night but the memories of the passion he'd awakened in her. Something she'd be reminded of with every ounce of gained weight and growing belly. Yet he'd barely mentioned that incredible time they'd had, as if it had never happened, and this pregnancy had been some sort of divine intervention.

This baby had apparently been created from thin air solely to provide him with the opportunity to become a father. A few days under the same roof would give them both an idea of how difficult it would be to carry on that pretence. If she couldn't manage it, they'd have to come up with a plan B. For now, this was the only one they'd come up with.

'What do you say, Harriet? You, me and baby for the rest of the festive season? It would mean you'll be here for our Hogmanay party too. Esme is hosting it this year so it's sure to be a spectacle you don't want to miss.'

She tried to convince herself it was the headache of facing a custody battle that finally persuaded her to stay. Not his smiling blue eyes or the thought of them spending time as a family.

CHAPTER FOUR

'ORANGE JUICE, CEREAL, toast and tea.' Charles ticked off the breakfast checklist as he loaded a tray to take up to Harriet. Since it was early in her pregnancy, he wasn't sure how she'd react faced with a cooked breakfast first thing in the morning and chose the safe option.

He still couldn't quite believe he was going to be a father. For the longest time it had only been him and Esme at the castle, wrapped up in their own careers. Now there would be a new focus. Okay, the suggestion of marriage had been a mistake but since he and Harriet had agreed back in London that they had no future together, he'd wanted something to keep her in his life. He was asking her to give up more than ever to move back to Scotland now, with nothing to offer her in return. For now he just wanted time with her and a chance for them to work this out together.

Family was something he never dared believe he could have after inheriting Heatherglen and knowing his whole life would be tied up in it. It was expected for the Laird to marry and provide an heir, but it had been more important for him to get the clinic up and running. Now he had no choice, and there was going to be a baby, it was a chance for him to be normal and have a role for himself other than running the castle and clinic. No other woman had lived up to Harriet, so it seemed only fitting that she should be the mother of his child.

'Someone looks happy this morning.'

He looked up to find Harriet standing in the kitchen doorway with much the same expression on her face as the one he was wearing.

'I was thinking how nice it might be to have a wee one running around the place.' He didn't need to lie to her when he was trying to persuade her to stick around. She had to know he was looking forward to it all, no longer fighting the idea.

'I haven't agreed to anything yet.' Her frown told him he'd jumped the gun, but he was determined to make her see this was the best place for them both.

'What are you doing up, anyway? I was going to bring you breakfast in bed.' He did his best to dodge another argument, even though he was miffed she'd thwarted his attempt to gain brownie points.

'I'm an early riser. I like to make the most of every day. Thanks, though.' She took a seat at the table and started picking at a slice of toast from the tray. Charles joined her so he wouldn't appear rude in leaving her by herself, then poured himself a cup of coffee and sat down.

'Ah, yes. My little lark. I'd forgotten how much you enjoy mornings.' It was a throwaway comment borne of past familiarity, but it brought back more recent, erotic memories, which made him shift in his chair. Images of their early morning tryst in that hotel bed burst into his thoughts and refused to leave.

Harriet was blinking at him, her toast hovering in mid-air, frozen by the inappropriate reference to her insatiable appetite for him. It wasn't as though they could avoid the subject altogether when she was carrying the evidence, but he realised he'd been indiscreet. Harriet had made it clear she didn't intend to let their past get in the way of a potential working relationship.

'It's only me!' Esme's timely arrival through the back door saved both their blushes.

'Morning, Esme.' Harriet sounded as relieved as he was to have someone break the sudden tension in the air.

His sister was going to lose her mind when she heard she was going to be an aunt.

'I've just been down to the therapy centre to pick up a few things. Charles said you could use a change of clothes so you didn't get yours dirty. I brought you some of our winter gear.' She plonked the pile of clothes and boots on the table, Charles whipping away the breakfast things a fraction of a second before she did so.

'That's very kind of you but there's really no need to fuss.'

'It's only a sweater, some waterproofs and a pair of wellies to wear around the estate. Nothing fancy, just practical.'

Harriet made no further protest. 'Thank you. I don't know how much longer I'll get away with wearing my own clothes anyway.'

She tested the give in the trousers, stretching the elastic waistband. Charles could see the very second she realised what she'd said as her wide-eyed gaze flicked between him and Esme.

His sister didn't miss it either. 'What do you mean?'

Worried he'd put his foot in it more than he already had, Charles left it to Harriet as to what to say next. There would be no going back once Esme knew about the baby. Although, by the excitement he could already see fizzing up inside her, she'd probably already guessed.

'I…er…' Harriet cleared her throat. 'I'm pregnant.'

Esme managed to contain herself a second or two longer until Harriet confirmed the paternity, should it be in question.

'Charles is the father.'

His sister's squeal almost deafened him. 'Oh, my goodness! When did this happen? How did this happen? Wait…don't answer that one. This. Is. *Amazing!*'

Another squeal and she launched herself at Harriet. Charles leaned back against the kitchen worktop, content to let them hug it out, only to have the breath knocked out of him too by an Esme missile.

'Are you trying to kill me?' He laughed as she squeezed him hard.

'I'm just so happy for you, bro.' She paused. 'It is good news, isn't it?'

He supposed neither he nor Harriet appeared to have as much zing as the auntie-to-be.

'Yes, of course.' There was no hesitation in his reply and he wished he'd been as positive about the news the first time around. That knee-jerk, defensive lashing out had damaged what little trust Harriet had left in him, but he hoped he'd have the chance to repair their relationship over these next few days. If only for the baby's sake.

'It was that conference, wasn't it? I knew something had happened. You couldn't wipe the smile off your face for a week. My brother has been emotionally frozen since losing you, unless you count being perpetually grumpy. You're the one person who ever seemed to make him happy.' Esme knew him better than he was comfortable with and the heat in his cheeks confirmed he'd flushed the same shade of scarlet as Harriet.

He flashed Harriet an unspoken apology for his sibling's lack of tact. This was their love life, the supposedly never-to-be-spoken-of-again fling they were now discussing over the breakfast table. A bit much for someone who hadn't set foot in this house in over a decade.

'I'm only here over the festive season so we can work a few things out.' If Harriet didn't see the need to satisfy Esme's curiosity with the details, neither would he.

'Well, I hope you do. Feel free to pop down to the therapy centre and look around or, you know, if you just want to talk.' As subtle as a brick, Esme shot a dark look in his direction that said she'd already pinpointed him as the source of their conflict. He'd prepare himself for an interrogation, followed by an ear-bashing, once they were alone.

'Thanks. I'll keep that in mind.'

'Yes, Esme, thanks for bringing the clothes over for Harriet. We wouldn't want to keep you from your work any longer than necessary.' He didn't need her siding against him too if she thought he'd been in the wrong. Which he had been. Besides, he needed every second he could get alone with Harriet to try and redeem himself.

'It's lovely to have you here, Harriet.' Esme ignored him and kissed her new favourite person—which obviously wasn't him—on the cheek.

'I'm only a couple of months gone, so I'd appreciate it if you keep the news to yourself for now.' It might've helped Charles's cause if Harriet hadn't enforced a news blackout, but he knew Esme would respect her wishes, even if she was fit to bust with the good news.

'I can't believe I'm going to be an auntie.' She skipped back out the door and he envied her carefree position in this situation.

'She's going to make a wonderful aunt,' Harriet mused.

'Esme will spoil the baby rotten.' She was bad enough fussing over those dogs so the second a baby was on the scene the place would be filled with toys and cute outfits. Strangely, the thought of the castle being turned upside down didn't disturb him as much as it usually did. It would be nice for it to be a proper home again instead of a memorial reminding him of everything he'd lost. His sister was right about one thing, though. He had been frozen here, never really coming to terms with his losses, including Harriet. Hopefully now, reconnecting with her would bring him some peace again.

'Yes, well, I'm sure we'll be glad to have an extra pair of hands when it comes to babysitting. *If* I decide to stay.' Harriet was quick to correct herself, but it was a good sign she was thinking about having support here at Heatherglen rather than being on her own. Letting the news slip to Esme could've been the best thing to happen. For him. With his sister on side he'd have double the chance of persuading Harriet to stay permanently.

'Why don't I give you a tour of the clinic and let you see everything we've achieved?' Perhaps if she saw why he'd sacrificed their future it would give them the chance to have another one.

Harriet cursed her big mouth. As lovely as Esme was, she wished she hadn't blabbed about the pregnancy. Now there was more than her and Charles involved it was bound to complicate things. Once Charles realised there was no way she was letting him dictate the rest of her and her baby's lives, a clean break wasn't going to be so easy. Not with a super-excited auntie in the mix.

She could do without Charles being all charming and thoughtful too. He'd thrown her last night by coming after her and begging her to stay. Even if it was for his own selfish reasons. That last-minute plea for a second chance, that offer of a future here at Heatherglen had left an opening for a flicker of hope she couldn't extinguish that he might still be the honourable gentleman she'd once believed him to be.

Their time together at that conference had reawakened feelings for Charles she had no business having when he didn't deserve them. She had confused past Harriet and Charles for their present-day incarnations because her hormones were all over the place.

So, she'd woken up this morning determined to

harden her heart against him. Only to find him making her breakfast, smiling to himself about the baby coming, and arranging for her to be more comfortable in this environment. That's why she'd spilled the beans to Esme. She'd been so comfortable she'd started imagining being here as part of a family.

All she could do to save herself now as he led her out for a walk in the grounds was to look at Heatherglen from a professional viewpoint. There was no way she'd be content with swapping the hustle and bustle of London hospitals for a country practice. Working on a casual basis in the middle of nowhere would be a demotion for her. A sure-fire way to ensure her career took a back seat to motherhood. Exactly what she'd hoped to avoid.

'I know the twenty-sixth of December is considered a holiday, but I hope you don't mind if I call in and see my patients? It must suck, being away from home at this time of year.'

They walked to the front of the clinic and it seemed odd to find everything still decorated for the season when Christmas Day had been something of a nonevent for her. Christmas night, on the other hand, had been more action-packed than she'd anticipated.

'I don't mind at all. I know as well as you do we're never really off duty.' If she'd been back in London she might've been calling in on some of her own patients. There weren't very many people in her life. At least, none who'd be spending time with her instead of with their own families.

Sometimes those patients having treatment were her

comfort as much as she hopefully was theirs. Hospital could be a lonely place with only sporadic visitors, if any. Much like her home life. A simple chat could reassure both sides there was life outside those four walls.

'Sorry, I didn't mean to be insensitive.' It took her a few seconds to figure out what he was apologising for. He'd mistakenly believed she might have been pining for the comfort of her own home when it was strangers in a different medical setting she had been thinking about. Not that she was going to have him pity her by explaining that to him.

He'd given up their relationship to remain here, transforming an ancestral pile into somewhere he and his sister could work and live side by side. Home was never somewhere he'd leave when he'd given up everything to keep it. Whereas her apartment was simply a base where she slept between surgeries and meetings. It could literally be anywhere in the world. Easily transferable. There was no real emotional connection. If that's what constituted a home, there was more attachment for her at Heatherglen already.

'Don't worry about it. There'll be plenty more Christmases to come.' Once there was a baby involved, things would be different. She was sure she'd want to spend all the time she could with her child rather than wandering around hospital wards.

It had been a long time since she'd felt the excitement other people seemed to draw from Christmas and she was looking forward to experiencing it for herself. Whether it was London or here at Heatherglen, Harriet knew next year would be the best one yet.

'Things might have changed since you were last here.' Charles showed off the renovations with pride, but Harriet couldn't view his achievements objectively when she knew they'd come at the price of her happiness. Every new fixture and fitting had been built on her heartache.

'So, how many patients do you take in at a time?'

'We can manage around twenty residents, but Esme deals with more clients at the therapy centre. We've got a good set-up.'

They wandered past a Christmas tree decorated similarly to the one in the private wing except it was missing those personal touches of home-made ornaments she was sure were Esme's handiwork.

'Didn't this used to be——?' She spun around, finding something familiar about the space they were in, except in place of the heavy velvet drapes she recalled, there were modern vertical blinds.

'Ah, yes, this used to be the lounge. We had to replace a lot for health and safety reasons, but we tried to keep the original features, like the fireplace. This one is only for the aesthetics now.' It remained grand and ornate in here, although it had been repurposed, but it was in this very room he'd crushed her thoughts of marrying him.

Perhaps that was why he'd gutted it. In the hope of removing all traces of her and what had happened. This place was proof that wasn't possible. You couldn't simply erase history because it suited you. There were always going to be reminders of the past intruding on the present, no matter how hard you tried to cover it up.

'I remember being in here the day of your father's funeral.' She hadn't said it to upset him. The memory of that day, the room full of people and chatter as they'd mourned his loss, was simply too vivid to ignore. It had been clear something other than grief had been plaguing Charles when he'd been so distant they could've been in different cities then instead of standing side by side. He'd done her the courtesy of waiting until the other mourners had departed before he'd ended their engagement, even insisting she keep the ring, but it hadn't lessened her humiliation or confusion.

'It was a long time ago.' Something he obviously didn't want to be reminded of when he was striding on towards the other rooms.

Harriet bit her lip when it wasn't as easy for her to dismiss it but opening up old wounds wasn't going to help either of them. She was supposed to be over it all, that's what she'd told him, or he'd probably never have slept with her again. They couldn't change what had happened then any more than they could alter their decisions, or lack of them, in London.

She wasn't sure he'd even do anything differently when so many had benefitted from the clinic since their break-up. Certainly, she wouldn't choose to change more recent events between them. Motherhood wasn't something she'd wish away now when it was a part of her. If she hadn't fallen pregnant by accident she might never have factored a baby into her life and she had no regrets about the prospect of becoming a mum. It was the most important event in her life she had to look forward to. They simply had to live with the decisions they'd made and make the most of whatever fate had in store for them.

'So, what services do you offer here?' Back onto more neutral ground, perhaps she'd stop getting so emotional about what this place represented to her and begin to see it as just another workplace environment.

'We run our clinics, of course, with state-of-the-art facilities. Along with more holistic therapies and emergency facilities for the community en route to the main hospital.'

'It looks as though you have everything you need here. I don't see what I could possibly add to your set-up.' Harriet wasn't being humble. She was aware that an experienced orthopaedic surgeon would be sought-after in a private clinic. There simply wasn't enough professional incentive in it for her.

While she wanted to help every person she could, she suspected the more challenging patients would be found in city hospitals and that was where she thrived. It was satisfying to improve a patient's quality of life by relieving pain and improving their mobility. Those with more insight into the human psyche might suggest a link to the mother she'd never felt she'd truly helped, and needed to atone for her perceived failure as a daughter. It was just as well she tried not to dwell on those things she couldn't fix and concentrated on those she could. With one exception. While the surroundings of her patients might be different, she wouldn't trade the number of lives she could improve for a matter of comfort or cash.

'You're the best in your field, Harriet. We both know

that. Waiting lists for surgery can be backlogged for years and most people come here because they can't face the pain for that extended amount of time.'

'Spit it out, Charles. I know you're building up to something.' It wasn't simply her sparkling personality and unborn child he was after, by the sound of it.

'You know me too well.'

'Once upon a time, perhaps, but I don't presume to predict what's going on in your head any more.' The barb successfully managed to wipe the grin from his face and suggested she could still wound him. Although that wasn't going to achieve anything except make it harder for them to work alongside each other if she kept dragging up past hurt. If she ever entertained the idea of moving.

'The main reason for my visit today, and for bringing you with me, was to meet a few people.' He stopped looking at her as though she'd shot him in the chest and started up the huge marble staircase.

'Who?' Her borrowed boots were squeaking as she hurried to catch up with him down the corridor. She might be dressed appropriately for the Scottish winter climate, or Esme's place of work, but compared to Charles and the clinic she was out of place and underdressed.

A city slicker transported into the birthplace of nobility, she could do without him trailing her around like a pet. She preferred to be the one in control of the facts and her daily schedule. Something she'd sworn she wouldn't give up for Charles or anyone else. Not even her firstborn.

Flora, the physiotherapist, was leaving the room they'd stopped at. 'Oh, hi. He seems to be moving a little better today. I'm sure he'll be glad to see you.'

'Thanks, Flora. We're just popping in to say hello.' He knocked on the door and waited for the resident inside to permit him entry. It was a simple gesture but showed the respect he had for his patients' privacy, treating them more as house guests than customers.

'Come…in.' A laboured male voice came from the other side of the door.

'I'm taking you in to see Gerry. He's recovering here after his stroke, so we're still working on getting his speech and mobility back on track.'

Harriet appreciated the heads up before they went in. A stroke could occur when a blockage prevented the blood supply reaching the brain, or because of a burst blood vessel. The resulting injury to the brain caused by a stroke could cause widespread and long-lasting problems. Including communication or irrational behaviour, caused by the psychological and cognitive impact of a stroke. It was always best to be prepared for such circumstances in case a patient became angry or resentful towards those trying to help them. Thankfully, such behaviour lessened as rehabilitation and recovery progressed.

The elderly gentleman was sitting in an armchair by the bed, clad in blue cotton pyjamas and trying his best to run a comb through his thinning white hair with a shaky hand.

'Hello, Mr Moore. I hope you don't mind me bringing a colleague of mine in to see you. This is Harriet.'

Charles made the introduction and Harriet stepped forward to say hello.

'Call…me…Gerry. Lovely…to…meet…you…Harriet.'

His speech was slow and slurred. The evidence of his stroke was visible where the left side of his face drooped, but he still had a twinkle in his eye that said he had a lot of life still to live.

'You too, Gerry.' She took his hand and gently clasped it between both of hers.

'How is it going with Flora, your physiotherapist?' Charles sat on the edge of the bed, giving more of an impression that he was a visitor than the attending doctor.

'Task…master.' Gerry grinned.

'You certainly seem to be improving.' He nodded towards the comb, which was now balancing precariously on the edge of the nightstand. Harriet knew how important physio was to stroke patients to improve muscle strength with exercises. Although recovery could be slow, these small goals, such as picking up objects, were important. They encouraged patients on towards longer-term, more demanding goals such as standing or walking. It was all working towards getting the person's life back where possible.

'Can…feed…myself…now.'

'That's fantastic. I'll see if it's possible to have your meals with the other residents. The company will do you good.'

Gerry smiled at that but even the effort of speaking was obviously already taking its toll on him.

'We should get on and let you practise the exercises Flora has given you. I just wanted to call in and see how you were. I know the team are working with you but if you need to talk to me about how you're feeling, just let me know. This can be a confusing, frustrating time and I'm here, along with everyone else, to help you through this. The same goes for your wife. This is a lot for her to deal with too.' Charles shook his hand and Harriet said her goodbyes too. By the time they reached the door Gerry had already closed his eyes.

It was clear Charles went above and beyond the call of duty for his patients and if he was doing this to prove to her he was a nice guy at heart…well, it was working.

'He's a lovely man and he certainly seems to be recovering well.'

'I think it helps to have a multi-disciplinary team all under one roof. There are a lot of us working together in cases like this. You know orthopaedics could be used in conjunction with physiotherapy to work towards the best recovery. Surgery could provide stability to increase function in some instances.' Charles didn't have to convince her of the benefits of having a skilled team tailored to the needs of individual patients. She'd witnessed it for herself on occasion. The problem for her in joining the team at Heatherglen lay closer to home.

'Uh-huh?' She didn't give him the satisfaction of agreeing with him, but she was enjoying having him try to convince her. It gave her an insight into the work he was doing here, and the sort of man he'd become in her absence. A noble, conscientious one who only wanted the best for Heatherglen and his patients.

'I have someone else I'd like you to meet. If you want

to?' He hesitated, perhaps picking up on her wariness about getting drawn into this.

'Of course.' She didn't want him to think she wasn't interested in his work when that was supposed to be the reason behind this visit.

He led her down the hall to another room and knocked on the door. A cheery, young voice shouted for him to come in.

Charles opened the door and ushered Harriet into the room. 'This is the Dawson family. Everyone, this is Harriet Bell, a friend who's staying with us at Heatherglen.'

'Hi.' The young girl in the bed could only have been about seven or eight with her parents sitting close by. Her adorable gap-toothed smile stole anyone's right to be in a bad mood when she was the one hooked up to hospital machinery.

'Bryony is my favourite patient but don't tell anyone else in case they get jealous.' Charles winked at the little girl, who giggled in response. He was charming a child as easily as he had her when they'd first met. It gave some indication of what an excellent father he would make. One more reason to like him she didn't need.

'Hello, Bryony.' Harriet greeted Mr and Mrs Dawson too, though she didn't know why Charles had brought her here.

'Is Harriet your girlfriend?' Bryony asked. The Charles-crushing apparently started from an early age.

Harriet found herself watching and waiting for his reply as intensely as his little admirer. Ridiculous when she hadn't held that title for a considerable part of her adult life.

'I told you, Ms Bell is a surgeon, like me. Except she works with people's bones instead of their noggins.' He rapped his knuckles on his skull and set off more childish laughter, successfully avoiding answering the personal question.

'Can you fix my legs?' With the directness only a child could get away with, Bryony challenged Harriet directly.

'I'm sorry, I...er...' Put on the spot, she felt compelled to answer without knowing anything of Bryony's medical history, or how long her connection to Heatherglen as a medical practitioner would last.

'Harriet's just visiting but I'd like to share your details with her, if that's okay?' He was checking with Bryony as much as her parents but all three nodded their consent.

Harriet had the ominous feeling of having walked into a trap.

'Bryony has cerebral palsy. At the minute she has a baclofen pump to help with the chronic pain. It's a small device implanted in her abdomen connected to the spinal cord by a thin tube under her skin. It continuously dispenses medication through the spinal column and delivers muscle relaxant to reduce tightness.' Undergoing surgery at such a young age made the children more special to the medical staff involved. There were always risks and no one undertook these procedures lightly on such fragile bodies. Bryony certainly seemed to have a special place in Charles's heart.

As an orthopaedic surgeon she had a lot of experience with CP too. Cerebral palsy—a group of conditions caused by an issue with the brain around the time of birth—led to difficulties with muscle strength and movement. The severity of the condition varied from patient to patient, but many came to her to address problems of muscle spasticity and contractures. With surgery, Harriet was able to help release muscles that were too tight or transfer strong muscles for weak ones. In some cases, she operated on the joints themselves, to aid deformity preventing basic motor function.

All of which Charles would've known before bringing her in here. However, the history of the patient's condition and potential for improvement had to be taken into consideration before surgery. She couldn't volunteer her skills without extensive consultation with a team of carers and specialists to set realistic goals. Something she was willing to do if asked.

'I hope the pump helps you feel better soon.' Although she didn't want to reference it for fear of upsetting the family, Harriet was aware it must've been hard to have gone through this, especially over Christmas.

'Recovery has taken longer than expected. Bryony picked up a virus from her little brother right after surgery, but we hope to have you home soon, don't we?' Charles obviously had been thinking the same thing and Harriet would've been surprised if he hadn't paid a visit at some point yesterday, as he was so fond of her.

'Santa sent me a letter to say he'll make a special stop at my house when I'm better.'

'Because you're such a brave and special girl.' Her mum rested a hand on her daughter's forehead, but Harriet didn't miss the glances exchanged between her and

Charles. She got the impression he might've had a hand in that letter. In fact, she'd go as far to say it was probably in his handwriting.

'We're going to have a second special Christmas once Bryony's home.' As Bryony disclosed the contents of her extensive, unicorn-themed Christmas list, her mother looked as though she'd enjoy it as much as her daughter, knowing she'd be home safe.

A sudden jolt of awareness at the role she was about to take on almost knocked Harriet off her feet. Every decision she made from now on, every emotion was going to be tied to this baby. Just as Mrs Dawson's happiness and peace of mind were centred around her child. It didn't matter what happened between her and Charles, Scotland and London, this baby's welfare came first.

Her hand automatically rested on her stomach, already protecting him or her. The movement didn't escape Charles's notice as his gaze followed the action.

'Bryony's suffering twenty percent spasticity in her limbs. She was mobile, but the pain has become too much for her lately. There's no guarantee on how long the pump will last, so that means another operation further down the road.' Charles shared that extra difficult news out of Bryony's earshot.

Harriet's heart broke a fraction more for the family she'd become attached to in such a short space of time. If it was her child she'd want everything humanly possible done to stop her hurting.

'How can I help?' she asked, knowing she'd committed to coming back to Heatherglen.

CHAPTER FIVE

CHARLES HADN'T BROUGHT Harriet here to guilt her into assisting him with Bryony's treatment. He would've been here regardless of his ex's presence, but he wouldn't apologise for wanting Harriet to see the difference she could make at Heatherglen. The little girl had had a tough time of it as had her parents, and he would do everything in his power to make things easier for them.

When he had the ear of an orthopaedic surgeon with Harriet's experience it made sense to get her advice. It was simply a bonus on a personal level if she got involved and maintained an interest that saw her return, or stay for good.

'I'm going to show Harriet around the rest of the clinic, but I'll be back to see you all later.' He shook hands with Bryony's parents, who knew he couldn't spend all day at their daughter's bedside when they had other children at home on a post-Santa high. But he'd do his best to call in and provide some company for Bryony when he could. He knew Harriet well enough to expect her to want to do the same. Perhaps spending quality time with a child would show her what could be gained by sharing parenting responsibility. She could easily walk away, deny him any access to the child she was carrying, after the way he'd treated her in the past, but he wanted her to see they'd be better as a team. That their baby would be better off here, with both parents. A family.

The triumphant smile he was wearing as Harriet was saying her goodbyes to the family died on his lips. A wagging, panting bundle of fur streaked past him as he opened the door to leave the room.

'What the—?'

'Isn't this Esme's puppy?' Harriet scooped up the excitable animal, which had been causing havoc recently.

'He's so sweet. Is he for me?' Bryony's voice matched the excitement of the canine intruder and he cursed his sister's generous heart. If Esme hadn't insisted on keeping this nuisance around, he wouldn't have to upset a young patient.

'Sorry, Bryony. He must've escaped from the house.'

'You can stroke him if you want.' Harriet stepped in with a compromise and took the dog over to her before the tears had an opportunity to fully form.

'He tickles.' Bryony giggled as Dougal licked her face. Charles wasn't pleased that Dougal had made an unscheduled, unsupervised visit but it was good to see her happy. Harriet too. Although the dogs were part of the ongoing therapy around here, he'd still have to have a word with Esme about keeping a closer eye on her four-legged friend. He didn't want Dougal getting in the way when staff were doing their rounds.

He lifted the hand sanitiser and passed it to her mother. 'I'm so sorry about this.'

'Don't worry. He's the best therapy we could have asked for.' Bryony's mother joined the group fawning over Dougal as though he were a newborn baby. Now, that kind of interest he could understand. When their child was born he'd expect the whole world to take notice. But a dog?

He understood their importance in terms of therapy here. He'd seen the results for himself. They calmed patients as well as providing a distraction from illness and treatment. However, on a personal level he didn't know what the fuss was about. He'd never been a dog lover. Probably because his parents had stressed how much mess and destruction they could cause in a place like this where every stick of furniture had historic and monetary value. As proved by their canine companion. Sure, Dougal was cute, but he didn't do anything for Charles except generally make his life more difficult around here.

'We should get him back where he's supposed to be.' Charles stood back and let Harriet and her new friend leave before him.

''Bye, Dougal.' There was a chorus as they left, indicating there was only one of them who'd be truly missed.

'Just wait until I see Esme. I'd prefer he had a bath at least before he starts wandering around the place.'

'Oh, poor baby, don't listen to the nasty man. You smell like home to me.' Harriet covered Dougal's ears against the insult and peppered him with kisses, completely losing her own professional image to let her soft-hearted mothering instinct take over.

'You lived in a kennel?'

She tutted. 'We always had a dog in the house when I was growing up with Mum. They're great company and totally devoted to their owners. If I wasn't so busy with work, I'd still have one, but it wouldn't be fair to leave one at home alone all day.'

'Exactly why he shouldn't be in the castle, unsupervised, while Esme is at work.'

Harriet had talked about her parents and how difficult her childhood had been, with an absent father and an over-dependent mother, but she'd never mentioned having pets. She took so much joy from being around Dougal, a picture of their little family, complete with raucous pets, flashed into his head and suddenly he didn't mind at all.

'He's only a baby. Esme is the expert and she only has his best interests at heart. How could you be mad at this little face?' She held Dougal out towards him. The dog's tail was wagging so hard his body nearly folded in two.

Charles stared into the pair of soulful eyes begging for his love. A little pink doggie tongue shot out and began slobbering over his face, making it impossible to remember why he was being a grouch.

Then a warm trickle of liquid soaked through his suit and reminded him.

'Dougal!'

'Whoops. I think he got too excited.' Harriet could

barely contain her laughter as the puppy promptly forgot all the house training Esme had no doubt instilled in him.

Harriet didn't know how Charles was going to react to a little pee as she laughed at his expense. It was understandable he would be upset at the dog running amok in the clinic but there'd been no real harm done, other than to his suit.

Charles rolled his eyes, took the pup from her, and held him at arm's length as he headed towards the front door.

'You can't abandon him outside. It's too cold.' Even with his jaunty Christmas jumper he'd freeze to death out there. She wouldn't stand back and let that happen. She'd never forgive herself and Esme would never forgive either of them.

'What do you take me for, Harriet? I'm not a complete monster.' Her accusation stopped Charles in his snow-covered tracks. It highlighted how much work was required on her trust issues with him before the baby arrived.

She didn't dispute his intentions were honourable in his desire for them to raise the child here, at least in his eyes, but sometimes that wasn't enough. This time she'd need more than promises to persuade her to change her life for him.

After all, this was only a helpless pup and a baby was going to cause much more disruption. She would do whatever it took for her child to have a stable home life and history had shown Charles couldn't always be counted on.

Nevertheless, she followed him to the canine therapy centre and was blown away by the changes there too. The old stables had been modernised with huge windows, opening the building up to welcome people inside. A huge investment of time, money and love had gone into the clinic and the centre. A commitment Charles hadn't managed to make to her.

'I'm sorry. You didn't seem very sympathetic to him.' If he couldn't put up with Esme mollycoddling an abandoned pooch in her own home, it didn't seem so farfetched to think he'd chuck it out in the snow.

'The dogs are a great asset here but they're Esme's responsibility. I don't want to spend my days chasing after them when I'm trying to work. It's my job to make sure the patients are comfortable during their treatment and Esme's to train the dogs. I'm sympathetic to a point but I can't have puppies running amok in the clinic. As well as the professional issue I have with what happened today, I guess I'm just not a doggie person. We were never encouraged to have pets in the castle because of the potential mess and damage they could cause and that has stuck with me. That doesn't mean I'm incapable of showing love and compassion to a baby. Despite whatever is going on in that head of yours.'

It sounded so ridiculous out loud she blushed. Charles was justifiably upset by the accusation. She'd overreacted. This was the real reason she'd agreed to spend time here—to find out who he really was now and decide if this was the right environment to raise their child after all. If his ego took a bashing in the process he'd simply have to get over it. As a father-to-be he was going to have to put the needs of the baby above his pride.

'Charles! Harriet! It's nice of you to stop by.'

'I believe this is yours.' Charles presented Esme with the canine criminal who didn't look the least bit guilty as he licked her face.

'What are you doing out here, mister?' Esme nuzzled her face into the bundle and Harriet wondered how the siblings could interact so differently with the animal.

'Good question. You can pay the dry-cleaning bill for my suit.' Charles arched an eyebrow at them both.

'Oh, dear. He didn't, did he? Dougal loves you, that's why he gets so excited to see you.' She too was doing little to hide the laughter at her brother's misfortune.

'Yeah, well, the feeling is definitely not mutual. You're going to have to increase his security detail.'

'He's not some sort of criminal mastermind. He probably slipped out through the door when you weren't looking.' Esme inadvertently tripped Harriet's guilt switch. It was possible she hadn't been paying close attention to anything other than Charles's sunny disposition when they'd left this morning. It seemed such a long time ago now.

'It might be my fault. I think I was the last one out this morning.' She confessed her misdemeanour, glad something more serious hadn't happened if it had been her who'd left the door ajar.

'It's not your fault.' Charles was quick to absolve her of responsibility, though he'd been keen to hold Esme to account for the same incident.

'It's no one's fault. What my brother has neglected

to tell you is that this isn't the first time this has happened. As much as I've tried to partner Dougal with Max, he prefers Charles's company. The dog, not Max.'

'Goodness knows why.' Charles brushed off the idea, but Harriet had witnessed the puppy's love for herself.

'We should've called him Houdini. It doesn't matter where we put him, he always manages to escape and track down his favourite person in the whole world.'

'I wish he wouldn't.'

'You're fighting a losing battle, dear brother. Just give in and accept you're the leader of Dougal's pack.'

'Never.' Despite his refusal the scowl had broken on Charles's face, hinting that he wasn't as immune to the cute little mongrel as he made out. It was nicer to imagine him sitting in his armchair with a dog curled up contentedly in his lap than a man capable of leaving a puppy out in the snow. Then it wasn't such a stretch to picture him cooing over a baby.

'He certainly made an impression on Bryony, the young patient whose room he barged into.' Harriet attempted to shift her thoughts to someone who wasn't a part of her soon-to-be family. She wanted to remain objective where a potential work environment was concerned and keep her confused feelings about Charles out of any career decision. He'd taken the last one out of her hands and now she wanted control of the next. Minus his influence.

Esme grimaced as she heard about Dougal's exploits. 'I'm so sorry. Max and I have been checking on him regularly. I don't want to have to lock him into a dog crate. It's important he gets used to a home environment.'

'Preferably without wrecking it in the process,' Charles added.

'Charles and I can take him with us and keep an eye on him until you've finished here. We'll have to go back anyway.' Harriet indicated the ruined suit, which wasn't going to do anything to improve his attitude towards Dougal with the constant reminder of his humiliation.

'Would you? That would be so helpful. I have my hands full here.' Esme passed the pooch parcel again as a dozen others sounded their demands for her attention.

'You owe me one, sis.' Even Charles seemed to re-alise her workload could do without one more demanding dog as he accepted his fate of puppy-sitting for the rest of the afternoon.

Harriet feared for Dougal's future if he got on Charles's bad side again or damaged more than the Laird's cool façade.

'Excuse me if I'm speaking out of turn, but there was one positive to come out of this mishap.' All eyes were on Harriet now, including Dougal's, begging her to save him from eviction.

'I'm dying to hear this.' Charles folded his arms and waited for the defence.

She ignored the cynicism and the childish urge to stick her tongue out at him. 'Bryony, Charles's patient with cerebral palsy responded well to Dougal and I know you train therapy dogs here. Is there a chance you could partner the two together?' It would solve the immediate problem by finding Dougal alternative ac-commodation and at the same time provide the young girl with a much-needed companion.'

Charles was so busy laughing it was left to Esme to explain the flaw in that plan. 'Unfortunately, I'm not sure Dougal is going to be suitable for training. Not unless we use Charles as an incentive. We can look into alternatives for Bryony if the family is interested. We train a lot of dogs to help cerebral palsy patients. They seem to get a lot out of having therapy dogs.'

Harriet nodded. She understood the joy of having unconditional love from a pet during tough times. A dog could only aid Bryony through the challenges she endured.

'I can mention it to her parents and get them to come and talk it over with you if they're interested.' Now they were on the subject of his patient Charles resumed his professional manner and took the suggestion seriously. Although it didn't help with the Dougal problem, Harriet was satisfied her idea hadn't been as ridiculous as she'd initially feared.

'Great. I can give them a tour and put them in touch with some of our other CP families.' Esme gave her brother a swift kiss on the cheek and did the same to Harriet before disappearing back into the kennels, leaving Harriet and Charles to mind her fur baby.

'Stay!' Everyone in the vicinity could've told him it was a pointless command by now, but Charles attempted to assert his authority all the same.

Dougal had that same goofball expression, tongue hanging out the side of his mouth, tail wagging, with no intention of doing anything he was told. Charles had no idea why he was so irresistible when there was a bowl of dog food and a comfy bed waiting nearby. He knew where he'd rather be. Especially when there were belly rubs and Harriet kisses on offer elsewhere.

Naturally, the little mongrel had made a run for it the second Charles turned his back and it was only Harriet's quick reflexes that had saved him from further dog slobber.

'I'll keep him company while you get changed,' she promised, burying her face in Dougal's fur.

'If you wouldn't mind, I think I'll grab a quick shower.' A cold one. Then he might burn his Dougal-scented suit.

'Go. I'll be happy to get some snuggles without you scowling at us.' He thought she was joking but he and the mischievous pup were going to have to get along if he was going to impress Harriet. Besides, if Esme had anything to do with it, Dougal was going to be a long-term resident. Charles was simply going to have to get used to changes around here.

Some breathing space between him and Harriet was good, he realised, casting off his clothes to step into the shower. He'd jumped in with that offer to Harriet to join them at the clinic on the basis he'd be closer to the baby. However, the more time he spent with Harriet the more he could see what he'd given up twelve years ago.

If that one night in bed had reminded him what they'd had together physically—and, boy, it had improved with age—being in her company today had brought out that caring side he'd admired so much in her. She was good at her job, that had never been in doubt, but it was her extra interest in Bryony, and that stupid dog, that took him back to the reasons he'd fallen for her in the first place.

It was a shame she'd made it clear she didn't trust him to commit to more than one night together. He didn't blame her but the reasons for wanting her to stay at Heatherglen were becoming more personal by the second.

He wanted to have it all—a successful career, a memorial honouring his brother and father, and a family of his own, including a partner to share it all with. Yet he knew it was selfish. Something that always spelled disaster for those closest to him. The ones he was supposed to love.

He was pushing her to transfer to Cluchlochry for the baby's sake because *he* wanted her to. Really, what was in it for her? There were better career prospects in London and that was the reason he'd sacrificed a life with her in the first place. It wasn't fair to pressure her. Hopefully they could resolve this with a proper conversation about what was best for all of them. It wasn't the first time he'd had to rein in his feelings for her and he'd survived. They both had.

Once the water had turned colder than he was prepared to subject himself to, he stepped out of the shower and wrapped a towel around his waist.

The en suite bathroom made his wardrobe accessible without having to compromise his modesty.

If he was spending the afternoon with Sir Pees-a-Lot, he wasn't going to risk another good suit. He bypassed the smart shirts and trousers, reaching for the comfy, less expensive option of a well-worn pair of jeans and a sweater.

The bedroom door burst open just as he was about to unfasten the towel. A flash of brindle brown, a tug at the hem of the towel and Charles felt cold air on his naked skin.

He exclaimed in exasperation, 'What the hell...?'

That was closely followed by Harriet's 'Dougal!'

As she ran into the room Charles was left cupping his hands over his privates to save both their blushes. Nothing she hadn't seen before but the way she was staring at him made him feel more exposed than ever. He should've been flattered by the blatant ogling but with a rogue puppy wrestling with his towel on his bedroom floor it was downright embarrassing.

'Well, this is awkward.' He sidestepped towards the clothes he had laid out on his bed, wondering how he could dress without flashing her again.

Harriet blinked at him a few times before she became animated again. 'Oh, my goodness. I'm so sorry, Charles. He slipped past me when I was putting the kettle on for a cup of tea. He's as fast as lightning.'

'It's okay. You need eyes in the back of your head to watch this one.' What else could he say to make this whole episode less embarrassing for both of them? This dog had a lot to answer for.

'Dougal. Drop it. Drop it.' Harriet attempted to retrieve the towel Charles would appreciate having back. Dougal clamped on tighter to his prize. Charles knew at first hand those little teeth were like needles.

'Leave it. If the two of you wouldn't mind leaving,

I might salvage some of my dignity.' An unfortunate choice of words given what he was clutching at the moment.

'No problem. Sorry. Again.' She reached for the dignity-destroyer, who saw this as some sort of game and dashed away every time Harriet came close. Eventually she managed to grab one end of the towel and entered into a tug of war.

It was all becoming ridiculous now. All they needed was Esme to walk in on this farce and she'd laugh herself into a coma.

'Give. Me. The. Damn. Towel.' Harriet gave one last yank and emerged victorious, clutching the now chewed towel. Although she did manage to land flat on her backside in the process. Dougal had bested them both.

'I'm not sure who won that one. I'd help you up but...' He shrugged, unable to come out of this situation as a gentleman.

She stood up and held the towel out to him. Even then he wasn't sure how to accept it without making another show of himself.

'You might want to close your eyes or something.'

'Don't be silly. We're both adults.' The twinkle in her eyes said she wasn't offended, or surprised, by what she'd seen.

She wrapped the towel around his waist for him, pressing her body to his as she did so. Close enough that Charles could hear the hitch in her breath, feel her warmth on his skin, and it was torture that he couldn't do a thing about it.

* * *

Harriet sensed his eyes on her before she saw him watching her so intently. So much for remaining emotionally detached. Now here she was standing in his bedroom with her arms wrapped around Charles's lower half with the most recent image of what lay beneath burned on her brain.

Her skin was flushed with the heat of arousal, not embarrassment, remembering the last time she'd had her hands on his naked body. It would be easy to fall into bed with him again and forget everything except how good he could make her feel.

'Harriet...' That husky tone of his desire shot straight to her loins, cutting off all common sense in favour of a more basic need.

She closed her eyes against temptation, but it didn't help her forget the softness of his lips, the memory of him kissing her fresh enough to make hers tingle.

'Don't.' It was a plea for him to stop. If he made a move on her she couldn't resist because she didn't want to. She ached for him and to share his bed again. It was only her long-held insecurities maintaining that last defence.

Sex with Charles would only complicate her life. London had proved that. Her seduction hadn't given her any sort of closure but instead had opened a whole new chapter between them.

He rested his chin on her head and sighed. A reflection of Harriet's own frustration at their situation. She wanted to cry but Charles continued to hold her as though he was drawing as much comfort as she was from this embrace.

Yes, he was wearing virtually nothing, and she was aware of every taut inch of him as she pressed her cheek against his chest. Even if he'd been fully clothed in a room full of people the moment would've been as touching, and intimate.

They'd made mistakes and suffered as a result, but they couldn't go back and change anything any more than they could predict what was going to happen. She couldn't remember the last time someone had simply held her, or when she'd let them. Accepting comfort seemed like a failure to her. As though the stresses of life had defeated her. She'd learned long ago not to give in and admit she couldn't do everything on her own. Growing up with her mother hadn't left room for two to wallow in personal hardship. One of them had to be strong enough to carry the other and in her case, the child had become the parent.

Later, when Charles had broken her heart, she'd been in need of a shoulder to cry on. With none available she'd soldiered on lest she let melancholy consume her as it had her mother. Since then, she'd cultivated pride in her independence and in taking back control of her emotions.

This warmth from his touch even without the physical attraction reminded her of everything she'd been missing in her pursuit of a self-sufficient life.

She sighed, and Charles continued to maintain the simple contact. Given their traumatic history and the break-up he'd told her he hadn't wanted, it was possible he'd been living in emotional isolation too. Even though he mightn't have replaced her in his affections, the thought didn't please her. Rather, sadness settled over her as she realised what they'd both lost.

A sharp yelp reminded them Dougal was in the room and they broke apart.

'I think someone wants your attention.' Charles was smiling at her, but his hangdog expression was tugging at her heartstrings more than the little one nipping at her heel. The fact Charles might crave something more than her attention was something she couldn't afford to indulge.

'He's due a feed.'

'I can see that,' Charles laughed as Dougal caught the bottom of his towel and tugged again. This time Charles was ready and managed to keep a tight hold of his modesty.

'This time I'll lock him in solitary confinement if I have to.' The dog was turning out to be such an excellent guardian against her making bad decisions she might just adopt him herself.

CHAPTER SIX

'It's my way of saying thank you for not driving Dougal to the nearest dog pound.'

Esme plated up the dinner she'd insisted on cooking, regardless that she'd only recently finished work. She was another one who didn't submit to a typical nine-to-five schedule but had made an effort to get home to cook this feast.

'Really, you didn't have to.'

Harriet would have settled for something as plain as a slice of toast. Her stomach had been somersaulting since she'd walked into Charles's room to find him naked. The sight of him sitting opposite her at the dinner table in his casual wear hadn't lessened the impact he'd had on her when she'd set eyes on him again.

Now, as well as the memories of rolling around in bed with him, his very presence reminded her of the vulnerability of being in his arms. When she'd let go of everything except the bliss she'd found in his embrace. It was unnerving that she'd lost that much control around him, yet she yearned to do it again and again. It didn't help when the four of them—Esme, Charles, Max and herself—seemed like they were on a double date. At worst, a family meal she was intruding on or anything else she didn't have a legitimate reason to attend.

Charles tucked into the home-cooked meal with gusto, his appetite greater than Harriet's.

'This is amazing.' Max reached across to squeeze Esme's hand in thanks and the pure love in their eyes for each other was so touching Harriet had to turn away before she started blubbing.

It was hard to believe she and Charles had ever been that oblivious to the world around them, though they must've been at some point. Certainly, Charles had blamed their relationship for making him blind to his father's struggles after Nick had died. That was what had made his blunt dismissal so hard to accept when she'd still been loved up. If Max turned on Esme now it would blindside her too, Harriet was sure. Love was a painful business.

'So, what did you guys get up to this afternoon after you left the centre?' As innocent as it was, Esme's question almost made Harriet choke on her dinner as a naked Charles sprang to mind.

He was smirking at her now, daring her to share their adventures in his bedroom, which, although without serious incident, were memorable all the same. It turned out to be something she'd prefer to keep private between them for more than one reason.

'We were…er…busy trying to keep Dougal out of trouble.' Eventually Charles jumped in with a truthful half-answer.

Harriet couldn't help but smile at him in thanks

and because of the memories of the pup running rings around them.

'He'll be out of your hair tomorrow. Max is going to install safety gates. You know, the ones you use for babies. They'll come in handy in the future anyway.' It was at the last second Esme caught what she was saying. Max too, judging by the expression of horror on his face.

'Harriet's pregnant,' Esme blurted out, probably before Max keeled over thinking she was the one planning a baby in the near future.

Charles dropped his knife and fork onto his plate with a clatter. 'For goodness' sake. Harriet asked you to keep it yourself.'

'Sorry,' Esme mumbled into her chest, but Harriet would've been surprised if she hadn't shared the news with Max at some point, given the close nature of their relationship.

'It's fine. Don't worry. We've just found out we're expecting, Max, and we're trying to figure things out at the moment.' She didn't know how much of their history he was aware of but there was no reason to make anyone feel guilty about the situation. The news had to come out some time.

Max nodded sagely. 'Sure. It's a lot to take in. I won't breathe a word to anyone.'

'Thanks.' For all Harriet knew, she'd be gone by the end of the week, with no need to put Max or Esme under pressure to keep their secret.

'Congratulations.' Max raised a glass to toast them and Harriet clinked her water against it.

'You too, mate.' He reached across the table to shake Charles's hand.

'Cheers.' Charles was beaming, and the simple acceptance of the unplanned pregnancy began to make her feel part of the family. Not the best environment to nurture that sense of isolation she needed to maintain control in her life.

Heatherglen was offering that support to her child she hadn't had growing up, but she wasn't convinced it would be a good move for her personally. A miserable mother, as she knew, did not a happy childhood make. It would take her to get past her feelings about Charles, positive and negative, to be able to face him on a daily basis.

'Harriet and I are going to take a trip into the village tomorrow.' Charles dropped the next bombshell into the middle of their meal.

'We are?'

'You are?' Esme echoed Harriet's surprise at the announcement when he hadn't consulted either of them.

He carried on eating without missing a beat. 'I thought I could show you around. The shops should be open again and I expect you'll need to get a few things.'

'I do.' The trip would take them away from the patients, family and four-legged friends who'd provided a necessary buffer between them today, leaving them alone. A dangerous position as this afternoon had demonstrated. Yet the gesture proved he had been thinking about her, about spending time with her, and anticipating her needs for her unexpected extended stay. She couldn't turn him down even if she wanted to.

Out of the corner of her eye Harriet could see Esme shaking her head.

'What?' Charles demanded to know why she disapproved of his plan. Harriet too wondered why such a thoughtful gesture should warrant the negative response.

'You never take time off. Yesterday was Christmas Day and you spent most of it at the clinic. It's so unlike you, bro.'

He shrugged. 'Maybe I have different priorities now.'

Harriet snapped her head up at that.

'Already? Wow. Fatherhood must be agreeing with you.' His sister teased him, their back and forth relationship dizzying, but it showed how close they were. Only two people who loved each other could generate such strong and varying degrees of emotion. One minute they were at each other's throats, gently joshing the next. If Harriet had had a sibling, she would've had someone on her side supporting her through the ups and downs. She might not have shut down emotionally over the years if she'd had someone giving her a kick up the backside when she'd required it. Annoying her when she hadn't.

It was a nice idea that her little one might have that family support but it made her consider what sort of relationship she had with Charles. Their lives had already been turned upside down without future family planning too. They weren't even together. In case she'd forgotten it, she was supposed to be putting him off the idea of her hanging around so she could return to London. It was ridiculous to go down the road of believing they could have a family together when their circumstances were so unstable.

Yet he was making an effort to convince her and Esme he was going to change and manage his time at Heatherglen so he could devote himself to her and the baby. This wasn't the Charles she'd anticipated finding at the castle, Laird of all he surveyed and unwilling to give up anything for anyone. Now every little thing he did for her, every concession was going to make it harder for her to walk away when the time came.

'Ready?' Charles waited for her to belt herself in, his hand on the ignition key as though he was giving her the opportunity to bale out. This venture was about more than replenishing her wardrobe. He was showing her he would prioritise her when he had to. The significance wasn't lost on Harriet, but anyone could make a promise. It was being true to your word that counted. Only with time and a history of seeing things through could she be convinced he meant what he said.

She couldn't expect Charles to drop work to take her on a shopping jaunt when the mood struck, neither would she want him to. It wasn't the commitment to his patients she had an issue with. Raising a child necessitated making small compromises on a regular basis for school runs, holidays or illness. Children didn't run to a schedule and Harriet would rather manage it all on her own than have him complain every time he had to make alternative work arrangements.

'As ready as I'll ever be,' she sighed, and buckled up for the bumpy ride they were about to undertake.

'The roads have turned icy overnight so I'll take it easy. I'm carrying a precious load after all.'

She didn't know if he was talking about her or the baby as he negotiated the frosty lanes with his foot hovering on the brake. They came as a package now but that would change, physically, in about seven months' time.

If she decided not to move and he wanted their child at weekends and holidays it was going to be difficult. Should she have other work commitments, or Charles no longer thought of her as part of the equation, the separation was bound to be stressful. She was already fitting in here way too easily, with everyone being so accommodating. In some ways it was like being a child again, only with people who were taking her feelings into consideration along with their own.

'It's like a scene from a Christmas film where they've thrown in every cliché they could think of to make it look festive here.' In the city, snow was a cold, slushy nuisance, causing accidents and slowing traffic to a standstill. Here in the country she was able to take the time to appreciate the beauty in the weather. The white undisturbed fields, glistening invitingly, made Harriet want to roll around and make her mark where no one else had.

As they approached the village, the cosy fairy-tale cottages coughed wisps of smoke into the freezing air and told of the families inside sitting around the fire.

'Different from London?' Charles would take this vista for granted when he had it on his doorstep. Gaudy lights, over-decorated trees and throngs of harassed shoppers would be as much of a novelty to him as this was to her. It was only the potential hazards of the season that linked the vastly different locations.

They stopped at a junction just outside the village to check for oncoming traffic, only for the car to continue travelling out onto the road after Charles had applied the handbrake.

'We must've hit a patch of black ice.' Very experienced in driving in these kinds of conditions, he did his best to control the vehicle, steering into the skid instead of fighting against it.

The car eventually slid to a halt and Harriet sent fervent thanks to the heavens that they were alone on the road. They would've been helpless should anyone else have been coming towards them. Instinctively she wrapped her arms around her belly, that mama bear already fully formed and protective of her cub.

'Are you all right?' Another hand covered hers.

'No harm done,' she assured him, but it was apparent papa bear was making himself known too.

'I'll take a different route back. It's longer but the roads might be gritted out that way.'

Harriet muttered agreeable sounds as shock began to set in about what could have happened. At that second she realised her baby's life was more precious to her than her own. She'd give up anything to ensure this child was safe. Including her job and her house if she was sure Heatherglen would be the best place to provide security.

It took several attempts to get the car going in the direction they wanted. That was mainly because Charles refused to let her get out and lighten the weight of the car. The result of spinning tyres as he attempted to get traction on the slick surface was the smell of burning rubber.

The spinning motion of the vehicle combined with the acrid air had her clutching her belly now for a different reason.

'I have to get out, Charles.' It was a warning for him to pull over before his car was filled with more than fumes.

'What is it? What's wrong?' He immediately pulled over to the grass verge.

'Air,' she gasped, nausea rising too fast for her to quell with willpower alone.

Charles unbuckled his seat belt and jumped out of the car before she could stop him. He slipped and slid around the side of the car in his hurry to get to her. 'Be careful. We don't want any more accidents.'

With one hand steady on the now open passenger door, he held the other out to her.

'I just need some fresh air. There's no panic.' Embarrassed by the sudden bout of nausea, she ignored the helping hand to stand on her own two feet unassisted. A plan that went awry as soon as her foot slipped on the ice and she had to accept all the support offered.

'I've got you.' He caught her and braced her against the side of the car with his body.

She closed her eyes and wished the world would stop spinning. 'I'm fine.'

'Look at me. Open your eyes and focus on me, Harriet. That's it. Now, take deep breaths. In...and out.' Charles called her back from the brink of oblivion promising to take her somewhere safe.

She followed his instructions, inhaling his familiar scent, so reassuring and irresistible. Despite her return to full consciousness Charles kept a tight hold on her.

'Has this happened before?'

'No, but I don't usually spend my mornings doing doughnuts in the car.' Sarcasm was her only defence when she was at his mercy.

'I'd never have come if I'd realised the roads were so bad. Do you want to go home?' He eased her back into the passenger seat so she was sitting sideways with Charles kneeling at her feet.

His feelings of guilt were almost palpable, but revenge wasn't something she'd ever wanted in coming to Heatherglen.

'No. It's probably just shock, or morning sickness, or motion sickness. It'll pass.'

'You know it's not a weakness to be sick or, heaven forbid, to let someone help you.' He was holding both of her hands and Harriet could picture him in the delivery suite with her with the same calm presence, coaching her through labour. She hadn't realised how much she needed someone like that in her life so she could take a breather once in a while and let someone be strong for her.

However, the birth was a long way off and anything could happen in the interim. It wouldn't do to become reliant on Charles for support if he wasn't going to be there at the crucial time.

'Honestly, I feel a lot better. I'd rather get back on my feet and find something to distract me. Now, you said something about shops?' With steadier movements than before, she exited the car and slammed the door, forcing him to take a step back.

In London the shops would already be bulging at the seams with savvy shoppers seeking bargains in the sales. Cluchlochry was quiet, as though in hibernation, waiting for spring before the inhabitants would emerge back into the daylight.

Charles huffed out a cloud of breath into the atmosphere, but he'd stopped arguing with her. If these past couple of days had shown him anything about the woman she'd become, he'd realised she was much stronger than the one he'd known previously. Headstrong, stubborn, she'd heard it said before from other people whose interference in her life she'd refused to accept. It was that self-defence mechanism that had protected her fragile heart from any further sledgehammer blows. She had to keep that superwoman cape on at all times. Especially around Charles.

'Christmas is over. People have a living to make. I'm sure they'll be glad to see customers in their businesses and we can always stop for lunch at McKinney's pub.'

Harriet was curious about the shops, which were missing the garish signs the high-street stores usually displayed. If anything, the shopfronts here blended in too well with the surroundings. Especially now it had begun snowing again in earnest and limiting visibility.

'Any suggestions about where we should begin our shopping trip?' Left to her, she was afraid of walking in on some unsuspecting local watching TV in her parlour because she couldn't tell the business premises from the residential buildings.

'There's a wool shop if you fancy taking up knitting.'

'Why would I?' She rounded on him, waiting for the explanation, which was bound to begin a debate about stereotypical gender association.

'It's the sort of thing wo…people do when there's a baby on the way, isn't it?' Charles's face was unreadable as he waved at the proprietor standing by her colourful window display of yarn.

Harriet hoped he was joking.

'Are you honing your carpentry skills so you can knock a crib together, then?' It was a jibe to get back at him for insinuating she should be sitting knitting bootees for the duration of her 'confinement'.

Not one to give her the satisfaction of winning an argument, Charles countered with a chirpy, 'Maybe I will.'

Now she was going to be plagued with a sultry montage of him in her head, his naked torso beaded with sweat as he lovingly crafted a masterpiece with his rough, strong hands. Looking for a distraction from her over-active imagination, she pushed open the next shop door.

'Hello, there.' The shopkeeper didn't need the jingle of the bell to alert her that she had customers.

'Hi, Joanie. This is Harriet, a friend of the family. I'm just showing her around the village.' Charles made the introduction and Harriet wondered for the first time if any of the locals would remember the scandal of the young Laird's failed romance. The rumour mill would be working overtime if they heard she was back, pregnant.

'Nice to meet you, Joanie.' Harriet shook her hand,

already getting friendly vibes from the pleasant red-head and her quirky shop.

The shelves were packed with all manner of knick-knacks and cute gifts tourists and children would lap up. Unfortunately, there was nothing in stock that would aid her quest for a bigger wardrobe.

'Your hands are freezing. Let me make you a cup of tea to warm you up.' Joanie wouldn't hear another word on the subject and disappeared into the back of the shop, ignoring any protest.

'Hot sugary tea is exactly what you need.' Charles pulled over a couple of chairs to the counter and gave the impression that impromptu tea parties here weren't unusual.

Despite the suspicion he'd somehow tricked her into this, Harriet took a seat and warmed her hands by the electric fire. The pleasant warmth seeping into her bones reminded her of how it had felt walking into Heatherglen after being so alone on the road from London. It was cosy, homely and she wanted to stay here for as long as possible.

'There you go.' Joanie returned with a tray full of tea things and Charles passed a cup to Harriet before taking one for himself.

'Try some of the shortbread. I made it myself.' She prised open a tartan tin full of sugar-dusted Christmas-tree shapes.

Surmising the sugar hit might help her wooziness, Harriet helped herself. One bite and she was in buttery, sugary heaven.

'You know, I should be sick to death of eating this

stuff, but this is really good.' Charles finished his short-bread in two bites.

Joanie blushed, as most women did when Charles paid them a compliment.

'Everyone seemed to like it. Perhaps I should start selling it.'

'You should. It's delicious.' Harriet took another when their host offered the tin around a second time.

Joanie beamed at the praise. 'You two finish your tea. I'm just going to take the rubbish out into the back yard.'

The sudden chill blasting through the building when Joanie opened the door was a stark reminder of the outside temperature.

Charles set down his tea and rubbed Harriet's shoulders up and down as she shivered, trying to generate some heat back into her body. It was the touch of his hands on her that managed to raise her temperature again.

A thud and the sound of broken glass outside startled them both.

'Joanie? Are you all right out there?' Charles called, on his way to find out for himself with Harriet following close behind.

There was no reply and when they were faced with the scene in the shop's back yard they could see why. She was lying unconscious on the ground, the contents of the rubbish bag strewn around her and a pool of blood staining the ground crimson around her head.

Harriet no longer cared about the cold or the snow as she knelt in it to take the woman's pulse. 'Joanie? Can you hear me?'

'I'll phone for an ambulance. Hopefully there'll be one nearby. Watch out for the broken glass. I don't want you getting hurt too.' His concern for her continued to amaze Harriet when it came so naturally to him to think about her. It took her right back to the time when they'd been in love and he'd have done anything to keep her safe.

Harriet carried out basic checks on Joanie, making sure her airways were clear, while Charles gave their location to the switchboard operator. He came to assist her once he hung up, covering Joanie with his coat to keep her warm.

'She's probably slipped on the ice and hit her head in the fall. We don't want to move her until we can get a neck brace on her.' There were all sorts of complications with head or neck injuries and there was a risk of paralysis if they tried to move her.

'We're going to need a CT scan to see what the damage is in case it's more than concussion. If the roads are too bad to get her as far as Glasgow we can make her comfortable at Heatherglen until it's safe to transfer her to hospital.'

'There's a good strong pulse and her breathing is normal.' Harriet reported her observations, but Charles didn't seem as positive as he checked the head wound.

'She has a compound fracture to the skull. The skin and tissue are broken, leaving the brain partially exposed.' An open fracture presented a risk of bacterial infection. If left untreated it could lead to permanent brain damage or even death. An open head injury also left the patient vulnerable to other conditions such as seizures and paralysis.

They needed a CT scan to assess the extent and severity of the fracture, but it was looking as though Joanie was going to require surgery to reduce swelling in the brain. This was time sensitive.

Harriet was applying pressure around the wound to control the bleeding, all the while talking to the patient and trying unsuccessfully to get a response. Charles got back on the phone to give an update on the severity of their patient's condition, but he didn't return with good news.

'The weather's bad out there. They don't know how long it will take to transfer her to the hospital and an air ambulance is out of the question until that blizzard outside passes.' He had a decision to make quickly as he could already hear the clinic vehicle drawing near. Joanie didn't even have any family around with whom he could discuss the situation.

'We'll take her back to Heatherglen and do a CT scan there.' If it proved he was worrying unnecessarily, they could take their time with the hospital transfer. However, something more serious would require immediate action. They didn't usually carry out major operations at the clinic, referring serious cases to the hospital, but they did act as a local A and E when necessary.

'Lyle will assess her, but we might have to ask for your skills here if we need to operate.' His fellow Scot was the one called on for any local emergencies, but Harriet was the surgeon here. This decision could prevent them wasting time and improve Joanie's chances of recovery. They could make a difference.

This was exactly the sort of situation he'd helped Lyle set the clinic up for in the first place.

CHAPTER SEVEN

THEY WERE GREETED at the front door of the castle by Dr Sinclair and Dr Kirkpatrick.

'I thought you might need some extra help on this one,' Max was offering his services too, which could only improve Joanie's chances with so many accomplished medical staff available.

Harriet realised she'd already been included in this band of doctors. She was no longer merely a visitor.

'Do you mind if I take the lead on this one?' Harriet asked as they wheeled Joanie inside.

'Not at all. You're the surgeon here.' There was no sign of territoriality from Lyle, which went some way to easing the pressure Harriet was suddenly under.

'We'll need a CT scan to see what we're dealing with.'

'Would you like me to assist if you do have to operate?

'The more the merrier, right?' Harriet soon found herself scrubbed in alongside the others prepping for surgery once the scans showed their fears had been justified.

'I'm glad we had so many hands available.' Charles

managed to lighten the mood a little as the team came together to provide access to Joanie's injury once she was under general anaesthetic.

He made the initial cranial incision to reveal the extent of the fracture, and he needed assistance to keep the skin flap pinned back out of the way.

Harriet worked quickly to debride the area, cleaning and removing the blood clots that had formed there and repairing damaged blood vessels. Once the bleeding had stopped, she used screws to hold the skull back together in place.

'We'll monitor for infection or secondary complications such as intracranial pressure and brain swelling. Charles, we'll need to keep her on a ventilator until it's possible to move her to a high-dependency unit.' Sometimes patients needed additional surgery to relieve pressure and drain any accumulating blood. In the meantime, she'd prescribe strong antibiotics and medication to reduce possible inflammation.

This wasn't her area of expertise, but she'd spent sufficient time in an operating theatre to be confident in what she was doing. Charles too had put his trust in her skills to make this call. Everything he did was with his patients in mind and whatever would produce the best possible outcome. The easiest option would've been for him to leave Joanie at the mercy of the time it would take to get her to that hospital.

Instead, he'd taken on the responsibility for her initial treatment and everything that would happen once she was at Heatherglen. Harriet was beginning to see there was a role here for her to perform emergency surgery when it was required. Along with the everyday cases which came into the clinic requiring her expertise as an orthopaedic surgeon. It was a good balance of cases which would hold her interest and provide a necessary service to the local community.

All the same, she'd be happier when Joanie was getting specialist care at the hospital and she was relieved of her responsibility.

With the benefit of hindsight, and an explanation for his behaviour, she was beginning to understand what had driven Charles to do the things he'd done in the past. It was a pity it had come so late.

She was the one who'd been selfish over the years, wanting him to herself when he'd devoting himself to improving the lives of countless others.

'I'm sure you weren't expecting to perform brain surgery on your holiday.' Unbidden, Charles brought her a cup of tea and set it on the table beside her chair.

'This was never supposed to be a holiday, remember?' She was keen to remind him that this stay wasn't about her taking some time out. It was for them to make life-changing decisions regarding the child they were to have in a few months' time.

He took the seat opposite, the glow from the fire throwing shadows on his face. It was the first she'd seen him rest since Joanie's accident. After the surgery he'd insisted she come back home while he oversaw Joanie in Recovery. She'd had the chance to shower, change and take a nap before he'd come back. If this was his regular schedule it was no wonder he didn't have time for a private life, but that didn't mean she was willing to pick up the slack.

'How could I forget when Heatherglen is all about family for me?' He was staring into the flickering flames of the fire, not seeing Harriet at all and making it difficult for her to believe she was part of that sentiment.

'Forgive me, Charles, but I don't understand that. We could've been raising a family together by now, but you turned your back on me and our future. I admire your dedication to your work, but I can't help worrying where you're going to fit a child into your routine? What's going to change?' It was all very well saying the words but what point was there in making promises he couldn't keep? Relegating her in his affections in favour of Heatherglen was one thing but she wouldn't let him do that to their child.

'Nothing. I'm going to remain as faithful to my family as I have been for these last years. That includes my son or daughter.'

A lead weight dropped into Harriet's stomach as he confirmed she'd never been, and never would be, included in that beloved circle.

'Being faithful, providing a home and financial stability is completely different from being a parent. I grew up believing my thoughts and feelings didn't matter in comparison to my mother's. I had to be the strong one and ignore those things every other child took for granted. I didn't have attention, affection or even an interest in what I was doing at school from my mother. So much of my time was taken up with her insecurities and demands for my attention and it was almost a relief when she passed away. I'm not going to subject my own child to the same treatment.'

Losing a parent was anyone's worst nightmare and she still grieved for her mother. It was difficult to reconcile that with the belief that her mother's heart attack had given Harriet her freedom. She would never have reached the heights in her career she had if she was still at her mother's beck and call.

Harriet would do her damnedest to ensure her own child's emotional needs were met. Something she'd missed out on as a child, and as an adult. Sometimes being read a bedtime story or an afternoon spent making cupcakes could be enough to prove to a child it was loved. Since she'd arrived here Charles had gone out of his way to make her comfortable, but it was impossible to know if taking time out when necessary could be sustained long term. There was no way she was going to move here if they'd end up resenting the intrusion into each other's lives, with their child in the middle of the feud.

'I'm aware I'm not part of the family, you made that abundantly clear when you sent me back to London.' It hurt, regardless of his reasons for behaving the way he had after the funeral, or her insistence she was over it.

Charles shook his head. 'Don't you see? I'm the reason my father died. That's why I had to stay at Heatherglen. After we lost Nick I carried on with my life in London without a thought to how my parents were coping. The long and short of it is that they weren't.

'Dad threw himself into work here, trying to blot

out the pain of losing his firstborn. If I'd been any sort of son to him I would've come back and helped then, lightened the load or given him something to focus on other than his grief. He worked himself into an early grave and I did nothing to stop it. I was so used to having my freedom, with none of the responsibilities resting on Nick's shoulders, I simply continued doing my own thing. Including proposing to a vulnerable young woman barely into her twenties who'd only recently lost her mother.'

He was clutching at the arms of the armchair so hard Harriet was afraid he'd rip them off.

'We were both old enough to know what we were doing. Yes, we may have rushed into things but don't use me to exacerbate your guilt. As to your father's death, what could you have done? You were grieving for your brother too.' She remembered the tears and sleepless nights in the wake of Nick's death. Unsurprising in the circumstances. What had happened to his brother had been horrific and traumatic for everyone.

Charles stopped worrying the upholstery and began pacing the room, coming to rest his hands on the mantelpiece and staring into the blazing hearth.

'That wasn't grief. It was guilt.'

Despite the heat of the fire, Harriet shivered at the coldness of his tone. So matter-of-fact and emotionless when she knew Nick's death had devastated him.

'How can you be to blame for his death? He was in Afghanistan on patrol. You didn't plant the IED. I know how much you loved him.' He'd always spoken of Nick with such admiration she was sorry she'd never got to meet the man in person.

'You don't understand...we rowed before he was posted. I said unforgivable things that I can never take back. I told him to drop dead when he tried to lecture me about stepping up and doing my bit to support Heatherglen. All because I was jealous of him. I didn't see why I should put time and effort into the place when I wasn't the golden child who'd be inheriting everything.' The sound that came out of his mouth was somewhere between a laugh and a sob.

'We all say things we don't mean in the heat of the moment. We shouldn't spend the rest of our lives beating ourselves up about it.' She was pretty sure she'd said she'd hated Charles on more than one occasion when emotions had run high, but she'd never stopped loving him. It was a way of lashing out, trying to hurt him with words she knew weren't true.

'We can when we'll never get the chance to take the words back again. I thought he was the one who had everything. He was the war hero, the heir to Heatherglen. Esme was the youngest, Mum and Dad's little princess, and I was nothing more than the spare.' There was such raw pain in his every word it was heartbreaking to listen to and Harriet knew deep in her soul he'd never shared his torment with anyone else. She felt privileged but she also hurt for him, and for herself. If he'd only confided in her at the time they might have worked through this together then.

Instead, they'd retreated to their respective homes and locked themselves away to recover from their wounds.

She wouldn't have been human if she'd sat back and let him pour out his heart without offering some comfort. With his mother no longer on the scene either, and his big-brother protectiveness of Esme, Harriet recognised the signs of self-neglect. Thankfully, she was able to prescribe the correct treatment.

Charles angled his body to meet her when she put a hand on his shoulder to let him know she was there, and pulled him into a hug. He was unyielding at first but soon relaxed into her with a sigh, letting that tension escape on a heavy breath near her ear.

They stood for a while, drawing comfort from each other, with only the sound of the crackling fire to break the silence.

'You have to leave the past behind, Charles. Don't let it destroy you. You're still entitled to a life of your own. Especially when you've done so much for others.' Her voice was cracking with the thought of him carrying so much unnecessary guilt.

'I couldn't bring Nick or Dad back, but I thought I could do the right thing by you, Harriet. Thinking I could get married and have a normal life was a fantasy and the nightmare of taking Heatherglen on was stark reality. I envied your freedom when mine had been taken away from me. I didn't want to ruin your life too by dragging you back here and now I've done that anyway. I know I broke your heart, but I broke my own too.' He broke the seal between their bodies to drop his gaze to her belly where their baby was growing by the day.

'I've never done anything I didn't want to do. Except leave you.' She was trying to smile but the overwhelming sadness at the memory wouldn't let her. She hadn't been truly happy since that day.

'I never wanted you to go, Harriet. I thought I was doing the right thing by you, Nick and my dad, by setting this place up.'

'I know.' She rested her forehead against his, wishing someone had bashed their heads together at the time. 'What about you, Charles? What did you want?'

'The only thing I've ever wanted, Harriet. You.' His hands were at her waist now, sending her pulse into overdrive. When she looked into his eyes, saw the blue fire of his truth there, the game was all over.

Her future was undetermined but, at this moment, she knew exactly what she wanted to do. Yet she hesitated, her mouth hovering against his, her breathing ragged, knowing that if she gave in again to temptation she'd never want to leave.

Then Charles closed the gap and made the decision for her, his lips hard on hers as he kissed her. She'd been waiting for this since London. Wanting him to kiss her and obliterate everything else around them. Now she was burning with need for more. Circumstances had kept them apart for too long and now that raw passion for each other was free to burn out of control.

Harriet tugged his shirt from the waistband of his trousers, undoing only a few buttons before yanking it over his head. Much to Charles's amusement.

'Here? Now?'

'Yes.' She didn't recognise the huskiness in her voice demanding Charles take her where she stood. Such was the intensity of her desire to have this man again she'd lost all inhibitions.

She let her hands roam over his torso, getting to know that terrain of hair and muscle. Charles kissed his way along her neck as he tore off her clothes. 'Max and Esme are in bed and Dougal is safely locked up,' he murmured against her fevered skin. So they weren't being totally reckless. This time.

The yearning to join together was as great as it had been in London. Yet that urgency to consummate their reunion before common sense prevailed had been replaced with a different longing. This transcended the physical, it was more than re-creating the best times they'd had together. Now they were going to be parents, making plans for some sort of future together, they were reconnecting on an emotional level too.

Harriet could try and deny it. Blame it on her hormones or a holiday fling, but Charles was the only man she'd ever given herself to completely. Her body and soul had always been his and in sleeping with him again she was playing a dangerous game with her heart.

To her detriment she'd always considered Charles worth the risk.

Hopefully, this time it would pay off. With the baby, the job and an offer to stay at Heatherglen, the last commitment he needed to make to her was himself. It was the only reason she'd stay. She loved him. Always had and always would. Without having that in return from him there was no way she could live here. It would be so much worse than never seeing him again.

'Are you cold?' He mistook her shiver as a symptom

of being left clad only in her underwear when she was burning for him from the inside out.

'Nervous,' she answered honestly. Anxious about what was going to happen between them after tonight. She needed to be more than a convenient distraction for him.

'Me too.' His admission surprised her. It suggested there was more on the line for him too than simple physical satisfaction.

Charles took her back into his embrace, brushed the hair back from her face. 'We can take it slowly.'

As if to prove they had all the time in the world, he gave her a long, leisurely, skin-tingling kiss that melted any nerves into a puddle.

He unclipped her bra and let it fall to the floor, freeing her breasts to his attentions. Her nipples were more sensitive than usual, and a shot of electricity zapped to every erogenous zone when he brushed his thumb across one. When he took the other in his mouth and tugged, she almost combusted with desire.

'Charles...' She was pushing away his boxers, ridding her of the final barrier to his body. So much for taking it slowly. Her body had decided she wanted him to satisfy her craving right now.

How could something they'd done a hundred times in the past still feel like the first time? Charles wanted this to last and to make it special. The night they'd conceived this baby had been passionate and urgent because they'd thought they'd never see each other again. Tonight he was going to make love to the mother of his baby, proving his commitment to her. No pressure.

He could already see the subtle changes in her body with the swell and new sensitivity of her breasts. It awakened such a love inside him for her it terrified him that he might hurt her all over again. He wanted to put her needs before his own so he could watch the pleasure on her face and know he'd put it there.

Not that Harriet was making it easy for him. Her confident command of his body as she slid her hands over his backside and around to take hold of him was seriously jeopardising his good intentions.

'Don't worry. I'm going to make sure you get everything you need, Harriet.' He quelled his own throbbing desire to focus on hers.

He dotted feather-light kisses across her midriff, felt her quiver against his lips as he moved lower until he was kneeling between her feet. With a gentle nudge he parted her legs and relocated his focus to her inner thighs, kissing and teasing the soft skin. Her sweet gasp of anticipation and the slight unsteadiness in her stance matched his own growing impatience for that most intimate contact.

She opened to him at the touch of his tongue and cried out as he lapped her sex. Hands braced on his shoulders, she encouraged his efforts and he lost himself in the quest for her orgasm with every venture into her core.

He was so dedicated to his pursuit that when Harriet climaxed he almost came apart with her. Through every tightening and subsequent release of her inner muscles he demanded everything she had, leaving her limp and breathless when the last shudder of her climax subsided.

He didn't give her the time to say anything, literally sweeping her off her feet to carry her over to the settee. Softly, he laid her down and covered her naked body with his. Kissed her until he drove himself to the brink of insanity with desire for her.

'Harriet, I can't wait any longer.'

'Good.' The coy smile was at odds with the wanton action of her legs as she snaked them around his hips. Pressed tightly against him, it was impossible for Charles to resist any more. Finally, he gave in to his own primal urge and took possession of the woman he loved. If he'd thought she'd believe him, he would've said the words. Instead, he wanted to show her the strength of those feelings in his every move.

He claimed her again and again, her soft moans increasing his steady rhythm until his restraint was hanging by a thread. Then Harriet secured her inner hold around him, building that unrelenting pressure inside him to the point where he could no longer hold back.

He roared as his love for her burst free, so loudly he was afraid they might hear him at the other side of the castle. Perspiration clung to his skin as the ripples of his release shuddered through his limbs.

Only then did he see the sheen of tears in Harriet's eyes and his racing heart almost came to a halt.

'What's wrong? Did I hurt you?' He'd been carried away on that wave of ecstasy, but he was sure she'd been right there with him.

She bit her lip and shook her head, letting him

breathe again. He'd never have forgiven himself if he'd done something to cause her pain for a second time in her life.

'It was amazing. It's just...' Her throat sounded raw with the unshed tears she was swallowing down for his sake. He understood then why she was so upset. They could have had this a long time ago and no one knew better than he what a great loss that had been.

'I know.' He kissed her on the lips, trying to show her how sorry he was as the salt water of her tears washed over them both.

All this time they could've been living at Heatherglen together, raising their family. The hurt he'd caused them both seemed senseless now in the scheme of things. The separation clearly hadn't diminished their feelings for each other. They were more intense than ever.

Dougal barked somewhere outside the confines of their reunion, reminding Charles that their privacy wasn't guaranteed. More so when he heard a bedroom door opening and closing, followed by footsteps on the stairs.

Without another word they scrabbled for their clothes like two horny teenagers about to be sprung by his parents. They dressed in silence, but remained undisturbed by his sister or her puppy charge. As he pulled on his trousers, and Harriet fastened the last button on her blouse, no one would've been able to tell they'd just had the most mind-blowing sex. Or that he'd woken up to the fact he loved her more now than he ever had as that selfish young student. Perhaps the time apart hadn't been a complete tragedy. If not for the life he'd gone on to have without her he might not have appreciated how much more enriched it was with her in it.

'We can go to my room. We'll have more privacy there.' Not only so he could share his bed with her but they had to talk about the future. Time was slipping away and he wanted to spend every second of it with her. To make her feel the same way about him so she'd realise this was the best place for her and the baby. With him.

'If you don't mind, I think I'll retire to my own room, Charles. I don't want to confuse anyone.' The willing partner he'd had wrapped around his body only moments ago was now keeping her distance, her hands fidgeting in her lap.

His earlier euphoria dissipated with the rejection, though he didn't think this was about revenge. It was much something much more serious than that. Doubt.

'I just thought—'

'Please don't put me under any more pressure. It's not fair.' She was on the verge of crying again and he would never willingly cause her distress again.

'I'll see you in the morning, then.' It was almost as difficult to walk away from her tonight as it had been all those years ago. Only this time he was leaving the next move to her. The decision about the future of their relationship was entirely down to Harriet. He was powerless. Something he was no longer used to.

CHAPTER EIGHT

'ESME IS LOOKING forward to meeting you to discuss the possibility of a therapy dog for Bryony.' Harriet had caught up with Bryony's parents in the corridor and taken them aside to discuss their daughter's needs. She didn't want to mention anything in front of her and get her hopes up in case things didn't work out.

'Yes, Charles said he'd make an appointment for us to see her at the therapy centre. We think it's a great idea. A dog will be good company for Bryony.' Her mother was much brighter than she'd been yesterday, and Harriet imagined the prospect of training a dog had caused much excitement.

'I'm so pleased to hear that before I go back to London.'

'I suppose you have your own family there.'

A denial hovered on Harriet's lips, but they weren't here to discuss her personal life. It was already confusing things at the clinic. Instead, she simply smiled, neither confirming nor denying the assumption she had someone to return to. She wasn't sure if it was sadder to admit that or the fact she was running away from the chance to have a family here because the idea freaked her out so much.

Bryony's parents thanked her for her help before setting off back home, leaving Harriet wondering where she could retreat for peace of mind from Charles.

She'd set out early this morning to avoid him. It was silly, really, when she was living in his castle and seeing patients. She couldn't dodge him, or what was happening between them, for ever. It had crossed her mind to do a moonlit flit and leave in the middle of the night. All because sleeping with him again had made her realise she was still in love with him. In reality there was no escaping that, regardless of her location.

She dropped her head into her hands, taking a moment to reflect on what the hell she was doing with Charles. Once she'd had that space from him to think straight last night she'd convinced herself that by refocusing on the professional aspect of her stay she could get away unscathed. It wasn't turning out to be that simple, though. There was no way to keep this solely about the baby now they'd slept together again.

It was one thing to tell herself she'd somehow exaggerated how great their last time together had been and she'd read more into it than she should have for a conference hook-up. The reality of being in his home and work life was very different. Those feelings weren't simply going to be cured by hiding from him.

She'd spent half the morning with Esme, playing with the dogs and discussing the merits of pairing therapy pets with CP patients, safe in the knowledge Charles was on his rounds at the clinic. She'd only come back here when she'd spotted him going back home. It would be childish, not to mention exhausting, to keep this up. He'd catch up with her at some point.

Then what? She couldn't tell him why she'd run off after their passionate encounter and expect things to carry on as normal. Either he'd try to take advantage of her wasted feelings towards him in order to maintain contact with his child or he could cut off communication altogether. One thing was for sure, he didn't return the strength of her admiration, he never had.

Harriet was stuck, trapped by her own emotions and bad decisions. The worst of it was she didn't regret last night, and she'd do it again given the chance. She was a danger to herself.

The quiet elegance of the lounge called to her. A room where patients were able to relax and interact and which had been empty when she'd passed by earlier.

'Sorry. I didn't realise anyone was in here.' She hadn't expected to see another peace-seeker but there was a man sitting by the fire.

'No problem. It's a good place to collect your thoughts.' Now he'd spoken to her it would be rude to walk out again so Harriet joined him on the opposite side of the fireplace.

'I'm not sure I should be collecting them. I might be better off throwing them in the bin.' That prompted a deep laugh and she instantly relaxed in the man's company.

'Are you staying here?'

'I'm visiting with Charles and Esme.'

'Oh, you're a friend of the family? You knew Nick, then?'

'Unfortunately, I never got to meet him. Was he a friend of yours?'

There was a sad nod of the head, which went a long way to explaining the extent to which his death had affected the man. 'I served with him in Afghanistan. Not an easy thing to get over.'

'I'm so sorry.'

'At least I can talk about it without breaking down now.' His self-deprecating humour was much appreciated by Harriet when she knew nothing she could say would ease the suffering he'd gone through.

'They've been helping you here, then?' If he was a friend of Nick's she knew Charles and Esme would have bent over backwards to assist this man with whatever ailed him.

'They've been life-savers. They literally got me back on my feet and now we're working on getting me integrated back into society. I've still got an issue with loud noises I'm dealing with. You know, with the whole bombs and explosions thing that I can't seem to get out of my head.'

'That must be awful but I'm sure you're making great progress. These things just take time.' It was great to hear first hand the difference they were making here, and she was sure Charles would puff up with pride when she recounted the conversation to him.

'I'm very grateful for the help Charles and Esme, and

all of the staff here have given me. We're working up to the ultimate test soon. They're planning a firework display for Hogmanay, so we'll see how I go with that.' He lifted a pair of crutches from the floor and heaved himself into a standing position. Harriet hoped she hadn't chased him away with her arrival.

'Good luck.'

'Thanks. I'm Andy, by the way. Andy Wallace.'

'Harriet Bell.' She couldn't remember the last time she'd shaken so many hands and made so many new friends in such a short time. It was a nice feeling, being part of the community.

'I hope I see you around again soon, Harriet.'

If the lounge was intended to give the residents here a time out from their stresses and allow them a space to simply relax, it had definitely achieved its goal today. It had helped to take her mind off her own problems to think about someone else's.

'I've just spoken to Bryony's parents. They're very excited.' Charles's voice disturbed Harriet's chance of peace and quiet.

'So it seems. I'm glad they'll have something to look forward to.'

'I wanted to speak to you about that.' He sat down beside her on the love seat, which was suddenly crowded now he'd wedged his large frame so completely into the space. There was no room for her to edge away from him when they were sitting hip to hip and thigh to thigh. It was ridiculous that in a castle of this size she couldn't put some distance between them. After all these years apart, suddenly they were drawn together at every turn.

'About Bryony?'

'Partly. I take it you've heard of selective dorsal rhizotomy?' They weren't the words she'd expected to hear from Charles today, but they managed to spark her interest all the same.

'Yes. It's a spinal procedure used to improve mobility. I've been involved in a few.' It involved cutting nerves close to the spinal column, which could not only reduce spasticity but give patients back their independence. However, it came with risks. The operation was irreversible and relied on only cutting sensory nerves. If motor nerves were severed it could result in total paralysis. It was a highly specialised surgery, but she had seen some life-changing improvements for patients who'd had it.

'So you know the difference it could make to someone like Bryony? A lot of CP patients could benefit from it so they're not relying on hoists for the rest of their lives, or they're able to do simple tasks for themselves such as feeding and drinking.'

'Charles, I couldn't make that decision. There's a lengthy screening process for those being considered for the procedure. Patients have to be assessed by physical and occupational therapists on their functionality. My involvement is mostly on a post-op basis should any problems arise with joint alignment. Ultimately the final say would be down to the neurosurgeon performing the procedure and there's no guarantee it would work in her case anyway.' Everyone was assessed on an individual basis and as much as she wanted to improve life for the little girl and alleviate her pain, it wasn't up to her.

'I know I'd have to consult a neurosurgeon too. If I hadn't had Heatherglen to run I might have gone into surgery myself. There's a lot of things I would have done differently given the chance but this is about looking forward, not back. I'd like to give families like Bryony's hope.'

'One of the problems is that there's very little funding out there for the procedure. We're in a Catch-22 situation where they won't approve it universally until they can see conclusive results that it works. Hospitals only have approval for a limited number who meet certain criteria.'

'That's why I want to look into part-funding it myself. Perhaps set up a research facility here, with your help, where we can provide the procedure to those who need it and catalogue the results.'

'Patients need intensive physiotherapy after surgery to help with their mobility too.' This wasn't something to be taken on without considering all the implications and the potential benefits had to be deemed greater than the risks.

'Of course. I'd have to look into extending the physiotherapy department too. I'll sound Flora out about that. What do you think? Would you be interested in being part of it?'

'It's an amazing opportunity, but there would have to be something more concrete in place before I could consider giving up everything in London. You would have to have a neurosurgeon on board or this whole thing is moot.' They could do so much good for patients across the board and it sounded like an exciting project. Every physician wanted to be part of something revolutionary in the medical world and Harriet was no exception. She simply had to be sure there was something career-wise worth moving for if things didn't work out for her here on a personal level.

'I know a few in the field who are interested in taking part if we have the appropriate after care in place, which would include an orthopaedic surgeon. In the meantime, I'll get a proposal together and get things moving. I'll make some enquiries with Bryony's consultant too and see if she could be a possible candidate.'

'It would be great for her and her family. They've been on my mind a lot.'

'I thought I hadn't seen much of you since last night.' He rested his hand on her knee and though it was an innocent touch compared to last night, her body didn't appear to understand that. Her skittish pulse was reacting as though they were still rolling around naked on the couch. It didn't help when he was expecting her to say something about the progression of their relationship now it was more than resolving custody of their unborn child.

'I've been busy sussing out the career potential here.' It wasn't a total lie. She'd simply been using that research to keep her out of harm's way. When Charles was close she didn't give any thought to the consequences of her actions. Knew only that she wanted him.

She'd never had much time for relationships, but it was different with Charles. Yes, she had needs, and goodness knew he increased hers every time she laid eyes on him but being intimate with him was about so much more than meeting her physical needs.

Perhaps it was their history, and now their future as parents, but she hadn't realised how incomplete she'd felt until she'd come back to Heatherglen and found that missing part of her. A return to London now would only emphasise what she was lacking in her life. If only she could be truly sure she could trust Charles again she would rather stay here in some sort of relationship with him than go back to a world without him in it at all.

'And? What's the verdict?' He lifted his hand as he awaited her response and even that loss was too great for her to bear for too long.

Harriet cleared her throat, but her mind wasn't proving as easy. She had to work hard to focus on her career prospects rather than on the man beside her. 'I can see the possibilities Heatherglen has to offer.'

'Such as?' His mouth twitched, and it was apparent he knew exactly where her lustful imagination was taking her.

She crossed her legs and attempted to stem the arousal threatening to wreak havoc inside her. 'The clinic provides a good base for my work. As you said, I can consult and operate at the hospital when I'm needed. Working with Esme at the therapy centre is appealing too. I think it would be mutually beneficial for us to confer about patients. Bryony's opened my eyes to the possibility of putting patients in touch with Esme and vice versa. We could do so much together.'

This was what he'd planned when he'd pushed her towards his patients, but she would've seen the benefits for herself eventually. Heatherglen was offering her the chance to continue her career at the same time as raising a family. The only thing casting a shadow over proceedings was that fear of having her heart ripped out again.

'And us?' He took one of her fidgeting hands in his, stroking the inside of her wrist with his thumb and sending shivers of delight across her skin.

A lifetime of denying herself the pleasures he could give her or trying to keep a lid on her feelings was a choice she didn't want to make but Charles hadn't voiced any desire to have a proper relationship. They were going to be parents. They'd already been lovers. It was as much commitment as he was liable to make and only Harriet could decide if that would be enough for her.

'I see no reason why we shouldn't carry on as we are.' The thought of sharing his bed regularly emboldened her gaze on him. Knowing if she wavered he'd see through the bravado and realise she wanted more than he was prepared to give.

'So you'll stay? We'll raise the baby here, together?' The hope and joy she saw on his face should've made her decision clear cut, but it caused a wobble in her confidence. He wasn't declaring his love for her, he was excited about having the baby here.

'I'll stay for now, but I still have to go back to London in the new year as planned.' Despite her unrequited feelings for Charles she knew this was probably a better environment in which to nurture a child than the lonely existence she had in London. As future parents that's what they both wanted.

'What about a permanent move?'

'I'm seriously thinking about it...'.

'You don't know how happy that makes me.' To demonstrate, he cupped her face in his hands and planted a kiss on her lips.

If Harriet closed her eyes she could make herself believe this was possible.

When Charles was kissing her, when his hands were on her, she was able to live in the moment. She could move here, raise their child, keep her career, and make love with Charles when the mood took her. The only thing she couldn't have was his love, but no one had it all. Perhaps she simply had to settle for what she could get.

'Morning, sleepyhead.' Charles nuzzled into Harriet's hair, tousled from sleep and their other nocturnal activities.

'Is it that time already?' she murmured, half-asleep.

This was everything he'd dreamed about. Waking up to a naked Harriet at the start of the day, falling back into bed with her at night was the perfect way to begin and end his days. He had the clinic and now, with Harriet here and a baby on the way, he considered himself the luckiest man on the planet.

''Fraid so.'

'Ugh.' She snuggled further down under the covers and Charles's heart swelled because she'd rather be here with him than anywhere else. Long may it last.

These past couple of days with Harriet had been amazing. It wasn't the traditional start to a relationship, beginning with a pregnancy and working backwards. In time he hoped they could repair their personal issues so she could trust him again and someday they'd be living here as a proper family. Not merely together through circumstances. So far Harriet hadn't given him any indication she wanted anything other than having her physical needs met. Although he was happy to oblige, he was still in love with her, he always had been. He hoped at some point in the near future she'd feel the same way about him.

'We do have a bit of time before I have to do my rounds.' Every part of him was wide awake now.

She blinked her eyes open as he nibbled her ear lobes and brushed his thumb across her nipple. He knew all her weak spots and wasn't afraid to use that knowledge to his advantage.

'I look a mess.'

'You look beautiful.' She looked so at peace he wouldn't want her any other way.

'I…have…morning…breath.' She giggled in between kisses.

'I…don't…care.' He didn't. Not that she tasted anything but sweet on Charles's tongue. All that mattered was that she was here with him.

'In that case—'

It was his turn to gasp as Harriet stroked the length of his manhood, making him aware she was up for whatever he had in mind.

His playful growl was answered by her squeal of surprise as he flipped her onto her back. Once he was covering her body with his, all joking was finished. Making love to Harriet was a serious business.

She was so ready for him Charles slipped easily inside her to find that peace he'd only ever found with Harriet. She'd been the only woman he'd ever considered sharing his life with. Although that thought process in the past had been behind the decision to break up, the idea now was akin to winning the lottery. Every touch, every kiss from her was a gift. Someday he hoped they'd both believe he was worthy.

He wanted to say the words, to tell her he loved her, but he didn't have the right. It would scare her off when she'd been wary enough of this set-up. After that first night together, she'd done her best to avoid him until she'd seemed to come to the conclusion this arrangement would be convenient. His feelings for her were anything but convenient. They'd complicated the life he had at Heatherglen and the one he'd planned with the mother of his child. If he kept them to himself, they couldn't hurt anyone. It was only thinking of himself that caused pain to those around him.

'Hey.' Harriet's voice broke through his thoughts. She took his head in her hands and forced him to look at her. 'Where did you go?'

He had to get better at pretending he could be casual about this if he expected her to stick around.

'I'm right here with you.' He kissed her long and deep, sufficiently that the tension ebbed away from her limbs again beneath him. Passion enough to distract them both from what was going on in his head.

They rocked together, clinging onto what they had

in the moment. As Charles followed Harriet over the edge, his last thought before oblivion hit was that since she had come back, his heart had begun to heal again.

In the end they'd had to rush to get ready in time for work, they'd spent so long in bed.

'I'm going to have to get changed. I can't turn up in yesterday's clothes.'

He'd tried to pull her back in for one last smooch, but she wasn't having any of it.

'You could borrow something of mine. I don't think anyone would object if you turned up wearing one of my shirts and nothing else.' He drew a finger down her spine as she leaned over the side of the bed to collect her discarded clothes.

'I would,' she protested, but he couldn't help going back for more when he'd made her shiver. He swept her hair from the back of her neck and danced kisses along that ticklish spot. Her response as she leaned back for more of his touch only added fuel to the fire in his belly. Charles reached around to cup her breasts in his palms, pinching her nipples between thumbs and forefingers so she groaned with appreciation.

'I really have to go,' she tried again as he nuzzled her neck.

'You don't have to. You're free to do as you want, and I hope to hell that includes me.' He knew he'd said the wrong thing when she stiffened beneath him and covered his hands with hers to stop them wandering any further.

'Charles, if I become part of this household I'm not

going to take advantage of my position, and neither are you. I'll be coming here to work, not be installed as your mistress.' Harriet pulled her clothes on with such jerky movements Charles could see she was battling to contain her temper.

'I know that. It was a joke. A bad one.'

She wasn't listening as she walked barefoot to the door with her shoes in her hands, no longer content to spend another second with him to put them on.

'I'll see you at the clinic.' The slamming door said everything about the offence he'd caused.

Charles fell back onto the pillows with a sigh. It shouldn't be a crime to want to spend time with her, but it wasn't something she apparently wanted to hear. Perhaps he'd oversold Heatherglen to her when it now held more appeal for her than him.

CHAPTER NINE

HARRIET KNEW SHE'D overreacted to Charles's teasing this morning. Especially when she'd have happily spent the rest of the day in bed with him. It was that niggling fear in the pit of her stomach that sex was all she was good for that made her snap.

'I'm going to have to tell him how I feel.' She ruffled Dougal's ears as he lay at her feet. With Charles caught up in admin work, something she couldn't help him with, she'd returned to his private quarters. It didn't stop him plaguing her thoughts.

Since coming here Charles had dominated her every waking moment, and a lot of the sleeping ones. It was no wonder when he was the reason she'd come here. He was always going to be her baby's father. For her own peace of mind she was going to have to face the consequences of these feelings, even if it meant the end of the affair.

'At least I'm not the only who's fallen for him.' As a last resort to stop Dougal running riot in the clinic in his pursuit of Charles, Esme had suggested using one of his old shirts as a comforter for the pup. It had done the trick. The scent of his reluctant master, lining his basket, settled him until the man himself was available. If things didn't work out Harriet might have to steal some of Charles's clothes to take back to London and do the same.

'It's a poor substitute for the real thing, isn't it?' Although, like the smitten pup, she was sure she'd tire quickly of the imitation.

Dougal snuffled deeper into the shirt, inhaling the scent she knew was intoxicating. They both just wanted to be with him. Unfortunately, it seemed he was only prepared to tolerate either of them on his terms. Yet Harriet had seen him soften towards the dog, sacrificing one of his shirts and fussing over Dougal when he thought she wasn't looking. He was getting used to sharing his space and she hoped that would extend to her. After everything he'd been through with his family, the personal struggles he'd shared with her, it was possible he was simply as scared as she was about getting hurt and losing someone else close.

Dougal let out a pitiful whine.

'It's time to be brave. We've got to show Charles what he could have here. A real family.' She took the dog lead from the hook behind the door and clipped it to Dougal's collar.

'Let's go for a walk.'

Either he'd already learned what the 'W' word meant or he'd picked up on Harriet's renewed optimism, but Dougal was panting with anticipation and jumping at her to hurry up and open the door.

She was going to have a word with Esme about taking Dougal on permanently on Charles's behalf. He'd be the family pet their child could grow up with and a commitment to her future at Heatherglen, where she was more than a staff member or a lover. She wanted to be here as a valued part of Charles's beloved home.

Charles couldn't wait to get back to Harriet after work. Things between them had been strained since his faux pas that morning and he intended to make amends. It had taken a lot to persuade her this was the place for her and their baby and it wouldn't take much for her to change her mind again. Joking that she was moving here to be a lady of leisure, or pleasure, wasn't going to do much to keep her onside.

As he stood at the window he could see Harriet walking Dougal outside with Max and Esme. His sister and her new beau were effortlessly comfortable together, hand in hand. Whereas he and Harriet veered back and forth in their affections.

Although history didn't paint him in the best light, they shouldn't have to struggle to want to be together in the early days of a relationship. It wasn't something that should have to be forced. Yes, they were compatible in bed, they always had been, but outside that confined space there was more than a physical distance between them.

There was always an excuse or a disagreement between them, sending her running after they'd made love. She was holding back from him and that wasn't a good place from which to start a relationship.

'Hey.' He greeted Harriet with a kiss on the cheek.

It was all he could do not to pull her in for a full make-out session after spending all day thinking about her.

The slight uneasiness he could detect in the way she was twisting Dougal's lead around her fingers and the sidelong look she gave his sister stopped him. Clearly, she hadn't been pining for him in the same way as the pup pawing at his trouser leg desperate for his attention.

'Hello. I thought I'd take him out for some fresh air this afternoon.' Harriet wasn't as hesitant about showing affection to the other male in her life as she showered the pup with kisses and petting. 'I didn't have anything else to do.'

He caught hold of her arm before she could follow Esme and Max inside. 'We could go out somewhere for dinner, if you like.'

The thing he didn't want was for her to get bored after only a couple of days here. Although he'd forgotten it over the years, there was a world outside Heatherglen.

Harriet moved on past him. 'Some other time perhaps. I have some things I have to sort out with your sister.'

She didn't elaborate or even acknowledge his desire to take her out. He was getting the brush-off.

'Is there something wrong?' He'd rather know now than go on pretending until after the baby was born.

'Wrong? No. I have to take Dougal in and feed him. Excuse me.' She ducked her head under his arm and scooted inside, trailing Dougal, who was fighting to stay by Charles's side. At least someone wanted to be with him.

Charles had that same horrible emptiness inside that he'd had that day he'd realised he was jeopardising Harriet's future happiness by making her follow him to Heatherglen. It was happening all over again. Today should have been proof that neither he nor Heatherglen were good for her.

Her time in London was precious, a whirlwind of activity. By dangling promises of a better life for their child he'd emotionally blackmailed her into agreeing. Only to have her spend her days walking stray dogs and slipping between his sheets when he wasn't at work. He'd virtually bribed her with that promise of a research facility. It was something he'd been considering since Bryony had come to the clinic but the prospect of having Harriet as part of the team made it even more of a priority.That kind of opportunity would grab someone as ambitious as Harriet, but how long would it take to complete? What could he offer her in the meantime?

He banged his head against the doorframe. He'd been the worst kind of fool, a selfish one. This time running the clinic and the estate had made him forget the implications of dragging someone into it along with him. These years in isolation were worth nothing if he hadn't learned his lesson and he stole Harriet's life anyway for his own benefit.

It wasn't for him to tell her she'd be better off here when he knew nothing of her existence beyond these walls. Only what he'd imagined, and that was never going to be something he considered more fulfilling than this when it meant he'd lose her.

This trial run was supposed to have been a test for her to work out what she wanted. No matter how he tried to convince her otherwise, it didn't include him or Heatherglen. Not long term. He was fine for a holiday fling, but her trust in him hadn't recovered and it never would as long as he continued to ignore what was best for her.

It suited him having her, the woman he loved, on site, looking forward to raising their child together at his family home. Exactly the sort of selfish behaviour that had driven his father and brother to their deaths. He couldn't bear responsibility for destroying the lives of any more of his loved ones.

Okay, Harriet wasn't in immediate danger but being somewhere she didn't want to be, with someone she didn't love, would be like a slow, painful death. Like the one she'd told him her mother had suffered. An existence she'd sworn she'd never submit to. He was making her follow in those footsteps and sacrifice her identity for his sake.

Charles had made that difficult decision to end things after his father's death because it had been the right thing to do for Harriet. Now it wasn't her feelings about him clouding her judgement, it was those she had for the baby. At his prompting. He didn't believe she was capable of loving him again and it was his fault she was pregnant. If he'd used contraception or common sense, she would never have tracked him down again.

As much as he hated to say it, the Charles who'd set her free the first time had been a better man than the one he'd been recently.

Harriet would've loved to have gone out on a proper date with Charles. She couldn't remember the last time she'd made time for dinner, or even a movie, with someone. Since reconnecting with him they'd spent their quality time together in bed and though she wasn't complaining, it would be nice to venture out as a couple. That getting to know each other stage was needed more than ever when they were such different people from before.

She was sure they'd get another chance for a bit of fun away from Heatherglen now she was making plans for a permanent move. Taking on the responsibility of a family pet would show Charles she wanted to be here long term with their family.

'I'm so happy for you both.' Esme's eyes were shimmering with happy tears as she hugged Harriet, then scooped Dougal up for a cuddle.

'I'm not sure your brother will feel the same but he's more fond of this one than he'll admit.' Harriet had come to Esme's quarters to discuss the adoption. Her living space at the far side of the castle was perfect for having secret puppy conversations.

She wanted to surprise Charles with the news later. It had been on her mind about Dougal for a couple of days but seeing Esme at work, training and teaching Dougal, and her, a few basic commands had convinced her they could tame this little one. After all, he'd become part of the family too.

'Being honest about his feelings isn't a strong point for Charlie boy, but I can see the difference it has made to him, having you here. I'm not about to interfere in whatever is going on between you two but it's obvious you're in love.'

'It is?'

'It's great having my big sis back again.'

Harriet had been so distracted by her relationship with Charles she'd neglected the one she should've been cultivating with Esme. She'd never supposed the few meet-ups they'd had during uni years would've had any lasting impact on Charles's teenage sister but clearly Esme had seen it differently.

'I'm sorry I didn't keep in touch.' Harriet rested her hand on Esme's, wishing she'd attempted to maintain some sort of communication over the years. She'd simply assumed she was no longer welcome at Heatherglen in any shape or form.

Esme shrugged. 'You weren't to know I'd put you on a pedestal and turned you into the big sister I'd always wanted. I was devastated when Charles said you'd gone, and the wedding was off. I had no idea what had happened. Only that I'd lost you on top of Nick and Dad. I was angry at you, and Charles, for quite some time.'

'I'm sorry. I was so devastated by the break-up I wasn't thinking about anyone's feelings except my own.' Poor Esme had been forgotten about in the midst of the family tragedy and drama. It explained some of the behaviour Harriet had heard about during Esme's teenage years.

'I think we were all floundering back then. Hopefully we've found what we've been looking for.' She glanced at the ring on her pinkie finger.

'You and Max certainly seem very happy.' She and Charles had some way to go yet but there was time before the baby came to work out those issues that got in the way every time they got close.

'It's a promise ring. We want to take our time.' Her excitement was evident, even in Esme's hushed tones. It sounded as though she was afraid to say it out loud and jinx things. Harriet could empathise. She didn't take anything for granted when it came to affairs of the heart.

'Good idea. Congratulations.' This time Harriet instigated the hug.

With Esme confiding in her it felt as though they'd formed their own secret club. A sisterhood. Suddenly thoughts of girlie gossip and shopping trips filled her head. Neither were things she did on a regular basis, but she'd always thought she'd been missing out. It was the promise of spending time with Esme and extending that notion of family that held so much appeal.

'We've all got so much to look forward to and Heatherglen is beginning to feel like a real home again. Can you imagine what it's going to be like when the baby gets here?'

Harriet didn't have the heart to express her concerns regarding Charles's commitment to her personally. She hoped that was something they could work out and signing up as Dougal's new guardians would show Charles she was thinking of them as a family already.

That fizz of excitement Harriet had been trying to keep under control was bubbling to the surface now she had someone else's enthusiasm to expand on.

'I can't wait until next Christmas and being part of everything here. First I need to talk to Charles and let him know about the plans I'm making.' By this time next year, she'd expect to be fully settled. She and

Charles would have taken some time off work to spend time with the baby for its first Christmas.

It was impossible not to get carried away by the idea of family in Esme's company, when she thrived on it. Each of them had suffered in their own way over the years but finally the planets were coming into alignment.

'Harriet?' Charles knocked on the bedroom door and waited for a response. He'd already checked the kitchen and lounge, but there was no answer from Harriet's room either. There'd been no sign of Dougal either since their return. He thought that by the time he'd showered and changed she'd have finished whatever she'd wanted to talk to Esme about without him present. A matter that wounded him more than it should.

She could talk to anyone about whatever she pleased, but it highlighted the growing distance between them if she couldn't confide in him.

He would do his best to reassure her she'd have whatever support she needed when the baby came, if that was all that was keeping her here.

'Are you there?' He inched the door open in case she was simply avoiding him, but the room was empty.

He took a seat on the end of her bed, expecting her to come back at some point. He didn't want to invade her privacy, but the partially unpacked bag was sitting nearby. She was living out of her luggage and ready to run at a moment's notice. He was hoping his news would give her a better sense of security here.

The pitter-patter of puppy paws sounded down the

corridor and the anticipation of facing Harriet made his stomach flip.

'We're going to have to face the music at some point, Dougal. Let's hope Charles is in a better mood than usual.'

He got to his feet, suddenly feeling like the intruder he was as he unintentionally eavesdropped on her talking to the dog. Harriet hadn't always seen him at his best, but he was doing his best to win her over.

'Charles? What are you doing here?' She pulled up in the doorway, so startled by his appearance that she dropped the dog lead from her grasp.

Cue Dougal and his over-affectionate fascination with Charles's trouser leg. This was one time they didn't require his canine antics providing some light relief.

'Can we do something about this dog so we get five minutes' peace to talk properly?' If this moment proved to be a turning point in their relationship, he didn't want it tainted by the memory of her being more interested in the dog than him.

'Okay. Sure.' She stared at him intently for a few seconds before retrieving Dougal and calling on a passing Esme to come and take care of him for her.

'I know I upset you with that stupid comment about being the lady of the house this morning so I put in a few calls to Fort William Hospital. I have a few contacts and I made enquiries on your behalf about transferring there.'

'You did what?' She crossed her arms, challenging him to spit out the words he was now wondering whether he should say at all.

'I wanted you to have a concrete reason for moving here. I thought securing a position for you at the hospital was the best way to convince you there was a life waiting for you here since the research facilities will take a while to get up and running at the clinic.'

'You didn't think to consult me on this first?' Harriet frowning at him was not the reaction he'd expected.

'I thought you'd be pleased. This is giving you the career opportunities you wanted as part of the conditions of moving here.' Unfortunately, neither he nor Heatherglen had been enough to convince her to stay, which was why he'd used his initiative to go further afield. Over time he hoped she'd develop a love for him on the same par as the one she obviously had for her job. Except the impatient tapping of her foot on the floor said she wasn't best pleased with this turn of events.

'Charles, something as huge as changing my career path is for me to decide, not you.' She huffed out an exasperated breath. 'This is you making decisions for me again, without considering the consequences. I know nothing about this hospital, what their practices are like, or what I'd be expected to do in that particular environment. Things that are down to me to investigate, if and when I'm ready to relocate.'

Charles was beginning to think he couldn't do right for doing wrong.

'I was simply trying to facilitate that move for you. All I want is for you to have a reason to want to stay here.'

'Is it me or the baby you want here?'

'I thought you came as a package?' He tried, and

failed, to make her smile because he wasn't sure which answer she wanted to hear. Of course it was important for him to be close to the baby but more than anything it was his desire to have Harriet here with him that had prompted his flurry of phone calls today.

'This isn't a laughing matter, Charles. It's my life, my future, and my career you're interfering with. If you can't see that then I really don't think we have a future together.' As she said those words he got some idea of the devastation he'd once wreaked on her. It felt as though someone had taken hold of his heart and squeezed it until the pain was so great he was sure he might die.

She'd been hesitant about starting over again here until she'd seen a commitment from him, telling her he would make a good father and he was no longer that man she'd believed had run out on her with no good reason. He'd thought he'd delivered with the prospect of employment at the hospital. Apparently not.

'I just wanted you to stay,' he muttered, feeling utterly pathetic that he'd failed her again.

'It's always about what *you* want, isn't it, Charles? You know I'd hoped we'd moved on from the past, but this proves we're no further on than we've ever been. Everything has to be on your terms, with no thought to how it affects me. You haven't changed at all, but I have. I'm no longer prepared to be that woman who'll wait until you get bored again.'

'Harriet, please, we can sort this out. I've messed up. Tell me what I can do to fix this.' He wasn't above begging if that's what it would take for her to give him another chance. This time he had much more to lose if she walked out of his life for good. He loved her more now than he ever had. Along with the baby he might never get to meet.

'If you'd changed from the man who ended our engagement without even talking to me about it, I wouldn't have to tell you what to do. We're only going to make each other miserable trying to force this relationship to work simply so you can have us where you want us. If it's okay with you, I'll spend the night and leave tomorrow. I have a few things to sort out and some goodbyes to say. We can work out access arrangements when the baby is born. In the circumstances you'll understand I want full custody. After all, I tried to do things your way.'

He sighed his reluctant acceptance. How could he object when she was right? If she loved him this wouldn't be so difficult, but he couldn't force her to feel the same way he did about her.

He should never have stepped out of his shoes as Laird and medical professional when he knew the heartache that caused from previous experience. Now he'd have to start the grieving process all over again. Grieving for the loss of the woman he loved, his child and the family he wasn't destined to have.

CHAPTER TEN

'I'M SORRY THINGS turned out this way.' Charles walked out the door as though he'd just cancelled a phone contract.

Harriet, on the other hand, had just had her whole world ripped out from under her. Again.

She managed to stay upright until he was out of the room, then her legs gave way and she collapsed onto the bed, too stunned to even cry. The moment she'd decided to seduce Charles in London she'd set herself up for a fall. If she hadn't given in to temptation she wouldn't have to go through this heartbreak for a second time.

Ending it with him was the last thing she wanted to do but she'd done so in self-defence. By making decisions for her without consulting her, it was clear he'd learned nothing. The relationship was never going to work. Especially once the baby was here and he started taking over there too. If he was incapable of changing, of considering her thoughts and feelings, she would end up the one getting hurt. There was a baby to think about in all of this too. The only option she could see now was to walk away and save what little there was left of her heart. It wasn't any easier to do second time around, even if it was through her choice this time.

She lay back on the bed and wondered when she'd started thinking of this place as home when it held so many panful memories for her. Now there was one more to add if she ever had the stupid idea of coming back. Whatever arrangements they made regarding the baby's upbringing, she couldn't put herself through this again.

Harriet curled up into a ball, her arm wrapped around her belly. It was only when she thought about their baby that the tears finally broke free and trickled from the corners of her eyes. It was just going to be the two of them from now on. Like her and her mum all over again. Except she'd make sure she had a job and a home to return to in case of this very eventuality.

Damn Charles Ross-Wylde for making her fall in love with him again. Now not only was she going to be a single mum, struggling to juggle motherhood and a career, but he'd damaged her heart beyond all repair this time. Along with her trust.

He'd offered her a job, a home and a place in his bed. The only thing he hadn't been able to give her was the love she so desperately wanted from him. Charles had waited until she'd fallen in love with the idea of being part of a family here with him, then snatched it away by repeating the same mistakes.

If she'd kept driving that first night and never come back, she'd be in a different head space than she was in now. A few days over Christmas feeling sorry for herself would've been nothing compared to this. She'd seen the possibilities of living at Heatherglen and becoming part of the family, but she would have to leave it all behind to look out for herself because no one else was going to do it for her.

'You're up early this morning. All that excitement with Harri must have kept you awake.'

Esme was refilling Dougal's water bowl when Charles made his way downstairs to the kitchen. Last night had left him drained but not in the way Esme probably imagined.

'Have you seen her?'

'Not yet. So, how do you really feel about the Dougal adoption plan?'

'The what?'

'Don't tell me you didn't get around to discussing it. Me and my big mouth.'

'No, we…er…had some other things going on.'

Esme stuck her fingers in her ears. 'Ugh. Stop. I don't want to hear what my brother and his girlfriend got up to last night.'

'Then tell me what it is you're wittering on about.'

She grabbed the two slices of toast as they popped up and began buttering them as though this was any ordinary morning and not the day after Charles had lost everything precious to him. 'Harriet had the bright idea that you two should adopt Dougal and keep him here at the castle.'

Charles stopped castigating his sister long enough to consider the implications of that news. 'Harriet wanted *us* to adopt Dougal?'

'Yes.' Esme munched on her breakfast, giving nothing else away about Harriet's secret pet project but it told Charles all he needed to know. Harriet *had* thought about staying on and making a life with him here. Taking on a dog was a commitment for the family they should have become. It was his blundering in, trying to secure her employment, that had messed everything up. If he'd left her to come to her own conclusion about what she wanted, instead of trying to force her hand, she wouldn't be leaving him.

He had been selfish. All this time he'd spent convincing her this was the place to raise the baby, he'd never once considered what would make her happy. He was asking her to give up everything she had achieved in London so he could have her and the baby here without disrupting his life. The truth was he didn't have a life worth living without Harriet in it.

He'd sent her away twelve years ago rather than make her fit into this world and now that's exactly what he was trying to do. She was the one expected to make all the concessions in this scenario he'd conjured up when it was clear it should've been him making the compromises to prove how much he loved her. He hoped it wasn't too late to do that.

With renewed determination to get their relationship on track he headed for the door. 'Esme, if Harriet comes through this way I need you to stall her.'

'What do you mean?'

'She wants to go back to London. I need you to keep her here until I get back, okay?'

'What is going on with you, Charles?' She was waving the remnants of her toast at him and if she knew how badly he'd screwed things up with Harriet, she'd be chucking it at him. He was going to do his best to fix things before Esme resorted to violence.

'I'm trying to get myself a life,' he answered, on his way out the door.

'Well, don't be long. We have a party to sort out.' Esme apparently had faith that he could do that in one afternoon. As Charles got into his car and set off for Glasgow, he prayed she was right. After all, he had everything to lose if he didn't get it right this time.

Harriet had intended to leave first thing, but she'd fallen fully clothed into an exhausted sleep so deep she hadn't heard her phone alarm go off. It had been the sound of a car door slamming outside that had finally woken her. Although she hadn't thought it possible, the sight of Charles driving away saddened her even more. If he wasn't even prepared to fight for her there really was no way back for them.

She took her time getting ready and packing up the last of her things. With Charles gone she didn't have the same urgency. Besides, she still had to say goodbye to Esme. Harriet was surprised to see her still sitting in the kitchen when she was usually at work by this time.

'Hi, Harriet. Can I get you anything to eat for breakfast?' Esme being nice to her was the last thing she needed. Much more of this and she'd start blubbing and tell her how much she loved her brother. She'd have to get out of here before she talked herself back into staying and condemned herself to a life with someone incapable of putting her first.

'No, thanks. I'm going to head back to London. I have a lot to sort out.'

She didn't enjoy keeping Esme in the dark, but she could do without any more drama. She was feeling too raw from the fallout to be exposed to someone else's pain. It was only fair someone considered Esme's feelings in these matters too, but she had to work through her own first.

'When?'

'Today. Now. As soon as I've woken up properly.' She wasn't looking forward to the long drive home, but she'd have to do it before she was faced with Charles again. There was no guarantee she'd maintain her dignity if that happened and her self-preservation was replaced with the overwhelming love for him she couldn't seem to bury.

'No! You can't!' Esme's outburst was so loud it send Dougal scampering back to his bed with his tail between his legs.

'I have to.'

'But—but it's—Hogmanay. We have our big Hogmanay party tonight. You can't miss that.'

'I'm really not in a partying mood.' It was one thing to pretend to Esme that nothing had happened to spoil her time here but putting on a brave face for a house full of strangers would require an inner strength she no longer possessed.

'It's wonderful, Harriet. Everyone comes together for the party. We have music and enough whisky that we can usually persuade Charles to sing.'

That did catch her interest. It reminded her of the

night she'd met him at university. At one of those alcohol-fuelled affairs where it had been too noisy to even think straight. Then Charles had picked up a guitar, begun strumming and that velvety Scottish accent had captivated everyone in the room. It was a long time since she'd heard him sing. The memory of it did nothing to alleviate her pain.

'I'm sure I wouldn't be missed.'

'Oh, but you would. Hogmanay is a time for us all to be together. You haven't seen anything until you've been to our Hogmanay party.'

'I'm due back at work.' She knew the lame excuse wouldn't work but she attempted it anyway, her defences at an all-time low.

'There'll be dancing and fireworks and don't forget all the men in kilts.' Esme sensed her weakness and pounced. There was one man in particular who'd look delectable in the family tartan, but even the promise of that sight wasn't enough for Harriet to prolong her inevitable departure.

'Please, say you'll be there, Harriet. It's our way of saying goodbye to the past and welcoming in a new start.' The way Esme described it, celebrating Hogmanay at Heatherglen was tempting. The closure she needed before starting over as a mother to this baby who needed her to love it enough for both parents. She could always slip away during the fireworks…

'You can't leave anyway. The caterers have stuffed up. I'm going to need you to go shopping for me.' Esme pulled out a pad of paper from a drawer and started scribbling a list on it.

'What? No. Can't you get someone else to do it?' She'd end up with a serious case of trolley rage if forced to endure the hordes stocking up as though they were preparing for the apocalypse on top of everything else.

'There is no one else. I'm waiting for the fireworks guy to set up and Max is helping the band with their sound check. Charles delegated everything to me this year, and I can't have people turning up without food to offer them. I need your help.'

She was getting stressed if she was admitting she couldn't do this alone. If the event turned out to be a disaster Harriet knew she'd blame herself. Esme deserved someone to think of her for a change.

This was turning out to be the worst New Year's Eve in history.

Everywhere Harriet turned she was confronted with families stocking up with copious amounts of alcohol and snacks. Some were arguing over how much they actually needed, others looked bored to tears, but they were all preparing to see in the New Year together. At the stroke of midnight, she'd be getting ready to leave Heatherglen for the last time. Faced with the reality of ringing in the New Year alone made for a depressing picture.

She found herself wandering away from the grocery aisles towards the clothing department. To the baby section. The tiny outfits drew her like a moth to a flame. Her eyes misted as she fingered the soft fabric and thought about preparing for the new arrival on her own. Something she and Charles should be doing together.

* * *

Charles no more wanted to host a party than he wanted to go back to a house without Harriet. It was a tradition he usually enjoyed, unlike the recurring break-ups. This year he was prepared to let Esme take over. With any luck she'd throw herself so deeply into preparations he could excuse himself altogether. How could he celebrate the start of a new year when he'd finished this one on such a low? Loving Harriet wasn't something he'd get over as soon as the clock struck midnight. Unfortunately, he didn't have a fairy godmother who could wave her magic wand and make him happy again, or make Harriet love him.

He hadn't seen her today, and he prayed his sister had been able to come up with a plan to keep her there for the few hours he'd been absent. It would be devastating if he didn't get to see her one last time and beg for her forgiveness.

Charles braced himself for the onslaught of Dougal love and whatever else waited for him behind Heatherglen's doors. If Esme was on her own and Harriet had gone, he'd never forgive himself and his sister would kill him once she found out how stupid he'd been. He could only hope with the upcoming party, the ear-blasting would be short-lived.

As predicted, as soon as he set foot inside the family home, Dougal was there to greet him. He reached down to stroke the only one who'd be pleased to see him, no matter what. When he glanced up from his crouched position on the floor he met those anguished eyes that had haunted him since last night.

'Esme wanted me to stay for the party.'

The sight of her when he thought he'd convinced himself he might never see her again hit him so hard it almost knocked him onto his backside.

'Can you give Harriet and me a minute, sis?' He was aware he was on borrowed time with Harriet now, especially if she worked out he'd been behind the ruse to get her to delay leaving for a while.

'I don't think there's any point—'

'Sure.' Thankfully, Esme cut off Harriet's protests and nipped out the door before she got dragged into the conversation.

'Can we talk?' He sat down at the table and pulled out a chair for Harriet. She remained standing.

'I don't think there's anything left to say, Charles.'

'I think there is. I hear you made plans for Dougal to become a permanent feature here?'

Harriet grabbed a cloth and began to clean down the work surfaces, which already looked spotless to Charles. 'It was just an idea I had. I'm sure Esme will find somewhere else for him.'

'You were going to make a decision like that without talking to me about it first?'

She spun around to face him. 'Rehoming a dog is not the same as transferring a person's job to a different country without telling her.'

'I know. I know. What I'm trying to say is that we were both doing things we thought would benefit each other. I wasn't trying to control your life, but I was guilty of not taking your feelings into consideration.'

'Why would you cut me out of decisions like that

again after everything we've been through? You know how hard it's been for me to trust you again and then you go and do exactly the same thing.'

'I realise that. Probably too late, but I swear I will do whatever it takes for you to be happy from now on. All that matters to me is you and the baby.'

'I wish I could believe that.'

'Surely the fact you were willing for us to take on Dougal said you were thinking about staying on here? Deep down you must know how much I care about you or you'd never even have considered that sort of commitment.'

'It wasn't my feelings that were ever in question. I love you, Charles. I've always loved you. Why else do you think this has been so hard?'

'Then what the hell are we doing to ourselves?' Hearing her say those words was all Charles needed to know he'd done the right thing in the end. He crossed the floor so he could be closer to her, wanting to take her in his arms, but she dodged around him and resumed her cleaning.

'I'm sorry but, ultimately, nothing else has changed. Except I called you out on your behaviour this time.'

'That's not true. A lot has changed. It just took the shock of potentially losing you to make me realise that. The clinic is up and running. They don't need me here any more. Esme could easily take over Heatherglen.'

'What are you saying, Charles?' Harriet stopped scrubbing invisible stains to stare at him. Knowing he was saying something she wanted to hear gave him the courage to carry on.

He pulled out a piece of paper and handed it to her. 'I went to see my solicitor this morning. This is simply a letter to confirm my intent, contracts are in the process of being written.'

She scanned the letter his solicitor had drawn up this morning under duress. He wasn't happy that Charles was willing to sign away his inheritance so easily, but this was a sacrifice he was only too willing to make if it meant he and Harriet could be together.

'I can't let you do this.' Harriet folded the letter and tucked it back into his jacket pocket. She was so close he could feel her warmth, smell her perfume, and he so desperately wanted to kiss her again. He wouldn't, though. Not unless he was sure he wanted him to.

'Oh? You're telling me what I can or can't do now?' He couldn't help but smirk at the irony in that. Really, he didn't mind when it showed she cared about him.

She gave him a sidelong look. 'This is different. Heatherglen is your life. I can't let you give that up.'

'You and the baby are my life now. I was asking too much of you, expecting you to give up your home, your job and everything else to move here. If you can still picture a future with me I'm fully prepared to follow you back to London. I'm sure I can find work there and we can come back and visit Esme anytime.' The answer had been staring him in the face all along. Harriet wanted him to make a commitment, a gesture big enough that she would stop fearing the worst. That he was going to leave her on her own again.

He'd fulfilled the promise he'd made to honour his brother and father and he'd seen Esme build a business and fall in love. Now it was time to focus on what was important to him. Harriet.

'This is all so…overwhelming.' Harriet wanted to believe she could have it all, but only a few hours ago she'd been getting ready to say goodbye for ever, convinced Charles didn't love her enough to change. Now he was offering to give up everything and go back to London with her. It was everything she wanted yet she was afraid of taking that final step with him again. Her head was spinning with the possibilities awaiting them but there was still something holding her back.

'I'll do whatever it takes to prove to you this family is all that I want. Say the word and I'll quit working altogether to be a stay-at-home dad. I just can't lose you again.'

She would never ask him to do any of the things he was willing to give up, but these weren't things he would say lightly. 'You'd do that for me?'

'I'd do that for us. For our family.' He stroked his thumb across her cheek and placed a ghost of a kiss on her lips. Enough for her to crave more. Except he let go of her again. 'I won't put you under any pressure to make a decision now. You need to do what's right for you.'

Sound advice. If only she knew what that was.

'Esme, this isn't the food I brought back from the supermarket.' Harriet saw the plates of haggis, neeps and tatties and homemade black bun, a rich fruit cake wrapped in pastry, and knew she'd been played.

'There was a bit of a mix-up. The caterers arrived not long after you left.' With the party in full swing, Esme had finally taken a break herself to get something to eat from the buffet laid out in the marquee.

'Uh-huh? You couldn't have phoned to let me know?'

Esme waved her away. 'I was busy. There's no harm done.'

As though Harriet wasn't suspicious enough about Esme's whole part in getting her to stay, she gave Charles a little wink before she disappeared with Max.

'Why do I get the feeling you had a rather large hand in the great catering mishap?' she asked Charles.

'I thought we needed more time to get our act together.' Charles slid his hands around Harriet's waist and kissed her neck.

'Well, one of us did.' She should've been angry that he'd concocted that supermarket trolley dash and wasted her afternoon, but it showed he had been fighting for them after all. While she'd been dispatched on a fool's errand, Charles had been signing his life away in a solicitor's office to prove his commitment to her. It was worth all the cloak and dagger shenanigans in the end when it made them both consider what was most important to them. Right now, she was content to be with Charles. The man who was willing to give up everything just to be with her.

He kissed her again. 'It's almost midnight and I promised I'd get up and sing. Although I'm not sure I've had nearly enough whisky yet to do that.'

'You have to. I've been looking forward to that all evening.' She turned around in his arms and fluttered her eyelashes. This Hogmanay party reminded her of that first night they'd met. Hearing Charles sing again would be the perfect way to end it.

'In that case, I wouldn't want to disappoint you. Now, are you sure Dougal's safely locked away?'

'Yes, and I left the radio on for him so he doesn't get lonely, just as you asked.'

'Thank you.' He dropped another kiss on her lips and went to join the band on the stage. Thankfully, the weather had improved over the course of the day. Although the ground was muddy, the crowd was able to move outside to watch the band. It had the atmosphere of being at a music festival. Especially when most of them were wearing wellington boots to enable them to move unhindered across the wet fields.

Charles looked so handsome up there, singing traditional Scottish folk songs, wearing his kilt and playing the guitar, Harriet had become his number one groupie. Especially when he locked eyes with her and made her feel as though she was the only person here and he was singing directly to her.

'This last song is dedicated to the woman I love. Harriet, this one's for you.' As Charles began singing the slow ballad that had made her fall in love with him in the first place, tears streamed down her face. It was only now she realised she'd been waiting for him to say those words before those last barriers around her heart fell away.

All too soon the song was over, but she'd make sure he kept that guitar and kilt handy. She wanted to see them both on a regular basis.

'Ten, nine, eight…'

The band began the countdown and Charles jumped down off the stage so he could be with her at midnight.

'Seven, six, five, four…' She pulled him close so he was beside her to toast in the new year. Andy, the guy she'd met in the lounge, was standing nearby with Esme and Max and she waved over to him. He looked nervous and was leaning heavily on his crutches, waiting for the cacophony of cheers and fireworks as though he was going into battle.

'Three, two, one.'

The place erupted as the sky lit up with explosions of colour and the crowd burst into a chorus of Auld Lang Syne, linking arms as they did.

'Are you doing okay, Andy?' She moved closer to where she could keep a closer eye on him even though he had people on either side to make sure this wasn't too much for him.

'You know what? I really am. I'm not in Afghanistan any more. Not even in my head. Happy New Year, Harriet. I think this is going to be the best one yet,' he said as he raised his glass of whisky.

'I think so too,' she said, and couldn't resist giving him a hug. It was so heart-warming to see another patient start anew after their recovery, whether from mental or physical impairment. As he joined Esme in letting off the party poppers and covering everyone around them in glitter and string, his laughter confirmed he'd passed his test and finally conquered his demons.

Charles grabbed her by the hand and pulled her towards the house.

'Where are we going? We're going to miss the party.' She looked back with longing at the throng of happy people celebrating without them.

'We can't miss the first footer,' He said as though she knew what he was talking about. Her expression must've given her away as he was compelled to explain.

'The first person to step into the house in the New Year.'

'Oh,' she said, still clueless as to why this was significant.

Sure enough they'd just made it inside before someone knocked. Charles opened the door to a tall, black haired man and welcomed him in with a, 'Happy New Year.'

The dark stranger presented Charles with an array of gifts. 'Whisky, to drink and celebrate the New Year. Coal, so that your house will be warm, bring comfort and be safe for the year ahead. Shortbread, to make sure those in the household won't go hungry and a silver coin to bring prosperity.'

'Thank you. Now go on out back and get something for yourself to eat and drink.' Charles accepted the basket of gifts with one hand and clapped him on the back with the other, ushering him towards the party outside.

Once the mysterious visitor had gone, Charles opened the whisky and poured them two glasses. 'Happy New Year.'

Harriet clinked her glass to Charles's. 'Here's to the New Year, and our new life.'

'I'm so happy you're here to share this with me. There's only one thing that could make the moment more perfect, Harriet. That's why I wanted us to greet the first footer and bless us with good luck for the forthcoming year. Harriet Bell, will you marry me?'

'Yes. A thousand times, yes.' She threw her arms around his neck, uncaring about the whisky spilling everywhere. This was the ultimate commitment and there was nothing she wanted more than to marry this man and have his baby. As long she was with Charles she didn't care where they started their new life.

The truth had finally set them free, enabling them to raise their family in the best possible place. A home filled with love.

EPILOGUE

'Do you think we should call off the Christmas party?' Charles was doing lengths of the living room with the baby over his shoulder, trying to settle him.

'Thomas is just teething. He'll be fine.' Harriet was more enamoured than ever with her gorgeous husband now he was as attentive to their son as he was to her. They were enjoying their time off together over the festive period, even if sleep had become a thing of the past recently.

'It's not just for Thomas's benefit. I think it would be nice for us to have a quiet evening together.' Once their son had stopped crying, Charles was able to lay him down on the activity quilt he'd received from Auntie Esme for Christmas. The baby's attention now on the bright-coloured jungle animals on the fabric and the noisy attachments, his exhausted father collapsed onto the sofa beside his wife. He still had enough energy to give her a passionate kiss. Thankfully, parenthood hadn't diminished that side of their relationship.

'That does sound like heaven.' Chilling out by the fire, spending quality time together, was more appealing than the idea of rushing around making sure their guests had enough to eat or drink all evening.

'Surely we could skip it for one year?'

'I don't think people would mind. Aksel and Flora are probably comfortable enough where they are without having to trail out here from the village in the cold. The same could be said for Lyle and Cassandra, even though they don't have as far to travel.'

At this time of year most people were content to stay with the ones they loved. The difference for Harriet this year was that she had people to stay at home with.

'What about Esme?' Charles gave her the face that said their plans for a quiet night had just been thwarted.

'You know she'll want to see her nephew and having Max and Esme isn't the same as hosting a party. We can still have a quiet night in.'

'You think? Just wait until she has us playing musical chairs and hide and seek.' Although he was denying it, Harriet knew Esme's excitement was part of the tradition around here.

'As long as I don't have to start cooking, or even get dressed, I don't care. I'm going to slob out today.'

'Me too.' Charles stretched out along the settee and put his feet up. They were both overdue a good rest after the year they'd had getting her transferred from London and making plans for the research centre. Not to mention their wedding in the middle of it all. Now, with Aksel building an adventure centre on the estate, the year ahead was going to be another busy one for Heatherglen. She would never have expected Charles to give up Heatherglen when it had become a family home for all of them.

They heard paper rustling in the corner and Charles lifted his head. 'Dougal! He's in the presents again.'

Harriet watched with amusement as the two did battle over the new scarf Joanie had knitted Charles for Christmas. She couldn't seem to do enough to thank them both for saving her life.

'Give me that back, you daft mutt.' Charles was growling almost as much as Dougal, who thought he was being treated to a new game, and Thomas was gigging at the spectacle too.

Yes, this was her crazy family, and she wouldn't trade it for anything.

* * * * *

COMING SOON!

We really hope you enjoyed reading this book. If you're looking for more romance, be sure to head to the shops when new books are available on

Thursday 26th December

To see which titles are coming soon, please visit

millsandboon.co.uk/nextmonth

MILLS & BOON

Coming next month

THE MIDWIFE'S SECRET CHILD
Fiona McArthur

'Let us see where this leads us, Faith. I will not let you down again.'

Her barriers quivered under the strain but held. 'As you say. We'll see.'

She watched his eyes narrow at her less than trusting response.

He held out his palm and reluctantly she took his strong fingers in hers and his warmth seeped into her like it had from the first moment they'd met years ago and did again – until their hands separated, slowly.

She tucked her fingers behind her back. Instead of stepping away he stepped closer. His bulk blocking out the light from the open door. His male scent coated with the salt of the sea. His strong jaw coming closer as he leaned in and she turned her head until he kissed her cheek. His breath warm on her face, his mouth even warmer, and despite herself her body softened even with that light touch. His hand came up and caressed the other side of her cheek. Cupping her face with more warmth and such tenderness that slowly she turned her head towards him. Towards his full, sensuous mouth, until their lips were a breath apart. Inhaling the life force between them as they hovered on the brink of the kiss that shouldn't.

Yet, it was she who leaned forward and offered her mouth, her first sign of trust, her first forgiveness.

But it was he who propelled them slowly but surely into a kiss that buckled her knees and sent her hands up between them to clutch his shirt. His arms came around her with a certainty and possession that jammed them together until her breasts were hard against his rock like chest. She wanted to be lost like this so much.

She pushed him away.

He stilled at once. Nodded, turned and left before she could make her feet move. Her breath eased out. She sagged against the door she moved to shut. Phew.

Continue reading
THE MIDWIFE'S SECRET CHILD
Fiona McArthur

Available next month
www.millsandboon.co.uk